UNBRIDLED BOOKS

M. ALLEN CUNNINGHAM

Unbridled Books
Denver, Colorado

Library of Congress Cataloging-in-Publication Data
Cunningham, M. Allen
Lost son / M. Allen Cunningham.
p.   cm.
ISBN-13: 978-1-932961-34-8
ISBN-10: 1-932961-34-8
1. Rilke, Rainer Maria, 1875–1926—Fiction.   2. Rodin,
Auguste, 1840–1917—Fiction.
3. Quartier latin (Paris, France)—Fiction.   4. Paris (France)—
Intellectual life—
20th century—Fiction.   I. Title.
PS3603.U667L67   2007
813'.6—dc22   2007000367

1   3   5   7   9   10   8   6   4   2

First Printing

Book design by SH·CV

For K, of course

and for the
"young person anywhere,
in whom something is rising up that causes you to shiver"

Contents

Three

Preface

RAINER MARIA RILKE (1875–1926) is widely regarded as the modern master of the lyric in German and one of the world's greatest poets. He is perhaps best known and loved in the United States for his *Letters to a Young Poet,* collected posthumously. He is the author of *The Lay of the Love and Death of Cornet Cristoph Rilke; Stories of God; The Book of Images; Auguste Rodin; The Book of Hours; New Poems I & II; The Duino Elegies; Sonnets to Orpheus;* and a single novel titled *The Notebooks of Malte Laurids Brigge.*

The following pages represent Rilke's life re-imagined as fiction. All epigraphs are Rilke's as attributed, and further Rilke quotes are incorporated directly into the narrative, distinguished by italics and full quotation marks. Other italicized passages herein attributed to the character of Rilke are invented. Inspiration for imaginary events has been in most cases the writing of Rilke himself, particularly his novel and some of his ten thousand letters.

We must understand one another or die. And we will never understand one another if we cannot understand the famous dead, those fragments of the past who sit half buried and gesturing to us on memory's contested shores.

Lee Siegel, The Atlantic Monthly, *April 1996*

I however, Lou, your somehow lost son, not for a long long time yet can I become a sayer, one who foretells his own way, nor a describer of my former fates; what you hear is just the noise of my footsteps, always drawing more and more distant on unsure paths, always drawing away, I know not from what, and whether my steps are bringing me closer to anybody I do not know.

Letter from Rainer Maria Rilke to Lou Andreas-Salomé,
November 9, 1903

THE VALAIS, THE RHONE VALLEY OF
SWITZERLAND: PRESENT DAY . . .

*B*y silent evening I drive down the vineyard road to Muzot. Stand in the narrow byway and stare through summer darkness at your gaunt tower rising from the grapevines. Ancient stone-hewn structure set against the distant granite mountains that rim this valley and look in these nocturnal hours like a phalanx of figures slouching closer at the end of some age-old restlessness. It was refuge from old restlessness you sought in this place. This tower then harbored you night by night in the long-burning work you'd awaited through years of war. Upon completion of your last great poems, you opened this rudely canted door to a February night punctured with searing stars. Stepped out into celestial air and stood stroking the tower's stones with thanks.

I linger in the dark at the tower's lee side. Bats whistling in their blind wheelery through the trees. The musk of grapes wafts from the tangled arbors, and somehow . . . somehow my night swings open to that very night: to you standing in the shadowed yard alone and relieved. How does it happen that eighty years may fall away to this moment? What hatch has clattered free? . . . I have no answer. But there you are: nationless figure in a world gone mad with devotion to country. And I, dark in your darkness, begin to grasp all that has led me here. In these days many things stand for me as they once stood for you, back in the years well before you arrived in this place, back in your haunted time when a young dream-figure by the name of Malte Laurids Brigge moved into your soul as into an ancient room and made you his confessor. I've been traveling after you and Malte, both. . . .

one

PARIS, PRAGUE ~ RAINER, RENÉ:

1874–1902

Far back in my childhood, in the great fevers of its illnesses, huge indescribable fears stood upon me—fears as before something too big, too hard, too near. Deep unsayable fears, I remember them well. And it was these self-generated fears that were now with me as at first, but now they didn't need night and fever for pretext, they caught me in the middle of my days, when I thought myself healthy and courageous, and they took my heart and held it over the void. Can you understand how that is? . . . I would be strange to everything as one dying in strange lands, alone, supernumerary, a fragment of other contexts.

*Letter from Rainer Maria Rilke in Paris
to Lou Andreas-Salomé, June 1903*

*I*t begins with a pale willowy woman of twenty-three. She lies propped on two limp pillows, the bedclothes rumpled at her feet because the cramped room has started to swelter again. She's been abed since her delivery a week ago. When not dozing she gazes past the footboard to the rail of wainscoting. A bar of yellow dust there, her eye constantly drawn to the spot. The discoloration is becoming a soft torment, beginning to signify some deeper discoloring. A tainted life. Her maimed wishes. She would call Josef in and tell him to be firm with the housekeeper—but could she possibly speak to him of such a trifle at a time like this, with the Madame coming in by the hour only to say the child is worsening? No, Phia fears she'd lash out at Josef should she summon him now—would let slip the melancholy she can hardly sculpt into thought, let alone into suitable words.

She digs her fists into the mattress and raises herself on the pillows. "Madame Wertz!"

A small bustling noise from the next room, the dull clacking of heels in the hall, then the midwife appears in the doorway, nonplussed, her uppinned silver hair frazzled like a tiara of smoke.

"Open the window please," says Phia.

"But Frau Rilke, the winter air."

"For a moment at least. I'm stifling."

Madame struggles with the latch. At last there's a thunderous crack as the sash comes free of the sill. A blade of November wind—so cold it seems to scorch—slices into the room and touches Phia's face. The rim of sweat at her nightshift collar tickles like a necklace, blue-feeling.

"Has she been sleeping?"

"In fits and starts, Frau."

As if the child has heard, a pained infant cry comes sawing through the thin wall.

Madame gives a grimace like a smile. "You see. Awake again already. I'll bring her to you, Frau."

"Yes, thank you."

Ismene is small in Phia's arms. Two cupped hands would hold her. So languid—and yet brittle. She makes querulous sounds but hardly moves beyond the heaving of her tiny frame. A deficiency in the lungs, Madame Wertz has explained. Nothing to be done but keep her warm. It's Josef's old infirmity, thinks Phia. His unsound health barred him from military distinction some years ago, and now that watery bloodline has enfeebled his daughter.

Oh Josef! Of what use is respectability in a man, if not balanced by *distinction* of a kind, or at least the will for it? Would that he'd followed his brother's example, for Jaroslav has done well by the Rilke name: a successful law practice, holdings in property, and last year a title conferred by the emperor: Knight of Rüliken. That knighthood took labor and time, piles of vague ancestral papers to scrutinize—no easy thing proving a lineage long lost!—but Jaroslav succeeded. What a gain for a man of the same bourgeois house as Josef the railroad inspector. Not that Phia believes herself bred of a much higher milieu than her husband. She's no aristocrat. But she does happen to be the daughter of Herr Carl Entz, who holds the sobriquet of Imperial Counselor, even if he isn't a proper nobleman—and she did grow up in that stately house not two blocks away. . . . Still, Phia remembers how she longed to be free of that life. And who could fault a young lady's belief that Josef Rilke, such a well-comported ex-soldier, might liberate her? But here now, a year after the wedding, Phia Rilke lies abed in a dusty room, stranded in the hope that her frail infant daughter will not die.

Phia nuzzles the child, careful not to squeeze her. Ismene quietens.

Phia prays: Christ in Heaven, keep our sweet daughter Ismene in this world. Give her life and we will consecrate her to your service. Let the earth profit by this soul's devotion.

The prayer spins and spins, finally unravels into sleep, and mother and daughter lie heart-to-heart in slumber.

Hours drain away.

When Phia stirs again the child is gone from her arms.

She blinks to find Josef's slim figure at the bedside. Still in his great-coat, he's worrying the lifeless black shucks of his gloves. Phia knows what he will say, and though it seems a gross sign of his incompetence that he should still say it, she feels strangely tender toward him.

"Phia, she's gone."

Her eyes go dull at the words. Smoke stirring in her gaze. "Is she."

"Yes. Father Schwann will come this evening."

A pyre smolders on the altar of her heart. Her daughter an offering wrested from her. But with quick and wincing certitude Phia sees what must happen now: they must bless the little body, bury it, and restore themselves in the faith that the Lord has been appeased.

Then try again . . .

December 1875. Seven months in the womb and the new child arrives in a hurry for the world. A son. The mother's quavering hands—each as large as the boy entire—molest him with fearful devotion meant to prolong the mercy of God who has lent her this child to measure her faith.

She has Madame Wertz gussy up the boy for baptism. Sheathed in snowy bunting, he is hurried in the mother's arms along the ice-grim street, his pink face haloed with white frill and her heart pothering in the narrow breast at his ear. Above the mother's pluming breath surges the Prague sky, cadaverous, impaled with black spires.

The father keeps pace at his wife's arm. He knows what danger it is to bring the still-feeble boy out in this frost, but voices no objection. Phia will not be dissuaded: a blessing must be seized whatever the weather. In the weeks after Ismene's death last year, his young wife wept beyond her supply of tears. *If we'd gotten her to church!* she had muttered one day, aghast at their unnoted error. He had replied, *We can't know such a thing,* meaning it gently, but Phia grimaced and her eyes went dark and she fairly spat: You *don't know it!*

They'd fallen quiet then, both knowing he had blasphemed, both ashamed for it.

No, the boy will be baptized today—that's that. Anyway, the church stands in sight at the end of Heinrichsgasse, just paces from their door. *But in time,* Josef thinks, *once this boy has grown sturdier, we must talk—my wife and I—about the daughterly garments she keeps the child in. All children are girls for a time, that's tradition. But this son is no surrogate.*

In Saint Heinrich's Church the barreled nave yawns bright and gilded like a summer sky. The boy sneezes at the wafted feathers of incense. Phia clutches him tighter. A priest's hand falls in blessing on the hairless pate. Oil and water to the hot little brow. A murmured paternoster, a rosary touched to the red gloriole of the newborn mouth. Josef the paterfamilias stands by, making all prescribed gestures. Finally a lather of names pours forth like the death-staving milk of Mother Maria Lactans herself: "René Karl Wilhelm Johann Josef Maria Rilke."

Little René Maria: the reborn. As long as possible he will be a reparation. Till true gender blooms undeniably. Or till his papa can stand for it no longer.

So Mama's effete and fastidious hands coddled you daily, soaked you in girlhood. You were costumed in ruffles and skirts, your fair thin tresses in curls, cinched with flowing ribbons.

Once beyond the age of mere gibber you went into the trust of a governess, relegated to days of business-like care, occasionally brought out before the chirruping ladies in Mama's circle to be ogled in a new frilly dress or display your daughterly affectations.

—*Who's come to see Mother and her friends?*

Answer: *Your Ismene, dear Maman.*

—*And is Ismene a good girl?*

—*Yes, Maman.*

All the ladies cheep and trill. You redden in your curls. Their small pretender, florid with delight.

Mama's blacksleeved arms stretch toward you. She pulls you near to scrutinize your skirts, your ankle boots (which she will not have you scuffing), and you sense the surge in her hands. Erratic, electric. She props you on the stiff sofa cushion beside her, leans forward to her teacup. The whisper of her dress, her thin black muslin sleeve stretching out again. Her other white hand floats to her hairclip, trembling over the ornate fanwork while her mouth moves without pause and the church ladies give audience to her mannerly gossip.

One listener wears the crumbs of a biscuit in the flaxen fuzz of her upper lip. The lady's mouth smiles and you watch the crumbs cling.

Still Mama's hand is twitching at the hairclip, twitching in a manner you will years from now recall: your first memory retrieved from the height of a distant future moment—memory lewd or libidinous, as though the hairclip were some warm organ pleasuring your mother's fingers. Pleasuring her, even in company.

. . .

And this girlhood of yours is captured in photographs.

Big hands shift you into place, prop you up in your girl-clothes beside a nursery chair.

—*Now rest your wrist here on the chair, like this. This foot forward. Fine. Don't move.*

The hands tilt your button hat just so. They tug at your skirts, fan your box pleats nicely over your knees. A knuckle digs beneath your jaw— *Head just so.* Your shoulders nudged back, chin prodded upward.

—*That's right. Now, are you sure you can't surrender the crop? It's rather unsightly, you know. Can't you let us have it? Think how it would please your mother over there.*

But the crop is your one condition. A buggy crop you found leaning in the shadowed studio corner. You grip it in your left hand, trailing it over the floor before you. As a boy might do. They will not get it from you.

—*Oh yes, the dog! That will be lovely. Let's bring it right over here please. . . . Will it lie down on this chair? Can we get it to lie down? There, yes. That's fine. All right now . . . nobody move!*

But the dog slumps. Its slack brow arches. Dark canine eyes part indifferent, part amused. A blunt canine groan explodes the silence as the exposure is made.

In the blinding burst of the flash your chin sinks. You peer up at the lens as from the low cupboard of the kitchen hutch where you like to hide. Big hands will continue to prop and posture you and you will acquiesce, but in this instant your eyes are caves and some deep refuge has welcomed you into its cupboard space. Only the dog is your ally in this retreat. Only the dog, free from reason, understands. Animals will always be just.

The impartial camera apprehends an unmistakably boyish face fringed with ribbons. Dark soul staring from a body not its own. Already an outlander's gaze.

"Don't believe destiny to be anything more than the heaviness of childhood."

Years later. Twenty-eighth August 1902. The girlchild in the photograph, now a grown man with cropped blond hair and a ragged arrow of a beard, sits up in the seat of a stifling train car. Seventeen hours of travel have brought him to Paris, his new and necessary life. Rain pounding down as the car creeps into the Gare du Nord—sheets slashing across the window beside him. Out there, the rocks that bed the rails seem to boil. Hot rain.

He studies the Baedeker map unfurled across his knees. His lodgings look to be adjacent to the Montparnasse area, and it strikes him as a terrific benediction to arrive to such a name: *Montparnasse,* domain of music and poetry.

I've arrived, Clara.

The train slumps to its halt and he rises to collect his suitcase and trunk, then descends from the airless car into an airless station.

I'm here, I'm climbing down off the train you and Ruth watched me board yesterday. Where are the two of you right now, as I breathe my first of Paris? Taking breakfast in our little kitchen, aren't you?

Above the swirling platform the gables of grimed glass roar like drums. The poet stands with his suitcase in hand and the heavy trunk at his feet. He is decked in his best clothes for this arrival. Starched collar and foulard tie and broad hemisphere hat. Highlow shoes with white cloth-tops. But even at a glimpse he looks a damaged vessel, as when he was a child. Something about him cleft bare and never closed. Twenty-six years in the world now, yet forever these countless cracks in his surface.

He hears a voice: thin stomach-punched words beneath the drumming rain. There's a blue-capped boy standing before him in waterlogged tunic and short pants, two kerchiefs knotted at his scrawny throat.

"Portier?" says Rainer.

"Oui."

The young porter bends to the poet's trunk. It's packed with books, but the boy levers his weight to heave it up and staggers ahead through the teeming station, tossing words behind him as he goes. The words mean nothing despite Rainer's Berlitz hours so he gives no answer, halting and veering to follow.

The boy deposits the poet and luggage in a queue. *"L'octroi, l'octroi,"* he says, and disappears. At the front of the queue each traveler in turn parlays with a French official through the window of a small booth.

Several shuffling moments pass. Then Rainer stands at the booth.

The official's remote and glassy eyes barely see him. *"Bonjour. Des comestibles?"*

Rainer hesitates.

"Avez-vous des danrees alimentaires . . . Ah, vous êtes Allemand? N'est-ce pas?"

"Non. Er . . . oui." He's certainly no German, but he needn't cause confusion just now.

"Alors." The officer leans and taps a finger toward the suitcases. *"Apfel, Brot, Schnitzel, Wurst?"*

"Ah. Non, monsieur."

"Alors, c'est bon."

Rainer is waved past the booth. The young porter returns.

"Désirez-vous une fiacre?"—the last word heavily guttural, a tiny clap of thunder in the throat. The boy seems to see it's lost upon him and tries again: *"Cabriolet?"* Makes the expansive gesture of horse reins shaken in driving manner.

Rainer smiles. *"Oui."*

The boy hauls up the trunk and the poet follows him through the station doors.

Outside, a dark drapery of rain. A world submerged and lusterless, kingdom created of stone and little else. Splash of traffic everywhere. The standing cab boasts no more than a shallow calfskin hood. Water pools on the seat. But the enclosed cabs cost more. Chattering to the driver, the boy hops up and runs a rag from his pocket across the seat, jumps down and makes a broad sweeping gesture. *"Montez monsieur, s'il vous plaît."*

Rainer clambers aboard and the boy hands him the suitcase, but the trunk and suitcase together won't fit.

"Le camion!" The boy holds back the trunk, gesturing vaguely to an area behind. *"Le camion!"* Rainer leans through the water tasseling from the hood and peers to the rear. In a deep puddle a big sideless cart stands piled with luggage. A corpulent man cinches down the edge of a bulging tarpaulin. Baggage truck. No other option in this rain. So Rainer nods to the boy, struggles to dredge up the right words. *"Ça . . . au lieu,"* he says, handing the suitcase down in exchange for the trunk. Better to keep the books close. Already the rain has soaked his knees.

"Quelle adresse?"

A pause as Rainer recalls the number.

"Destination?" says the boy. *"Dez-tin-ah-see-oh."*

"Oui, oui. Er—onze rue Toullier."

"Toullier?"

"Oui. Panthéon." He's been told the Panthéon is a block from the place.

The boy vanishes. And with a sudden iciness in his stomach Rainer recalls Clara's wreath laid away in that suitcase. Little magenta wreath wrought by her sculptress hands from the fresh moorland heather around their house. He almost calls the boy back but feels it foolish. No retrieving the wreath now, not without opening the luggage in this downpour.

—Because everything remains unbroken, Clara said yesterday as she laid the braided wreath in his hands. She meant it to be an image for what would bind him and her and their daughter together, no matter where he must travel.

"*Voilà, monsieur.*" The small porter reappears, handing up a luggage ticket. The boy's knuckly hands are caked with filth. Into the cupped palm Rainer presses a silver coin. The boy, already turning back to the station doors, shouts to the driver: "*Onze rue Toullier, Quartier Latin!*"

The harnesses jangle and Rainer swings forward into a morning like night, roadwater spitting upward off the wheels in glutinous hoops that splatter his trousers.

A moment later the cab is whirling onto a water-lashed boulevard, the frenzied city spilling away far before him. And for years and years ahead Rainer will recall the abrupt and baleful extravagance of this first plunge through the Paris streets.

With lethal mindlessness traffic seethes in all directions. Dark-garbed pedestrians hunch and run the gauntlet, scurry along the sidewalks. Great blocks of buildings line the way in endless martial formation, prisonous brown walls hemming high. Rainer feels a shudder again. Clenches his coat closed at his throat. It seems the chill in his core means to linger, though the August air is heavy and hot. Clara's wreath drifting away behind, a retreating talisman, and the poet now glooming forth through curtains of dark vapor rising from the gutters, a dull reek of sewage, mildew, the stench of urban summer, into this Paris of which so many have spoken. And yet can this be the same Paris? Rainer squints through the glopping rain, the begrimed hustle around him. He's wanted to come here, or so he's been telling himself in the time since his departure became a necessity, and yet already, somehow, it seems something here will use his want against him. How promptly he senses it, like the faint press of a hand to his chest. Something maledictive.

But this surging boulevard is all he's yet seen. *Mustn't recoil so quickly,* he tells himself. And repeats to himself the praises of Paris sung by numerous friends: Arthur Holitscher, Heinrich Vogeler, Paula Becker, and Clara of course—she worked here once. Of course. He's been here less than an hour. It will take some time to accustom oneself, as in any place, that's all.

The cab turns. Someone shouts from an oncoming cart. Flurry of words, unintelligible. The cab driver volleys a fierce retort and shakes his fist.

Rainer braces himself atop his tough seat. In truth his fast unease is a thing purely native to him. He's never been one for measured appraisal of place or experience—not with those cracks in his surface through which the outside comes always flooding in: his senses soaked by the temper of a place, the state of its people. For this, all cities have equaled torment. He's fled from several already—beginning with Prague, city of his birth. Prague, for years a labyrinth of spidery streets he could not unpuzzle in order to free himself, and always its forked spires stood bludgeoning the sky as in gestures of horrific warning. Prague, which was Mama coming at night, crucifix in hand, to pray fervently over the bed where René Maria lay wide-eyed and clutching the blankets. So quick from Mama's womb that seven-month soul, so breakable. The child would watch Mama's lampcast shadow swelling huge and tumorous from her back, a blacker self threatening to swallow her up. Her voice always gravity-stricken in its tremble, as though she fought to lift her words through the night-heavy air. The tiny Christ a silhouette in her hand, Christ's bronze elbows sagging below the crossbeam. And always Christ seemed to be slipping, tiny hands and feet tearing free of the nails, palm flesh ruptured like rent stockings. But René Maria didn't want Jesus to drop on him and prayed with Mama, prayed silently that Jesus would not drop, would not come crawling spiderlike atop the bedclothes—wouldn't be naked wouldn't be wet with blood wouldn't bleed through René Maria's blankets. At length an *Amen.* Then Mama bent toward the child and Jesus sank close in the watery light and the child in his frilled cotton bonnet touched each of the five cool wounds with a kiss. Summer and winter that small god was cold to the lips.

Prague was the second crucifix too, the one mounted on the wall above the breakfast table: Christ so large he was nearly the boy's size, though impossibly thin. Head slumped to one emaciated shoulder, he hung there watching with leaden eyes as René Maria ate soft bread or a bluish egg. A burgundy starburst bloomed from the crushed bonework of the hallowed feet, intricate paisleys of blood adorned the breast and stomach, and in each impaled palm a hard red calyx stood like a frozen flower. Christ kept staring sadly as if to say, *I can't come down,* and years later the boy would learn the reason: this god meant to screen the Heavenly Father from sight by those injured arms.

With this Prague for his provenance, most cities have been quick to find a passage inside him, to tear at the black gum of Rainer's nerves and agglomerate the forms of old nightmare. Why should Paris be different, in spite of whatever he'd hoped? Even the best cities accommodate only briefly.

The buildings go by and go by, blear and brown. Under limp and drizzling awnings, heaps of ungainly goods stream past. Flaccid shoes by the hundreds. Dolls in tawdry echelons, tattered or eyeless or bald. Mounds of produce with bony cats curled amidst the turnips and skulls of wilted lettuce.

It's not cities alone that get inside him. Hardly. Rainer has long since come to ask himself: How can one possibly hold it all—the past the future the love of other people the world's overwhelming scenes the soul-incised faces of strangers everything everything everything?—*how,* when it *all* gets in at once? Ah, but now this city's pressing hugeness, its jostle and jamming of fates . . .

The cab carries him clattering down a ribbon of cobblestones. Deep dim crevasse that echoes back from its sunken quietude the clanking of the chassis, the complaint of the seat springs. Smell of stove smoke and kitchen grease here. Every slanted shutter flung open and scraps of forgotten household cloth flapping there or from the sills in sorry swags. Onward with the walls rising and rising till the sky is but a seam above, every surface plastered with crumbling notices, corners weathered to warts of pulp. *Belles Femmes!*—*Opium!*—*Absinthe!* and other seedy promises drearing away in a quarter rarely graced by daylight.

In the deeper dark of certain thresholds faint faces come forth like tinplate images. Pale consumptive children. The greased eyes of whores. They loiter in doorways. Leer from panels of soiled glass. Their gazes hard upon him as he judders by.

Is there some other Paris, Clara? Is it just in these few quarters? Or did you never think to tell me how the city would look at first?

But could Clara have known how it would look to *him?*

A sense of error haunts me already, Clara. So soon. And now I am seeing you at home in Westerwede: you and Ruth, the bright dream on the other side of this one. Could you have known the quick effect this city would have on me? . . . Clear weather in Westerwede, is it not? The sun is shining. I can see it. Why should I envision this and not be living it now?—not be awake in that other world? We both know this to be the unignorable question, Clara. For we had our work. For a time. Our cottage garlanded in grape bowers, and so much accomplished in my attic study with its small Russian shrine, its candles burning as I wrote. I did good things in that room, stationed at the handsome Biedermeier desk and fed by our dumb-waiter in my most unstoppable moments. And you also were working well. Why did we believe this work would fail to return to us? There were many troubles that first year, of course, but did it mean our work had escaped us for good? . . . And now I keep seeing Ruth, Clara. Ruth, who came and delivered us from the winter last year. No, she delivered us unto the winter, did she not? Had you or I ever believed as wholeheartedly in winter as we believed in this last one with her? Her small hands carried, in radiance, the warmth of the milk you shared with her . . . all the while the snow shawled everything beyond the cottage windows. It hung like ornaments from the eaves. We were deep inside that winter, past its coldness as past a fear. . . . And now my thoughts must flow backward to reach you both. And now Ruth's hands will drift about when they're not touching you, Clara, won't they? Because those dear hands know their other receiver has gone. Vanished, Clara, knowing nothing of this place he was headed, the bleak dream awaiting him out here. And, oh Clara, didn't this person write, barely a year ago, these words?

> *"those who leave the village drift for a long time*
> *and many die, perhaps, along the way"*

On and on through canyoned streets, the wheels sending up their filthy spray.

At a cluttered junction the cab skates round an overturned cart. A pale horse fallen in its traces and writhing on the puddled stones, its rear legs splayed wrongly, kicking not at all. A wheezing snuffle as the horse tries to rise. Its driver stands with one foot on its straining ribs, chattering and waving his hands. Bystanders have gathered. Rainer does not look further.

Finally the drenched neck of his cab's horse veers left, the cab tilts right, and a blue-gray cupola looms high and preponderant amidst the buildings ahead.

"*Panthéon,*" mutters the driver.

The hard dome overshadows the sky. But now the cab slews again and Rainer goes darkly into another narrowing passage. The horse slips to a halt.

"*Onze rue Toullier, monsieur.*"

Through the haze of rain the poet sees the housefront's blue number. Crude blue rectangular door.

The driver has jumped to the street. Rainer hands down the trunk and climbs from the cab. His coat sleeves hang heavy below the elbows and he's completely soaked from waist down, but the driver is a pile of lifeless garments, something once fierce within the man now withering by the minute. A dim candle sputtering in its sconce. His pruney hand accepts the poet's pay. He mounts to his seat and stirs the horse again and the cab slides away down the lane and Rainer is left alone in the thrashing air with a suitcase full of books and knocking at a foreign door.

I'm thinking toward you, Clara. It does me good. Out of my many premonitions, I think toward my wife who is perhaps a dream. Perhaps a stranger. But I knew her yesterday. She pressed a fresh wreath into my hands. She kissed me goodbye in the Bremen train station, holding our daughter in her arms.

Suddenly Rainer feels his own verses pebbling down upon him hard as the rain. Lines he wrote last year at Westerwede. He listens as if hearing someone else's words. And can't deny their prophecy.

"You believed you'd always recognize the power
when you seized the fruit;
now it becomes a riddle again,
and again you feel yourself no more than a guest.

The summer was like your house,
you knew where everything stood inside it—
Out into your heart you must now travel
like one who sets off across a plateau.
The great aloneness begins."

A long time and no one answers the door. The rain falls and falls. . . .

From far off in the saturated city comes the slurred knelling of a church bell.

*Y*ou first met Clara two years before. To the day, in fact. And what does this strange synchronicity betoken?—to have come twice round the wreath of years and back to the moment you first laid eyes upon your future wife, and to find yourself alone in such a place as this Paris?

Twenty-eighth August it was, 1900. Walking down the Worpswede highway at twilight with Heinrich Vogeler. Smell of countryside. The north German moors reclining to the horizon, the whole terrain purpled in the failing light. Behind you to the west: the fern-furred mountain-in-miniature—the Weyerberg. Everything of that twilight remains intact yet. It's like this:

You're wearing the blue Russian tunic that so perplexes Vogeler's elderly housekeeper. Shirt with billowed sleeves and cummerbund and a swatch of red fabric across the shoulders.

"He doesn't mean to wear that in the village, does he?" the house-keeper had murmured to her master while proffering the tureen at dinner. Vogeler merely smiled and caught your eye across the table.

A good fellow, Heinrich—you'd felt an immediate fondness while first shaking his hand on an Italian veranda two years ago, the painter promptly urging you to visit him in Worpswede. Now you've come to accept his long-standing offer, Vogeler's burnished cane tapping at the dirt as you walk beside him through this treasured landscape of his. He wears smart black gaiters and a dandy Biedermeier coat.

"We're a family out here," he says. "In fact, that's what we call ourselves. *Die Familie.*"

He means the colony of Worpswede luminaries, a handful of young artists with a provincial style all their own. They were first drawn to these moors to gain the tutelage of the famed painter Fritz Mackensen, but now they flourish here in their own right, a family of creatives. And Vogeler intends to make you, it seems, a part of *the family.* He's given you your own lovely red room in the lovingly furnished mansion he's dubbed the Barkenhoff. You really couldn't have hoped for any better sanctuary for the work that lies ahead of you. You've come west to Worpswede from Berlin, from Lou, after a second summer of travels with her in Russia.

Russia's wonders rendered you dumb. Strange to be in a place so exotic, and yet to experience it in every moment as a *homeland,* everything standing too close to your heart—impossible to express it all adequately. No doubt it didn't help for Lou to abandon you in Saint Petersburg as she did: nearly a month alone in your lodging at the city's thrumming heart, pining all the while for the Russian countryside from which you'd just returned. But now, now you intend to sit down in your new red room for days on end, to mend the great gash in your diary and give voice to the watershed of Russia. You *intend,* but plans will change, and in this very moment—as you and Vogeler come upon a small cottage standing amidst grapevines—it's already happening. Already you've been diverted.

Boas of tendril and leaf hover darkly before the cottage, trellised in the indigo evening. Beyond, the frame of the lamplit door holds a tall womanly figure in silhouette. She murmurs something and comes down into darkness.

"Clara," says Vogeler. "She's a sculptress."

She remains but shadow and shape as your threesome draws together in her yard. Vogeler introduces you.

Reach to press the sculptress's hand.

A moment or two of cordiality, but Clara Westhoff is shy, talks little and quietly. All across the moors the crickets have raised an elaborate chorus.

Vogeler says, "Rainer's just returned from Russia." And so in that Worpswede night you begin talking of Tolstoy, the River Volga, the peasant villages whose people say God abides beneath one's left arm. The words flow from you as they've refused to do in your diary. At length Clara Westhoff offers her own quiet remarks about the spiritual traits she finds unique to Slavic folk. Their faces, she says, ignite something inside her—faces deeply expressive of that people's chiseled soul.

So this is how a sculptress talks. You like her voice, her soft-spoken, selective words. She is shy, yes, but in a manner that suggests harbored power rather than meekness. She interrupts herself—"Look at us talking in the dark"—turns back through the cottage door and brings out a lamp. The light bathes everything in yellow. And now you see something halting in the sculptress as she looks upon you: your high boots and loose Russian smock, the features of your own pseudo-Slavic face as she described a moment ago.

"Oh," she says. "I thought you were German. Or Austrian, perhaps. But you are not?"

Vogeler chuckles. And now everyone laughs a little.

"A long story," you say.

Still Clara Westhoff's arm stays raised with the light. The lamp-glare carves her own features into breathtaking relief. A face as from some old and noble myth. And you feel that her surprised and searching eyes are somehow molding you, making you, from the shapeless clay of the moorland darkness.

Shortly after this night, you wrote of Clara in the diary where you thought you'd write of Russia:

". . . her whole dark liveliness which is strength upon strength and displeasure wherever there is lack of occasion for strength. One should permit nothing to be as finished as it seems—everything must come more and more into one's hands, each hour must want to be crafted better."

Alone in a tiny room at number 11 rue Toullier, collecting your thoughts. The close ceiling compels you to sit. For to stand at the center of the tattered carpet, as you did when the fat *hôtelier* woman brought you in, produces an unnerving sensation of compression, your hair nearly grazing the low-hung beams. The *hôtelier* had noted your wetness and warned you in icy French not to soil her furniture. A warning mordantly comical with this stained chair brooding in its corner—but she was clearly not to be challenged, so you stood about and didn't even mention the crusted tablecloth, the bits of paper inexplicably strewn across the carpet, the jammed rolltop desk.

The woman had appeared at the front door only after you'd bruised your knuckles in knocking. Blunt turtle face thrust from the musty hall and glancing around as though she judged you no more than some inept porter delivering the trunk of a guest you'd failed to keep in tow. You introduced yourself in halting French and watched her walleyed face shrink back into its wattle. In a kind of weary condescension she waved you inward. You followed as she thumped away up the narrow stairs, the black-caked hem of her skirts dragging ahead. Four, maybe five breathless flights, pulling the trunk up behind you. Discolored gray walls. A meager daylight lurking upon the steps.

Clara. What did I say to you in our last few days together? What kind of talk filled our last weeks? Talk of work and money and faraway cities, but mostly money. And all the time the summer was bright outside our house. The heather was festive with sunlight.

Standing behind the woman as she opened the room's door you tried not to look at the bulbous carbuncle on her nape, a sort of boil bedded in the mallowy flesh.

This city—how can I explain it?—already holds great malevolence toward me. And you know I have the sense for such things. You understand the way everything gets fast inside me, whether I want it or not. . . .

And now you are alone in this sordid chamber which some joke of fate has ascribed. It seems the real tenant has merely stepped out—or maybe been forced out, judging from the consternation of that torn-up paper on the floor. You are sitting stiffly in the soiled chair because standing is not an option.

You lack a change of clothes, your suitcase presently strapped to an overburdened luggage truck trundling down a dismal lane somewhere. Clearly you will need to burn a little something and get dry. Best to first go out, though, and wire your safe arrival to Clara . . . and what can you tell her? How describe this room?

Between the dusty black stove and the washstand a small blackened maw is dug into the wall. A tin refuse pail stands there. ("Don't use that fireplace," added the *hôtelier* with a didactic look). At the mantel tilts a tarnished mirror. Before the mirror a sallow clock, the minute hand locked at the twelve and vainly twitching. Side by side at the mantel's corner are two silver candlesticks, each with a nub of melted wax. They seem a source of light in themselves. The whole of this abject chamber stands contained in the slender hips of silver. And what is such contradictory finery doing here? . . . It must be that your predecessor invested these candlesticks with great importance. They lavished a tangible glamour on his squalid life, whoever he was.

Stoop-shouldered beneath the beams, you rise and touch the candlesticks. Your hand in a jellied distortion of silver. You will care for these things now. Everything their brightness has kept at bay shall stay at bay. Yes, go out and wire Clara—and you needn't cause her worry. Before leaving, crouch to collect the scraps of paper. Turn them over in your hands, these fragments of someone's former life. All of them are blank.

Telegram to Clara (in your nascent French):

> *"One can't doubt: I am in Paris. . . . I am all expectation: What shall become of this? My room is on the third or fourth floor (I dare not count) and what makes me proud is that there is a hearth with a mirror, a clock and two candlesticks of silver."*

Even more sopping when you return, and no harbor but this garret chamber. Light the stove, disrobe, drape your clothes here and there. The corroded window opens only with force, but now you've got it hinged to the hissing rain and the tight heat begins to drain from the room. Beyond the sill: nothing to see but the opposite building with its twelve shutter-flung eyes.

Heat some water in the blackened kettle, wash in the sullied basin (the bottom plaqued brown as tea). But in spite of the basin your clean-smelling soap brings relief.

Now in singlet and knee breeches you unpack the books, amongst them a copy of *The Book of Images* for Rodin. He won't be able to read it in the original German, of course, but it's important that you be allowed the gesture of giving him something; that something of yours might rest amongst his things. Packed with the books is your small Russian icon, an ogival diptych brightly painted. The serene gazes of Christ and His mother both swart and ebony-eyed and nimbused in gold.

Prop the diptych on the broken desk and immediately Westerwede leaps to mind. Your attic study and its Russian shrine. How you and Clara furnished every room of that house in an act of hopeful devotion. The finishing touches came in gifts from family and friends. Like the picture of

Saint Cecilia from Clara's parents. You had hung it above your desk. The saint's gaze upcast to the clarion angels above, a broken harp hanging from her fingers and a number of broken instruments scattered at her feet. Saint Cecilia: chaste Christian who consented to marry a Roman on the condition that he accept a sexless union. How uncanny that such an image came to you as a wedding gift—with all that it spoke of your recent past.

"Shall I tell you about my husband?" Lou had said.

Remember: rumpled in her long shirred sack dress, Lou reposed in a weathered deck chair like an empress. Summertime air in the Isar Valley. The garden vivid in sunlight. Her eyes floated upward to the stirring trees and one hand moved to the goblet of milk nearby, then abruptly returned to her lap. "He forced me—" She sat forward in her chair. "You see. He forced me to marry him." Her confession in your best weeks alone together.

As fleetly as she'd arrived in your life Lou took herself away again, held herself beyond reach. And then came the modest wedding ceremony in the dining room of Clara's girlhood home. Then months of anxiety. Ruth's birth. More anxious months. And now this little diptych is the single thing left of the Russia you'd known before all that. Oh, to think now of the good work you'd sworn would result from your time in Russia. Six months spent there in the space of two years—and how many more months of preparation, study, discipleship?—and all that time lived in the presence of Lou. Whatever came of that? . . . There *were* those one hundred poems you thought of as your "Russian Prayers," true, but what human connection was ever gained? What besides this everlasting homesickness, this unshakable alien feeling now surging up again in Paris?

You and Lou had sailed north on the River Volga, a voyage of more than a week, penetrating to the country's very heart. Her husband had come along on the first journey of the previous summer, but this second Russia was yours and Lou's alone. You still hold the names inside you: *Saratov. Samara. Stavropol* and *Simbirsk. Nizny Novgorod.* Yet that landscape had been so much more than names in the hours and hours you stood marveling from the steamer's deck.

Flat timber rafts skimmed past you downriver, piled high with trees felled in the upcountry woodlands. From each shore the country rolled away immense and unnamable, untrammeled by the dark boundary lines that mankind in frenzied forgery throws like dragnets across its maps. The vast outer landscape seemed to mirror the vast one within you, which Lou had helped you discover. It didn't matter that you had never before been in Russia—it was *home* to you. The world's different terrains flowed together into one, inner and outer, irrespective of nations. Nowhere could a person see this more clearly than on a river journey. And what *was* a *homeland,* after all?—the cartographic coordinates at which one's birth had accidentally occurred?—or a reverberation, the spirit of a place vibrating deep in the spirit of a person? And how Russia reverberated in you! No matter that you'd never been there before: to be in Russia was to *return.*

And to be there with Lou meant everything. She stood beside you on the deck, sometimes for an entire morning. Together you watched the landscape rippling from blue to tawny-gray to green to blue. Here and there it lay fleeced in white clover. And the great plains coursed away to the horizon, and those monumental burying mounds—*kurgans,* they were called—swelled upward and shrank back again. Above the huddled villages pale gulls swarmed in phantasmagoric clutch and retreat, the bark huts smoking darkly beneath, and amidst the huts the golden teardrop spires rose like huge buds. And then the mythic steppes, those desolate seas of grass, and off in the depths of the scene: a wild yellow horse in a bolting gallop, a cloud of chaff pluming like chalk at its heels. *That* was Russia as you and Lou created it together. That was Russia before it became but names lined up in your memory like antique urns—remnants of some world once significant, now lost forever.

But no, names are not the only remnants, for you still have this diptych and that is something. Little wooden icon carried halfway across the world. You vowed not to forget the circumstances of this gift. *Remember now* . . . that small peasant village of Krestá-Bogorodskoye high upriver. The young girl whose mother was called . . . Makaróvna. Yes: Makaróvna, whose birchwood *izbá* sheltered you and Lou for five idyllic nights.

Makaróvna's young daughter must have been thirteen or fourteen. She wore a headscarf like her mother's and hung about the woman's heels, never daring to look guests in the eye. She squatted in the dirt floor of the hut and stoked the fire beneath the samovar while her mother freshened the big cloth sack with new hay: the humble bed you would share with Lou.

But later, when Makaróvna sent her daughter back to your *izbá* with cups for chai, the girl forgot her meekness and locked her eyes on yours. Lustrous eyes she had, pools of darkest honey. She stood there barefoot in the sawdust before your threshold, staring. In each hand she held forth a ceramic cup. Village hens jerked about her feet, dealing her toes a few inquisitive pecks, but she didn't notice.

"Remarkable!" said Lou when the girl had gone. "Has anyone ever looked at you that way?"

"What was it?" you said. "Did I frighten her?"

In a moment the girl returned. She ducked through the *izbá* door and stood close before you with solemn eyes. "For you," she said in deep thoracic Russian. Words of so profound a timbre that one could not doubt the soul to have its seat in the chest. With both hands she held out the painted diptych. Christ and His mother offered up on the bed of the girl's palms. The gift itself made in a gesture of receiving.

The girl was poor, her family was poor, but for you to decline acceptance would deprive *her* of a gift. So you lifted your hands in like manner and she laid the diptych across your fingers.

"Because your eyes," she said to you. "Because your face." Careful, slow words meant to command your understanding. And then she turned to Lou that Lou might understand as well. "Because his face."

Lou gave a silent nod.

The three of you stood still together, the fire popping softly, the smell of birch resin perfuming the *izbá* like incense.

Finally the girl spoke again: "How many twenty-four hours from here does your home make?"

By the manner of her asking, it seemed she suspected a spirit such as you to have journeyed from some corner of her native land whose language was unaccountably strange. You blinked, shot a dumbfounded look at Lou. She gave the girl an uncomplicated reply while you just stood there. The *Liebfrau* and Blessed Child stared up from your palms with close-set almond eyes.

"What did I do?" you asked Lou later. "Did she think I was Russian?"

Lou merely smiled and would not answer. And for days after, you felt intensely humbled, like one who'd been touched by some undeserved blessing.

Homestruck. That, you know now, had been the feeling that touched you in those strange moments with the Russian daughter. And how long has it been since this feeling has returned to you? After Russia you've felt *homestruck* on very few occasions: at Vogeler's Barkenhoff in Worpswede, if only for a month or so—and then later in your cottage with Clara. Yes, however ill-suited you've recently proven to be, your brief Westerwede life was no blatant error: setting up home, laying down seeds—else why should you feel so many things kicked away in coming here to Paris? Else why should it so pain you to be without Clara's wreath in these first hours?

You did begin to *fear* it was all in error, though, didn't you? Even the marriage, maybe. Last year, one month before the baby's birth, you wrote to a friend: *"I am a bad money-maker."* Clara was tumid with child, nearly bursting her blouses—and you no more than her beleaguered husband, penniless at a time when manful prosperity was most direly needed. For months you had dispatched fretful letters to every promising corner, but all prospects had dimmed while Clara's delivery neared—nothing yet resembling a steady income. Your play, *Daily Life,* would be produced, but not till Christmas.

Then, in the ice-blue noon on twelfth December, the unforestallable miracle occurred. You stood watching your daughter's slick reddish limbs flailing between Clara's knees. Awestruck at the obstreperous noise of new life filling that tiny bedroom, you were transformed to paterfamilias.

A week later *Daily Life* premiered in Berlin. You did not attend the performance, but the audience's rude guffaws rang in your ears even in Westerwede. The actors could hardly hear one another, it was rumored— maybe just hyperbole, but what comfort if it was? The play's run was quickly cancelled: another stave of hope ripped from the ground where it had so tenuously lodged.

And then. *And then,* promptly, came the worst: Papa's piteous letter from Prague. Twenty brief lines scratched blackly on the thin stationery of the Turnau-Kralup-Prague Railroad Company:

> *'The allowance endowed by your Uncle Jaroslav, so his daughters wish me to inform you, shall be discontinued come summer.'*

—and up ripped the final stave. Papa's blithe and deadly guarantee fol- lowed; he would secure you a clerkship in a Prague bank, should you sim- ply have the sense to return "home" and commit to stable employment.

Oh, nothing to do but rail at that proposed fate. You hadn't been earn- ing much, but you *were* surviving—thanks largely to your prolific pen, which must someday (mustn't it?) be the means to a sound existence. And God knows you'd been writing: a book of novellas just published, followed immediately by *The Book of Images.* And a single magnificent week back in September had tenured the outpouring of an entire thirty-four poems. It had been like a trance! Poems so astonishing in their power, their flooding speed, that you quickly recognized them as prayers. Russian-style prayers

somehow a continuation of the sixty-six others that had flooded through
you two years before while living with Lou (those were still in Lou's keeping). Those first prayers had used you like a medium; some monkish spirit
intoned his devotions through you. These new prayers were different somehow, but they were of a piece. They too had used you. You *knew* they were
beautiful.

And what of that?—to go on producing such unserviceable things as
poems? Immeasurable things, beautiful no doubt, but not fit to become
commodity, not prized enough for exchange. What to do in gainful employ when one feels oneself employed by *poems?*—by this rare work that so
far surpasses the notion of value it can only be *ungainful?* Such a person
does not become a bank clerk. Such a person is an *economist of the spirit*—not
a toter of figures, an automaton in office attire! Such a person resists—no
road but one lies open to him. So you resisted, despite the precarious state
of your young family. For what would you amount to should you forsake
this unserviceable art of yours? What sort of father, husband, man, *soul?*
Deadly questions, all. *"Spiritually alone,"* you wrote to a friend, *"this would
be a complete resignation, a frost in which everything must die . . . I would sooner
go hungry, me and mine, than take this step."* These words in one letter
amongst many written early in the New Year. And at length these letters
yielded a modest salvation, for come spring you were scratching away on a
monograph about the Worpswede artists, a commission from a Berlin publisher. Clara was busy with commissions too. The Westerwede life might
have seemed tenable at last—but the final stave, already uprooted, would
not stick again, and you and Clara had conceded that your household could
not stand. With the Worpswede monograph finished, a second commission came from Berlin: another monograph, this one on the subject of the
inimitable sculptor Auguste Rodin (with whom Clara had briefly studied
two years ago).

So: Paris, to meet the Master. So: Clara's wreath laid ceremoniously atop the garments in your suitcase. And then the quiet breakage of farewell in the Bremen station, a parting kiss for Clara and one for Ruth, the child clinging about her mother's neck. Paris: this dismal room, this broken desk, this vengeance of rampant memories, all with the juxtaposed purpose—*preposterous* were it not already guaranteed—of meeting the world's great Rodin.

"Are you sure this is right?" Clara had said to you in the station, a flash of distress in her eyes as she held Ruth close. "Sure you should go just now?"

What could you answer? You kissed her again and told her she'd join you in Paris before long.

"Ja," she said. "Before long. The wreath will keep till I come." Then she stood watching you climb the steps to the car.

Westerwede was finished. There could be no discussion, just yet, of where little Ruth would go when Clara came to Paris.

"The city was against me. It rose up before my life and was like an examination I could not pass."

Three long days alone with Paris. It seems a lifetime of sorts. Rainer walks about in a troubled thrall. The dim crevasses of the Quartier Latin digest him and even for his Baedeker he is lost. He must widen his stride to overstep lank piles of trash heaped in the streets, pockets of dross and litter amongst the cobblestones. Rag pickers trundle toward him steering their rude and wobbling carts and he must stop and turn himself flat to a wall to let them by. In the grim fissures of lanes or alleyways sallow people stand amidst the puddles in sagging clothes, back between the houses where the huge worms of the pipes droop from the walls like vermin killed and curing. He sees small children peering up from sullied basement windows: pale hairless wastrels like moles. And just as the gutters along every street bear the sluglike flow of fluids, so does a strange and abounding fear coagulate in the very air, hardening into sound till it seems some discarnate voice is spluttering the name of this place with malfeasant insistence: *ParisssParisss-Parisss!* A name somehow reptilian, infernal in its pop and hiss: *Parisssss.* Fork-tongued city. It's fast becoming his private capital of fear.

And yet it is a great city, and not without beauty, certainly not—and isn't that natural: for such dread to be bedfellow to such beauty? At the end of this momentous apprenticeship beginning now in Paris, Rainer Maria Rilke will write:

"The beautiful is nothing but the beginning of terror, which we still
    unguardedly endure,
and we admire it so because it spurns us, stopping short of our
    destruction."

But these streets. These streets engulf the poet as they have long since engulfed the gaunt gray man he sees daily guarding the door of Saint Etienne du Mont: the man's rheumatic hand cupped in front of him, his dumb mouth contorted in an effort toward words. The man tries and tries, but never speaks. And it seems he means to utter some inexpressible gratitude, with never a thought of whether a single charitable coin has fallen to his big-knuckled hand.

Rainer sees at once how easily he himself could go under in that manner, this city's sea of anonymity churning him down and his every word snared fast in its greasy undertow.

He's to meet Rodin on first September, when the sculptor expects him in his Paris atelier. Till then, in his sordid fifth-story silence, the poet wrestles with the need inside him. Need that incessantly makes itself felt but cowers when he gives it leave to come forth as work. He sits at the broken desk, the window open at his side, and the need is a confused shudder; he cannot tell its meaning. He waits at the desk, full of readiness. The need won't slacken, and neither will it bring anything forth. But Rainer does not move from the desk, for this time spent at the desk is the reason he's come to this city. For this he's abandoned everything, in order, perhaps, that everything might return to him somehow.

Outside, far below in the street, people are laughing. Laughing and running. Feet tromping by in breathless clatter. And it's the laughter of something big and profoundly contemptuous. The clatter of everything within him: running away.

He writes to Clara with angry determination, cudgeling words meant for himself.

"This city is very big and full to the brim of sadness. And you will be alone and poor in it and very unhappy unless from the first hour you cultivate through your work a happiness, a stillness, a strength. . . . Heavy your life will be. . . . But it is true: it will then be your own heaviness that you have to carry, the heaviness of your heart, of your longing, the burden of your work. And therefore be happy, deep inside, behind words and thoughts rejoice."

Be happy, deep inside, in the heaviness of your heart, in the burden of your work—yes, this was the lesson that brought him to Lou, to Clara. He must remember it now.

But he longs for Clara's presence as he writes. Her face hovering before him. Her wreath within reach at the edge of his desk, its wild magenta already dimming to purple—or is it just the wrong-colored light in this room, the cast of this city's emberous fear? And can a soul have more than one capital of fear? Was Rainer's escape never conclusive?—for he thought he'd escaped in fleeing Prague, that capital of his early years. . . .

In Prague within the stroke of a day, little René Maria's girl-clothes had failed to convince. His face too featured, his limbs too long, and the squares of his bony shoulders already framing themselves out of his blouses. Boyishness no longer quelled by dresses.

"It's time these games come to an end," said the father.

So curls were snipped, hair combed down straight and neat, the child garbed in dark trousers and jacket. Suddenly a schoolboy.

The mother sobbed, but the father was pleased. They seemed hardly to note one another's differing states. Mama and Papa had always been quiet in each other's company. Else they kept to different rooms. Except when guests came—then there was chatter. Or except when Papa was strict—then they were tangled in noise.

Papa spoke plainly to the boy now, instructed him how to carry himself: breast straight, shoulders back. Spoke to the boy of his military days: *What fulfillment! How I miss them! But you—if you keep your neck straight and if you listen—you have the promise of an officer. Don't you want that, son? Have I told you the role I served in the Italian campaign? Just twenty-one years of age, still noncommissioned, and given command of the citadel at Brescia. Ja, your own father. And you are made for such a thing too, my boy. You are made for it, but for one thing that will hold you back if you allow it: this unhealthy condition your mother has encouraged in you, this . . . sogginess. A boy ought to love and respect his mother, of course—but it's peculiar and girlish, as one grows older, to coddle and need coddling.*

Yes Papa yes Papa yes Papa. Propped in his seat with shoulders back, René Maria says he understands. Rainer sees that faraway self avowing his understanding, but even as the words leave his mouth the small boy has begun to quiver. The big brocade chair growing monstrous, wanting to swallow him. And Papa will soon find it all in his face. The boy cannot dissemble. So René Maria gets up and goes out of the study. With stiffened shoulders he fights off the tremors. Papa has not seen his face. Good.

The boy seeks Mama in the parlor, finds her at the glass-fronted cabinet where the wine is kept. She's filling the finely labeled bottle with the cheap red claret from the carafe. He draws close and gazes at the ruby rope of liquid.

Mama says, "Hello little boy." Slow words spoken in the minor key of disappointment—and now a dim recognition dawns inside him. Nevermore play the daughter for her. *But I would do it, Mama. For you!*

Her familiar skin-smell seeps toward him, buried white muskiness escaped from black garments, odor he breathes like inhaled peace. She gives him the funneled paper to hold at the bottle's mouth while she pours. The shadowy volume rises in the glass.

Every day now Mama clutches his hand and walks him to the Piarist School, though it's not far from Heinrichsgasse. Briskly along the streets where gamboling schoolchildren clump and scatter. The boy is free from danger with Mama. But in the absence of grown-ups the Bohemian children curse him and his Christian Brother teachers. "Rotten Christers!" they jeer.

Prague's streets are a maze of coiled apartheid, and the boy, a German speaker, is unwittingly part of the ruling minority. His tongue cuts him sharply off from the more numerous Bohemian children, guarantees their contempt. Austrian by nationality, Bohemian by milieu, German by language—just as gender has come to him like an illegible missive, a smear of letters on a splattered page, so a nation will never be his. Nor a culture.

In the schoolyard by day René Maria remains aloof, daintily lurking at the edge of the yard, eyes on his feet. Else he stays indoors and draws pictures: horses and canaries. Else he becomes absorbed in fantasies the girls enact. Girls are not so foreign.

And yet a deep-dropping question now lies in the vacancy where *his* girlhood was, question like a hole wherein he has lately fallen and fallen. Only in Mama's presence does the question ease and shrink. And then a bulging fear remains buried under his clothes. Fear of falling, it protrudes like a tumor in his chest, but Mama soothes it. Tames it.

. . . oh Mama who was Prague who was nightmare who was Jesus pinned in helplessness who was salvation always kept at bay—in those days she was also the wellspring of wonders.

Rainer sees her now, an outlandish pile of black as always. Frilled widow's costume she wore daily. Down the dim kaleidoscopic cave of Paris and the surging memories it brings, he comes again to her queer thin form. Her hands and face stand out bloodless against her dark garments, and across her knees are the bright pages of the Schiller book laid open.

She is reading aloud:

Zürne dem Glücklichen nicht, daß den leichten Sieg ihm die Götter Schenken, daß aus der Schlacht Venus den Lieblung entrückt.

Evenings in the parlor while Papa shuts himself away in his study. The words of Schiller in Mama's voice, and the boy wandering about in obedience to the *things* and their strange drawing power.

He's long been surrounded by them. *Dinge. Things.* The potpourri dish with its thread-thin scallops of blue paint. The china doll. The pear-shaped perfume bottle. The miniature gilt-framed pictures of Papa as a handsome officer candidate, of Mama as a bright young woman. Now that René Maria is older he's permitted to take the *things* in his hands, to turn them over and feel their animate qualities. So he lifts them, sets them down, lifts them, runs his fingers over their textures.

In truth these Heinrichsgasse rooms boast nothing but second-rate *things*—much-touched *things* wounded by hands, not the fine array Mama would like. See: this potpourri bowl's yellowed porcelain, this Monsieur Parrot of heavy glass whose dolorous white face once flaunted a most brilliant green. The boy pities them. Already he knows to pity them.

Over time he has learned of the strange regard *things* have for him as for everybody, though most people never notice. How *things* sometimes shrink the world and make it more bearable. How in the absence of *things* the world would tower frightfully. He has noticed that most people pay them little heed, and yet while a person converses at a table, converses nervously with someone still a stranger, he sees how desperately the person's hands seek *things:* a fork, the rim of a plate. It happens by instinct; one gets anchored again in the world without quite realizing. And then one just moves on thanklessly amongst *things*—when all the while it was the small round napkin ring that kept one from feeling the world's hugeness.

Mama reads: *Alles Menschliche muß erst warden und wachsen und reifen.*

René Maria pictures the words just as Mama now sees them on the page. Powerful nouns bounding forth to pummel the air:

Menschliche—humankind.

Götter—gods.

Zeit—time.

Geburt—birth.

The nouns stand up in potent German capitals, full in the mouth. *Dinge.* And already he can feel the *things* in his hands tremoring strangely at the words. Tremoring like wounded relations.

"With every line one broke off the world."

Take the words from the Schiller book. Lift them by memory off the pages. Channel the words to your mouth and carry them about on your tongue. Own them.

Siehe! Da weinen die Götter, es weinen de Göttinnen alle,
Daß das Schöne vergeht, daß das Volkommene stirbt.

Go to Papa in his study. Slip in silently; he doesn't notice. For a moment you may watch him: the different manner his face and body assume when he believes himself unobserved. He is hunched over papers and his big neck is bent and his thin hair is neatly combed. Two fatherly hands, white and matted with dark fuzz, lie unmoving amongst the papers as though asleep. He is silent. He too seems a *thing*.

Now break the silence, cautiously. Watch Papa's eyes come up. Begin.

Pronounce the words arranged within you. Recite with melody and care, all the time watching Papa's *thing*-like hands, the way they thaw and change and stir: listening. All the *things* of the world listen.

And the words are threading themselves in the carpet beneath you. They are sidling up against Papa's ledger books, railway stamps, inkwell and pens. The words are entering Papa's bristly beard, softening it. Instinctively, he moves his hand to stroke that beard.

"... *the* things *vibrate into each other, across and out into the air, and their coolness makes the shadows clear and the sun into a lucid, spiritual vision. Then there is no main* thing ... *every* thing *is everywhere, and one must be in all that in order to miss nothing.*"

The words draw to an end. Papa's hand falls back to the desk. He says nothing. His lips are like the neat seam of a mitten. But Papa's light-colored eyes move heavily in their sockets, lids drooping, black pupils sinking slow from your face to your feet—slow, like dropped things sinking through water. And before Papa speaks, something seems to flop open in your belly. Something cold floods your limbs. Then Papa's mouth is moving:

"Fetch your mother please."

Scuttle away—quick to the door. Slip out and shut the door upon the words. But the words, left alone with Papa, begin caroming about. You can hear them blindly thudding in there: noise like moths against a window.

Where is Mama? You've been alone with the words and she's been distant.

But you find her after all. In a chair somewhere. Convey Papa's message.

Mama looks shrunken, faraway. Your voice can barely reach her. Very slowly she stands up and plods into the study.

Noises leak through the door after that. Mama's high and quavering voice—then Papa's like an eclipse: *Kleinigkeiten!* And: *schwach!*

Later the study door flies open, slams shut. Mama sweeps into the parlor. Sweeps past you without a glance, her eyes dull and dark as florins. And now Papa's silence grows swollen behind the door. And now something is rattling in your chest. As though you've been running.

Stand up. Go directly to the kitchen. Look above the table and find the crucified one hovering there as always: twisted arms outstretched. Did you come here just to look at Him? *He,* hanging sadly, *He* surely knows why you've come.

Pull back a chair. Clamber up to kiss the shattered feet. The Lord staring down the bloody length of His own body. Blood-encrusted eyes half closed.

Frequently now the boy finds himself adrift on the great lake-like silences between Mama and Papa. From memory he starts copying down the words of Schiller. Watches the words bleed out of nothingness into visibility, trailing down his arm to the pen tip.

Soon he begins rhyming his own words. They trickle through his limbs from some indeterminate source. He looks behind the words for a source and finds only darkness.

Mama learns of his rhymes and praises him. *Bubi Dichter,* she calls him. And words continue growing, rooting themselves inside him and stirring noiselessly like flowers. Soon there are fields of them in that dim terrain within.

May 1884. Mama and Papa tear free of one another and Mama makes plans to leave. René Maria, nine years old, gives his parents one of his first poems. An anniversary gift.

*R*ainer writes another letter to Clara, his stationery spread on a book across his knees as he sits in the Jardin Luxembourg breathing the pungent waft of the ceaselessly tended flowerbeds.

Now and then he looks up from the page to watch four small children bent at the pond's edge prodding their sailboats. He's confessing to his wife this day's short-lived hopes, describing the Saint Michel rooms about which he's just inquired. Not more than a block away from his current quarters, these rooms seem part of a wholly different Paris, a brighter, airier city. And for a few hours this morning it had appeared that one could simply move quarters and find his lot greatly improved—for why *shouldn't* things be as simple as that?—simple as a well-lit room with a vista of these royal gardens, *une chambre sans* smoking lamp, *sans* soiled ceiling plaster? Or simple as *two* rooms, even: one for oneself and another for one's wife? He needn't sink to squalor after all, not if it only meant taking two rooms that were ever so slightly past his means. Other people seemed to manage it without worry; why should the poet's lot be so much harder? He'd come to Paris to meet the great Rodin, after all—shouldn't that entitle him . . .

But no, Rainer tells Clara now, he had to cease from those thoughts. They were mere distraction, such thoughts of wealth. Thoughts he often uses to run away from himself and from important things.

Lifting his pen, he looks up toward the Luxembourg gates, past which Paris churns in its feverish way. All the doomed fury of this capital with its skirling wheels, its pounding hooves, its condemned ones who do not even know to gnash their teeth. And how many they are who loiter at death's curb in some old sullen lethargy long since mistaken for life.

Just beyond the gate a blind man stooped with age stands begging. Long white hair, stringy as corn silk, falls to his shoulders. His eyes but smoky blue pockets in the slack unmuscled brow. People going past him without a glance, their glances hooded and everything within them fisted tight.

In these last few hours Rainer has told himself that he will bear out this lurid city, this Breughel-world which wants to disrobe itself before his appalled heart. Yes, bear it out while he awaits his wife. For to endure it is the important thing. To let himself be poor and to endure it.

An hour or so sitting in chill sunlight redolent with flowers, and a feeling of brittle peace forms within him. The children leave their hired boats doddering across the pond. New children arrive to launch others. Restless knife-tip light stabs up through the dark water. Rainer bends to the letter again.

"Don't believe that I suffer disappointment here. On the contrary, it surprises me sometimes how readily I give up every expectation for the sake of what is real, even if it is terrible."

*M*ama leased an apartment. Papa agreed to a permanent separation. All things diverged, and the boy tumbled toward whatever destiny the parents would dictate. Papa wanted military school. There seemed a good chance René Maria might be enrolled without cost, son of an ex-cadet as he was. So the child stood before his father in the motherless Heinrichsgasse flat.

"Well, my boy. It's decided. You shall begin as junior cadet at the Militär-Unterrealschule of Saint Pölten. You ought to be highly anticipant."

"I am, Papa."

"Good. Now, most of the other cadets, you know, will be twelve while you are ten. But you needn't worry about that. If you stand straight and put yourself wholly to your schooling no one will be the wiser."

"*Ja,* Papa."

Upon completion of his final year at the Piarist School in Prague, the boy's hair was snipped to military order, a uniform obtained, and with Mama he rode the train into southern Austria to the Kadettenschule at Saint Pölten.

Later he would call it *"ungeleistete Kindheit,"* an unaccomplished childhood. Would call it *"the daily despair of a ten, a twelve, a fourteen-year-old boy."* Call it *"a singularly foreign, most unrecognizable life."* Call it *"a first painful training in solitude amongst the crowd."* Call it *"that long, violent plague of my childhood."* Call it *"one single and terrible damnation, from which I was thrown up like one from the deeps of a roiling sea."* He would say, *"I had to lift myself out over it."*

Mama stood over René Maria at the gate, sobbing. She raised her hand and like a solemn priestess traced a cross in the air, then turned and walked away choking into her kerchief, her form growing smaller as he watched, he who'd been this woman's daughter just yesterday. Standing there looking after her, he felt his slender boy-limbs, encased in the stiff wool of the uniform, swelling to man-sized proportions of grief.

The dormitory: a sea of stiff beds all impeccably neat. Just after lights-out, while the many bodies roll restively in the squeaking cots, stern boots come clacking down the hall. The noncom's clipped Slovenian voice: "Turn onto your right, recite the Lord's Prayer, go to sleep!" Repeated over and over till it draws down to a distant murmur and the dormers have fallen silent.

Nights the long room heaves with breath. René Maria lies awake. Someone turns and groans. Someone mutters something: a vehement oath apparently meant for the figures in a nightmare. And the sleeper's terror comes coursing like gas across the bedlocked terrain of dreams.

Lying here is hard. Keeping one's eyes shut and keeping silent and pretending slumber while the terror slinks from sleeper to sleeper and oozes into one's ears to burrow in one's head: somebody else's nightmare. But René Maria cannot possibly hold it. He has no room. He knows he must pretend sleep and it will pass. Will find him locked inside his own nightmare and will slither back and spill from his ear and glide onward—at least till it comes round a second time—and by then he hopes to be asleep truly. He'll have his own wretched dreams, but that's not new.

The hardest thing is morning: the bugle's brazen rupture and the hurtle into consciousness. There's the shock of the cold dormitory floor beneath René Maria's feet then, but something stands yet between him and sensation. He watches the other cadets don their uniforms, train their bed-clothes into place with hardly a thought. Their night-fear behind them already. But he is root. He is root, for some part of him, somewhere deep, still has its pores wide open to a powerful intoxicant. Unfinished nightmares go with him into the day, bleed like sweat through his crisp uniform. And so he seems peculiar to the others. That naked terror he carries disturbs them: a thing too familiar.

Not far from the Kadettenschule, in the tangled copse at the brink of the southern field, stands a small forgotten cemetery. René Maria slides from amidst the jostling cadets, shrinks to a slim figment as he crosses the vast lawn and disappears into the trees. The place receives him with silent indifference. Fractured gravestones protrude like antediluvian bones from a fur of weeds.

At the foot of an apple tree is a ledge of woven roots resembling a chair. Hemmed in by forsaken graves, René Maria sits here with hands folded just so and strives to lose himself in prayer.

Mama writes sometimes, always on fine blue paper that feels nice against the fingers and floats lightly in the hand. Always when he unfolds the paper it resists the earth and flutters upward. He reads the letters out here in the graveyard, sometimes over and over. Mama's thin ink slanting across the page. She thinks of him in his uniform and cannot help but long for the baby she knew. It makes her weep to remember the daughter he once was—little "Ismene" in soft boots and pantalettes. But now René Maria is an upright, sensitive boy, so handsome in his uniform—and this makes Mama proud. *'Do not worry, René Maria, if you grow homesick,'* she writes. *'Don't worry if you must cry, Jesus is always listening.'* Mama says she often wishes he could come live with her forever, but of course this isn't possible. She knows he understands. *'Always remember how I taught you to pray on that day when you were three. Remember not to complain when you suffer because the Savior gives us our suffering. Remember: if your prayer is not answered directly, it's because God is terribly busy.'* She is having a lovely time in Vienna, such a cultured city. So many lovely people . . . *lovely lovely lovely* . . .

René Maria falls deeply into the letter and his fingers slip and the pages fly: blue papers somersaulting through the weed-eaten monuments. Up he goes, scrambling to catch them.

"And you wait, you expect the one thing
that will endlessly increase your life;
the tremendous, the immense,
the awakening of stones,
depths sweeping toward you."

Beyond the rooftops the mantis-like Eiffel Tower rears weird and unignorable, standing in for the remembered spires of Prague. Three o'clock on Monday, first September: just an hour and a day and a month, same as ever—but how momentous these ciphers can become, for here in the tower's lank shadow stands 182 rue de l'Université, a building of parchment-colored stone. Just inside, in a single atelier in this city of a million buildings, you will find Auguste Rodin at work. He's expecting you.

At first the sculptor appears much smaller than you imagined. He has his back turned as you enter, and what impresses you foremost is the broadness of the shoulders in his compact frame. He wears a colorless waistcoat of natty cotton, workmanlike trousers to match. His sleeves are turned back and he's cupping a little plaster piece in his hand, scratching away with a pen-like tool. His gray hair is trimmed very close against his heavy-looking skull. At the base of his bent head is a wiry fleece—dark against the whiter hair: a leonine kind of fur, intimating strength and vigor. Already you cannot doubt his force. Then he turns—gray broom of beard sweeping around, farseeing eyes traveling over and stopping with a look silently demanding but in no manner unsolicitous. Look of a man yet encaved in his heavy work.

"*Oui?*" he says.

He has a model before him. You hardly noticed her: young woman in a drape. She too is looking over now.

You step inward from the doorway. "*Mon maître.*" It feels very natural to address this man as your master.

"*Oh, oui oui oui,*" he says. "*Le rendez-vous, n'est-ce pas?*" And already he is approaching, all else dropping from him, one great hand coming up to clasp yours.

"I needn't interrupt your work," you say.

His grip is in every way the grip of a sculptor: strong, but full of conscious gentleness. His powdered palm leaves a grit of plaster in your own. He doesn't notice.

"*Si'l vous plaît,*" he says, waving to two armchairs nearby. "Let's sit." He sets his small object down, murmurs some words to the young lady, and sits, working a cloth between his hands. Sits, somehow, without coming fully to rest—and yet he's in no manner distracted or inattentive. "You have just arrived in Paris?"

"Recently, *oui.*" And how bizarre to give this answer. *Recently.* Paris has thrown you so far backward into yourself.

"And where are you staying?"

"Rue Toullier."

"Toullier? Near *le Panthéon, non?*"

"*Oui.*"

"I lived in that quarter as a boy. Have you gone there yet?"

"The Panthéon? No."

"I have a commission for the monument of Puvis de Chavannes—do you know him? *Un peintre très grand.* His work is in the Panthéon. Very great work, murals of enormous beauty. You should see them."

"*Pardon?*"

"You should see them."

"Oh, yes, I will."

"*Oui,* see them and then, who knows, maybe you will write something about Chavannes next." From his godlike beard comes a very human little laugh, boyish and almost shy. A smile lights his shrewd eyes.

You smile back. Then silence.

Tall windowlight, smokified by the residue of the Master's art, pulses whitely amongst the surrounding works of marble and plaster. Off in one corner the idle model twirls on the balls of her feet, shoeless on the dusty floor, long balletic arms cathedraled above her. The purple drape hangs from her shoulders in Grecian pleats. Rodin is watching her, his plastery hand moving in his beard. His gaze is controlled, assiduous, no gesture lost upon it.

"This is why I have her here," he says. "It's why I have any of them here. I've made it a rule to keep them around as much as possible, even if they are not working, even if I'm busy with other things. One can learn much just seeing them like this."

You watch the model too, and all at once it seems possible to see her as the Master does. Perhaps his presence has that prompt effect; perhaps everything becomes significant in such a presence.

"Where in Germany do you live?" he says.

"I don't live there anymore. It was in Westerwede, near Bremen. But that time is over. I had to leave all that to come here. My wife will leave soon as well."

"This home did not suit you?"

You give a slight roll of your shoulders, a moment of thought, then: "It's extremely difficult, *mon maître,* to live by one's art."

Rodin's throat rumbles in agreement. "Ah, *c'est vrai,*" he says, and now he stares squarely into your eyes, an earnest warmth in his face as of long friendship. "One must work very hard. Always work. Do you have a family?"

"A daughter, yes. A little one of ten months. My wife, by the way, sends her greetings. Clara Westhoff, the sculptress. She studied with you here for a time, two years ago."

"*Oui,* you recalled her to me in your letter this summer. She came to me through Klinger. *Oui, bien sûr.* She will come to Paris too, *non?*"

"We hope so."

"That is good. You will be lonely till then, eh?"

"Yes—though, with our work . . . we shan't live together when she comes."

"*Non?*"

"*Non.*"

Not till now have you said this to yourself, let alone spoken it aloud. These last days you've thought of Clara's arrival, nothing more. And yet already, somehow, it's become clear, with the Westerwede life dissolved as it is, that neither you nor the sculptress should stake your hopes on a conventional life together. All too overwhelming now, in light of this city's oppressive atmosphere, to struggle once more toward keeping intimate quarters. So quickly this grim city gets inside oneself. The single sure protection for each of you will be the solitude of a room in which you may work at any hour. And yet the marriage will continue. That needn't change.

"It's difficult, *mon maître,* you understand. . . ." Your slow French prohibits further explanation. But still the Master's eyes show you he's listening, so you say, "We both need our work, my wife and I. That is foremost."

Rodin makes no reply to this. With an air of irrefutable resolve he turns and speaks out into the studio where his work awaits: "I must continue now. But tomorrow you can come to my home in Meudon. Many of my sculptures are there."

"Demain?"

"Tomorrow, *oui.*"

"I'll be honored, *mon maître.*"

Rodin rises, all his upward motion contained in his great laborer's shoulders. And as you stand to face him you feel his power, his presence, in a manner strangely intimate, almost empathic. It's like standing before a cheval glass. As though this gray-bearded sculptor is some bizarre patriarchal mirroring of you in your smaller Germanic beard.

"I hope you won't hurry off," he says. "Please feel at liberty to look around. Look at everything."

He retrieves his plaster and calls the model back and at once he's deep in his work again.

You move through the atelier, light-footed and slow. A great deal to look at here, the Master's creations bristling on all sides, and it's very strange to have the creator himself close at hand all the while. The rasp of his stylus is the only sound in the room. Passing amongst the works, you have a strong sensation of being waterborne, of drifting. It occurs to you now that each of these figures is an island of sorts. Rodin is alone in his work, as is most every artist. These figures stand up out of his aloneness. Yes, so an artist has rights to nothing but his solitude, from which he raises monuments. Though the whole world may give its heart to an artist's creations, his loneliness shall never be circumscribed by love. Rodin's fame bears no connection to his greatness—nor even to this work of his; to watch him now, across this terrain of his labor, it seems very clear: fame is but a thing that tries to circumscribe his loneliness. Meanwhile, he keeps working day by day, quietly as in this very moment. This Master whose name pours from the mouths of countless men—this Master goes on working as if unknown, as if nameless, alone to himself in his Paris atelier on a Monday afternoon.

On a waist-high turntable here is the *Hand,* which you've seen only in photographs till now. Massive five-headed organism straining upward from the corded muscles of the wrist, thumb and fingers splayed apart as if each longs to fulfill some destiny entirely its own—and yet every finger is united in the furnace of the palm.

"That's a hand like this!" calls Rodin from across the atelier. He takes some shapeless clay from a nearby worktable and raises it shoulder-high and squeezes. "Like this. It's holding a chunk of clay." And as he looks at his own mimicking clutch there is a breathless energy in his eyes, something in him yet awed by the spectacle of such a hand: four bent-knuckled fingers striving to emulate the shape-giving power of God.

"It is very beautiful to see him working. The connection of his eyes with the clay. One thinks one can see the many lines of his gaze, which go with such certainty like a net into the air. And how everything is then of a oneness: he and the thing to which he gives life—you would hardly know how to say which one is the work."

It's like enacting a confused and unquiet dream: crossing the great jumble of Paris toward the high cramped room at number 11 rue Toullier. Can it be true that you were with Auguste Rodin but moments ago? You will see him again tomorrow—you must remember *that* if today insists on sliding into unreality and fear. For already, though you've only just met him, you feel with keen conviction that Rodin himself is the country to which you've traveled. Inward country vaster than France. In the Master lies the worth of coming to this place. His life will be a deep lesson to you—it's a single life, yet it's a *thousand* lives, all from two solitary hands!

In the late-day air you can sense a strand of the approaching autumn. Autumn always portending one infirmity or another, some inventive sickness meant to cripple your work. You've not been wholly well since your arrival in the horrendous August rain. And in your mean quarter you are surrounded by hospitals: the Hôtel Dieu, the Salpêtrière, the Maison de Bicêtre, the Val de Grâce. They are in abundance, the hospitals. They're right there whenever one should need them—and what if you should actually *need* them now?

You must put away thoughts of your own health, while your course leads past the innumerable restaurant windows in the boulevard Saint Michel and the boulevard Saint Germain—past those miles and miles of glass wherein your figure streams in meek and sidelong reflection, a lean faint form sweeping across the tables at which people dine in great finery. Mustn't think of your health. Must keep well till Clara comes.

And yet beyond the gray windows of the Hôtel Dieu as you come past them by day, you've seen invalids standing in pale shapeless shifts, looking out. Looking out as if awaiting you.

But of course they can't know how René Maria lay in his own oversized shift, back in his hard Saint Pölten days. . . .

—*For godsake, Rilke, won't you get up?*

Jogging in rank. Legs give out and the boy collapses to the icy lawn. A few cadets curse as they go veering by, the air above streaming with one and another ruddy face. Then the sergeant's face leers low.

—*For godsake, Rilke.*

The sergeant's eyes red and watershot in the stinging air.

—*You won't get up, Cadet?*

—*I can't run, sir.*

The sergeant hollers across the field. A corporal comes trotting in a clatter of stickman limbs.

—*This one can't run. Help him to the infirmary.*

So within the hour the boy lies floating in an invalid's shift far too large for him. And the Regimental Doctor's bloodless fingers clasp the boy's legs, wander chill along his throat, prod at the flesh beneath his jaw, sniffing for infection. Hands are always falling upon him. The air itself seems to endlessly manifest hands. They all leave their marks. It's been this way since the beginning. So is one's life not one's own, but a thing for picking up and turning over by countless curious fingers? How does one move with care through a world so thick with hands? How sense one's own destiny if one has become no more than a palimpsest of strange imprints?

December in Saint Pölten. In the dead of night, René Maria kneels shivering at his bedside. His birth night now, and the boy praying earnestly for death while the dormitory sleeps.

Someone stirs. An angry voice a few beds down. "For Christ sake, who's sniveling? Go to sleep!"

René Maria tumbles back beneath his covers and shuts his eyes.

Death does not come. At morning he's startled by the dormitory's new brightness.

The *réveille* begins. The cadets spring from their beds into the raucous charade. But something seeks him from amidst the tangle of boys. René Maria can feel its encroachment as one feels the dimming of a cloud across the sun. Soon Karl is standing before him. Karl, whose night-terrors are loudest of all. His face looks bloated with dream even now.

"You're René, huh?"

"*Ja.*"

"I saw you fall down during laps yesterday."

Nothing to say to this.

"You kept a lot of us awake last night with your whimpering." Karl steps closer. "Heiner says you refused to help him with his algebra."

"Yes."

"Why?"

Bite your lip and say nothing.

"You said if you helped him you'd be deceiving the teacher. Where do you come from anyhow?" Karl stoops slightly, tugs the thin bottom hem of René Maria's knee breeches. Embroidered blue *Unterhosen,* they match the edging of his bed linens. "Did your mama make those?"

"Yes."

Now the noncom sweeps into the dorm on his first round, barking out orders. Karl disappears and René Maria hurries to dress.

Later, the dormitory murmurous in the moments before lights-out and Karl rumbling toward him again. Then Karl stands very close, his body a wall. He snatches at the chain around René Maria's neck, inspects the small medallion. Two greyhounds leap to flank the Rilke family seal.

—*It begins with the Rielko family, said Uncle Jaroslav. Carinthian nobles, sometimes called Rülkho. They go as far back as 1376.*

Jaroslav's strong fingers pressed the medallion into René's hand, and René thought his own hand looked very small under Uncle's.

"What is it? A coat of arms?" Karl tugs and the chain digs at René Maria's neck. "Are you somebody special, Rilke?"

Onlookers engulf the boys now, clumping up with great suddenness.

Ancient names, grand and dithyrambic: Rielko . . . Rülkho . . . Rülike . . . Rilke. Uncle's deep voice had been profoundly reverent.

Karl yanks at the medallion and René Maria stiffens close against the larger boy's chest, locked in that frightful intimacy. Down below Karl's undershirt, a rigid thing presses like a narrow second heart.

Something floods to René Maria's head. Febrile heat. Bulge-and-pulse in his eye sockets, his stomach crumpling like paper. Karl's body emits a sickly-sweet smell. René Maria must turn away and try not to breathe it— but Karl holds him close.

"All done with prayers for the night, Rilke? I don't want to be kept awake again."

René Maria feels fingers pressed hotly to his chest. Karl shoves, and the chain, still caught in his other hand, slices at René Maria's neck, breaks with a brittle pop. The necklace clatters to the floor as Karl moves away.

Troubled laughter from a few onlookers, but most of them merely stand there, quietly agog as though just awakened.

René Maria cups his palm to the stippled gash at his nape. Feels the sticky line of blood but does not bring his hand away to look. He bends and picks up the medallion and chain. It swings from his fingers like a rosary. He lies down on his side, pulls up his blankets, thinks quickly of Jesus. Mama says Jesus knows all that the boy suffers. Above the boy, stretching away down the great length of the hall, the gas lamps burn brightly.

At night now, René Maria lies open-eyed and longs for Jesus, the stubbornly rigid Jesus of the crucifix so often tendered in Mama's soft hand. He knows this Jesus to be stuffed amidst the used handkerchiefs and greasy bills in Mama's handbag, bronze face smashed to her passport as she trots about Vienna—but this is no matter. The boy takes refuge in Christ, trusts Christ. And is fully aware that the figure he trusts is but a *thing*. The Saint Pölten dormitory gapes four years long and four years wide, and in the absence of solace the boy adores a broken god.

No, but still René Maria's verses keep gestating. With his verses he speaks and speaks the mute world—world always feigning muteness, but he believes it is not mute, not mute, only pretending. Soon he's permitted to read his efforts in class. He stands up before lessons, orates from his notebook with wavering voice.

And then one morning he turns in the dreamlike fog enveloping the southern field. He is bent for the solitude of the cemetery, but a hand has clapped his shoulder, and there stands Karl with a ring of cadets behind. Words are exchanged—no more than wisps in the numb white air—and suddenly everything is blanked from sight. René Maria's eyes sheeted in

ice, white surfaces roiling, a purple heat spreading in cheeks and brow—
then the frosted lawn shudders into vision and something streams down,
streams out of him with impossible warmth, plopping lightly at his feet.
He sees his own hands moving in a flurry of black: his black gloves catching at the flow, scarlet soaking darkly in dark wool. *Blood!* His numb nose
stops the upward sweep of the gloves.

Karl is stepping away with one fist drawn back at his side, red face
twisted almost to tears.

René Maria's legs tremble. Liquefaction, everything dripping. But
now muffled words are forming. He's talking into his wet gloves: "I suffer
it, Karl, because Christ suffered it. While you were hitting me I asked God
to forgive you."

But Karl is already walking away, the ring of boys rolling after him.
Six or seven figures no more than irresolute streams soaked up in the cotton of the fog. They vanish. And René Maria stands there alone in his dim
piety, swabbing at brilliant blood.

"Who shows a child

> *exactly as it stands? Who places it amidst the stars and gives the*
> *measure of distance*
> *unto its hand? Who makes the child-death*
> *out of gray bread that becomes hard,—or leaves*
> *it there in his round mouth like the core of a beautiful apple?"*

*R*ainer alights upon a grimy platform at Meudon-Val-Fleury. The village lies beyond the southwest limits of Paris, twenty minutes by train from the Gare Montparnasse. An ungainly knot of roads twists upward along a modest mountain of kinds.

As he climbs the lanes, the little homes packed side by side along the way appear to him vaguely Italian: tile-roofed and terraced. At points the hilltop road curves off to afford a vista of red rooftops cluttered in the valley below. The sight calls up his time in Florence, four years ago. The young poet alone in Tuscany, armed with awestruck eyes and a journal. Lou had dispatched him there that he might garner the riches of the Renaissance. He was to fill in the journal, present it to her on his return.

"Whether I am yet calm enough, ready enough," he wrote upon arrival in Florence, *"to begin this diary which I want to bring home to you, I do not know."* Then arrived days of confusion. The muscular spirits of Renaissance art came to seem more than his powers of observation could manage. And finally he fled west to the Ligurian Sea, sheltered himself in the small village of Viareggio. There the journal took shape in a mighty way, the young poet roaring into its pages with a new command of his powers. But when it came time to bestow the journal upon Lou, she failed to see all he'd borne forth in those words of his. Already back then, he and Lou were growing at odds, though the real estrangement would not gape between them for some time still. . . .

Rodin's estate stands near the end of the long hilltop road. The poet passes through a gate onto a lane lined with chestnut trees—a distinctive sort of promenade, but somewhat derelict too. Old elegance long since starved. At the lane's end the trees shuffle back to reveal a tall slim house, a faded reduction copy of some grander country château. Peculiar structure: just two rooms wide and two stories high, with implausibly tiny garret windows gabling up out of the declivitous roof. House for a boy-prince.

From beyond the house come the clipped shouts of dogs, then human voices, and Rodin appears wearing a high-crowned hat. He sees the poet and smiles, his palm raised in greeting. Two large long-furred creatures come galloping from his heels, black gums flapping with dog smiles. They swirl around Rainer in nostrilled joy while the Master draws up and clasps his hand. "I'm just getting back to work. You won't mind being on your own a while? Come with me."

At the rear of the house, lawn and footpath drop away to a sloped garden, and in a great span below is the jumble of red roofs again.

"That's the Sèvres Valley," says Rodin, "but here is my museum."

They stand before a grandly arched garden pavilion, a kind of classical temple adjoined improbably to the weird little house.

"It was my showcase at the World Exhibition a few years ago. I had it moved here from Paris." Rodin leads Rainer inside, and the poet finds the long airy hall teeming with creations.

The Master leaves him to wander as he will. Immediately again Rainer feels himself afloat on the sculptor's sea of work. It seems everything is here. The powerful nude figure of Victor Hugo halts before him, life-sized, forward-striding, bearded face furrowed with long reckoning, his right forearm raised across his breast as if bearing a shield. Here stands the lone figure of *Adam,* demure and earthbound. Here are *The Kiss* and *The Thinker.* And here is an arrangement that draws the poet's focus for close to an hour: two identical figures, identically posed, each but twelve inches high. An aged woman, nude and slack-shouldered. She sits in a small grotto with her double, both their heads bent beneath coved rock, hair bunned limply at their napes. They are reversed to one another, twins in opposite posture. Together with herself, the old woman gazes downward, the back of one hand pressed lightly to the base of her spine. Her loose paunch folds forth atop her thighs. Flaccid purse where her progeny once grew. Her breasts wilt like lumps of saturated moss. She seems to be hunched in listening manner, heedful of everything softly withering within her.

In their doubled act of listening these figures end completely in themselves. Each is a soul, though each is a *thing.* One faces the rear of the grotto, contained in the cave's penumbra, turning her brittle spine to the world as though in renunciation—but she's just as complete as her double, in spite of this withdrawal. Rainer kneels down to peer into the enclosure's darkness. Yes, she's there inside with lowered head. And he feels it an impropriety to impinge on her aloneness, plaster though she is.

Even the countless unfinished works treasured in this pavilion seem somehow complete. Amongst the sculptures stand long glass cases filled with plaster fragments. Here are hands—very human hands of all sizes and all gestures. Hands without mates, without wrists or arms, but hands with destinies all their own. Here: a narrow tapering hand of tawny clay, dropped on its side. In size it resembles the hand of a five-year-old child, yet the entire eloquence of a grown woman is expressed in the graceful rivering of the carpal tributaries, the sensual stepping-stones of the knuckles. The fingertips lie clustered, arcing toward the thumb in the gesture one makes when fine fabric slides through the touch. Hand that tastes. It's true of each hand here: each tastes and sees, hears and smells, wants for nothing. On a lower shelf lies a row of small individualized arms. Another case holds nothing but rows of legs. Fifty or more legs fashioned of bleached white plaster, each bent at the knee like a rigid comma, the arch of foot taut or rounded, toes cramped or curled or rearing like tiny heads.

It's as though Rodin has gained a secret from the plastic world's very

soul, has heard the whisper of that which is *part,* that which is bound always in its service to the *whole.* Hands have said to him, feet have said to
him, heads have said to him: *I wish I could drop from the body and have my
wholeness known. I am more than limb, more than nerve and muscle—let me show
you!* So in this Master's fearsome power even fragments cease to be fragments.

*"When he shapes a hand, it is alone in space and it is nothing other than a
hand; and God in six days made only a hand and poured out the waters around it
and curved the heavens above it, and rested over it when all was complete, and it
was a splendor and a hand."*

Rainer's eyes grow weary with looking. Time slips by. Rodin comes in
once or twice, disposes himself should the poet have questions. Rainer
doesn't have questions—the Master's work is vast with answers—but still
they talk a while, then Rodin goes out. Near noon he returns to invite the
poet to stay for lunch. Before they retire to the table, Rainer presents the
gift of the books he's been toting in his valise. Three slender volumes, carefully inscribed. Again from the Master's beard comes that blithe laugh. He
is pleased. He leafs attentively through each book in turn, though the
printed words are foreign to him. Rainer watches his eyes as the pages shift.

Then, a garden repast. A table clothed in glaring white, set for five in
a hedged enclosure. Rodin is going to the city soon and has changed out of
his working clothes.

An aged rumpled woman in a floral dress comes bustling from the
house streaming unintelligible French. She seats herself at the table's end
opposite the Master. Madame Rodin perhaps. Her colorless dry hair sits
lumped in a haphazard nest atop her skull, shorter strands drifting freely
about her ears. Toward Rainer and the others she throws a distracted look
of acknowledgment apparently meant as greeting, but no one is introduced.

A young girl, maybe ten years old, sits at Rainer's side playing aim-lessly with the hem of the tablecloth. Across from him sits a French gentleman—evidently here to accompany the Master to the city.

Rodin touches his fork. "This lunch is rather late."

"We just sat down," says Madame. "The food is coming."

"I'd hoped to sit to a ready table. You know I'm going to the city."

"Yes, and Madeleine's aware—"

"And yet we're all here with empty plates."

"You expect me to be everywhere at once. Speak to Madeleine yourself."

"I think you could be more clear with her."

Madame's small shuddering hands begin to crawl about the table, touching this and that. "You think she doesn't listen to me. You think she'll only listen to you, then *you* should talk to her. How can I do *everything?*" Her exasperation flurries forth, hard to follow. And Rodin is talking too, though with less fervor and not so much volume. Their words collide above the table.

Madame lifts her plate and sets it down, lifts again and again sets it down. She reaches out and moves her glass six inches forward as if it disgusts her. Nudges the fork—nudges, nudges, till it lies perpendicular to the spoon, then shifts the spoon too. She moves the rose vase from the table's center, sets it a foot out of place. All this time the stream of argument continues—till quite abruptly the lady and the sculptor both drop into silence. Madame stares at the tablecloth. Rodin's eyes wander toward the poet and his tablemates.

The little girl and the French gentleman seem unperturbed.

The food arrives, several dishes borne on a big platter by a disheveled manservant whose wrists look somewhat grimed. Everyone begins to eat and now the *déjeuner* is altogether ordinary. Afterward Rodin takes his leave. Madame approaches Rainer, smiling.

"You must stay for lunch whenever you come again."

"That may be a great deal, Madame."

"All the better," she says, curtsying a bit, her palms diverging in a gesture of welcome. She has made her French very precise for his benefit. She seems to mean: *We are not so strange. Don't be afraid.*

"*Merci, Madame.*"

The poet revels alone in the great pavilion for several more hours, his brain aswarm with plastic life, his eyes fuzzy and burning.

A dream: An ache in Rainer's hands, his fingers locked in rheumatic clutch—and big-knuckled hands of another kind prying and prying at his grip. He's seen this happen in the Jardin Luxembourg. The park attendants—three of them—prying that shoeless woman's fingers from the bench to which she clung in witless abstraction, that hoary white-haired shoulderless woman whose arch of slick red gums gawped at the world as her fingers stood up one by one in obedient rigor mortis. The attendants at last unseated her and bore her to the gate and put her out onto the bustling street. And now in his dream it's happening to *him.* They've found Rainer clinging to his chair. Mustn't let go now, though the numbers of their prying hands increase. The owners of the hands have seen him for what he is—oh yes they know what squalid quarters he keeps and there's no use trying to explain. But mustn't let go. The name *Rodin* rises to his lips, but he can't make himself any clearer. All night long they are working away at his fingers and at last he splutters awake, bolting upright from the pillow into the deathly yellow murk of his Paris room. Faint haze from the gaslamps in the rue Soufflot, his window flung wide that he needn't suffocate while he sleeps.

His heart is beating hard. His nightshift limp and wet.

"Clara," he says to the empty room. "Clara." Without a thought, her name has risen to his lips. And instinctively his hot hands have begun prodding at his face, where her softer touch would be were she there beside him. She would have heard him writhing and gentled him awake. In their bed in

Westerwede he'd wrenched conscious from nightmare more than once. Clara had given him water to drink, had laid him back down and touched his face till he was calm, breathing: *Shhhhh.* Her breath at his ear. *Shhhhh.*

Now, alone, once his heart has settled, Rainer lies prone again. Blinks at that dim gaseous glow across the ceiling beams. "Shhhhh," he breathes to himself.

Though Clara will come to Paris, he'll not have her near in moments like these. His hands quiver slightly in the sheets at his sides. He must have been clamping them. Sleep itself exhausting.

He thinks of Rodin. Thinks he must know something of the way Rodin's hands often feel, hands set hard in the constant labor of creation. But what have Rainer's own hands accomplished? What, beyond warding back a nightmare?

Clara, innocent wife, could she ever have seen how quickly her little household would come and go? . . . Remember . . . April 1901: how you lay bedstricken with scarlet fever just a week before your wedding. Wasn't your inadequacy as a husband foretold in those days of sickness? Blurred days in the care of Johanna Westhoff, your mother-to-be, at Clara's family home in Oberneuland. Tap of Westhoff family silver to your teeth as Johanna spooned soup into your slack mouth. Obscured in the murk or fever-smoke behind your new mother, your new father paced: tall, regal, silver-bearded. Stymied patriarch forced with his family to postpone the wedding, wait, watch you convalesce. Murmurs in the hall whenever the mother went out. You drifted and slumbered and sweated.

At length, now and then, your eyes would snap wide from sleep to find Clara materialized beside you, her strong sculptor's wrist close before your face, twin tendons pulsing as she laid a compress to your scalding brow.

Lifted . . . pressed. Slow sensation bled through the fever's gauze till you could feel her touch, its healing effects. Words bubbled meekly from your mouth: "Not the heartiest groom, I'm afraid."

She smiled. Magnificent Clara Westhoff smile. Drew back her hand and plashed the cloth in the steaming basin. Last year's scar still sloped across her knuckles: dark pictogram of the hammer's violence. She had bathed the hand in water that night too—*cool* water—and together you had watched the fountaining of her blood: water frothing pink, then red.

"I wouldn't blame your parents if they remembered this," you told her. And watched Clara's eyes flit toward the hall. "I mean if it made them more cautious toward me. It must look like a very complicated kind of . . ." you floated in search of the word, your raw throat clamping.

"Ruse?" said Clara, smiling again.

"*Ja,* thank you. A complicated ruse."

No, but the fevers had always been there. Fevers rattling the floor-boards—those big broad-shouldered fevers invading René Maria's bed-room—charging right through the door like reckless housebreakers. Through the walls. Or exploding down through the ceiling in sprays of splinter and dust.

The fevers had lain upon the boy with their darkness, had smothered him like a candlewick: the flame within him crushed from both sides and a gray ghost of smoke pinched into shivery flight. And the boy's inward fire went into the fever, burning in that outside darkness. Yes, and Mama coming to the boy in the bedroom which had grown strange with sickness. Mama lifting and setting down his hollow limbs, swabbing his hollow forehead. Her hands at the blankets were rustling echoes: noise of some-body rummaging in an airy room.

Mama would leave him for what seemed hours at a time. In the still-ness the fever gained strength, and somewhere in that world of black, in the vise of the fever, the boy's dislocated self managed a prayer, pleading with *Himmelpapa,* his father in heaven, for surely *Himmelpapa* saw the terror the boy endured.

At last, after days and nights, the arbitrary hour of healing would come: René Maria falling back into the sheath, coughing life into his suffocated body, stirring to awaken . . .

"But what do you mean *more* cautious?" said Clara.

"What?"

"You said if it made them *more* cautious toward you."

"Did I? I shouldn't have."

Clara's scarred knuckles surfaced from the basin and brought the boiling compress to your brow again. A loving sidelong look in her eyes.

You remembered then: *Her wounded knuckles, the dull plunk of the hammer falling to the ground, the flap of damaged skin folding back and her blood that seemed so loud in the quiet September night, blood welling up like a word spoken again and again. But how you came together, suddenly—you and Clara Westhoff—over that grimacing pain . . . Memory within memory . . .*

The previous September it was. Your first of those twilight parties at the Barkenhoff. Several of the Worpswede luminaries had come. Otto Modersohn the painter, Carl Hauptmann the writer, and yes: Clara Westhoff, arm-in-arm with a second young woman. Both in white empire dresses, these two had moved bright and svelte in the dusk which blued the moors around Vogeler's house, figures emerging from that peaceable landscape with impossible sprightliness. You stood at your window watching them, a strange fervency awakening within you. Who *were* these people? What *was* this place, that everything, *everything* became pure image here? And then you were standing in Vogeler's entryway pressing the sculptress's hand again, and the girls' dresses were skirring in your ears, a white affetuoso of muslin and chiffon.

"This is Paula Becker," said the sculptress. "Paula is a painter."

You turned to press the second girl's hand. She was auburn-haired and smaller than Clara, but they were sisters of a kind: vestal mothers to things of art.

As the boisterous *family* began to funnel toward Vogeler's white-walled music room, the sculptress touched your arm. "No Russian shirt tonight?" Her eyes skimming down your collar and black lapels. You smiled.

The group arrayed itself in Vogeler's empire chairs. Milly Becker, Paula's younger sister, made the girls three. A shy little creature with lovely wrists, she seemed most content when poised at the piano, so she sat and played and the arpeggioed keys toppled like shuffled cards. *The family* fell silent in a collective act of listening nearly sacramental. Schubert, Strauss, and Franz. The parlor candles listed and wavered with the flickering notes. You watched Paula Becker and Clara Westhoff all the while. Somehow, the music seemed to extract the girls from their bodies. These shored shells in which every gesture of sound reverberated.

After the music Vogeler invited you to read. You rose and took footing beside the piano and recited from memory. Felt the euphony of Milly's music to be suspended in each spoken line. The white room lay silent but for your voice, and the two girls in white remained very still. The auburn-haired one seemed to grow especially solemn.

Afterward Milly returned to the keys: a playful minuet suggestive of loosened collars, upturned sleeves. A quicker frolic followed. The night plunged forward, *the family* becoming more awake, more restless.

Modersohn and Hauptmann and Vogeler commenced an eager search for wine. The Barkenhoff cellar provided. By midnight the gathering had turned Bacchic. Vogeler started nudging you for a drinking song. You demurred. Soon his nudging was almost lurid: *Someday you'll see, Rainer, someday you'll see the big fat hole in your poetry. No Dionysian song! No hymn to the holy vintage!* And later: *A big fat hole, Rainer! (wink wink)* And still later: *Believe me man, you'll write it someday—and you'll have me to thank, you'll say:*

That Vogeler told me all along!—his cup thrust high, wine leaping to splatter the carpet.

And now even the girls had joined the hijinks, cavorting through stumbling dance steps, twirling violently off their partners. You merely watched, sitting apart. Clara Westhoff spun from Carl Hauptmann's snapping arm, came back, spun again—till Hauptmann's mien grew serious and he stopped without warning, stood bowlegged and said gravely, "Dizzy, dizzy."

The fairytale night, lovely at its commencement, seemed to you tattered then, these people but parodies of the people who had come together so completely just hours before. How had that ceremony of music bled away into this cheap beer-garden scene? Disillusioned, you slunk off to your red room. Moved to the window without lighting a candle, shoved the chilled pane and let the night purl inward. A mist had started out there. The Worpswede country was faintly cerulean in its depths.

After a moment you sensed a presence of a kind, turned to find the girls coming wordlessly into the darkened room. As if the scent of nocturnal dew had lured them. They drew close beside you at the window, each talking quietly, their white dresses glistering blue, Paula Becker's light-colored hair rendered silver in the gauze of moonlight, Clara tender-looking in her shyness.

Later, the night still aging, you found yourself walking across the dark heath with the two girls and Heinrich Vogeler. The country whisperous around you, the muslin fog shifting soundlessly across the moors. The girl's dresses rustled like hushed exclamations. Up ahead in a brief black gap the moorland canal rippled milk-white.

Through the feathery night to Paula Becker's studio. Paula herself walked beside you, Clara Westhoff and Vogeler lilting behind.

"This country," you told the auburn-haired painter, "is like nothing I've ever known before. I've never seen colors like these. Even in the dark they keep emanating." Your own voice sounded dreamlike in your ears, a thing emblazoned on that empty nightscape. Before you the canal water warped again, opalescent.

"Did you see that?" you said.

"*Ja.*"

"Don't you love this place?"

"I do, yes," said Paula. "It's somber country though. One doesn't laugh much here."

"I think I'm without memory in these moors," you said. "I think that's it. This landscape won't allow me to dwell in the past. All I can do is look around me. Look and be changed by my looking. Every day is new and different. Every day *I'm* different."

Paula said, "It's true, it's a magical place. I'm sure that's the reason we all stay. I remember being in Paris and missing this. Even in Paris."

You turned to see her. "What was that like?"

Tiny agate crystals glinted in her eyes. "Paris, you mean?"

"*Ja.*"

"Clara and I were there together as recently as June—you'd think it wouldn't seem so distant already."

You watched her fair face as her memory wheeled back. Myriad things shifting behind her eyes.

"It's a very foreign city," she said at length. "At first it seemed *far* too foreign. But then I think it must seem something different to every person. I think the question must be: What were *you* like in Paris?"

"So?"

Paula turned and met your look as she high-stepped through the tangled moorland scrub, her skirt lifted slightly in two fists. She was small-shouldered. Cautiously, she said, "In Paris . . ."

"Yes?"

"In Paris I was like someone waking up." She left off, but you felt there was something more to come. Then her voice rose to a timbre altogether new, edging toward intimacy. "May I tell you something?"

A silent thrill within you. "*Ja,* Paula."

"It sounds childish maybe, but I remember walking down the long Paris boulevards. People streaming past me, and me thinking: *Not one of you has before you the kind of beautiful life I do. Not one.* I remember more than a few days that way. But every time I thought such things, I immediately realized how far I had yet to go. How much work I must still do." Her eyes were shining now. "You could say I was like that in Paris."

In Paula's studio a mask of Dante hung high on one wall, great jib-sail nose flapping in the kerosene light. On a richly colored jacquard cloth white lilies uncoiled like strands of moorland fog.

Coffee was made and everyone drank earnestly. Suddenly Paula sprang up, gulped the coffee in her cheeks and said, "The goat!"

A stunned silence. Then a chorus of laughter burst out.

Paula's landlord's goat was penned in back and needed milking. The girls passed through the rear door into the night, taking the lamp with them. You sat with Vogeler in the darkened studio. Listened to the animal's stuttering chortle of relief as its udder was made to shrink.

The girls themselves were chortling when they returned. Paula planted the lamp at the center of the table and held something forth in the light. "Look!" In an earthenware bowl in her hands a black liquid lapped like thin molasses.

"*Was ist das?*" said Vogeler.

"Milk!"

"Milk?"

"Midnight milk," said Clara.

"*Es ist schwarz!*"

"*Ja!*"

A bizarre hush fell over the group. Everyone staring into the bowl where the black Worpswede night stood in starless liquefaction. Then the bowl was passed around and one by one each person drank the distilled darkness. Nobody cheapened the miracle with theory or question.

At three o'clock Paula Becker retired, but you and Clara Westhoff and Heinrich Vogeler set off down the black highway to Clara's house, soon passing through the dark grape bowers of the cottage yard. In Clara's parlor your threesome encircled a lamp, languid and wordless. Talk seemed unessential now. The night had bound you all in its stupefaction, and to remain in vigil together seemed enough. Before long Vogeler was snoring into his fist. You exchanged a smile with the sculptress.

Brightly she whispered, "Let's go into the studio!"

"All right." But when you rose to follow she led only as far as a cupboard in the rear of the house.

She was rummaging about. "We'll have to break the lock of course." A moment more and she produced a hammer, which she nonchalantly carried to the door. "Bring the lamp."

Outside at the studio door you raised the lamp and Clara Westhoff pounded at the lock. There was a squabbling noise from the black country beyond the cottage: a slaverous yap and growl—some small predator murdering smaller prey. Death by tooth and tufted claw just beyond the radius of your light. The dark of these peaceable moors whose deepest night hours still countenanced ancient instincts.

Clara stunned the lock again. You drew in with the lamp. Near enough to smell the skin-warm scent her movement radiated, the frictional heat of the hammer at its task.

"The landlord unlocks it every morning," she said. "He won't give me a key."

And then with a horrible dull noise of breakage the hammer crashed across her left hand. She gasped away from the door into darkness and her hand leapt back to her shoulder. The hammer thumped to the lawn. She was saying: *Oh oh oh.*

You brought the lamp close. Her blood was already welling.

"Inside," she murmured. She meant the studio, and you swung the lamp that way to find the fractured lock dangling free. So the broken noise had been the lock's. Good. Push the studio doors. Enter.

Clara was clutching her wounded hand, releasing, clutching—all ten fingers bloody now. "Water," she said.

"Ja." You were already looking.

"Over there."

In the corner you found the bucket, whipped back the cloth and quickly filled an enamel basin. Clara made a wincing staccato noise as she dropped her hand into the cool water. A downy pink plume expanded, then the blood ran from her knuckles like unraveling thread.

You sat down beside her. "May I see?"

She nodded wordlessly, so you clasped her wrist, braceleting the warm slenderness below her sleeve, and lifted the hand from the red pool. She could still move her fingers.

"You'll be able to work?"

"It's not broken," she answered. "Just the skin." She had a comforter's tone, though her face was still tensed.

You kept your hand cupped beneath her wrist, loath to withdraw it. You had the fanciful thought that her healing might be quickened this way. Clara Westhoff accepted the hopeful touch. For a long time you and she remained conjoined, unmoving.

At last you said, "We must never be like the hammer. That's important, isn't it?"

Clara had the deep listening look again. "Like the hammer?"

"Invulnerable."

It wasn't a new thought, but it was the first time you'd spoken it aloud, affirming in words your own congenital state. For since boyhood you had known you lacked the self-protection most persons possessed. *Because your eyes,* the young Russian girl had said, holding forth the gift of the icon. *Because your face.* That barefoot peasant child living so near to God in her poverty—hadn't she, immediately upon looking into your eyes, seen this truth about you—seen, in some way, your soul? In your three years with Lou you had learned, learned wholeheartedly, to embrace your un-shielded condition. No choice, really, but to embrace it. Your art would forever after come of it. Nothing surprising, then, in finding yourself fever-stricken at the Westhoff home seven months after that night of Clara's wound, leveled before the threshold of your wedding.

Holding the ceremony in Saint Jürgen church was out of the question, but the date could not be pushed back—you and Clara were of one mind on that. So on twenty-eighth April, still fever-weak but alert, you buttoned your gaiters, belted your jacket, and met your white-garbed bride in the Westhoff dining room downstairs. The sculptress was statuesque and grand in her window-lit dress. Her Artemis eyes embraced you bravely. That soulful beauty you loved in her.

A space had been cleared in front of the window, the mahogany sideboard pushed to the corner. Mother and Father Westhoff and brother Helmuth in attendance. No Rilkes. The pastor stood at the ready in his austere Protestant surplice—and he might solemnize without misgiving, for the groom's withdrawal from the Roman church had been certified several weeks before.

Thus, a few days later you stood in your Westerwede cottage gazing at Saint Cecilia in the painting the Westhoffs had given you. Inevitably the figure brought Lou to your thoughts: coerced bride refusing her husband's bed. And did you have any inkling of what that image presaged of your coming year and its lonely departure? Cecilia in thrall, all earthly music scattered in the broken instruments at her feet, her upcast eyes wonder-struck by some more ethereal music which plucks one out of life and makes of one a wanderer.

I'm sorry, Clara. And give Ruth my apology in the tenderest kiss. It was a poor man that made you his wife. Now has he made you a stranger? Don't blame him, please, for believing he could have a home. For wanting just what everyone wants . . .

Rainer is not well. A bitter reaction is occurring in his bowels. Cinders tumbling within him. The work of a horrendous allergy. Fiery stool and aversion to food of all sorts. Only water goes down with ease, bewilderingly cooling. In the discolored toilet bowl as he rises, a lean dark matter lies in coils. Foul mimicry of his inner mappings.

"'How has your life been?' . . . Rodin has answered: 'Good.'
　　'Have you had enemies?'
　　'They could not hinder my work.'
　　'And fame?'
　　'Has obliged me to work.'
　　'And friends?'
　　'Have required work of me.'
　　'And women?'
　　'Through work I have learned to admire them.'
　　'But you have been young?'
　　'Then I was like anybody. One understands nothing when one is young; that comes later, over time.'"

.　　.　　.

Another garden lunch with the Master and Madame. Again the little girl is there. Again Rodin and the lady seem out of sorts. She is a saddening, ill-gathered person. Perhaps years in the presence of this mountain-like husband could only unanchor her thus.

Later the poet walks in the garden with the Master. The little girl skips after them along the gravel path. The men sit together on a bench, the Sèvres Valley falling away at their feet: the river a length of gray yarn dotted with tiny buildings.

"I worked down there at one time," says Rodin. "In the Sèvres porcelain factory. I was younger. That sort of heavy manual work is good for a younger person. People forget this, since work is now understood to mean other things—having ideas or thinking this or that. These days people think labor of the hands is not so important."

The Master's own hands hover palm-up before him.

"But wasn't it difficult?" says Rainer. "I mean to develop your own work and do that other labor too?"

Rodin shrugs. "It comes very slowly at first, work of my kind. It needs great patience. You *have* to be patient, you see, if you must do *other* work all day. I hardly know anybody these days who really works. A handful of people in Paris, maybe. All the schools teach thought and craft. But you can't learn about nature, about form, by thinking, by making arbitrary shapes. I went to Belgium, you know, before I was thirty. I stayed there a good while, made many paintings, took a few commissions. In Belgium I learned that one cannot approach nature as if it's prey—which is precisely how I sought to make my paintings then. I would pounce on nature, try to subdue it on the canvas. One may make a few fine landscapes that way, but one doesn't learn much about the character of the natural world. About *Le Modelé*. Do you know this word? Always there is beauty everywhere— everywhere around us because *Le Modelé* is all around us. If you look at a stone, or at a woman's torso . . ."

As the Master talks, the little girl comes up from the grass where she's been playing. She clings to Rodin's knee. One of his hands has fallen to rest there and she lays upon its back a violet she's picked. The violet falls. She stoops and finds it and tries very delicately to press it to Rodin's finger like a ring. He does not move his hand, does not notice the girl's attentions. He is deep in his own words, his eyes roaming out to the distances before him. Eyes which seem to see nothing but *world* and the work it gives him.

"It seems," says Rainer, "that you were very alone in your work."

"*Oui.*"

"That only in Belgium, in your profound solitude, did *Le Modelé* reveal itself to you."

"*Oui, c'est vrai.*"

"Wouldn't you say it's very good to be alone? Don't the best things happen when we are most solitary? I came to see the results—in Worpswede—of too much society, too much joint endeavor. It holds those artists back. Do you know Worpswede?" And Rainer tells the Master something of the moors and the young painters there, tells how he lived in that landscape and was—for a while anyway—a part of all that.

"It's not so good to make groups," says Rodin musingly, "this is true. Friends get in each other's way. Best to be alone. Oh, but a man can take a wife, of course, because a man simply must have a wife! Your wife is coming soon, *non?*"

"*Oui,* next month. She must leave our daughter. It makes us both very sad."

Rodin's gray eyes lock upon the poet's. It seems he's taken the poet's words with grave understanding. He sets his bearded mouth and looks out again, into the distance. "*C'est vrai,*" he says, his voice deep and monumental. "One must work. Nothing but work. And patience. It takes great patience. I have given my life to it, you know. One must find joy in his art—that is where his joy is."

And the Master's meaning seems very clear: between one's life and one's art lies no middle road.

Just outside the gate as Rainer takes his leave of Meudon for the day, his eye snags on a spot of color: a broken surface with a glint like crumpled goldleaf. He crouches and finds a squashed scarab beetle, greenish-golden, flattened in the bed of pebbled rock. Someone has trodden it, yet the cracked plates of its wings still seem perfect: so many intersecting surfaces.

"*Voilà,*" Rodin had said, just moments before. The gift of her violet failing, the little girl had brought the Master a partly crushed snail shell. He received it with such sudden delight that the girl went twirling down the lawn. In gentle fingers Rodin raised the gift against the sky. "Here is the gothic renaissance, do you see? Right here in this shell."

So it's true: the Master *sees* beauty in everything. This tireless one. Rainer leaves the scarab where it lies. Soon he is juddering along in a train carriage, returning to the city. The broken shell of the city.

"And now, too, this old illness—the one that has always touched me so strangely. I am sure it is underestimated. Precisely as the significance of other illnesses is exaggerated. This illness has no fixed characteristics, it adopts the characteristics of whomever it grips. With a sleepwalker's certainty, it picks out each person's deepest danger, that which seemed passed, and props it up again before him, quite close, in the closest hour."

Rainer wakes and is not well. Snakes from his bowels again. The basin's tepid morning water causes a repulsive shiver. Smell of soap brings no comfort, conjures only sterile things, memories of loss. There's a hunger inside him that food cannot appease. There's an ungovernable quaking in his hands.

Here is the poet abroad in the Paris lanes again like a castaway. Sea-swell of streets heavy with humanity, and this city a listing galleon on some wayward course.

Unmistakable need has overshadowed him. Despite his fear he will see a doctor. Toward the regal dome of the Val de Grâce. People are helped there, aren't they? Old venerable hospital. Why shouldn't he be helped too? Eastward along the boulevard Saint Michel, past the windows of curio shops, dealers in antiquities and ancient coins. Flavian's aquiline profile on a little circle of stamped gold or bronze. Age-old penny sold for the price of four days' food. Inflation of vanished empires. It provokes a clenching in the pit of his stomach. Whole epochs swallowed up in the interval of inhale-exhale, and the poet's own epoch traveling that course this very moment, sucked into some infallible godlike lung.

The first thing seen is the glister of embossed coat buttons. Military brass of the gendarme, and the uniformed one in regulation stance, manning the door. The poet is not to pass by. Rainer couldn't have expected this.

The guard notes his hesitation. A clean-shaven mouth clips a single word: *"Oui?"*

"Bonjour. Perhaps I'm in the wrong place. I'd hoped to see a doctor."

"Military only. Unless you've got a pass, you'll have to go to a civilian facility."

"The Hôtel Dieu?"

"Oui. Or the Salpêtrière, the Maison de Bicêtre, there are many."

"The closest?"

"Salpêtrière, near the Gare d'Austerlitz. A mile, maybe two from here."

"But if I were to need help now?"

A slight shrug. Hard eyes braced against conspiracy. "Hire a cab. It's faster than walking."

But that seems too great a task for one day, trying all over again.

Start back then. Back along the way that led here. The impossibly large dome of the Val de Grâce folds hidden into a clump of streets behind. Rainer rounds a corner and there beyond the rooftops rises the other dome of the Panthéon. So many grand things to shrink a soul.

He passes a shut pharmacy. Blue delft vases displayed behind the window. *Cocaine,* says one. *Opium,* another. Must go by, mustn't think of medicines.

In a stone lintel above heavy gates stand the chiseled words: MAISON

D'ACCOUCHEMENT. And here on the sidewalk trundles a pregnant woman, her belly hugely distended beneath a soiled blouse, something outsized and overripe within her. How violently being burgeons!

She is alone. One hand cups the torso's bulge, the other lies splay-fingered against the wall, the woman coming on slowly, slowly, with immense concentration. Her face pinched. She does not see him. She is hurrying, though her cargo impedes. Her hand coming off the wall, slapping the wall, coming off as she goes past. And her dusty skirts are wet in back. Something rustles to the pavement, something dribbling from her body: the liquid trail of her need.

The poet stops.

"Madame?" He goes toward her, reaches to touch her. *"Madame?"*— other words escape him now. Anyway, she does not seem to hear: her face still squinched and everything turned inward to the pain. But she halts. Stands there braced at the wall, not looking anywhere.

"Madame?"

Nothing. Rainer touches her elbow, her back, moves to impel her forward.

"Madame, mustn't you hurry?"—this in German, but she must understand.

She is very still, seems to want only rest. She fixes him with gray glazed eyes, desperately silent. Her chapped and crackled lips come open. A shudder of shocked pain. Something has been rent inside her. At her feet a pool of dark bluish murk is forming.

And this whole episode not even a dream . . .

Tonight, *tonight:* safe again in the contained danger of his Toullier quarters, Rainer will lie feverbound, captive to his memory and its convoluted echoes: the reiteration of his fists at the hospital gates, the flight of his cry into the locked courtyard. Though in life the orderlies appear at last and speed the woman inside, they do not come in the memory. They do not come, and the bursting woman's wet gray eyes remain fixed and unseeing upon him. In the worst moments the great outside need leaves him no chance of evasion. Every need becomes *his* conclusively, sits upon his heart like a stone. Does he dare require a doctor for himself amidst such need?

"The main thing was, one was alive. That was the main thing."

Next morning Rainer is better. The anxious feeling gone. Sensations not so bitter now. Yet one must try to get help if he is able, mustn't he? Clara will be here by next month; he must try to be well when she arrives. So he will walk to the hospital—the Salpêtrière. And he needn't even go in, not necessarily. The walk itself may be enough to clear his conscience. A doctor may be superfluous by the time Rainer gets there.

A half hour gone and then he is standing outside a factory-like building. Rows of small windows in the walls of oppressive stone. An angry arch reads CONSULTATIONS in rigid tombstone letters, an open door beneath.

Something sucks the poet inside—it's not a matter of decision. Something recognizes him and draws him through the door. That he may meet his brethren. And they are all inside, all arrayed in a deep, purgatorial corridor: two long benches heavy with them, one bench to each wall. Lined up like that, the wounded ones sit there and stare at their opposites as at a mirror.

Someone has given Rainer a slip of paper, the selfsame paper clutched by the many hands in this hall. There doesn't seem to be a place to sit, so he walks to the end of the corridor and as he passes in the space where their gazes meet their *seeing* breaks before him like a surface of water. Then they are all seeing him. *And the lanky child of Prague goes ambling over the old Karl-Brücke—the bridge with its rows of opposing saints ranked above the muddy river, figures chiseled life-size from stone and blackened with soot. Their serried gazes meet above the boy as he passes between the pedestals, their grimed eyes still rueful in martyrdom. . . .*

Toward the end of the row a man rises. A blanched and speckled face. Egglike skull where clumps of hair cling without pattern to a pink scalp. The man waves a feeble usher's hand toward the slot of surrendered bench, his mouth contorted weakly—something like a smile. An imbecilic, wandering look.

"*Merci, non,*" murmurs the poet, and goes by.

"*Upon this bench they sat, those that knew me, and waited. Yes, they were all there.*"

"You say you don't have any particular pain?"

The doctor is a gentlemanly fellow with colorless thin hair, his face and hands pale as a priest's.

"*Non, monsieur.* Besides a stitch in the bowels now and then. And of course the headache."

The headache—ruthless force, and Rainer plunging headlong through thickening silt—ah, the vise-grips of earthen plates and that space all closed and airless—

"How often does the headache come?"

"Every few weeks, I suppose."

"Always with a fever?"

"Not always. Sometimes yes, sometimes no."

"And for how many years have you been prone to the headache?"

"As long as I can remember."

"And your bowels?"

"*Oui?*"

"Has this stitch in your bowels always troubled you too?"

"*Non, monsieur.* That's more recent."

The doctor has not touched him. The doctor sits at a table with papers fanned flat before him. A pen lies there, but he does not write anything. The poet sits in a small wooden chair, sweating hands folded in his lap.

This room is not a room, it's merely a partitioned space just off the corridor where so many wait. The wall behind, in which the door stands, does not even meet the ceiling. The doctor's words travel over and ring clearly in the hall. Besides the poet's chair, the doctor's, and the table, there's nothing here but a metal tray against one wall, erected on four long metal legs each shod with a little caster and in the room's far corner a big square-mounted sink fashioned of some unreflective metal.

"Your occupation?"

"Poet."

"And why do you come to Paris?"

"I'm writing a book about Auguste Rodin."

"Who?"

"Rodin."

The doctor kinks his brow, swings his head to stare at the concrete floor as though the name might be stenciled there. He seems to see it.

"Ah, *Rodin,*" he says, the second syllable distinctly nasalized. "*Rodin,* yes . . ."

He touches his pince-nez with very careful doctorly fingers. "Well, Monsieur Rilke, would you tell me once more what ails you exactly?"

"I beg your pardon, Doctor, I've told you already. Perhaps if you were to examine me—"

"Consultations only here. Examinations come later in the H wing. And from what you've explained, monsieur, I'm afraid your condition, if condition there be, is very slight. Indigestion perhaps, probably resulting in a bilious disturbance of the blood from which come headaches and . . ."

So the good doctor needs the poet to say his malady. And how can one *say* such a thing? How? . . . But the doctor is rising now, extracting something from an inner coat pocket.

"If you'll be good enough to draw back your jacket, monsieur, I might see whether your pulse has anything to report."

The doctor bends and sets a small cone against Rainer's breast, leans his ear down, attends. Against Rainer's back, attends. And what can one's heart be thought to say when hearkened to in no manner but this?

Another slip of paper like some dubious consolation prize. Ciphers printed blackly. The doctor instructed him to wait, but for what?

The speckle-faced man is still in the corridor, or, like the poet, has left only to return. The man hastens over, smiling his contorted smile. The clumps of hair affixed at his domed head are tightly coiled as moss, vaguely pubic. "Ye can sit in my place down there," he says. Sprightly words more breath than voice. Shy childlike generosity. Does he offer his seat to every newcomer? And how long has he waited in this stifling atmosphere? Does he even have a number?

"*Merci, non.* I think I'm leaving now."

"Leaving? Wait, but did they tell ye the secret? Oh, ye talked to Monsieur Lepage, *non?* Well, he never tells. But let me say it—can I say it? *Oui?* Listen." The man's spotted head declines, his eyes tilting in surreptitious perversion. His womanly hand clutches the edge of Rainer's coat. A sally of stomach-rich breath in a whisper: "It's not a hospital, it's a prison!"

Rainer pulls away, but the man's grip closes fast, his words now scant of breath, contracting in hiccup or laugh. "They was whores—*hyt-hyt*—that come here! Look in the books—*hyt-hyt-hyt*—they'll tell ye, whores is what they'll say, and a whore is one that'll open her juicyjaws–*hyt-hyt*—for anyone can part with two or three sous!"

Rainer is moving back now, but the man has adhered himself and moves with him.

"They put 'em in chains they did. Right here. Hundreds of 'em all in one place right here, thems and the idiots—*hyt-hyt-hyt*—and the shakers and the droolers all together. It's a—*hyt-hyt*—prison, I'm telling ye!"

Rainer wrenches away. Something drops with a tiny clicking noise.

"Your button, sir, your—*hyt*—button!"

But the poet is door-bent and deaf to everything. The harsh daylight stands ahead of him at the corridor's end as if whitely vomited from the gut in which he thrashes. And may he be vomited too.

*Y*our letter to Major-General von Sedlakowitz: composed ninth December 1920, in your forty-fifth year. The Major-General wrote, in light of your fame, to remember himself to you from your days at Saint Pölten. He recalled your early predilection for poetry and was proud to recollect that he himself had once encouraged you.

> *"Dear Major-General . . .*
> *I could not, I believe, have been allowed to realize my life . . . if I had not, through decades, disowned and suppressed all memories of the five years of my military rearing; indeed, what is there that I haven't done for this suppression!"*

A pale-green surface, scoured spotless, redolent of bleach. A gas chandelier. A ceiling. But not the gymnasium ceiling. The clapping of feet—a hollow sound. He heard that—just a moment ago, wasn't it? *The beating of countless excited feet. The hum of voices. Somewhere a whistle.* Now the press of cold fingers at his wrist. An orderly stands by him in white.

"Hallo, Kadett."

The orderly has a dull expressionless face. Mouth like a line drawn in pencil. He holds René Maria's wrist and looks at the boy as one looks at a picture, then lays the boy's hand aside and goes out of the room on business-like heels.

René Maria looks down along his own body: the shapes of his legs under sheets and woolen blanket. *His knees cracked with every declension as he sank and rose. Twenty knee-bends. Odor of boys in movement. Every figure bobbing as one, bright blue gymnasium shirts lifting, falling, and the grim instructor pacing up and down*—Achtzehn! Neunzehn! Zwanzig!

Someone sweeps into the room—the Regimental Doctor, looking flat-faced and shrunken, an officious board and papers beneath his arm. "Kadett Rilke," he murmurs, and scribbles something down on the papers. He sets the papers by on a table and leans over the boy.

Smell of leather and talc. There had been a long sliver of light overhead, a seam where the ceiling would open. Something within him had gone vaulting toward it, even as his body fell backward.

The doctor's suspicious fingers grope at René Maria's throat. Mild sterile pressure. The doctor stands back again, mutters a little something to himself, snatches the papers from the table and strides away.

Long hours. The boy lies on his back under the fizzing gas chandelier. The room's light does not change. He dozes and wakes. Dozes . . .

The Regimental Doctor's squeezed and pliant voice clatters in the quiet infirmary hall, waking him. *"Ja, Herr Rilke . . . seiner Gesundheit ist zart." Health is delicate, but . . . needn't worry . . . normal in time.* Then Papa's voice murmuring thanks. An interim of quietness, footsteps slowly growing louder. Then a dark shape comes streaming in the green floor and the father stands at the boy's bed, looking down upon him.

"Papa."

"Hello, Cadet."

Papa seems inhumanly tall and well constructed, his long wool coat very crisp along the line of his high shoulders. He strips off one black glove and touches René Maria's forehead, his eyes drifting ceilingward as though he prays to discern what so enfeebles his boy. Then he turns from the bed, draws up a chair, and sits. "I think I've seen you this way before, René."

"I know. It can't be helped, Papa. It just comes."

"I've spoken to the Adjutant, René. Your record speaks well for you, he says. Says you are good-tempered and orderly. I like to hear such things."

"Thank you, Papa. Was your train ride comfortable?"

"Better than expected. And prompt—that always makes a railroad man happy."

René Maria smiles. The mask of his face throbs mightily.

Papa doffs his bowler, brushes a gloved hand through thinning hair. The bowler bobs and floats along the fingers in his lap.

"I've heard from Mother, René."

"Yes?"

"Yes." Again Papa's eyes float toward the ceiling. The gas chandelier high above the bed. "I fear Mother has much . . . much to answer for in this. In your illness. The two of you write often, don't you?"

"Of course, Papa."

"Yes, well . . ."

"Papa?"

"I'm afraid so many letters from her, so much of a woman's voice, can only garble all . . . everything that ought to take effect while you're here. You see, René, it doesn't do, does it, to have girls around the Kadetten-schule?"

"No sir."

"Of course not. But your mother's letters. All that softness."

"Papa, I—"

"In speaking with the Adjutant, René, I must say a number of things dismayed me. He tells me you required extra testing in fencing and gymnastics."

"Yes, Papa."

"And I'm concerned about your class rank. The Adjutant has it presently at thirty-eight of fifty-one. Now, you see, don't you, how it will not do to excel in academics while you let other things flag? Of course you do, my boy. And that's why you mustn't give your mother's letters so much heed. It's—it's garbling, you see. And where are we now because of it? The *infirmary,* of all places."

Papa's eyes go grazing across the room. His glance will not adhere to any of these slick scrubbed surfaces. He seems bewildered by the place. Looks down at the bowler again, flips it over and runs his fingers along the brim. "Lord knows I understand what it means to be in the infirmary. But in my case it couldn't be helped. I've still that ailment in my throat, you know. With you, my boy, we've no such impediment. These headaches, what are they? Why do they come? I think we've answered that, haven't we? And couldn't things very easily be otherwise?"

"Yes, Papa. I see."

"That's my boy. I knew you would."

Maybe a dream, maybe not—regardless, its meaning remains. Rainer is walking along the lower Quai des Augustins at midday. The water of the Seine purls just a few feet below him.

The arch of the Pont Neuf, as he comes beneath it, shelters two or three misbegotten figures in its shadows. Stench of urine so rude here it gags him. In the puddled space beside one wall a pile of rags shudders as though unsettled by searching hands. A scraggly skull comes up and the pile transmutes to a shriveled woman squatting in her tattered garments to defecate on the stones, her knees bared white and bulbous at the clutched skirt-hems. Her rheumy eyes follow him past.

Into daylight again and now a second hag comes forward to thrust something upon him: a near-empty drawer proffered in two dirty hands. A few ignoble pins and needles roll about inside. The stub of a broken pencil. Two or three buttons.

The poet stiffens, tries to outpace her—but the dislocated drawer is there and there and there, blocking his path wherever he turns. Rainer grips his coat seam where the button was torn. Must go by her and not look. She cannot *make* him behold the thing he needs in that clutched drawer of hers. His torn button amongst those others.

Somehow he gets past. The woman shrinks away into the excremental stone, like some memory the city itself has called back into the soiled deeps of its forgetting. Rainer walks on. Must keep walking. But he knows that ragged figure came so close to him, got so nearly inside of him, as to understand that she carried a piece of him in her drawer.

And yet there are salvations—yes, even in Paris. It is a great city, and not without beauty, certainly not. In the hushed sanctum of the Bibliothèque Nationale reading room, Rainer peruses illustrations of the French cathedrals in all their medieval splendor. Or he spends hours immersed in the works of Flaubert, Verlaine, Mallarmé, Baudelaire: names like benedictions, for *they* struggled here too—even *made* something of their struggle, transformed it to gold, to silver, in the smithies of poetry or prose.

Rainer is safe in the reading room. Admission is not granted to just anybody; one must apply and win a special pass. He sits in the huge murmurous chamber, given reprieve from the roiling streets outside, and the words of Baudelaire whisper under his hands:

> *My soul without mast, old and disheveled,*
> *danced, danced athwart*
> *a monstrous, boundless sea.*

When the library closes Rainer emerges like one freshly awakened to walk the teeming streets of the Rive Droite toward the river. Narrow channels of streets walled high by the close buildings, traffic raging through like storm waters. Somehow he is still safe as he walks, the hush of the library still enfolds him. Twilight waxes everywhere, a darkening steam sent up from all sides of the city.

It's nearly full dark by the time the poet comes past the ancient structure of Notre Dame, its floriform buttresses vaulted from the fertile history of the Ile de la Cité. The great blackened towers, strangely humble for all their immensity, seem to sing now of the young night clasping them. Self-same vespers sung these eight hundred years.

He came by here in a rainfall once and it was the same then: this sense of the silence embracing all that lofted stone, the ever-deepening loneliness of this great *thing* that has out-tenured how many generations? The cathedral is perhaps the greatest of all this city's *things,* and it unifies all that surrounds it. Stands together with Haussman's housefronts and with the river and with the destitute humanity roiling in the knotted streets. What beautiful power it is that this Notre Dame in its grand *thing*ness can take such discordant elements and draw them all into a pure harmonic. Rodin's body of work has a similar power: his sculpture seems to have gathered everything, *everything* into itself. And Rainer wonders now: How may a *poet* acquire such ingathering power? How not merely understand the power but *acquire* it? How *construct* as the Master does?

Rainer knows he's nothing like Rodin—no sculptor, no craftsman. Enormous hunks of stone arrive frequently at Meudon. The Master orders the stones set down on the lawn that he may circle them with his thoughtful topheavy stride, his hand wandering in his beard. The poet has watched his eyes and seen the visions kindling there. In blocks of intransigent stone, fragments of mountains that move only with the strength of several men, Rodin gratefully receives the heaviness of his work.

Rainer, though, is no sculptor. By what handcraft, then, could *he* possibly make work of this city's *things?*—of this city's fear, even, which stands three-dimensional amongst the *things?* The fear, he sees now, could be a unifying power should one muster the strength to make it such. But what immeasurable quantities of strength would be required? How might he get outside himself and make of himself a hand to grasp Paris and everything Paris stirs up inside?—to give it all a form, a shape?

"He who creates has no right to choose. His work must be imbued with steady obedience."

Rodin's atelier in the rue de l'Université. Monumental figures stand everywhere about in the pleasant warm snowfall of windowlight and plaster dust. Rainer wanders amongst them, looking. Looking. Though he has studied them all so long already, his looking never becomes repetitious. Instead it becomes, somehow, *sculptural.* As though the works themselves teach his eyes to shape and hew.

In this moment the Master is deep in his labor at a pedestal near the corner window. Rainer has accustomed himself to silence in his presence. Natural breathing silence, like that between friends. The poet stoops to study a small hand-sized piece amongst the scattered antiques on a shelf: a stone tiger in midstride, powerful shoulders humped above the head, the muzzle sniffing low. Front legs and rear parted in the twin arches of the hunting pace, the long rope of tail flowing behind.

"That's beautiful!" calls Rodin from the corner. "That one is everything!"

He drops his tools and bustles over, seizes the artifact and turns it this way and that in a dust-blanched hand. His eyes invest it with immense significance. Rainer's eyes try as well.

"It's everything, this one," says the Master with a kind of helpless astonishment, waving his hand across the tiger, its self-evident grandeur. Then he braces the poet with his stare. "Have you gone to *la ménagerie?*"

"The zoo? No."

"You must go there." A grave look now, and Rainer can feel Rodin's sculptural glance fettling his rough edges, wanting to scrape him down to clean lines. "You must go there. It's in the Jardin des Plantes. Visit the Animaux Féroces. It means very much to watch those great cats. You'll see then the significance of this little antique."

The Master sets the stone tiger on its shelf, starts back toward his pedestal, has a thought, turns.

"And it's not just the cats. *Non,* everything is there. *Everything.*"

And could one have imagined such things as flamingoes, tortoises, gazelles?

"The resourceful animals notice it already,
that we are not very firmly at home in the interpreted world."

Rainer arrives in the Paris *ménagerie* to find the many improbable and vibratory realities of form that excite the Master's art. *Le Modelé* in abundance here . . .

Two enormous gray creatures stand swaying in a bare dirt clearing. Before them, a half-dozen people are pressed to a chest-high iron fence, arms outstretched, imploring the beasts to approach. One comes forward. Tree-trunk legs displacing rings of dust with every slow step. Gentle earth-heavy gait, the stump of the gray foot dragging in a whisper. The other foot is tethered to the rear fence by thick chain. Great ears flap like tent eaves. The blunt trunk-tip sweeps circles across the ground, nibbling, curling to scoop. A digitless hand. The trunk rears sniffing, lithe as a serpent in water. Long-lashed heartsore eyes drift in the creature's vast skull—registry of the trunk's experience. The trunk sinks to a human hand, ginger mitten-lips frisking across the palm, plucking it clean. The people press against the fence, against each other, sigh and effuse as they stroke the ancient hide. Laughter. The trunk rolls back soundlessly, curls, bears the food to the wet triangular mouth.

Elsewhere: a lion and a tiger lie heaped in separate cages, massive paws flung across the floor. From one or the other drifts a heady musk like carnivorous sex or breath or sweat-bedded fur.

In the next cage: a tireless panther walking and walking and walking. Tight violent curve of the spine forever turning back—wall to wall this way and that. Colorless jewel eyes like sunlit bottle glass. The bars blur to a dim mesh as Rainer follows the creature left and right and left and right.

No stopping no pausing the breath jetting out in hot lungheavy bursts beating the dangerous pulse of the feet falling and falling in huntlocked fervor and the blind brain muzzled and reeling in its muscled skull ah fantasy of the night-thick hunt in this city's magnesium glare and nevermore the wild murdering chase in the crazed light of the moon . . .

A mother and child passing stop to stand before the pen and the creature's hard skull drops beneath the shearing gears of the shoulders. Predator-gaze fixed on the child, but even then the panther does not cease. And suddenly the poet feels himself out there—*out there,* encaged behind the screen of bars. Frightfully animate. Bereft of destiny but wild with will.

He watches long. So much bespoken by the animal's ruthlessly cognizant eyes as it paces past the bars.

Finally Rainer must rip himself away. Away from the panther cage. He is hastening to the gate. Again impression has seized him. Again the *outside* power has encaged him before he could think to master it. Though all along it was *he* who ought to have done the seizing.

"Oh, it would require no more than some little trifle, and I could comprehend

everything and call it all well. Only a step, and my deep wretchedness would be salvation."

Out of the Jardin des Plantes now and into the strange will of the city. Cage of another kind.

"Dear Clara, And now you are coming soon, aren't you? I am waiting."

Yes, she is coming. And now one may take action to set things in order. To make things, perhaps, better and more conducive.

At number 3 rue de l'Abbé de l'Eppée a fifth-floor room is available for rent, along with a second suitable for Clara. Lodgings not extremely better than Rainer's Toullier room, but out of the crush of the main student quarter. The building stands almost directly adjacent to the gray church of Saint Jacques du Haut-Pas. And the two rooms have small balconies. From one, a corner of the Jardin Luxembourg can be seen—also the Panthéon dome, which appears strangely benevolent from that height.

Rainer promptly quits his room at number 11 rue Toullier. But that first ignoble address, lingering in his brain like an afterimage, shall be ascribed to a figure already linked to him in fate. Already the figure is fermenting inside. In the rue de Richelieu every day, emerging through the gate of the Bibliothèque Nationale, the poet sees the small hotel across the street, its name drawn large and neat along the white lintel: *La Malte.*

Reduced to its crudest form, Rainer's life could seem a blur of railroad platforms. Long wait for incoming trains, and then the reiterative shuffle of departure-arrival-departure—his and others. Endless dumb show played out against shifting backdrops, the players endlessly transposed. In these first cool days of October the poet stands on the platform of the Gare du

Nord, watching Clara's train slide to a halt in a gasp of smoke and steam, and the dumb show is real—perhaps more real than ever before—as the current of discharged travelers opens to afford him his first glimpse of his wife.

Tall and dark, cloaked in her long black traveling mantle, she glides down from carriage to concrete, turns to receive her bags from the porter, turns again to start along the platform. In the parchment-light from the gabled panes above she looks grand and sculpturesque. She catches sight of him and smiles.

For all his waiting, he could not have known what richness the moment would hold: to be recognized, to receive a familiar look in this strange Parisian sea. The space closing between them is a dream space, surreal and liberative.

"Rainer," she says.

"Clara, dear."

He takes her luggage only to set it down directly that he may kiss her. And her mouth very warm, and much softer than he remembers. This kiss a stamped impress of his former life—life so seemingly far he'd begun to doubt it for a dream. It's here now, immediate and vivid for all its dislocation. And yes, he has a daughter too.

Clara smells the same. Her breath is the same. The scent of her hair. And yet in her eyes there is a new loneliness, a mildly sad kind of contentment. Already he can see that.

"Are you very tired, my dear?"

"*Ja.* Is the hotel far?"

"We'll take a cab. Come."

Sluggish mortar-colored sky above the racket of hooves and wheels and skirling streetcars. Rainer grips Clara's hand as the cab judders into the swarm. Strands of hair trail and waver across her eyes. She gathers and gathers it, but finally gives up and lets it blow. She is lovely, her high Teutonic features windswept and darkly muslined. And related vividly in her face is Rainer's memory of the child Ruth, now at home with Clara's parents in Oberneuland.

Clara's head drops sidelong to his shoulder. She is watching the sky quaking above the cab. "It's such a city sky," she says. "Isn't it."

"It is, yes. Ah, I remember the Westerwede sky now, darling—just like that, you've brought it back to me. I'm so happy you've come, Clara."

The driver turns sharply and Rainer must plant a bracing hand to the hood-wall. He recovers himself, stretches his arm around his wife's narrow shoulders. "You're happy to be here, my dear, yes?"

"Yes, Rainer. Only tired." She squeezes his hand. Smiles a fatigued smile. "There was so much to do to sell up the house. So much furniture, it seemed."

"I wish I could have come."

"Heinrich helped a great deal."

"Vogeler," says Rainer. "How kind of him. I hope he doesn't blame me for not being there. I've written to him. Told him what things are like with me here. How I've been like one serving a sentence." The pleading letter to Vogeler dashed off in misery last month:

> *"You know well what has become of us. You've seen how unsuccessful all that we've tried has been. . . . Please, please . . . advise Clara Westhoff, help her with your presence, stand by her in these days when she will begin to live without our dear Ruth in the ruined house. . . . The distance removes nothing of the difficulty of these days,—I feel everything, suffer everything, and hope for almost nothing."*

Silence now. And Rainer is suddenly struck by the irreversibility of everything, now that Clara has come. Joint exile, and nothing behind them, and their daughter islanded back there in that waste which once, not long before, tenured their misguided wishes.

"So it's done," he says.

"What?"

"It's all behind us now. It's all gone."

"Ja." Murmurous, sleep-heavy word. Clara does not move as she says it.

Swallow this and be done with it. This: that the last dim, illogical hope still vestiged within you has become but a sterile seed—lifeless as a pebble in your heart.

The cab clatters onward through turgid traffic. Clara sleeps.

While they are coming up the last few blocks of rue Saint Jacques, where the broad street withers to no more than a lane, the sky begins shedding bullets of water. Rain sent down in humorless reprise of Rainer's arrival five weeks ago.

Separate quarters. They've agreed to that for the sake of their respective work. Rainer shows Clara to the room he's carefully arranged for her.

"It's nothing special, of course," he says. He can see she's not delighted. But not disappointed either. And what's important is that she not be disappointed.

The sight of the tall window draws her across the room. She stands there silhouetted in the steely light, the rain thrashing in deep dimensional effect behind her.

"Strange to be here," she says. Her quiet words drift and hover. "I mean to be here so *suddenly.* After being at home all this time."

"It's a very strange city, my dear. Very strange."

"But I'm glad, Rainer. Don't think I'm not. Only tired."

She turns and finds the flowers. He brought them up from rue Mouffetard this morning. Red matronly roses in full blossom. It gave him great joy to ready this room for her—he sees this now that he's about to leave her alone to it.

"Thank you for these," she says.

He steps forward and kisses her gently. "I'll let you rest." Another kiss, and then he is stepping out into the hall, drawing the door closed behind him. But he hears a murmurous noise and looks in again.

Clara stands near the bed's headboard, looking down at the pillow where he's laid her heather wreath.

"Oh, Rainer," she says. "You've kept it all these months."

"Of course, my dear. Didn't I say I would?"

He watches as she extends a hand to touch it. Then something shivers through her. A sharp small spasm, unignorable. She does not lift the wreath.

"Oh . . . oh, but it's dry. You didn't think to soak it, Rainer?"

Her tired eyes come up to touch him—and now there's a sudden pang within him, like a bitter hunger of kinds. He holds Clara's look only long enough to see her disillusion, then demurs to the dried wreath, the buds of heather an autumnal tan. An answer eludes him.

"Please rest, darling," he says. "I'll see you in a little while."

He draws the door closed. Moves down the hall to his room, jabbed with remorse as he remembers Clara's words of parting in the Bremen station. *The wreath will keep till I come.* But why remorse? Hasn't he kept the wreath? Though its color has dulled, hasn't it held its shape? It was the wreath's *shape,* after all, that made it an effective talisman. Yes, and now Clara is here. They are bound together yet.

Rainer reaches the end of the hall and opens the door to his room and the heightening ache in his breast becomes unmistakable. Sensation of self-imposed exile. They are bound together, yes, but he and Clara have agreed mutually to this arrangement of separation—agreed to it as artists. Now there must be little else but work. And Rainer will work as he's never done before, that he might honor this arrangement.

Yet he stands in his noiseless room and Clara's recent presence stirs like a swirl of heat around him. And has he not underestimated the task that lies ahead of them both? For Clara has brought *Home* along with her in coming to Paris. Yes, and now *Home,* which Rainer has longed for since his arrival in this city, which Westerwede has shown him he will forever desire but must never keep, resides just a few doors down.

How can one move on past need of a home? Or keep one's allegiance to— and yet not *keep*—a home? Did he ever really believe that was possible? Did he think he'd be able to set to work, free and untroubled, while all the time the allure of *Home,* in the shape of his wife, remained just down the hall?

"What is necessary is only this: solitude, great inner solitude. To go into your-self and to meet nobody for long hours—this is what one must be able to achieve. To be alone, the way one was alone as a child . . . It is good to be lonely, for solitude is difficult; that something is difficult gives us more reason to do it."

He begins the Rodin monograph. The air in his room very close and silent, and the triangle of dust and grime in the nearby corner somehow fitting, somehow not squalid now, but rather the attribute of a life becom-ing overgrown—life left unkempt in one's service to art.

But he doesn't wish to drive art away from life. For art—long, long road that it is—ultimately leads the way home to life, to the best and most fulsome of lives, does it not? Art is the one road open to those whose senses overawed them early on, whose senses drove a quiver into their hands. This road of art runs alongside the one the steady-handed walk, and the two roads enrich each other by their proximity—don't they?—and somewhere ahead the roads converge, for each is a way to life. He's learned from Rodin that there is no middle road—yet the roads converge, do they not?

The day darkens. Rainer lights a lamp—better for work than the bluish electrical glow from the ungainly fixture overhead. All the while outside his open window the falling rain sounds in sodden largo, his small balcony slick and somnolent.

The Rodin book is like a letter to himself. He starts with one good lucid sentence, suddenly ashine within him like a mirror: *"Here was a task great as the world, and the one who stood looking at it was unknown by everyone; his hands reached for bread, in darkness."*

Later. Still raining. Something leads you out of your room. Into the hall to Clara's door. *Clara's door:* strange how it has suddenly become such a thing.

Tap tap. From within, her quiet call: "It's open."

Her black cape hangs over the chair back. She's lying on her side on the bed, facing away. She twists her head to see you.

"Are you rested?" you say.

"Tired, but can't sleep. I've just been lying here."

"Perhaps a walk."

"Not yet. Maybe later."

"I'll leave you then."

"You don't have to go," she says.

She has rolled to her back. Her dark hair pools about her face in the drowsed light. Those deep clear eyes in that Artemesian countenance. Is this woman not your lover? Would that you and she could just come together. Was Lou right, two years ago, in her forewarnings about your marriage? Right, if even for the wrong reasons? Ah, Lou . . .

Step in. Shut the door.

"You look a bit different," Clara says. "I didn't expect that."

"Different how?"

"I don't know. Thinner, perhaps. Yes"—she seems to see it clearly now—"yes, more gaunt."

"I've been ill. Every autumn is like this for me."

She's concerned.

"It's only a trifle," you say. "A persistent trifle."

Her sculptress eyes remain steady. "No, it's something else too. It's like you've changed—matured already. I mean your appearance."

She puts out her hand and you step forward and clasp it. The spreading warmth that comes of this contact. Those gray scars still run across her knuckles, another imprint of the past you share.

She says, "Do I look different too?"

Appraise her carefully, wordlessly. Shake your head.

"No? Why shouldn't I?"

"Well, I do see more of Ruth in you now."

The child's name brings quick water to her eyes. "Do you?"

Touch the swell of her cheek. "We'll be all right, Clara."

"Will we?" Her tears begin to run.

"Yes."

"How do you know?"

"Because. Look." Kneel down beside the bed, press her wet cheek to yours. The gray window gleams dimly before you. "Look. The rain pounds down but we don't feel it. We have shelter. And Ruth has shelter. It's difficult, Clara—everything is, I know—but what's difficult is not bad. And as long as we have our work, we'll be all right. Our work is our shelter."

"We'll be all right?" she says. "You believe it?"

"I do," you answer. For what choice is there but to believe it, in spite of everything?—in spite of this scurrilous city and Ruth's distance and your own silent longings. You must believe it, that's all. For Clara's sake.

And now you've said everything, so you lower your head and kiss the scars on your wife's warm knuckles. And then you are cradling her hot face in your hands and kissing her tears, her eyes. Her mouth.

.   .   .

An hour later Rainer and Clara sprawl together in a sober aftermath of silence. Their slow-fast lovers' ritual already lies far below them, as if it happened not within the reach of an hour but eons past: their bodies interlocked like shapenotes in a plaintive sort of music. Confessional dirge. And why does this sense of shame hover between them now, unspoken? What sin was it to feed the needful hunger in a spouse's soul, to comfort loneliness with loneliness? They vault the canopy of solitude over one another. Love shared selflessly, without attachment or demand: two artists giving each other back to themselves. No use for self-chastisement now, thinks Rainer. But he knows they must not collapse into each other, despite this love which continually tugs them together. If they are both to live as the artists they are, they must keep one another free. He wants that for Clara: freedom. As he wants it himself. The great danger of love is that it hems the beloved in. He's learned this well in those days since Lou.

"For this is guilt, if anything is guilt:
not to increase the freedom of a love,
to surround everything with a freedom one has called up from inside.
We have, where we love, to affirm this only:
letting each other go: because to hold on
comes to us easily and requires us to learn nothing."

They must let their separate quarters enforce their separate disciplines, separate solitudes. Then, on the occasions when they meet—once a week or so—they can come to one another pure and whole. Invent a more expansive love.

But now Clara starts to cry again, wriggles over and nestles her wet face into his throat. And no need to ask what's the matter. Rainer can see little Ruth as Clara is seeing her now. The child drifts about in the gloomy air like a wraith, confabulated from the remorseful thoughts of her parents.

He moves to rise.

"Where are you going?"

"Shh. Don't worry."

He crosses the room on naked feet. A scrim of gray-black streetlight hangs across the windowglass like gossamer. The rose vase stands before it mutely, its color sucked away. But the flowers' fragrance has increased in the diminishing light, as if to fill that absence of red. In the darkness behind him Clara is muffling her sobs in the bedclothes. Rainer touches one of the blossoms, plucks off a big petal nearly the size of a playing card. Velveteen leaf concaved deeply, still molded to the carolla.

Back in bed, he sweeps the straggling hair from Clara's eyes, hushes her—*Shhhh*—and her pinched face begins to relax as he delicately lays the petal to her brow. She closes her eyes. Rainer draws the petal across her lids. This caress invented in a life altogether different. *Lou had lain there with parted lips, her girl-teeth showing sweetly as he swept the gentle rose down between her eyes and along her cheekbones, her breath turning long and deep with slumber. And he had leaned forth to breathe that breath from her very mouth.* Caress administered now with less hope, perhaps, but greater courage.

Eyes closed, Clara whispers, "It will be impossible, won't it? To accustom oneself to this. This life apart. Impossible."

He doesn't answer.

"Ruth's changed so much already, Rainer, since you've been away."

"I know. I think I can see her. You've brought her in your face, my dear. She's beautiful, isn't she?"

"*Ja.*"

Now he watches Clara's face falling toward sleep again. A girl's face, pained and tender. He sees how she tore herself away to come here. The courage that required. It ties a knot around his ribs, cinches hard. He holds such impossible affection toward her, this young sculptress who strives to be so many things. Wife, mother, artist, friend: she encompasses multitudes. And what has *he* become?

Clara seems better the next morning. He finds her in her room, standing at the open window inhaling the city in deep draughts. She wants an outing, so they set off together toward Montmartre: long, long walk across the river, stitching their way through cluttered streets, upward toward the unfinished Byzantine elegance of Sacré Coeur in its blinding whiteness atop the butte.

Finally, winded and slack-muscled, they mount the marble steps of the church and turn to gaze over the city's terrific chaos below. Treeless sea of rooftops. Here and there in the distance a gargantuan edifice alurch: Le Panthéon, Saint Sulpice, Les Invalides. The river is completely lost in the jumble, and even the nearer buildings stand so tightly packed that Rainer can't see the hundreds and hundreds of streets howling down there.

Something dizzying rolls through him, a dark and aqueous power. He must sit before he falls. His head aswirl in a shock of recognition. For the first time he's above it all, but how many weeks now has he been locked shoulder to shoulder with the poor and the perishing in that vise-grip down there?

Clara bends, touches his arm. "Are you all right?"

"*Ja.*" He smiles weakly. "Tired."

He's beginning to see the peculiar service Paris has done him. The city demonstrating conclusively how devoid of protection he shall forever remain, just how little choice he has in the matter of whether or not, and with what power, the world's pain, the world's beauty, will get inside him. Daily, impression almost lays him flat. No alternative but to reckon with all this in his art.

.   .   .

Your letter to Arthur Holitscher, seventeenth October 1902:

> *"I will stay in Paris for the time being, precisely because it is difficult."*

Clara finds a good atelier in the rue Leclerc, not far from the rue de l'Abbé de l'Eppée. Now that you've both steeped yourselves in separate work, you hardly see one another during the week.

On Sundays, though, you come together like two people returned from divergent journeys. Sometimes you sit in the airy quietude of Saint Jacques du Haut-Pas, gazing at the faded parquet flooring or casting your thoughts adrift into the sanctuary silence. Sometimes you stroll in l'Observatoire gardens, the square-trimmed chestnut trees quavering greenly above. Frequently Clara stops short in the path to watch the city children tussling around her. To watch the young mothers whose faces, though drawn and pallid, possess a homely joy. In Clara's own face you seem to see her very thoughts, and it brings you a sharp inward wince. You must continue to work, though, you and your gentle wife both: this conviction comes fast upon you whenever you feel her distress. It's the sole answer, you're sure of it.

Throughout November, your Rodin book grows and grows.

> *"No strange voice came to him, no praise to confuse him, no reproach to bewilder him. . . . Always his work spoke to him. It spoke to him in the morning upon waking, and in the evening it resonated long in his hands, much like an instrument he had set aside."*

You've decided you will dedicate the book to Clara.

.   .   .

In the Master's pavilion one day, while the sculptress makes sketches of some plaster figures across the row, you stand long before a haunting work: a man on his knees falling forward into great plumes of pale marble. A female figure manifests herself there, stern and deific, like a ghost relinquished from that mass of steam or stone. Half her body is visible, and already the man has pressed his face to her breast. Already, before she has appeared completely, he seeks to sink through her to some kind of absolution—*the smell of his homecoming, the feminine musk of fennel and lily* . . .

Man and His Thought, the Master calls it. But a strange proprietary feeling grips you as you study it. This work seems, somehow, yours. You would call it . . . *Lou.*

L O U : *1897*

"Zwar du erschrakst ihm das Harz; doch ältere Schrecken
stürzten in ihn bei dem berührenden Anstoß."

True, you frightened him to the heart, yet older terrors
plunged within him at the jolt of your touch.

The Third Duino Elegy

MUNICH: 1897. AGE
TWENTY-ONE . . .

'Come to tea next Sunday the Twelfth, seven o'clock. Be done with those books by
then and bring them along. L.A.S. will be there.'

*F*ive years before his first arrival in Paris, René Maria Rilke moves
through the rooms of a fashionable apartment in Munich—modest
quarters three floors above his own, fashionable solely for being the
dwelling of Jakob Wassermann, a writer. . . .

Several people in the apartment now—not a great number, yet somehow a small sea. Strangers. You've just come from your meager flat downstairs. Wassermann, the host, is nowhere to be seen. A large copper tea
service stands on a table against the wall. Around you, a murmurous noise
like lapping water. Clink of porcelain, the granular chime of cups seated to
saucer rings. From a coved window the late light comes bronze and carti-
laginous—it sprays an instantaneous blue at your black sleeve as you pass.
Dust motes riot like tiny kelp. In the duller light ahead, in one of Wassermann's wooden chairs, sits the figure you know immediately, though
you've never seen her before. The haze of her loosely gathered hair has
somehow caught the recessed windowlight and effulges blondly.

She's cloaked in a shapeless frock, all pleats and drapes. Outfit somewhat clerical, almost androgynous. But there's something potently feminine in the fall of the slack collar about her throat. A feathery boa hugs her
neck in a blur. She holds a saucer in one hand. The other hand raises the
cup to her lips as she listens to the woman seated across from her.

Perhaps you stand there several moments, watching her from four paces back. She is fourteen years your senior, famous, and possessed of a musky sexual frequency intense enough to scramble the stoutest masculine confidence. She has scrambled many. You can look to be little more than a boy before her. The groomed urbanity captured in your first Munich photograph, not quite a year past, has softened in favor of looser, windblown hair. During a recent trip to Venice you've sprouted a fuzzy mustache and the ragged arrow of a beard. Dark visage, somehow closer to the face that stared from your childhood photographs.

She turns now. Her eyes touch you. She will write that her first thought, upon seeing you, was that there was no back to your head.

A gap has opened in her conversation. Venture forward. Say something.

"I have read you," you tell her. "I have written you." Your hand goes toward her—"I am René Maria Rilke"—and then she is taking your hand, pressing.

"Hello." Her eyes seem very large and clear: blue irises like geodes, bedded with flints of every color. "You say you've written me?"

You are wheeling inside. Some dizzying power shrinks her. Eyesight scrolling up. "Yes. I was very taken with your essay in the *Neue Deutsche Rundschau.*"

"Ah, was it *'Jesus der Jude,'* or—"

"Yes."

"Ah," her chin rising a little. "Thank you." And now her eyes drift down again, her head turns—and someone else has won her attention.

Something slides away beneath you. Suddenly several moments have vanished. You've been drawn off in irresistible retreat. Barely a few words exchanged with her, and yet the beautiful lady was not dismissive. Her glance was indulgent. Her face had a gothic kind of sweetness. . . .

．　　．　　．

Dark evening. Alone in his room, the young poet again writes the famous author a letter. Presents himself to her as an artist of words. Reminds her that today was not the first time they met, for he had read her *'Jesus der Jude'* and it had seemed to him like a blessing and a godspeed. He too has penned some work on the subject of Christ, he writes—but *her* work was an immense fulfillment of all that *his* merely struggled for. He'd wished to express his thankfulness in person but had been thwarted by the presence of others. In the ceremonial silence of a letter, however, he hopes she can hear his gratitude. And maybe she will allow him to read his *Visions of Christ* to her sometime? That, like nothing else, will ensure he's properly offered his thanks.

He dispatches the letter to her Schellingstrasse pension early the next morning, but it does very little to cure the fervency coursing through his limbs. He's heard it said the lady will attend the theater tonight—and his own friends, Nora and Sophie Goudstikker, will be in the party. Come evening, then, René Maria has starched his collar and cuffs, brushed his coat sleeves and burnished his shoes, and finds himself steeped in the plush maroon stalls of the Gärtner Theater with Lou Andreas-Salomé and her Munich retinue.

Dinner afterward at Schleich's—a gloriously long evening. The window shutters stand open to the street, but the restaurant is thronged and hot. Wrists rise and fall above the tablecloth: glasses lifted and lowered, bread passed round, smoke aswirl. Lou presides at the head of the table, the talk continually looping back to her. Above her the Saturn-like chandeliers drift in their flaming rings and she seems some planetary spectacle. Object of many orbits. The plates are whisked away, glinting bottles refreshed. The dining room jostle slowly subsides. The men of the party doff their coats and slouch white-sleeved into the tireless conversation. The long table stands vacant of all but glasses, ashtrays, rumpled napkins.

Half after one, when the evening at last sighs to a close and the party begins to break, René Maria wades toward the head of the table. Lou is lifting the great fur boa to her shoulders. As her arms come down he inhales her sapid musk: ineluctable waft of fleece, coffee, lilies. He steadies himself, begs to escort her back to Schellingstrasse.

"Too late, my friend," says the thin bespectacled man at her side. "The lady has granted the privilege to me."

"Nonsense, August. I never gave you sole proprietorship." Lou pulls a small black tippet atop the boa. "René, isn't it?" she says.

"René Maria, *ja.*"

"This is August Endell. Forgive his opportunism. I'd be happy to have you *both* walk me back." And now with a confidential air she leans toward the young poet. "Thank you for your letter this morning."

Down the gas-lit street toward Schellingstrasse. René Maria and his cohort flank the lady. Passing under some plane trees, she tosses back her head to take a draught of the evening air and René Maria steals a glance at the bare length of her throat, lustrous in the muddy bronze of the streetlamps.

"There was a time in my life," she says, "when I might have refused any man's arm. The problem, of course, was in being expected to choose between the arms offered. I'm beyond such conundrums now."

"Lucky for us," says Endell. "Eh, René?"

"We are very fortunate."

René Maria's elbow links tight to the great lady's. Her skirts beating softly at the side of his leg. But all too soon he and his fellow escort stand shoulder to shoulder on the sidewalk outside the Pension Quistorp, watching Lou vanish into the bright lobby. Their chivalry done, they turn to the lamp-lit quietude of Schellingstrasse and August Endell says, "That, *mein*

Freund, is the only Lou Andreas-Salomé in the world." For a moment Endell stands there motionless, hands in pockets, chest thrust to the stars. Somewhat pensively, he amends, "I'm not pursuing her, you know."

"I see."

"She's married, you understand."

"Ah. Yes."

"Anyway, I'm much too timid for her. But I do love her charms. What man wouldn't?" He lets out a long audible breath—it seems a slow treasuring gesture toward the splendor as manifest in the mild night air as in the subject of his thoughts. "Over in Weimar, Friedrich Nietzsche is lying deep in his deathbed. Has been lying there for nigh eight years. People say *she's* to account for that. I think it's overblown, of course, but still I bear it in mind." Endell's hooked index finger dances at his brow. "I bear it in mind. A woman like that could unhinge any man."

Endell falls silent and stares away along the street. At length his ruminations seem to cease. "Well, which way do you go?"

"This way. And you?"

"That way. Goodnight."

"Goodnight."

And now nothing to do but depart. So the young poet glides from the Quistorp's light into the shadows pooled between streetlamps. At his back Endell's footfalls trail away in a low percussive shuffle till the late silence engulfs them. Half-a-dozen paces more, then René Maria halts in the warped gaslight. From his waistcoat pocket he withdraws a small notebook, a pencil. Steps up to the chest-high pedestal of a lamp and spreads the book there. Writes: *'Do I seem timid in your presence? I must assure you it's like the timidity of one come from the northern provinces to a city such as Venice. He is silenced as though he's entered a church. But like a song that is full of God, his gratitude wells up inside him. If only he could sing his thanks. May he? He still waits to know.'* . . .

Two brisk blocks back to the pension, and the young poet hands the folded slip to a woman at the desk. "For Frau Lou Andreas-Salomé."

He's late to breakfast in the morning. Next to his coffee cup the landlady places a trim envelope. *'To the poet René Maria Rilke'* in elegant lavender script.

'I suddenly recognized your handwriting. Why didn't you sign that very first letter of yours? Come to the Quistorp for lunch. We'll steal a table to ourselves.—Lou'

A great hatch clatters open, René Maria falls through the turning day, and then—what seems an instant later—he is seated in a rear corner of the Quistorp dining room with Lou Andreas-Salomé before him, and she is listening as he reads.

A huge eighteenth-century mirror dominates the wall behind her, its smoky pane marbled with threads of bronze, but the lady stands out of that—vibrant, salubrious—and every time René Maria looks up from the page his eyes fall on the spiraled hair at the back of her head, loose *chignon* above the downy chevrons at her nape. Ah, and the bare white length of her neck where two knees of spine undulate as under silk. Deeper in that tarnished mirror-space a second figure moves slightly. A slight dark shape recessed in the backward-thrown room: a poet and suitor. A nobody, really.

He reads three Christ visions. Lou is silent. When he's done, her clear eyes sway closed, she nods a small smile and thanks him. He can sense the note of restraint in her response. He says, "They are the most I have. You see how far they stand from your work."

"You shouldn't apologize. I'm glad you've shared them."

Something is glinting within her. She's been moved. Not by the poems, no, but by *something*. Astonishing how clearly she conveys this. Does she perceive something of the man in the wounded boy who sits before her, something of the future grandeur sheathed in his cheap suit?

"I knew I'd feel these were lacking in themselves," he tells her, "so I've brought you this other gift. My new book. *Dream-Crowned,* it's called."

In the mirror's blurred periphery he sees his doubled motion: the thin volume floating forward from his hands into hers and the book skimming seamlessly across a threshold, warped into the flatter world of the mirror without the slightest ripple—and now the mirror holds it.

"*Dream-Crowned,*" she says. "Is that meant to describe the author?"

"It would suit him now more than ever, Frau, being in your company."

Again she gives a small wry smile, barely a twitch of her mouth. "Are you sure it's completely proper to dream so in the presence of others?"

"One doesn't always have a choice."

"It's inscribed, I hope."

"Yes, to Frau Lou Andreas-Salomé, with thanks that I was permitted to meet her!"

"And is this another poem inside?"

"Yes."

"Did you write this for—"

"Just for the inscription, yes."

He watches as her eyes glide down the page. Then she closes the book and lays it flat on the tablecloth, one palm pressed to the cover as if to sense warmth from the pages beneath. She lifts her teacup, drinks with down-turned eyes.

He sits before her in the noiseless mirror-space.

Her cup chimes softly at the saucer. "Why René Maria?"

"Why?"

"Yes. Why not just René?"

"My mother is very devout," he says, blushing.

"I imagine, then, she's innocent of the Christ poems her son is writing?"

"Naturally, I'm afraid."

"And if she knew?"

"Impossible."

"It doesn't seem to fit, somehow."

"What doesn't, Frau?"

"René Maria. Somebody with such a name writing these ungentle things."

"Well, *you* may call me what you please, Frau."

"René then," she says, with a forthright look. "It's still not what it should be, but it will serve for now."

"And what should it be?"

She holds him with her imperious, warm, almost smiling gaze. "You are very eager."

He meets her gaze, still awaiting answer. Their joined eyes do not waver.

She says, "Something more vital, certainly. A name not so . . . curtsying." A new thought seems to visit her. "I believe I'd like for us to talk at length."

"Yes?"

"Can we do that now that I've heard your poems?"

"Now?"

"From now on, I mean. Not just in notes and poetry."

"I would be privileged—"

"Don't be. Just come to see me."

"Of course, Frau."

"Good."

Her elbows coming up, the white napkin lifted from her lap to the plate.

"But if I can't find you?" he says.

"Can't find me?"

"Yes, I'm afraid notes and poems will be inevitable then."

Lou's chin draws back a little: a nearly startled look in her spectral eyes. Then, despite herself, she smiles. "Very well."

Very well. With these simple words René Maria Rilke is given the courtship of Europe's famous Lou. Not a week since they've met, but they seem to recognize each other as from an era long passed.

Spring in Munich. Great spring within you—your first such season. It's clear to you now: every preceding spring has been but a lantern show in the dark theater of your being. *This one,* however, is germination, ebullience—something knuckling upward through the fallow ground inside you—and you mean to bear witness as never before, to feel this vivacity in every limb.

You call on Lou Andreas-Salomé as she requested. And now, and *now:* hours alone with her—company of two, while the impetuous spring days vibrate with terrific sunlight through the trees beyond her window. Lou stands with the window at her back, her hands a glimmer of motion while she talks, that bright world alive behind her. Other days, unruly May rain batters the glass and Lou sits at ease in a wingbacked chair. Or at a table in the Quistorp dining room, the flatware gladdened by her animating touch.

She's read *Dream-Crowned,* yes, but she doesn't understand your poems. Late one evening she tells you this, bluntly, leveling her gaze from the chair where she slouches. Dusk blackens the window at her back, a charred paper pasted to the glass. You listen to her judgment, then stand up and walk to the window and look out into that lusterless evening: light curling like flakes of singed carbon across the deeper darkness, all the day's color still implicit in that gloom.

"I knew how you felt," you say, "the first time I read to you. I could see it."

"Could you?"

"*Ja.* In your face."

"I don't know what it is. The verses seem to speak at first, but then . . . then they become just music."

"Just pretty, you mean."

"Yes. Very pretty."

Her voice soft and bold behind you. The words ought to devastate you, but somehow you're free of danger. As if she has celled you safely between her palms. As if she can make anything holy, even abasement.

Her judgments have soon impelled you to new beginnings. Repeatedly you fly from her presence into the rude enclosure of your rented room on Blütenstrasse, knock yourself over like a cup and let poems flood off the sides of your shabby desk. Again and again she accepts these poems—silently, else with some small gesture, some small word, from which you may gather the work's weakness.

In but a brief spring fortnight your days have been tugged back under the gravity of Lou Andreas-Salomé; to you it seems morning and always morning now—even the Munich nights, which previously looked so dark. Questions rise around you like so much water. You swim in questions, but one thing you know, one thing like a firm floor to the sea in which you kick and wave: despite her criticism, her embarrassment at your fledgling ways, Lou welcomes you, even takes pleasure in your presence.

One night you await her at the theater, but she fails to appear. You are standing in the lobby with ticket in hand when Nora and Sophie Goudstikker come in.

"But wasn't Lou coming?" you say. And the girls' averted looks show you the measure of your own ardor.

The first bell sounds.

"I'll wait a few minutes," you tell them, though you've waited half an hour already. You watch the girls drifting down the red aisle into the dim velvet stomach of the stalls. They seem to advance quickly to great distances. Strange, but already they are becoming mere figures to you, even these girls you've counted as friends, already they are passersby on your interminable path.

The ushers begin to close the doors and you find yourself sinking to your seat just as the lights go down.

"Not here?" whispers Nora.

"Not here."

The famous actor enters. In your ears the applause is a noise of great fibers rending.

Impossible to know what happens onstage. Bodies jostle here to there. Footsteps clatter and clatter across the boards. At last: the interval.

"I'm leaving now," you tell the sisters. "Sorry. Not well tonight."

Carefully their faces try to cover their comprehension; your real ailment is known to them.

It's not yet twilight in the streets, the late-spring day brazenly bright and long. You hurry to the Quistorp but Lou is not there. From a nearby flower stall you buy two roses, and somehow it gives you a shock of strange hope to hold those flowers.

For an hour you wander the streets. Spiraling walk. You are certain you'll find her. She will appear. In every step, every thought, you are calling her forth—and why should she fail to heed? At last you come to the green Englischer Garten. A world rudely alive. Roses stand up robust and defiant in the tended beds. The ones in your hand were wilting before you bought them, your silver exchanged in a gesture of flimsy romantic hope. Last youthful barter—somehow you know it as such.

Twilight breathes above the lawns. You sit on a garden bench, watching as the grass softens to blue. Wind stirs fitfully amongst the trees.

White papery blossoms tremble down and splatter the path. Soon an attendant will come along sounding a bell. You will be ferried out and the tall gates locked behind you. But to *look* at all this first: to see it and know it and one day, perhaps, to *say* it. To grow up toward simple things. Simple things expressed and believed. That is what Lou has been urging you toward. You'll get there, you're determined now, and then she won't make you go searching for her.

An hour later in the Quistorp lobby you are handing a note to the girl behind the desk when Lou steps through the entrance. She's alone—that brings relief. At the sight of you she slows considerably, easing forward into the yellow waver of the wall sconces. Then she stands before you. Looks at the girl and the small paper rustling in the girl's fingers.

"Is that for me?"

"*Ja,*" you say. "Another poem, I'm afraid." And you see this causes her to blush.

Lou plucks the paper from the girl's fingers but does not open it, just holds it in two downturned hands like a tiny purse. Her fingers slide back and forth along the folded edge. You can see the tautness in her limbs. A kind of cold resistance.

She says, "I'm sorry I couldn't come tonight." She is watching her own moving hands. She looks almost timid, as you've never yet seen her.

Silence. No further explanation.

"I'd like some tea," you say abruptly. "Shall we?"

Lou's eyes flutter. Her face hardening. An affronted stare.

She starts past you across the lobby, her inimitable musk stirring in the hurry. You pursue her to the stairwell door. Already she's started up the stairs as the door swings shut behind you. You stop there in the vestibule and blurt, "I want you to read it now."

Five or six steps above, Lou halts. Turns to look down upon you. She is statuesque, monumental in her shirred frock.

Her hands move, the paper crackling. And in her face as she reads, despite her transgressed intellect, you can see a buried smile—a flicker of pleasure, her discriminations be damned. So you rise toward her on the dim stairs. A yellow sconce-light from the vestibule below sends your shadow wobbling upward upon the steps, plunging forth into the narrowing darkness, your dark head and hers pooling shapelessly above you black in black.

Pause, standing close before her. Breathe the dusky fennel-scent clinging all about her like smoke.

"Lou."

The fingers of her left hand curl at the banister.

"Lou," you say. And touch her, cup your hand to her torso's curve.

She winces. Shiver of broadcloth and gossamer. Her heat has imbued the fabric. She's warm as day. And she's smaller than those garments attest. Your hand, shaped to her side, is *seeing* her. Your heart beats in that hand as in an eye.

Lou unclutches the banister. Her scent pours over you as she brings up her arms. Her fingers come fanning deep into your hair, cradling your skull, tugging you close—and now you are enfolded fast and embracing the backs of her knees, your face against her ruffled slack collar. *The smell of your homecoming!* Burrow your mouth to the hollow of her breast. Her heart hammering beneath your kiss. You are murmuring into cloth: words like muffled sobs. Say it again, more clearly: "You alone are real."

You remain locked to her. Watching the joists of shadowed bone below her throat, so close and motionless. A moment . . . another . . . and then:

"René." Her hands compelling your head backward. "René, go home now."

"Lou—"

"I know," she says. She is holding your face in her palms—*the mauve scent of her wrists!* "I know. We'll be all right. Go home now."

"Lou."

"We'll be all right. I promise."

With a mild shove, she separates, begins to flow backward up the steps as though sucked away by some powerful past. "Wait to hear from me," she says. "Don't worry."

She fades in the high darkness.

$\mathcal{T}$he train rockets them south from Munich. Great glittering needle plunging through the city boundary. Night train, yet the spring sun hangs implausibly festive above the fields, and rungs of light veer through the carriage with vertiginous speed. Lou sits very still. She does not speak. Only locks her arm in his and waits.

René Maria listens to the train wheels beneath them, heavy gears ecstatic in roar and clatter. *Now-now-now-now-now-now.* Does Lou hear it also? For days this incantatory byword has thrummed in the young poet's brain.

The morning after they stood together on the Quistorp stairs, Lou sent a note: *'We must find some place to go. We will. We must!'* But he was made to wait while she fulfilled her immediate engagements in Munich. *'A few days more,'* said a second note. Because he sensed he was a danger to her, he kept away, didn't call. Meanwhile his fervor poured into poems by the score. Innumerable hours confined in his small apartment, and yet he was past himself for the first time.

At last, this morning, came her leave: *'Waiting is over. Train tonight to Wolfratshausen. 6 o'clock. I'll come to you.'* She knew nothing would keep him from such a flight. She arrived to find him in his Blütenstrasse privations, stood in his door looking upon the brute accoutrements of his life and still—*thank God!*—she was charged with forward momentum. Beginnings do not frighten her.

Now-now-now chants the train—then suddenly: Wolfratshausen. Storybook mountain village.

Always startling to be somewhere for the first time. The world rears. What is ancient is not ancient to the newcomer, mute things speak, and local moonlight is the world's eighth wonder. In the dim linen sky above the Wolfratshausen treetops hovers the moon in silver. Below it the young poet and Lou are tapestry figures escaping, damasked with the light as with silken threads.

Her grip is strong and man-like in its clear need as she pulls him along cobblestone paths that seem to surge underfoot in their bodied weave of rock. Along village lanes hemmed by gloaming woods, by noise of evening birds. From somewhere above comes the riotous clangor of a church bell strangely baroque. Here and there a villager shambles past bundled in cloak and scarf and woolen cap. René Maria has barely noticed the Alpen chill. Lou's hand is the only thing—that streaming heat, so communicative.

She pulls him around a corner and here beside the slanting pickets of a pasture fence she stops and draws him close and kisses him and *now-now-now* in the deep dream of her musk and mouth his time falls short. For they've come together at the whirling center of something they've stolen each other to get here but already the hours are flaring away like water displaced like the plumes of their desperate breath like everything that slides off the slick hard surface of eternity—and the thought of return hangs in him like a threat. . . .

A chapel-like chamber, the narrow ceiling vaulted with blackish Bavarian wood. Not a furnishing but for the high altar of a single bed. The young poet turns back the blankets—old faded fabric, edges shaved thin with generations of sleep. His feet are bare in the soft rug. Lou, so quiet all day long, silently shudders.

He touches her hips: once more the almost slight body beneath the cups of his hands, but unswaddled now, delicate as a curved carafe, vessel wrapped safely in cloth by day. She seems to lean back in her nakedness, consents to being led. So he leads her to the bed and presses close till her feet leave the floor and now she grows easier, seeing how the bed will hold her. Now her eyes begin to rove and in the fulcrum of her throat the skin palpitates with audible beat. Now her knees rise to embrace him and he is closed in the clasp of her shape-giving hands and *now-now-now* like a sudden pronouncement he erupts upon her in molten white need iridescent as a pearl. Released at the jolt of her touch. But this is no more than the splash from a chalice that's been filling his whole life long. The chalice has not spillt oh no hc is still brimful and so he goes deep into the spandrel of her thighs and her ankles join to lock him close and ah she is warm even within—*amazement!* An eye opens in the young poet's loins. How warmly she gives forth what she has never yet given forth. For he is in her blood now, and now her blood is upon him.

> *"As one holds a cloth before gathered breath,*
> *no: as one presses it to a wound*
> *out of which the whole of life, in one flow*
> *wants to force itself,*
> *I held you to me: I saw*
> *you become red from me."*

Her maidenhead broken! Her eyes wide at his newness. What grandeur in the poured-out cup! *Now-now-now-now:* they struggle aloft through the membranous canopy of the word and the word means *Yes* and in their returning tumble he receives the impress of her fall, her intaglio stamped deep into the lime-gray shelf of his heart.

"I have a home." He shudders the words. *I have a home.* His mouth grazes hers and the words are a kiss gentling to her tongue, down with her breath, breathed into her inwardness. "I have a home at last."

.   .   .

Lou, in much later remembrance, will say that whenever she thinks back upon this time, she feels she could devote the rest of her life to telling Rainer and herself all about what happened in these Munich days and after. That she would be able to reveal in this manner the very essence of poetry.

The shutters slightly parted. Out there: the rarefied night, glassy moonglow. The poet is passing a white handkerchief up and down her snowy thighs—blood swabbed in ceremony—and they both grow fervid again. Again she pulls him. *Again:* the limb-locked beat of their breath the wheeling back of epochs the seasons twirling like saucers on edge—then everything shattering everything seized in the long-sustaining ring . . .

Afterward: stillness, but for the tiny sweep of his caress, his compassing thumb in the groove of her back as she lies.

The night is not for sleeping. His voice trickles in the dark like a touch.

"I've been loitering somewhere—I don't know where. Where could I have been before this?"

Silence.

"I've known such fear, Lou."

"Are you afraid now?"

"Sometimes I think I'm made of fear. It's always inside me."

"Try to tell me."

"There's so much."

"Just name one or another. Just say *I fear* . . ."

"All right. I fear . . ."

And he tries to name it all for her. One ear to her warm breast, the blood flowing hotly there like milk. The tonal meter of her heart, to which he drifts and drifts . . . to sleep.

.   .   .

I am a soft slow-moving boneless thing. Like a mollusk . . .

—one of those incessant boyhood nightmares as he describes it to Lou
upon the warm altar of the bed to which they've flown:

*I am inching along the earth, my mouth clotted with dirt and moss and sharp
pine needles. Humus that tastes like blood . . . I excrete a silvery glue as I go.
Clumps of debris adhere to my sides and tail. The way is hard. I have . . . no lungs.
Breath comes slow, comes heavy—it sits . . . sits thick in all my pores. A sense
of . . . suffocation. But the worst is when the stone comes down. It always comes . . .
down upon me. A stone not dropped, but gripped and then pressed, pressed, pressed,
against the earth with full deliberateness. I am ground between stone and earth. I
am crushed. Intently. Crushed. Like . . . like a film of mucus . . . rubbed long . . .
between two fingers . . .*

His time falls short. The first night almost gone already, the hours flaring
away like water displaced and now the threat of return—

"What is it, René? Why so startled?"

He has awakened in a jolt of limbs. "They've called me to Prague. I
just remembered. The Draft Board. A military examination. Oh God, Lou,
the Kadettenschule. Those fears I was telling you—"

"Shhhhhh." She slides close in her conch of sheets. Wash of her breath
as she speaks. Earth-fragrance. "Don't worry, René."

"Shouldn't I?"

"No, it will pass. Then we'll come back."

"Back here?"

"*Ja.*"

"To Wolfratshausen?"

"*Ja.* Won't you do that with me?"

"Of course, Lou, but—"

"Shhhhhh." Her hair is fanning across the pillow, rays aflare from naked temples and brow. Her arm floats upward and a fingertip grazes his chest, the base of his throat. He begins to sink toward safety again.

"Shhhhh."

Her body is edgeless and beautiful in the spill of bare moonlight. He doesn't ask about her husband. That she bled tonight is answer enough.

Shhhhhhhhhhh—the long sibilance of the train a few days later, as the young poet is sucked backward to Prague. Out of Munich to that dark little city which draws him repeatedly without his consent, René Maria an insensate piece of filing to the insuperable magnet of his birth.

There are but two or three other people in the carriage, and he rides alone with a restful mind, enclosed by the train as by a single long thought in which Lou still sleeps. How strange, then, for the thought to end—to open its doors and eject him into the dim expanse of Prague's Hauptbahnhof as into a wildly irrelevant memory. Papa, standing there, raises a gloved hand.

Later, in the blackness of night, René Maria lies restless on the stiff parlor sofa at number 19 Heinrichsgasse. From the sideboard nearby, Papa's railroad clock clicks out its seconds like a tongue, astonishingly loud in the silence of the flat. All through childhood the clock sat right there, but never has René Maria heard it as he hears it now.

Just two hours ago he stood talking with his father in this room and the clock's metronome tapped and tapped unheeded. But now Papa sleeps behind a closed door and in the night-heavy parlor the clock testifies at the top of its lungs to absence astir.

It's as though in recent years the harmless sprockets have learned to assert themselves. And how does Papa manage to sleep with such a noise?

Surely it's not sufficient to merely shut oneself off in a room—the doors all thin in this thinly built flat. It can only be that this welter of absence has increased imperceptibly; Papa, over time, has grown inured to it through gradual deafening. What other defense could he have, living alone in this emptiness? And nightly now the clock sits here in its rage, slashing at the darkness with a clamor like bursts of lesser cannon fire.

René Maria throws off his blankets and stands.

The clock is an antique thing of yellow wood, barely larger than the palm of his hand. A perfect square but for the flared elegance of its top corners. The face-glass, encased by a ring of silver, has blurred to a calcareous grain, like the base of an old salt jar. René Maria tips the clock back. Feels the weighted pendulum fall against the small rear door with a tap. Lays the clock down prostrate. Silence now. Time stunned to a stop. He'll wind the gears in the morning, as Papa has done every week for how long? In the lampless dark, the bulge of the face-glass gives off a sickly shimmer. As if the clock has just suffered the worst of indignities.

René Maria lies down again. But instantly, as a crackle wakes in the wall beyond the hearth, he sees his error. No muting that which now stirs. What gapes in this parlor, in this flat, is more prodigious than anything a clock alone might attest. That greater unquiet cannot be subdued.

Again: a crackle, instantly interpretable. A small sound like stale bread broken in two hands. It's as real and ineluctable as human memory—this room's memory. It has stirred for generations.

No use closing his eyes. As a child, fever-stricken or restless, René Maria would pull the blankets to his face—and of course the blankets were of no real use either, for it was under the blankets just as it was standing over the bed. One's eyes didn't see it, one's *body* saw it. One's *being.* Tonight, in his twenty-first year, it's still at large. The plaster cask has crackled open in the wall, has let slip its undeniable shape, and the shape is melding to the shadows in every corner. Oh, that presence. It cannot be pointed out but is everywhere enfigured—enfigured most blithesomely and most frightfully in the young poet's brain.

—*What is it, dear? I'm here, René Maria. What is it?*

Mama, pale vision, comes flying from the absences of darkness. She sits at the edge of his boyhood bed. He's awakened himself with a scream.

—*Shhhh, quiet, darling. You're dreaming.*

—*Mama, you forgot to do it again! You forgot, and it's come back!*

Already she is stroking his brow, cool fingers smoothing his long fair hair atop the pillow's curve. *I didn't forget, my sweet. You just didn't see me.*

—*I don't believe you. It came back, Mama! Why would it come back if you did it tonight?*

—*Listen to you. That a boy should talk this way to his mother! You were dreaming. It couldn't have come. Impossible.*

—*Do it again, Mama, please! Show me this time.*

—*All right, René Maria. Come see.*

In the parlor, in the corner beyond the hearth, the boy stands with his mother in the light of her clutched candle, clinging with one slight fist to her nightshift. The hump in the wall swells and shrinks as the candle-flame strobes, rough plasterwork roiled in the shifting light like water boiling.

Mama has the small glass dish. She crouches and sets it on the floor. The priestly water glistens, unspeakably clear. A sacerdotal rose petal floats there like a wafer of hardened blood.

—*Watch now, René Maria.*

Her voice assumes the ceremonial sound. He watches her fingers stir the water, pluck up the rose petal, and now she is flinging droplets at the swollen plaster, her thin hand shooing and shooing. She murmurs a prayer all the while. Soon a blotch of wetness darkens the wall. The stale rose-scent touches the boy's tongue.

And then it's done, and Mama sits beside the bed till his eyes begin to droop again. But as sleep arrives, so do the questions, files of questions that must be asked now that the fear abates.

—*What is it, Mama?*

—*I've told you. Don't you remember?*

—*I don't understand.*

—*One of God's poor souls, René Maria.*

—*A person?*

—*Yes. A revolutionary.*

—*But why is he in the wall?*

—*It happened often. Better a wall than a common grave.*

—*Why better, Mama?*

—*Shhhh. You're sleeping already. You're sleeping.*

Again René Maria throws off his blankets, rises to his feet in the clamorous silence. Stands to the presence and feels himself met.

Not an enemy, whatever it is, but neither is it a friend—though they knew one another when he was very small. Does it recognize him now? Or perhaps it goes on and on in some ever-recurring present tense which is really a past, and is incapable of recognition.

He steps toward the corner. The parlor air pulses with something more than his motion.

What to say? Just one thing occurs to him. His mind blurts it.

I am René.

He stands at the wall before the swollen cask he knows to be hollow now—not because the lank remains were never curled away in that cavity, those wisps of hair and flesh like clumps of lint strung so long from the bonecage—no, but because the thing's essence is free in the room. At his own side perhaps.

I am René.

He touches the tumid wall. His hand looks large against the plaster. From the cool surface comes a shock that sets the joists of his spine aglow.

A thrill like he feels in the presence of Lou. But he's been dragged from Lou's presence now and this is the texture of old inconquerable fear. Not even *his* fear. Nor is it Mama's—it originated with neither of them. It's a free-floating thing, a kind of humidity. It cleaves to the skin. No banishing it. One wears it day and night in this haunted place. In this haunted realm of his boyhood. And doesn't one carry it elsewhere too, always?

In the morning: the probings of the military doctors. In one colorless waiting room after another, René's name is called repeatedly.

Repeatedly he is made to undress before them. To bare his limbs to their meticulous tests, their unscrupulous instruments. But cold fingers and steely tools leave no marks on his spirit now. Lou is alive within him. Lou is awaiting him. These people could never know what it's like.

"I want to see the world through you," he has written to her,

"for then it's not the world I see, but always only you, you, you! . . . I want to be you. I don't want to have dreams that you do not know, nor wishes that you are unwilling or unable to fulfill."

He must wait in Prague, the Draft Board informs him, while they determine whether or not they'll make use of him. Young lover made to loiter in a homeplace never home to him. But everything has been—*hasn't it?*—a backward journey. Every event has pulled him back to these coiling streets of Prague. It was never any different before Lou, before he fled to Munich. But now, now he's arrived at she who was his destination through those long disordered years of becoming, and all things shall be different. All things.

TOWARD LOU : *1890–1897*

You are not a destination for me; you are a thousand destinations. You are every-thing and I know you in everything, and I am everything and bring you everything in my going-toward-you.

Florence Diary, 1898

*G*oward Munich, toward Lou. Seven years younger and still enmeshed in those disordered days of becoming. The Saint Pölten Kadetten-schule behind him now—four full ages of his boyhood gone to darkness. Again René Maria's body fails. High erratic nerves and a case of pneumonia occasion a summer journey to Salzburg for a saltwater cure. In September, despite still tenuous health, he's enrolled at the Senior Military Academy of Mährisch-Weisskirchen, arriving late and struggling to adapt.

Again the bark of officers, the ragged shuffle of boys, the rigors of drill: snap of heel, slap of limbs, the fierce controlled spasm of the salute.

He writes to Mama: *'The ailment hasn't gone. Headache and fever worse than ever.'* By November he's taken to the infirmary. Gray ceiling above him: rough plaster like a big wound poorly poulticed. Lying on his back in a stiff sickbay bed, compresses constant on his brow, the white sheets so grayed with sweat it seems his shadow has bled from him. Two weeks he is there: waking, sleeping, waking. Trying all the time to stay very still. Cursing his bladder when it grows full and tight for then he must shift to accommodate the bedpan.

But they discharge you from the sickbay at last. The Regimental Doctor, under pressure from the Sergeant, scribbles a perfunctory, disbelieving sig-nature on your release sheet and you stagger back to barracks.

Once again standing in the tightly buttoned high-collared uniform amongst rows of identical senior cadets. Once again jogging in rank, saluting with firm wrist, lying in a stiff dormitory bed, crashing headfirst out of dream at the blare of the *réveille*. But your limbs encounter resistance at every gesture, as though you're moving underwater.

The New Year descends. Once again the sickbay with its gray walls and starved light and the truncated language of the Regimental Doctor. It is all like a regurgitated dream, one you swear you've already awakened from, one the world spits back at you as if to say you have no ownership of these things.

The Regimental Doctor lays a chill hand across your scorching forehead, frowns into his charts, orders compresses. You lie there burning and now the conviction rises hot within you: *no peace as long as I'm in this place.*

You write to Mama—Mama, of all people, she who could never rescue you from anything: *'My illness is more spiritual than bodily.'*

Mama's nervous response arrives promptly: *'I've written your father with my fears for you.'*

So you send a letter to Papa, a few defeated lines that are nevertheless a start toward all the things you must eventually express.

With little choice left, Papa makes an official application for your discharge. Fourth June 1891, at exactly fifteen and a half years old, you are dismissed from Mährisch-Weisskirchen and put aboard a train for Prague. The end of your academy days.

As quick as that: five dismal years snapped off, a long-dead branch dropped from a now differently leaning tree.

 LINZ, AUSTRIA: 1891.
AGE FIFTEEN . . .

Just six months after your defection from the military college you are photographed in a uniform of another sort. You've been made a business-
school cadet at the Linz Handelsakademie, garbed in high-cut waistcoat,
black suit jacket and tie. In your left hand is a bowler cap the color of ash.
In your right hand a thin walking stick with silver top and silver tip. But
this is the same sallow countenance, same inside-out gaze that has contra-
dicted the costumed body all these years.

Your young girl-face is still submerged in this one. Stare of the young
soul made malleable in spite of his unmalleable fate. And yet his immovable heart already beats with a violent demand. Already this jaundiced face
insinuates the heart's resolve—a poet's heart commencing the decades-
long journey that shall first flourish in the presence of Lou and years later
culminate in the homely grandeur and over-life-sized loneliness of a remote stone tower in Switzerland.

 MAY 1892. AGE SIXTEEN . . .

Again, in a kind of backward fall, you find yourself traveling to Prague. Out of Linz. Austria retreating from you.

The train groans, groans like something falling into sleep after long running, groans to a stop. The people of Prague scurry quick and dark over the platform, the engine's gusting steam ghosting them out. And standing there in the dissipating cloud is Papa.

Papa is grayer—and isn't he smaller somehow?

"Hello René." The words trickle darkly from his mouth, plop like jelly on the platform at his feet.

Later: sitting in the parlor on the stiff brocade sofa, and Papa stands before you at the hearth.

"This Olga girl," he is saying. "She wired her brother from the hotel in Vienna. Otherwise we might not have found you."

Ah yes, returning from the publisher's office, through the thrumming Vienna streets to the hotel—and there was Olga in the lobby, in gloves and traveling attire already, waiting. Her lips looked bloodless. She handed you the fateful telegram. "A wire from your father. I read it. The clerk seemed alarmed when he brought it." You took the telegram and read the small, distant-looking words, Papa's smoke-like anger uncoiling there: *'Leave Vienna immediately. Return to Linz and collect effects. Take first possible train to Prague. Police alerted of your disappearance. Do not tarry.—Josef Rilke.'*

"I trust I needn't tell you that you won't see this girl again," says Papa now. And you blush at those words coming from Papa's mouth like an oath: *this girl.*

"Yes, sir."

Remember your father just weeks ago: how he stood by the mantel in Herr Drouot's drawing room in Linz. The ice ticked in his glass. His mellow voice:

—*I have your word? I have your promise to let this liaison go?*

He had come from Prague—all that way for fear that you were succumbing to distraction. Frau Drouot, in whose house you've lived while studying at the Handelsakademie, had wired Papa with her concerns.

But even after he had traveled so far for your sake, what could you give him but silence? Sullen silence enfolding you both like a mist. For the answer he demanded could be nothing but a lie. And yet he demanded it. So finally the silence ended with your false promise to Papa. He would accept nothing else. Dark-spreading promise like a nightfall.

And hardly weeks later: you and Olga Bergfeld taking mad flight to Vienna. You and she together in the cheap Viennese hotel room with the yellow water stain in its wall and the bed that creaked beneath the weight of your bodies—your bodies grappling and awkward, like muddled words spoken one over another. *Say it,* your bodies whispered. *Say it, say it.* But the right word would not come to you. You tried and tried but Olga's eyes looked flat and pale and meanwhile your own heart sprang ahead of you and went hurtling out of your body into a million fragile stars, little paper stars quickly scattering like cinders swept up a flue.

Olga made an angry grunting sound, a bitter noise almost flatulent, pulling herself away. But with that fast and fluid element a great shape had come unlodged and launched free of your heart—and you knew this to be *Himmelpapa* flung from you and rent to pieces in flight. And knew there to be nothing left inside, after that, but freedom, emptiness . . . beginning.

You stepped fully into your own life then. Yet you could already see the complications you would face: at last you were *yourself* and no longer merely their dreamed-of daughter, their obedient son—but they would go on seeing you as they'd long since decided to see you. They would not promptly believe that the son who stood before them was something other than the one they'd always looked upon. How *help* them to believe? How after so long a time does one muster the courage, the grace, for such a task?

"The Handelsakademie has dismissed you—not that there was much chance, anyway, of you remaining in Linz after this scandal. But now a business certificate is out of the question."

"I understand, Papa."

The Vienna publisher had a round face and pockmarked cheeks.

—It's kind of you to consider us again, Herr Rilke. We're always on the lookout for new verse.

The publisher's frosted window held a constant shuffle of color as people passed by on the street outside. The publisher's huge desk held your manuscript before him.

—I hope you don't mind, Herr Rilke, if I ask how old you are.

—Sixteen, sir.

—Sixteen. I see. Well, you show a great deal of promise.

—Thank you, sir. I feel it's meant for me. To be a poet, I mean.

—And you're still at Gymnasium, I take it?

—Business school, sir. I attend the Handelsakademie in Linz.

Strange how there had been no choice but to say it as if rehearsing the peculiar terms of someone else's existence. Handelsakademie. Linz. And yet with your manuscript before him, this man could not possibly confuse you with that business school cadet. And you had just said (hadn't you?) that other important thing, the very important thing you had yet to say to the people at home: It's meant for me.

"You do know, René, what you've done? The opportunity you've destroyed? The people you've disgraced?"

"I know, Papa. Forgive me." It's the most you can say, though clearly you must tell him something more of yourself now.

"Your Uncle Jaroslav was deeply upset when he learned of all this. He's as troubled by you as I am, René. He takes great interest in you. So you see, whatever you do matters more than you think. Matters not just to me."

"I know, Papa. I'm sorry." The most you can say—but why, why should it seem impossible to tell Papa the rest? And what is it that so powerfully compels us to divide ourselves? For already you are someone else entirely, *entirely,* and yet you cannot but give your father the words he expects, as though for fear of injuring him.

"He's coming here tomorrow, your uncle. He wishes to see you."

"And the house did the rest. One had merely to enter into its full smell, already most decisions had been made. Some little thing or other might still be altered; on the whole, though, one was already that which the people here held one to be—the one for whom they had long ago confabulated a life, from his small past and their own wishes; one who was but a confection of their spliced selves, who stood day and night under the suggestion of their love, between their hope and their suspicion, before their reproach or applause.

"So no use climbing the stairs with whatever unspeakable caution. They are all in the living room, and the door need only be nudged for their glances to find him. He stays in the dark, he will await their questions. But then comes the worst. They take him by the hands, they drag him to the table, and all of them, as many as there are, stretch themselves inquisitively before the lamp. They have it good that way, they keep themselves in darkness, and on him alone falls, with the light, all the shame at having a face."

Voices murmuring in Papa's study. The study wall, thin like all the others, is a fabric soaked with sound as with murmurous sweat.

Papa's voice, low and somber: "You're terribly generous, brother. I'm at a loss with him. Nothing's ever simple with René. If it isn't his health it's his willfulness."

"Is he often ill?"

"I can't say, really. He tells me it's not as regular as before, but he came home with that ashen face and lay in bed half the day."

"In that case, I think he should go away for a while. There's a tutor in Schönfeld. It would give him time to recover beyond excuse, and he could set right to work on his studies."

"But brother, if it happens that—"

Silence . . . then a small pained noise like a cough.

"What is it, Josef?"

"If it happens that he's . . . I fear he's weak, brother. I fear I've passed that on to him."

Silence again. Papa's slow steps along the crackling floor, his shoes in tense and measured pacing. "You're right, of course. *Ja.* It's high time he shake this ailment off. I've tried to tell him a hundred different ways, he just won't see how it holds him back."

"The boy's not sickly, Josef. You should have seen him last summer in Smichov—every day he stood straight and tall. I've told you before, Phia has done him a great deal of harm. Too much unguided reading. Too much praise. His head's clouded with all that. But there's good stuff in him, Josef. There's promise. First, his education—that will set him straight."

The muffled voices become like thoughts you're thinking as you sit listening from your small room, a colossus amongst the furnishings of childhood. Then Papa calls you out.

The men have come into the parlor. Uncle is sitting on the sofa, knees crossed. Cufflinks glimmer darkly at the heels of his hands. His cool eyes hang upon you, his mouth stern in its distinguished beard. Papa stands by the hearth in shirtsleeves.

Step forward onto the carpet. Be gentle in your gestures before these men. The air in this room feels brittle, breakable.

"Hello Uncle."

Jaroslav uncrosses his knees, sits up at the edge of the cushion. A slight frown releases words from his beard: "Hello René." His voice deep and quiet and slow. "So you've come home again."

Your eyes burning—blink away the sudden water. "*Ja,* Uncle. Forgive me."

"Well, René, we must start anew, mustn't we?"

"Yes, sir."

With a motion of his chin, Jaroslav indicates the chair behind you, the heirloom chair forbidden to you as a child. You sit.

"You've given us a bit of a go-around, René."

"Yes, Uncle."

—*So you plan to run a business? the publisher asked.*

—*Sir?*

—*After your commencement.*

Oh, so he meant that other life, still speaking to you as the Handelsakademie cadet.

—*No, sir. I don't expect to be at the Handelsakademie much longer, you see.*

And is it because you answered the publisher with such conviction that you cannot answer these men in like manner now? Must one's courage be rationed? Did you exhaust yours already in summoning up all that it took to call at the publisher's office?

"But you've still got good stuff in you, my boy. What most concerns us now is your education. You've fallen behind significantly in that matter, but you do wish to attend university, do you not?"

"Yes, sir. Of course."

"Of course. Then it's essential you complete your *Arbitur.*"

Jaroslav rises, steps toward the hearth. "I'm going to enlist some private tutors, René. We can't have you going off to school amongst students so much younger than you, can we? No. You'll set to work straight away. There's a tutor in Schönfeld, in the north. You'll spend the summer there. I'll make the arrangements."

For a moment Uncle stands with hands in his pockets, staring into the dark fireplace. Beside him Papa is enshrouded in silence. He stares out of this silence at you, as if staring from someplace very far away. He and Uncle bear a striking resemblance.

"Your father tells me you've been ill," says Jaroslav.

"Yes, Uncle."

"Well, you'll have a full recuperation in Schönfeld. We can't let this illness interfere any further, can we? No." Uncle draws a deep thinking breath through his nostrils, his great shoulders rising. He turns and leans over the sofa. "You remember, don't you, my boy, all that I've told you of our family heritage?"

"Yes, Uncle. And I still wear the medallion, the Carinthian device."

"Good, René. I'm glad to know it. And do you recall what I said to you the day you showed me the broken chain on that medallion?"

"Of course, Uncle. You said that to lose your lineage is to forget—to forget something for the whole world."

"To lose your lineage, René. *Yours.*"

"*Ja,* Uncle. Mine."

"Good." A grim smile flashes in Jaroslav's beard. "Just like I've said, Josef, we have much hope in this boy."

Now Uncle draws close and wraps your shoulders in one heavy arm, pulls you till you are leaning sideways off the heirloom chair. "Listen to me, nephew." His voice rich and warm in your ears, his breath that savors of tobacco. "You understand that I have no son. That both my boys left me from illness when they were still very small."

"Yes, Uncle."

"And you understand that you are your papa's only son."

"Yes, Uncle."

"And behind you stretches a lineage of more than five centuries."

"Yes, Uncle."

"And you wear round your neck the emblem of that history."

"Yes, sir."

A sudden draft seems to touch you. And behind you an immense and airy salon of sorts recedes to a tiny divot of black. In its endless walls stand doors upon doors. Beyond those doors: great patrilineal canyons through which family blood flows like rivers. *Rielko . . . Rülkho . . . Rülike . . . Rilke . . .*

"I'm going to finance your schooling, René." Uncle has released you. He's seated himself at the sofa again. "Your father and I have settled on an allowance of two hundred gulden a month, save school holidays. This will cover your tutoring till you've earned your *Arbitur.* Then it will cover law studies at university."

You flinch in your chair—some silent detonation within you. *Law!*

But Uncle and Papa are unmoved, they are very far from the implosion, still fixed in the cool fatherly dialogue. And now they are staring at you. Waiting. Your turn to speak. Ah yes, so you scour the ruptured terrain for words—but what can one say what can one say what can one say? For something has shattered . . . how can one say it? Language shattered too. And how much there was that couldn't be spoken in the first place. . . .

—I feel it's meant for me. To be a poet, I mean.

The publisher's eyes held something like a charmed bemusement, and you had really said it aloud . . . and yet had it all been spent in that moment? Had you squandered it on a stranger?

"Well, René?" says Papa.

Your stomach in a blue quiver and your face darkly blushing and you feel this with nauseating clarity as you turn to look at Uncle Jaroslav. "Thank you, Uncle. Thank you dearly."

Uncle's eyes thaw, even glimmer somewhat. "I know you'll do well, René. We have plenty of hope in you."

The Schönfeld summer comes and goes. The young poet returns to Prague, healthy and studied. Returns as if everything is just beginning and nothing at all has happened in these long years away at academy. Prague: gray spiderwebbing streets where green copper domes lie netted like hapless beetles, church spires snagged like antennae.

He is given a back bedroom in his aunt's low-ceilinged apartment at number 15 Wassergasse, less than a block from his boyhood home. Here Aunt Gabriele lives alone in a few dim rooms recessed from the street. Like a burrowing creature she shuffles from chamber to chamber, scooping the close confined air ahead of her.

In the nephew's bedroom a single dust-darkened window stands like a blind eye, giving onto a drab rear courtyard and the brick backside of a neighboring house. Time to time, servants from the street-front flats bring their employers' carpets back here and whack them with heavy staves and brown dust plumes to coat the windowpane with a poisonous kind of resin.

René hunkers at his desk, his daily tutors squeezing in beside him, leaning close, their breath pregnant with coffee or yeast or unspecified breakfast meats. From half past six till noon they come one after the other and René soaks up everything that has for so long stood back from him. He excels particularly in mathematics, watching the tutor's pencil sweep down the columned figures, then watching his own hand conjure those doubtless dark lintels that shelter sums. The tutor assures him he'll be finished with six years of learning in one if he keeps on at this rate.

In his first days at number 15 Wassergasse, in an act of proper gratitude, the young poet sits nightly with Aunt Gabriele for supper. The Aunt erect in her purple dress, needling food between fork and knife as though torturing it. Her voice flat and plodding, as if lumps of earth are falling from her mouth instead of words.

"Flew to Vienna, did you, little birdie?"

"Yes, Aunt. There's a publisher there."

"Scores of them, I'd suppose."

"Yes, but this one, you see, has printed my verse."

"So you still write poetry, do you?"

"Yes, Aunt, and Herr Kastner—that's this publisher's name—he was happy to receive me."

"You *and* the little governess?" Gabriele thrusts her nose high, as if sensing him by smell.

"He allowed me to give him my manuscript."

"Poets are always absent-minded, don't you think?"

"Of course not, Aunt."

"Well, it's really not *your* fault, I suppose, making a stunt like that. Not very different from what your mother did, after all. And you've learnt your lesson, I should think. Here you are, back where you started."

"Not at all, Aunt. I'm quite far along in my studies already."

"Yes, well that will please your uncle. That law practice of his bought this very building, you know. The practice means a terrible lot to him. A terrible lot."

"And to all of us, Aunt." The words escape the young poet's lips only to stand in the stifled air, burning his ears. Words not shaped by anything within him, yet they have used his voice for their transmittal. Now they hover above his plate, fading slow, and he looks through them in bewilderment at Aunt Gabriele, her slack jaws mashing food, this woman against whom he has no defense except to say what he said.

A chill wind whips through the tangled streets of Prague. In the Stadtpark and the park along the Graben the late-November trees have dropped their leaves like scraps of burning paper. The young poet dines with his father and Uncle Jaroslav at number 19 Heinrichsgasse. Two tall candles flame at the center of the dining-room table. René sits upright like the men, one hand at his lap, one hand fishing a spoon through his stew. He wears his black jacket and tie.

Silence. Clank of dinnerware.

"Well, René," says Jaroslav, stabbing at a hunk of beef, "how's it coming with you?"

"Very well, Uncle. I'm studying hard."

"That's my nephew." Uncle jabs the beef into his jaw and chews heartily, shoots a grin at Papa. "That's our boy, isn't it, Josef?"

"*Ja,* brother, your nephew's doing well. Gabriele says he's quiet as a mouse. Your Aunt says you're very quiet, René. Like a mouse."

René stares down at his stew: thin rings of oil swirling across the surface of brown broth. "Aunt is quiet herself, Papa."

"You do get on, I hope," says Uncle, "you and your aunt."

"Oh, yes." The lie burns lowly in the young poet's blood.

"Lord knows she's not the easiest soul to please. But we'll show her, won't we, my boy?" Uncle clutches René's arm, gives it a fraternal shake. "We'll show her that the Rilke name is far from failing yet."

René smiles. "*Ja,* Uncle."

"'*Ja* Uncle, *ja* Uncle'—listen to your boy, Josef! What a fine young man. He's got the old family dignity in him, by God. We'll show that sister of ours. First the *Arbitur,* then university, then the legal practice glides into trusted hands."

"You might like to know, Uncle, that I recently met a university professor. Made a very favorable impression upon him too. He had me into his office. A German literature man. Extremely kind. I believe I impressed him."

"No doubt you did, my boy. Well, this is capital news. Did you know this, Josef?"

"You didn't tell me this, René."

"His name is Doctor Alfred Klaar. He writes often for the papers. Heads the Concordia Society. I brought him a bit of my verse and he had me read to him for an entire quarter hour. Afterward he was utterly encouraging."

"Does he often do such a thing?" asks Papa.

"He'd like to but hasn't the time. He had me in, he said, because he saw particular promise in me."

"So you're still at that poetry of yours, eh, my boy?" says Jaroslav. "How on earth do you keep at it with all your studies?"

"I make the time, Uncle. It's extremely important to me."

"You are an enterprising young man, by God."

"Yes, Uncle. I mean to make something of my efforts."

"No doubt you will, René." Jaroslav gives the grave patriarchal blessing of his nod. Then raises a blunt forefinger. "So long as you keep your sights to the main prospect."

"Of course, Uncle."

"The task at hand—that's the important thing. Law schooling. When that's settled you'll have the privilege of poetry and such diversions."

"René and I," says Papa, "have come to that understanding already, brother. Haven't we, René?"

"Yes. I'm earnest in my studies, Uncle."

Jaroslav's hard candlelit eyes flicker an approving smile. But at the head of the table Papa suddenly looks shrunken and sad: a graying man sitting there silent while his only child tells loving lies at his coaxing. And René seems to see him sitting there in some not-so-distant future as well, sitting like someone very alone in a public place. Someone waiting at a vacant table for a person who never arrives.

First December, three days short of his seventeenth birthday, René is sitting in the tiny hatbox of his room, neck-deep in thought, when Aunt Gabriele's fleshless knuckles come tapping at his door. "René?"

"Please let me be, Aunt. I'll take supper in here again tonight."

But he hears the door opening and turns in his chair to find Gabriele's face leaning in. "René," she whispers, and then waits, as if to let the name fly gently through the shadows to his pool of lamplight.

"What is it, Aunt?"

"Your father's here." She nudges the door. Papa's tall figure steps in from the hall.

"Hello, Papa."

"Hello, René."

Papa looks sallow in the meager lamplight. He drifts over to the bed and slouches at the mattress edge, hat in hand, and gazes down into the blackness pooled about his ankles. "I've come," he says, "because your uncle is dead."

René jerks to grip the chair. "Oh, Papa."

"A stroke. Very extreme." Papa's face contracts as René has never seen it do: a puckered look of extreme puzzlement. He's like a scolded child. His left hand swims sideways across René's blankets, absently caressing the blankets like fur. Aunt Gabriele remains a slim shadow in the hall.

"Dear Uncle Jaroslav." René slides his fingers between shirt buttons, touches the medallion strung flat against his breast. Amulet radiant with his own heat. Suddenly it seems very difficult to picture Uncle, though René took supper with the man no more than a week ago. Already some monumental eraser has rubbed Uncle away. The young poet feels something shaking loose in his chest. He clenches his chair. *The two hundred gulden!*

Papa just sits there, keeps his blue eyes fixed upon René's, seeming to await a word. But a word of what nature? A slogan of comfort from his last fellow Rilke?

"The legal practice?" says René.

"Finished. You're three years short of the *Arbitur* yet."

So René is cut loose. And yet the long road toward the legal practice had made it possible—Uncle's benefaction had made it possible—for René to sit in this room with his notebook. . . .

Papa says, "Most likely your cousins Paula and Irene will sustain Jaroslav's allowance. It's what he'd want. Just as he'd want you to stay the course in your pursuit of law. I expect your education will not suffer. Of course there's no knowing just yet."

Papa's feet shuffle and he shifts his weight as if to rise, but stops. Stops and slackens and lets his hat lie capsized in his lap and stares into his palms upturned on his knees. René has never seen him falter this way. His wide sideburns look blanched, silvered against his white cheek. Fading things.

"Papa?"

"I can't say what it is, René. I can't put my finger on it, but . . . but it makes you think there's something in our blood. Your poor sister. Your fevers. Jaroslav's boys, both of them. And now it's failed even *him*, even your uncle."

A flash, and René's brain blazes up an image: Uncle's mustache flaring above a grill of gritted teeth. His body clenched in seizure, fatefully betrayed but fighting, fighting his blood's fierce treason. The medallion presses heavily at René's breast. "Poor Uncle."

Papa rises. Stands there a moment in the constrictive room. One hand floats forth and settles at René's shoulder. Words come down in a trembling fall. "I see you're working hard. That's good, son. Just as he'd want it. You made him proud, René. 'Josef,' he'd say to me, 'Josef, that boy of yours . . .'"

Papa's hand slips off, slides away like his words, and then he's stepping out into the hall, murmuring something to Gabriele. The door clicks shut.

They have left the absence behind. It crowds René's close room.

And so there you stand as in a photograph: one in the dark clump of mourners milling in the airy foyer of the Villa Excelsior, Uncle Jaroslav's home in Smichov. Whitewashed walls agleam in a smoky December light. Murmurous words grazing the tile floor. Beyond the doorways that lead from this hall are a number of flowing rooms where the furniture stands tense and motionless as though on display.

Beside you stands Papa in his crisp black coat. He's touching the hand of your widowed aunt, whispering condolences. His every gesture looks extremely decorous. And now he's guiding you into the company of your two cousins.

"Paula," says Papa. "Irene." He presses their hands in turn, shows them his mournful face, eyes momentarily shut.

The cousins' dark skirts sway as they extend pale hands. "Uncle Josef," they say.

And that they have all named one another seems enough. So when Papa steps back, you move forward and send your own gray hand toward them. "Cousin," you say, clasping Paula's cool fingers. And again: "Cousin," turning and touching Irene's hand.

"René," they reply.

These ladies and your two aunts—the new widow Malvine and the bereft sister Gabriele—are the sole women in the hall. The guests are otherwise entirely male: an array of broad, dark-suited shoulders amongst which the females cut slender tapering shapes. The collective murmur, too, churns out a manly baritone. Only now and then is the low drone nuanced by a woman's expressive timbre. So death bears a cogency entirely male. Death is a virile event.

You can recall the very different character of the Villa Excelsior two summers ago, when you stayed here for several weeks before going to Linz. How much less oppressive everything was then: the main door wide open and a languorous August light spilling in, each of the large rooms summery with leisure as Uncle strode from here to there, the papery summer air never seeking to restrain him.

Now it seems as if all the invisible molecules between floor and ceiling have been stacked and mortared together. One feels them pushing back at every gesture. The self conscious furniture stands about, awaiting the slightest trespass. The whole house emits a starched admonitory "Shhhhh!"—and everyone keeps limbs stiff and head lowered and moves slow so as not to affront the decorous molecules or the rigid furniture.

So spaces have wills of a kind—they *command,* they dictate, they prescribe one's behavior. Yes, isn't this the reason one is helpless to say certain things while standing in one's father's parlor?

The milling hall seems to sigh. Someone has opened the doors to the drawing room and somewhere a barometer is dropping, pressure unpent like liquid from a broken jar. A silence falls. Every person turns toward the drawing room.

Candlelight shudders upon the colorless walls ahead. Papa's hand touches your back and now you are shuffling with him and the guests out of the foyer, past your two cousins and your widowed aunt, who don't care to come in. Aunt Gabriele, at Papa's other side, appears to be the sole woman amongst this shuffling brotherhood. And it seems perverse that she should elect to enter this deep-voiced, hairy drawing room where one can feel, already, the weight of something completely unfeminine.

The drawing room is not like a room at all, rather like a motionless vessel, ballasted on each side by rows of candles—tall tapers in glinting waist-high candlesticks. You stand there on the strangely leveled floor, sensing how those candles anchor down the darkness, restrain it—for the darkness, if it could, would warp upward and curl everything into itself. Someone has closed the heavy curtains, and just now the doors draw shut behind you.

A few paces ahead, the guests are converging. Yellow light arcs above them like a big saintly nimbus, flinging their shadows backward upon you. Papa stands very still at your side. Aunt Gabriele makes a guttural gurgling sound; it erupts now and then into a minor hiccup. Her black-sleeved arm floats upward, downward, upward, dabbing a kerchief to her mouth, her eyes.

At length the congress of guests adjourns, the shadows slide away, and a big candelabra sparkles before you. Eight wrist-thick candles upraised like a pair of huge thumbless hands.

Papa presses softly at your collar and you step forward, feel the thick black elastic of your shadow stretching behind. In the candleglow, seeming to float elbow-high on that thread between darkness and light, are Jaroslav's two feet, shod in polished shoes, toes upturned. For a dizzy moment he appears to be standing laterally in the air—but then you remember. *Of course, he's lying down. He's stretched on a bier as dead persons are.* You scan the length of him: shoes to trouser seam to jacket hem. And where you expect to see his big hand reposing along the thigh there is no hand but just the faint seam of the jacket running upward and then the strange joint of the elbow bent to suggest volition. A pose incongruous to the will-less, gestureless density of Uncle's supine form. And Uncle's hands are clutching something just below his throat: fingers curled at the edges of a small oval object. Still higher, Uncle's great charcoal beard lies bristling at the collar, curving upward into the flared mustache; then the flared nostrils rimed with whitish fuzz, the ashen membranes of the eyelids, the flat forehead dusted with powder.

Still gurgling, Aunt Gabriele stands beside the flaccid face, one restless hand fluttering across her mouth. Uncle's fingers seem to bear the oval object to his lips, as a toddler grasps a biscuit in hungry hands. And now you recognize the thing: the Rilke family device, with its two capering greyhounds of the fourteenth century. So even inert blood cleaves fast to its heritage; even a lifeless body will claim its rights.

A long time you remain there, Papa standing motionless nearby. You seem to hear him muttering something—brief prayerful words—but you do not look. You stare at Uncle's two polished shoes glistering black, stiff with formality. Did you dishonor this man while he lived by failing to speak clearly of your aims? No, for you said all you could, all that was possible for him to hear, same as you've done with Papa. This uncle loved you in his own hard way. He gave you to understand the depth of your origins. In your own way you'll honor those origins yet, and honor that love as well: things you could not do while Uncle lived, not without causing him injury.

Papa breathes a deep, shrugging breath and turns back toward the double doors, mumbling something in Aunt's direction. You hear the word "doctors" and Aunt says simply, "*Ja,*" and thrusts her kerchief to her mouth again.

The doors swing open. Desecrative light slices the sacral darkness. Papa leans out, summoning someone from the hall. The light widens as Papa steps back, and a tall man enters the room gripping a bulky satchel in one hand. He wears a homburg hat, a greatcoat in which remarkably angular shoulders render him a perfect rectangle. Behind him follows a younger man with the eager gait of an assistant. The tall man strides up to

the bier, throws a cursory glance up and down Uncle's body, then takes
note of Aunt Gabriele. To Papa the man says, "Perhaps the Madame would
like a few more moments?"

Gabriele flinches, moves to the door as if prodded from behind. "No.
Please," she says through her kerchief, "carry on." And disappears into
the hall.

The assistant lifts Uncle's hands one at a time away from the breast.
Heavy senseless things like oblong lumps of dough. He sets the hands at
Jaroslav's sides.

Papa closes the doors, neatly sweeping the light back into the hall.
You step toward him. "Papa?"

"Ah, René," he says, his scattered look collecting itself upon you.
"This is customary for many people. Your uncle requested it."

The men remove the medallion from Uncle's breast, place it at his
belly. Then they are tilting back his bearded chin and unfastening his coat
buttons, talking rapidly all the while in hushed clinical fashion.

"Requested it, Papa?"

Uncle's creamy throat arches above the table, the Adam's apple a
knobby fist held high in stupefied protest.

"Yes, René. For certainty, you see."

From his satchel the doctor withdraws a glinting thing. Thin clean-
looking implement of indeterminate length which he lays beside Uncle's
languid hand. The assistant unslips the buttons of Uncle's shirt, bares the
immobile breast fleeced with gray hair. The steely instrument glints again.

Papa clutches your shoulder. "René? René, you're not alarmed, are you?"

The men pause. Their dim-lit faces twist back.

"Is the young man quite all right?" says the doctor.

Papa interposes himself between you and the bier. Shakes you gently.
"René, perhaps you should wait in the hall with your aunts, yes?"

Yes, you think. *Perhaps.* But you don't make a sound. Just nod your head and swivel toward the door as Papa turns back to the conspirators. That's precisely what they are—*conspirators:* these strangers disheveling Uncle's clothes. Hard to believe Jaroslav knows of this business, let alone requested it.

As the first sliver of hall light strobes across your hand you hear the doctor's voice behind: "Hold him, will you? Ready?"—then the door draws shut at your back and you are standing in the milky light of the hall.

Gabriele's reddened eyes lean close. She moves the kerchief from her mouth. "Is it done?"

And now you see how it is: the men attend to certainties in the drawing room, the women remain outside, waiting. And what does René Maria do?

"Not yet," you say.

But then comes a sound from somewhere deep in the generations beneath you. Low fibrillating shudder like a great eye opening. So an eye has been opened in Uncle's chest. The eye is weeping an ounce or two of blood. The untrammeled spirit flies to its portal. All at once the body means very little—the body becomes no more than an inscrutable sentence, written once and scratched out.

And already you have taken yourself away. The shut door at your back is conclusion and commencement at once. The red eye in that chest will watch you henceforth. And you must show the watchful eye, show it courageously now, who you are.

Something is pressing at the door. Release the knob, step away. Papa emerges and the men come quick on his heels, intent upon rapid escape.

"*Danke, Doktor,*" Papa says. He squeezes both their hands in turn, watches them go, then turns to the ladies and nods with closed eyes. "It's done."

The heart impaled, punctured with a snap like a bitten kernel of corn. The body doesn't flinch, the pale trunk impassive, purely willing. A last dim specter of doubt perforated. A brother bears witness: intimate red honor. The instrument's ease surprises him: the walls that keep us from spilling out are just that paper-thin! He watches the silver thing slide out again, red and sleek, sees the new wet orifice in the naked breast, keeps his eyes open, feels a tickle at his chest but does not scratch. And beyond the door, in the hall, his son is already on his way. . . .

"Your studies shall continue," Papa tells you a few days later, with a look of obvious relief, "till you've earned your *Arbitur.* Your cousins say their father would wish it so."

"And beyond that?" you ask.

"We can't be certain."

Papa doesn't know—though before long he'll see—that deep inside, you've already given it all up.

 MUNICH: LATE AUTUMN 1896.
AGE TWENTY . . .

$\mathcal{T}$he young poet sits in the Elvira Photography Studio garbed in the suit he purchased upon arriving in Munich: velvet-collared jacket and neck-high waistcoat and satin cravat. Nora Goudstikker, a pretty young woman to whom he is nothing less or more than a poet, engulfs herself in the velvet hood of a camera to become the eye that drinks his image. For the first time it will be *his* face locked in the contours of light. *His* face and *his* wishes.

This morning in his small apartment, while kneeling at the stove door prodding cooled embers and watching strips of paper curl in a flameless heat, he'd been reminded of how it felt to walk on the Graben with Papa: that slow charring at his very edges. That's what life in Prague was like— as if his own crematory rite had already commenced. That's what René had submitted to. That and all the questions, the incredulous furrowed faces, the inconquerable pragmatism: *A poet?* as if they couldn't imagine a person might become such a thing. *But what does a poet do? How does he live? Where does he take his meals?*

How could he have brought himself to give answers? They weren't really asking anyway. They were in truth working to ply him and shape him to something resembling themselves and all those others who peopled their world. So Prague meant being forged in a foreign crucible, and at last there was no choice but flight.

After posing, René finds himself bathed in vermilion light. Standing behind a curtain in the Elvira Studio, watching Nora Goudstikker distilling two solutions into a tray. The liquid murmurs from the bottle, settles glassily in the rectangular dish. Smell of vinegar.

"Now watch," says Nora. Her vermilion hands round off into a dream-like blur, bare wrists and forearms lightly downed below her pushed-up sleeves. A glossy plate slips into the liquid. Nora's fingers tickle up tiny waves that slip across the surface, touch the tray wall, wrinkle backward. Suddenly, like a small mirror submerged inside a larger one, the plate is giving up an outline—an intimation of a shape. Wind-tossed phantom.

"See it?" says Nora.

"Yes." His voice is shrunken in wonder.

"Here it comes."

Two days ago René was unwell. Snow had begun falling in Munich. After just twenty-four ice-locked hours the winter pallor started reflecting back the young poet's isolation and by nightfall he lay in the silent solitude of his room, touched with the old insidious fever and chill, the plastic fingers of the fever-dream. Crucifixes sliding through the night air above his bed, their fake gold falsely lustrous and somehow nauseating, and each seeming to grate across the solid darkness with a noise that put his teeth on edge while he sunk submerged in some warm-cool jelly. Mama haunted his thoughts all the while, Mama to whom these fevers belonged—she who was not there, who had barely been there at all, pale absent one who must open her breast like a blouse and gather the fever in again—no one else could do it.

By some good fortune the fever gave way late this morning and René opened his window to snowy air. Then the chill daybreak hours went whirling down him, vanishing fast, and this afternoon, as if awakening again, he found himself sitting at his shabby desk staring at a scribbled letter addressed to his mother. Callow, trustful words giving Mama the whole of his thin and sickly heart.

Something shifted inside him as he read the letter over. And he knew he must burn those degenerate pages. Burn them fast. For already he'd fallen back. He'd gone seeking that which he'd sought on countless occasions before. And what had he ever found in these searches? What, beyond a mother's faraway caress?—all his inner turmoil soothed, or rather made into something Mama *believed* she could soothe, something expedient. No more of that. He hadn't fled his childhood home in body only to remain there in spirit. No, Mama would not soothe his turmoils now, for they were not the old turmoils of the girlchild she'd once called Ismene, and to believe that Mama could counsel him now would be to behave as if nothing had changed—and yet how much had changed, yes, how much must continue to change!

"Here it comes," says Nora.

An unseen lung has fanned its breath across the glass, pluming up a silvery image. Light, syringed from ether and mixed gently in the genie's lamp of a camera, blooms like ink from the depths of a glass plate. A perfect likeness coalescing there: the young poet lapped up by the lens ten minutes before, his light hair coiffed in a tall pompadour.

"My God," he says.

And there seems something eucharistic about this process. Transmittal of essences. For one is fashioned of light, of time. Both things are no more than energies. But a record might be kept. A shape construed. A work of art. And so now he is staring at his own image: himself in profile ready for rendering, for capture of his new life's commencing moment, rife with hopes as it is.

"My God."

"You like it?"

"*Ja!*"

Amidst the blur of René's initial months in Munich, a new book of poems, *Traumgekrönt,* is published. *Dream-Crowned.* On the endpapers of one copy he writes a dedication to his father:

"You are, Papa, my best friend, and you have many concerns about me. You think that day after day I should have fear of the morning to come. No, you will see: I will meet with good fortune in my attempts. I will borrow silver from the stars; the sun himself comes and gives me gold, brings it not to the professor, not to the judge—only to your grateful, loyal son, the poet!"

In the New Year his mother comes to Munich. She brings her god with her as always—the tiny-limbed Christ pinned to the crucifix, and *Himmelpapa* who is like a dull character from a fairy story badly told.

René meets her at the Hauptbahnhof.

That Mama speaks frequently of her god does not disturb him as much as her belief that Christ is somehow portable, an object conveniently tucked into her purse, like a hairclip or tweezer. And worse is her stilted manner regarding her toy-deity: her conceit, intimated in each pious word or gesture, that this god pays her heed at every moment, is every moment gladdened by her trite devotions. Despite René's wish to regard her gently, he finds her ridiculous and saddening.

It begins immediately upon her arrival. She climbs down from the train carriage, wiry marionette of a mother, awkward in her dark finery, silver cross twirling against her breast. Scampers toward him across the polished marble: God's own little marionette.

But what if Mama should glance upward along the strings that animate her?—should find herself looming in gigantic duplicate, her huge puppetmaster hands aflutter up there?

Smaller black-gloved hands come forth to cup the young poet's face. Lace chafing lightly at his jawline.

"My dear boy!"

Her kiss planted thrice to his cheeks. Then long fingers grip his shoulders that she may study him at arm's length. Her chaste girl-like eyes scanning him crown to toe. Eyes completely free of calculation, they repulse René—but immediately his repulsion shames him. And in spite of everything, Mama's ardent touch is strangely pleasurable. It seems to him a very long time since he's been touched with such abundant love.

"My my, René, we do look fine, don't we! I tell everyone about you, you know. 'My son René is a poet,' I tell them. 'He writes books in Munich.' It never fails to impress." She sighs a proud matronly sigh. "And if only they could see how you look the part!" Her fingers twitter to his waistcoat. "Is this satin? How very debonair."

Outside on Höhenfeldstrasse, René hails an omnibus. Mama grips his hand frightfully hard as she hoists her swirling skirts, lifts one high-heeled boot to mount the high step, raises her elbows like wings and wobbles upward aboard. Her cross clinks at the handrail. She sits with her back to the side windows, outlandish figure in a row of passengers. René sits across from her, watching her narrow schoolgirl face as Munich flickers behind: soft Alsatian nose and chin colorless against her frilled blackness. Her little domed hat, fashioned of some sleek pelt and fringed in fur, tilts low down her forehead. The deep plumage of her dress calls to mind the downy blackness of a swan, but she lacks the swan's imperious grace, looks mute and small. This slim mother who once stood with him at the gate to Saint Pölten holding the tarnished crucifix above his head. Her skirts dusted a broad path in the gravel behind her as she turned and took her leave. In earlier years she passed the soft brush through his locks, smiled whenever he answered to a daughter's name, yet failed to see what demands that phantom sister made—that carping specter birthed directly into his brain. She sits with hands daintily folded. Small unfinished lady. Birth-giver to unfinished things. Her whole costume is an unfinished thought that began as some wild idea of elegance. Her glance skitters across the windows, collecting half-sketched images destined to remain uncompleted inside her.

René lets his eyes sink. He watches the brisk boulevard wind fluttering Mama's skirt hems and feels himself touched with a powerful desire to weep. What cruel capacities he must possess to think such thoughts of his fawning mother. Would that he could love her without judgment. Always his thoughts do war with his heart.

The omnibus stops and it is time to help Mama down into the street. Again she wobbles at the rear step, puffing and sighing. The omnibus slides away like a set piece and the young poet is standing with his mother at the juncture of his new life.

"Oh dear," she says, "not even a curbstone to step down upon, is there?"—as if the atmosphere has already commenced to offend her.

She gives him her arm and they trundle across the street and around the corner to Blütenstrasse.

"These quarters are far better than my first," says René—though immediately he sees his veiled admission and regrets it.

In his apartment, Mama sits in the desk chair. René perches on the edge of the bed. His kettle slowly boils. She asks questions about his latest book and he tells her a little. But he can say nothing of the fey and fearsome sketches that have pulsed within him since his arrival in Munich: scenes of Christ, or someone like Him, wandering the city as an urban pariah—Christ derided by city children who taunt Him for a fool. Christ as a waxen carnival curiosity in a tent at the Munich fair. Christ lying a night with a city whore.

Mama rises as if to explore the room—but there is little of it, so she just pivots here to there.

"Do you eat in?" she asks.

"Yes, usually."

This fact she takes with an aimless nod. "And do you go out very much?"

"Besides to the university, you mean? Yes, often enough. A walk in the Englischer Garten or an hour or two in the Café Wien not three blocks from here. There are a great number of writers in Schwabing. And some poets too. We're hard workers, most of us. Laborers really. All of us live in quarters like this, if not more modest."

"Of course," says Mama. Her gloved hand hinges back from the narrow wrist, self-conscious fingers tugging the lobe of one ear. "One can't expect Versailles, can one? And anyway, no one need really know."

Then her eyes flee upward from soiled walls to ceiling and meet with the big crack in the plaster above: unignorable flaw in her son's eggshell world.

The kettle sings. René pours out the smoking tea, gives Mama the cup that is not chipped.

So the young poet shudders to recognize what will henceforth be the pattern between them: in the smudged elegance of her Hapsburg dresses, Phia Rilke will periodically return to his life, still enacting the role—for nobody's benefit but her own—of Viennese Lady of Leisure, Matron to a gifted poet, Faithful Soul at once saintly and modest. And when she withdraws again, she will leave behind in long sinuous deposit the stain of her presence. Stain in the shape of René's muddled past, right across the center of his new life—like a darker human variant of the mucus excreted by snails.

And how can one rub out such a mark? How rub it out in order to return to one's painfully achieved present?

From Munich now, in the weeks surrounding Mama's visit, you wrench free and write the haunted Christ of your mother, of your boyhood. See him listing out into the world to wallow in this alleyway and that house of shame— for he is the poor man that Mama and innumerable others have made of him. You see now how you will never understand the full extent of the suffering this figure has borne, nor the length of his internment in the stony work camps of so many souls. For did he ever ask to be made a God?

The *Visions of Christ* lift you up out of your past. Off that faulty scaffolding and into the free dark ether of imagination and memory. You are twenty-one years old and through these bleak visions you are already, unbeknownst to yourself, speeding toward May 1897 and its unparalleled encounter. . . .

Weeks later the writer Jakob Wassermann stands before you, a stout silhouette in his ill-lit rooms three floors above your own. You've climbed the dark stairs to his door, hoping to borrow books.

"Here's something you ought to read," Wassermann says, "since you're writing of Christ. 'Jesus the Jew,' it's called."

You tilt the curled publication to the lampglow, unscroll it from the edges and read the name: *Lou Andreas-Salomé*. "Who is he?"

"She," says Wassermann. "Who is *she*. You don't know her? The lady who broke Nietzsche's heart? Why are you moving to Venice anyway?"

"Not moving. Just visiting."

Wassermann is busy rummaging at a shelf. "Turgenev!" he says suddenly, loudly, as if scolding someone. "You *have* read him, haven't you?"

"No."

"Take this then." Curt commanding tone. He brings the book over, retreats to the corner again. Then, taking something up from the shelf, stands for a long moment bent over his hands.

"This," says Wassermann at last, turning and holding out a slim book, "this is my only copy, and it's much underlined." His voice has slipped into a new, much graver key, almost forbidding.

You read the faded gold leaf of the spine. *Niels Lyhne*.

The young poet takes the borrowed books with him to Italy. *Niels Lyhne,* with its turned-in corners and inked margins, most fascinates him. How can a slim novel like this reflect so much of its reader's striated inner life? And who is this brilliant Dane—Jens Peter Jacobsen—who's fashioned such a clairvoyant work? For the first time in René's life it strikes him: to read means *to be read.*

On the return journey north he studies the strange and powerful essay from that scrolled copy of *Neue Deutsche Rundschau: 'Jesus der Jude,'* and again feels himself read. For here he finds his own *Visions of Christ* refracted through the words of this author with the name of the biblical dancer: Salomé.

Arriving back in his Blütenstrasse room, a folded slip of paper shuffles along the floorboards as he opens the door. A note in the same slantwise script that adorned Wasserman's lent books: *'Come to tea next Sunday the Twelfth, seven o'clock. Be done with those books by then and bring them along. L.A.S. will be there.'*

René will have time enough beforehand to send the lady a note

—and then: his hand going toward her, and she is clasping his hand. "You say you've written me?"

THE LOVER:

1897

"Brich mir die Arme ab: ich fasse Dich
mit meinem Herzen wie mit einer Hand."

Break my arms off: I'll take hold of you
with my heart as with a hand.

from an untitled poem
for Lou Andreas-Salomé, 1900

 SUMMER 1897. AGE
TWENTY-ONE . . .

*A*nd so you've become, by some great grace, the lady's lover. And yet it's destined. It's clear that you've been moving toward her all these years. You are not even surprised to receive your liberating notice from the Draft Board. Your telegram to Lou Andreas-Salomé from Prague, dated fourth June, 1897: *"Free and soon happy as well. R."*

Munich's city trees, when you return, seem to bear summer up in their full branches. But you've come back only to take flight for Lou and for the mountains. Out of Munich now, out of the university, off the path long since prescribed for you, onto the distantly rolling road in your heart. Road you will walk with Lou. There is no other road.

Wolfratshausen again. The village effervesces, every color standing up and asserting itself. So the place is more than a recent memory, more than a short-lived idyll. And what color there is in the stones of these mountains, the hue of the village church—hue of plaster and tile known only to the provinces.

Lou has leased a small cottage. You find her there in the company of August Endell and Frieda von Bülow. She takes you aside to show you to your room.

"It's better that August and Frieda be here too, René. You understand, don't you? At least that they be here at first."

"Yes, of course. And when can we be alone?"

"Very soon, don't worry. This is your room, and mine is just over there."

"Tonight then."

She stops in the doorway, stands there staring and for a moment says nothing, but you can gauge the effect of your words by the intensity of her look. Then a whispered: "Yes." Her face breaking into a warm smile. "Tonight. *TonightTonightTonight!* Do you think I could wait?" Her eyes radiant, like a girl's eyes.

She leaves you alone in the rustic room to unpack. Chamber even smaller than your Blütenstrasse quarters—but how sacrosanct already. A wooden floor. Narrow pallet of a bed. Single arched casement with little panes of watery glass diamonded between mullions of lead. The window stands open, white daylight reiterating a larger phantom arch. On the sill you find a teacup with two red rose blossoms in a bit of fresh water. You smile. A cool thrill of arrival at play in the backs of your knees, in your spine. In the room's corner stands a short shallow desk of peasant make, pegs of no uniform size doweling the various parts together. You arrange your few books on the desktop.

Lou and the others are gathered in the garden at the rear of the house. On your way out to them, you slip through her bedroom door to find a room only slightly bigger than your own. Double bed, dressing screen, desk. Two windows with shutters drawn, light slatting through the angled blinds. Her things lie scattered about. On an elegant washstand with porcelain rails sits a small glass decanter of her rosewater. Bend and unstopper it. Inhale. The nape of her neck immediately conjured. The notches at the backs of her ears.

You've brought one of the rose blossoms. Lay it on the waist-high bureau below the mirror. So she will smile secretly too.

In the garden August Endell bends above a wicker table, absorbed in work of some kind. Beyond him stands a gazebo with a shingled roof and a belly-high girdle of birch rails still barked. Quaint shelter nearly engulfed by a tangle of trees. Inside sit Lou and Frieda with a pot of tea between them. Lou sees you coming along the leafy path from the house.

"Oh August, show René what you're making, won't you?"

Endell jacks straight, drops a brush into a jar. "I believe it's just finished," he says, and steps back.

On a big cloth weighted down by stones, careful gothic letters glister brightly: the word "Loufried" in brilliant turquoise paint. The ladies have come to look.

Lou says, "Wonderful, August. Will it fly from the gazebo?"

"Of course. Soon as the paint dries." Endell turns to you. "The fabric's from an old valance in the parlor. The landlady was going to throw it out—but it's good eighteenth-century cloth."

"Loufried!" Lou delights. "What do you think of that, René? It was August's suggestion, of course. It makes this our little kingdom of friendship, doesn't it?"

"A kingdom indeed," you say. "What is Austria to our Loufried!"

Endell slaps your back. "That's the spirit, my friend."

Hours in the Loufried garden. You are one in a society of four.

Frieda von Bülow, ardent feminist, is staunch and exclamatory. Lou's liberalism, though, favors the natural or self-evident; she recoils from anything resembling the dogmatic. The women become very disputative in each other's company. Now and then August Endell chimes in with a deadpan remark, nibbling a cookie or waggling a crossed leg in a manner that belies his archness.

Balancing a bottomless saucer of tea in your lap, you remain attentively quiet, sipping away, laughing softly in the brief increments where the tensions break. Novitiate to the passionate candor of these three bohemians, these acrobatic role-reversers. The garden wavers richly on all sides. Occasionally Lou's glance skims toward you and from the glimmer of her miles-deep eyes you perceive that your quiet manner meets with her perfect understanding. She instinctively defers to the artless, the unpredominating.

Frieda regards you less trustfully. This lady's fame in Europe matches Lou's. She's pioneered the establishment of hospitals in East Africa, knows intimately of the remote actualities behind mythic names like *Dar es Salaam* and *Zanzibar*. But perhaps she cleaves to a colonizer's mistrust, constantly at arms against an irrational world. Now and then she subsides from her breathless talk in order to elicit your opinion. You demur, ill at ease with pronouncements, at least of the verbal kind—else you improvise some equivocal phrase to which Frieda responds with a look of sidelong dismissal before taking up her declamations again.

You can't help but wonder if you've aroused her suspicion. Perhaps she can see what's brought this wide-eyed René Rilke to Wolfratshausen, this young scribbler of indefinite achievement, magnetarian to her friend and fellow arguer. Maybe she and Lou have talked privately—they're very intimate, after all. What confidences might Frieda enjoy? Lou, slouched in her wicker chair across the gazebo, watches you with a bemused smile.

Hours flood past. Conversation churns and eddies. Then suddenly, as if you've been borne downriver into a still pool, you come awake to the arrival of nightfall.

Goodnights quietly mouthed all around, and you find yourself sitting alone in your lamplit room, perched stiffly on the edge of your bed, listening as the cottage quietens. And now: that the turnings of things will slow again, that this night will widen and lengthen like a great warm lake.

You wonder if Lou will signal somehow but soon cease wondering and slip from your room. Move noiselessly to her door across the hall. Do not tap—keep the silence—simply press the handle. Her room swings into sight, lampglow oscillating ornamentally on walls and ceiling. And there she is: seated on the edge of the bed, still clothed, staring straight at the doorway.

"Get in," she says, already rising.

Shut the door, latch it, and when you turn again you are in her embrace. Her mouth against yours, steam of words flowing across your tongue.

—*You see you needn't have worried. We're here now.*

—Ja, *we're here. I've arrived, Lou.*

And you are in her mouth, deep in the drink of her kiss. Ah, drunkenness!—yet every sense is neither dulled nor blurred but heightened to utter sharpness. Words stream quiet and rapid, but it seems it's your bodies that are speaking:

—*You were waiting for me, Lou, weren't you? As I knew you would be.*

—*Of course. And see, you opened my door. You didn't hesitate.*

—*No. Not a moment.*

—*My Rainer.*

—*What?*

—*Rainer. That's what I've named you.*

—*Rainer . . .*

—*Yes. Man and poet. That's what you are. René is too small, too timid a name for you now.*

—*Yes, Lou. Rainer. Yes, I am the name you give me. And you are my June night. I'm in you, the way I'm in this room.*

She draws away from you—*Come here*—moves backward to the bed and gathers her lank skirts and reclines atop the blankets.

—*Wait. Close the shutters first. Then lie down next to me.*

To the shutters, the slats tugged shut. Then snuff the lamp and find her in the dark. The pillow already carries the fragrance of her hair. You feel her form expanding with her every breath. A weak braille of moonlight hangs upon the wall, like a faint memory.

—Do you know, Lou, I feel as if I've died. . . . I'm like someone who has died and is walking forward into eternity—

And abruptly you begin to cry. It comes upon you unawares, bulging up and released with a cough. Lou clenches you close and you muffle the outpouring at her breast. A sea-swell mounts and expands, overwhelming the darkness. You are sheltered in her as in a warm cave.

At last you gain back your breath. Then you are telling Lou of all you feel to be falling away from you, everything you've known till now, every person. Some of these people, you tell her, have been good to you and for that you are thankful, yet your thanks to them is a thing sent behind you to great distances, and whatever these people have said to you, good or ill—it is all but one and another scratching on your headstone now, for you have died, René Maria has died—*and awakened to* this, *Lou!*

But you do feel thankful, you tell her, to everyone in that underlife, to *all* of them, even those who dealt with René Maria wrongly.

—Do you know why, Lou? Because all together they've formed a great long path that has led me—to you!

She says nothing. Still she is holding you, stroking your hair, her silence a dark penumbra to your body atop the blankets.

Rainer: name that waited in her as in a reliquary. Somehow, wrapped in Lou's embrace in the high awareness approaching sleep, you see your life going out before you: life like a river bedded between the twin R's of your new name as between twin levees. *Your* life. *Rainer's.* Lou, this miracle of a woman, has opened the way.

An hour has passed, or maybe an epoch. Her voice comes whispering. Her breath at play on his face, moist in his eyelashes.

—I found the flower.

—Hm?

—*The rose. I love that you left it for me.*

—*I knew you would. Where is it now?*

She reaches out in the darkness, her limbs aglow in that faint nonlight. Rainer catches scent of the blossom as she brings it close, passes it into his hand. He raises himself beside her.

—*What are you doing?*

—*Shhh. Just lie still. Now close your eyes.*

He begins to draw the rose across her lids, down the soft ridge of her nose. For a moment she chuckles but then grows quiet, quieter, and soon her face slackens as she falls to the trance of the flower's touch. Her lips parting in sleep, the breath rolling deeply, and Rainer leans to draw that breath into his mouth. . . .

. . . Adrift again. A century clicks by . . . then:

—*Rainer, I'm worried. . . .*

He stirs. A slumberous gasp. *What—what is it?*

—*No, no. Shhh. Just listen. It's René Maria. The way you talk about him. As if he's a different person.*

—*Yes, Lou, because he's just that. Because René Maria was something they . . . René Maria was what they called me, but it was never my name. I couldn't arrive, couldn't be anything till you gave me a name. This is my destination. Here, Lou. With you. And now there's a name, and René Maria can die away.*

—*But he'll remain, don't you see? You are Rainer now, yes, but René Maria will never die away. Neither he nor Ismene.*

—*No?*

—*No. Their fates have still to be determined. They're tied up in Rainer, in whatever he becomes.*

Silence. Her heart is tapping gently in her throat.

—*You're right, Lou.*

—*Do you see?*

—Yes, I see. You're right. That past remains unfinished.

Still he watches the hollow of her throat, like the membrane of a tiny drum. Her heart beating steadily there. That's *his* rhythm somehow.

"And I know that nothing fades,
no gesture and no prayer,—
things are too heavy for that,—
my whole childhood
stands always around me.
Never am I alone.
Many who have lived before me
and striven away from me
wove,
wove
at my being."

Awake to her hands upon you. Morning, and so you have slept a sleep like another life altogether.

Lou sits on the bed at your side, hips at rest in the curve of your prone body. Her sleepwarm fingers trace the rim of your ear. She still wears last night's clothing. The dawn glow is yet filmy and nonreflective: glow that gathers, grips things in its silence. The closed shutters behind her hold the light in serried threads.

You fold down the blankets and sit up. You've slept in your clothes too. Your whole body bristles with a cool sensation that seems to originate in the small of your back or in your loins: hipbones buttressing some abdominal gleam. And Lou is here. Still here.

"Listen to the quiet," she says. "Everything's still asleep."

She takes you into the garden. A vast silence opalescent in the predawn, everything grayed in a gray mountain-breath. Dark leaf-luster and hush of soil. Within the hour will come the liturgy of color. You stand beside her, you and she barefoot on the dewy earth. It seems you're both waist-deep in a still pool. Lou's voice riffles the stillness.

"Friedrich taught me about mornings. How every day dreams itself awake."

You seem to see her words blooming outward into multiple rings. "You mean Nietzsche?"

"No. Friedrich, my husband. We have a glorious garden back home in Schmargendorf. You'll have to see it someday. Friedrich always works through the night. Always off to bed just as I'm rising. We sit in the garden and watch everything come alive around us."

"Is he in Schmargendorf now?"

"*Ja.* I'll tell you more about him. Not now. Come."

She clutches her skirts and trots ahead along the garden path. You move after her. Watching the tender rails of her ankles as they tauten at every step. The mossy earth sends a shock of pleasure through your naked soles as you go.

It's an expansive garden, bleeding fenceless onto the forested hill behind the cottage. The morning light, yet bedded in the soil, rushes upward through your feet and it seems the day's dawning begins in your very limbs. The light quietly suffusing the garden is but delayed evincement of that glow within.

Now and then Lou stops and stands still, raises a listening hand, attends to the convening birdcalls. You feel your ears opening like flowers to that sunlight of weavering sound.

So begins the morning ritual at Wolfratshausen, your long ceremony of solitude. And what a very early prelude all this makes, for your final retreat in the Alpen splendor of Muzot will somehow conclude, in bizarre and lonely inversion twenty-eight years from now, the all-too-brief idyll started here.

The weeks begin to flutter by. Frieda von Bülow and August Endell return to the city. After every dawn walk, Rainer and Lou bring a basin of warm water from the cottage and bathe each other's earth-caked feet. At the gazebo's peaked roof above them the Loufried flag stirs gently. These days, they know, are like a kingdom, a country. Theirs alone.

And how have we managed this? Rainer wonders often. *How achieved such a high reality? How is it that one can come from nothing into everything?*

If people shall be like provinces in his life, Lou will remain (Lou alone) a continent.

The next few months will be spent here in Wolfratshausen. Most of the summer. Color and light and even birdcall transmute slowly through the passing weeks. Endell and Frieda pay infrequent visits, arriving only to depart before long. No doubt they can sense the intimate nature of all that transpires privately in their absence. They go away half embarrassed, half privileged to have witnessed it.

A summer of study, and Rainer is under Lou's tutelage. Together they read of Italian Renaissance art. Venice has continued to burgeon within him since his brief trip to that place earlier in the year, and perusing monographs with Lou brings a powerful sensation of convergence. He's on a path—his surest path yet. Everything around him flowing together into singularity.

Daily the sounds of the Alpen village rise and fall beyond the cottage yard. The knelling of a church bell in its measured intervals. Rainer writes love poems by the score, his lines moving ardently toward the simplicity Lou longs for—less complicated expressions no longer bloated with feeling but anchored in the solid profundity of actual *things*. He understands now, as he has never before understood: *things* give us names.

"And each word you say is my belief,
like an image of prayer raised on my silent path.
I love you. You recline in a garden chair,
and your white hands sleep in your lap.
My life turns like a silver spool
in your power. Unravel and release the thread
of my fate."

Through these weeks Lou has about her an air of quiet awe, of surprised fulfillment—some dormant expectation within her finally brought to pass. She tells him she's long wished for a time like this one.

"Just like this," she says. "Working side by side in perfect peace. Reducing everything to its essence."

They are sitting together in the garden. A bowl of apple slices and a glass of milk stand on a small table beside her.

"I almost had it once before. With Paul Reé. Do you know about him, Rainer? A wonderful man. Very brilliant, very gentle. Paul and I tried for a while in Berlin. For a short time we were almost happy, but it was impossible in the end."

"What happened?"

"Before that we'd been a threesome—I and Paul and Nietzsche. When things fell out with Nietzsche, Paul convinced himself he'd won the favor of my affection. Paul's interests were always mixed, you see. Our Berlin arrangement couldn't last that way. His pretences kept clouding up between us."

"You mean he loved you."

"I'm afraid he hated *himself* more than he loved *me*. He wanted something to throw back at his self-hate."

"And your husband?"

"Friedrich? What about him?"

"Wasn't it possible with him? This kind of work?"

"No," she answers flatly, without the slightest hesitation.

Then silence. Her eyes leveled hard upon him.

At last she says, "Shall I tell you about my husband?"

The garden vivid in sunlight. Greenery shivering bright and quiet behind her as she speaks.

"We were at war—Friedrich Andreas and I—for the first several years of our marriage. He is a strange, brilliant man. I'll never know anyone like him."

Her eyes float upward to the stirring trees and one hand moves to the goblet of milk nearby, then abruptly returns to her lap.

"He forced me—" She sits forward in her chair. "You see . . . he forced me to marry him."

Rainer expects something more, but Lou's face glazes with silent thought.

"Forced you?"

Some dark past is burning in her look. Her voice takes a grayish timbre: "We were sitting there in the kitchen with the small oak table between us. He'd been terribly persistent with his proposals. I should have recognized how agitated he was. His pocketknife lay in front of him. He always carried it, often took it out to play with. Suddenly—quite calmly—he picked up the knife, unfolded it and bludgeoned himself in the chest."

There is a hissing noise, as of something punctured. Then Rainer feels the bullet of breath escaping him: the stab of the image to his own chest.

"He meant to kill himself," says Lou. "And he very nearly succeeded, but that the knife slipped partly closed. Still, so much blood! The blade came very near his heart."

"My God, Lou!"

"*Ja.*"

Her small word drifts ruefully through the rustling garden air. A guilty smile steals across her mouth, then her eyes turn glassy in thought again. "He gave me no choice, you see. I had to consent to him. But even with wifehood forced upon me, I knew I needn't surrender my whole self."

"You forswore him," says Rainer. But somehow the words don't seem to reach her. He has said the words aloud for his own sake.

"That was ten years ago," Lou says. "The start of a long battle."

RainerRainerRainer!—the name comes pouring through the briny dark. The poet's inner eyes shudder open. Night burns them like salt.

—*I'm here, Rainer, I'm here. Shhh.*

—*Mama?*

—*Shhh. Be calm now, Rainer.*

But it's not her. Both the voices are his own.

—*That isn't you, Mama, is it?*

—*Shhh. You're dreaming, Rainer.*

—*But it was never Mama, was it? Never her at all.*

—*Don't say such things, Rainer.*

—*My fear was so big between us. She couldn't have gotten through.*

—*But you understood, Rainer. Think back. Wasn't it always like a game we played?*

—*You mean a game I played alone.*

—*Yes, very well. But a game.*

—*My God, I made you up! I created you, Mama, didn't I? As though you couldn't exist on your own.*

—*Of course.*

—*But out of what? There was nothing inside me then.*

—*Of course there was, Rainer. You've already said it.*

—*What did I say?*

—*You named it. The one thing you had inside. We all have something. There's always something in the beginning.*

And now he sees it. In the hollow murk of sleep, Rainer sees the secret clay, like something gobbed from the meaninglessness of saliva and dust.

—*You mean fear! I made you from my fear.*

—*If that's what you call it, yes.*

—*But what else might it be called?*

Now a laugh, huge and chittering in that void. Meteoric sound caroming off into vastness, hinging back from the distance in shapes like words. Words cryptic, defiantly meaningful—

—*Rainer!*

He comes plummeting into Lou's presence. She's beside him in the bed, shaking him. The room's darkness is daylight compared to that other.

"You were kicking, Rainer. You were dreaming."

"Oh, Lou! It's all inside me. Everything. I've never had but what's inside me. I've dreamt it—everything."

"Was it your mother again?"

"No, this time it was *me*. Just me. And it's always been this way. Now I know—"

Something chokes back his words. Lou waits, listening. The night in this room is like a fur, grazing Rainer's limbs.

"Without me, Lou, it couldn't have . . . been real."

"What couldn't?"

"Anything. Mother, Ismene, Saint Pölten, anything."

"You helped create it, you mean?"

"Yes. And that doesn't make it unreal. None of it. It's just that it all *needed* me, you see."

She pulls him close. *"Ja,"* she says. "It needed you. And I think . . . those things of your past, Rainer. That darkness. I think your work awaits you in all that."

"My work?" He's eager to hear this prophecy.

"Ja. Those things need you still. Your work will come of them."

"Yes, because . . . because *everything* needs me, Lou. That unfinished past and everything else. At every moment, I help it to be. And I can do that consciously. I can help it to be—*all* of it now. That *whole* past and not just the fear. Back then, when I was little, I didn't understand the way those things all used me to *create* themselves. They . . . sat so heavily upon me. I had no defense. But all the time I was their point of entry—without me they had no hope. Nothing has ever existed without my help. So I can be like that for everything, I can help anything express itself. Things present or past, *anything!* I can do it deliberately. Can't I, Lou?"

But she is silent now.

"Can't I?"

Oh, but one can fail. Is this the reason Lou does not answer you? It has not yet occurred to you, but despite one's awareness one can fail to take the weight of all that surrounds oneself and lift it into expression. And here lies the long frightful lesson that your time in Paris, years from now, shall hammer home. What happens to one who absorbs the world, who becomes sodden with impression that makes him heavy and pins him down such that he cannot lift himself, let alone transform his new mass into art? How does that unexpressed world avenge itself inside him? Are these the questions that cause the tree in the Wolfratshausen forest to seem so terrible to you?—the tree past which you refuse to walk on the afternoon that so frightens Lou?

You and she are climbing the sloping forest path toward the hilltop and its vista of southern mountains when suddenly you clutch her arm and pull her to a halt.

"What is it, Rainer?"

"The tree."

Up ahead, ten yards distant, stands the magnificent acacia. While walking this path with Lou three days before, the presence of this tree struck you like a fist. On that morning the path had lain sun-dappled, hypnotic. You'd just awakened in Lou's arms and danger seemed very distant, so the instant the acacia announced itself you touched her hand and pointed and said . . . what did you say?—jostling the moment's feeling into half-formed words that staggered out and immediately lost their way in the greening forest light. You had to stop yourself. You turned to Lou with terror: "I shouldn't say it, should I? It's too fast."

Together you continued along the path—but already, *already* in the lacework of treelight you saw your error. You had lopped away the stem of something very fragile, something that had hoped to blossom in the dark eventuality of silence.

And now the acacia stands before you once more. The acacia remembers.

"Let's walk this other way, Lou."

"Rainer"—a quaver in her voice, and so you know how bad you look. "Rainer, what's the matter? You won't tell me?"

But of course you know better now. Keep silent. Clasp her hand tight and pull her out of the path. She knows not to ask anything further. The acacia remembers, *for already it is changing, changing, transmogrifying in the injury you have done to it and it will not forget oh no it will go on changing and it wants to get inside and grow, grow to something black and clotted—yes a bundle of murky phlegm in your brain in some soft groove of your brain a ragged seed to overgrow the truer perceptions a seed to outshadow it all . . . And who were you to think you could capture this power so casually?*

A telegram arrives from Berlin. Sitting before you in the shade of the garden gazebo, her bare feet interlocked in yours, Lou unfolds the blue paper, reads, lays it down. "Friedrich is coming."

You flinch. "Coming here?"

"Yes."

"Your husband?"

"Yes."

"But does he know I am here?"

"Yes."

A chill in your feet. Draw them together and sit up. This shade all at once inordinately cool. "What shall we do?"

Lou makes a tiny motion like a shrug—but not a shrug at all. She turns her head and looks off into the garden. Her powerful profile just as it was the first time you beheld her. Her clear untroubled eyes absorb the surrounding color.

"You must understand about Friedrich," she says. "I can probably explain this to no one but you, Rainer. Friedrich . . ." She draws a breath, stares down into her palms. "Friedrich is like . . . like a magnificent animal. Very capable of wildness, but always innocent."

She turns to you. A strangely inquiring look. Surely she sees how you've begun, already, to shudder. But she seems to know she cannot comfort you.

"During those first ten years," she says, "when Friedrich tried to subdue me—"

"When you forswore him, you mean?"

"Yes. During that time, things were . . . were much as you'd expect. We squalled almost daily. Awful, awful. One afternoon I was asleep on the couch and woke to find him pressed upon me and had to throttle him till he surrendered."

She waves back the bleak memory with a slow sweep of her hand. Again breathes deeply.

"We fought and then we had our impasses and then we fought again, and when I said the word *divorce* to him do you know how he replied? 'But I would never be able to forget that you are my wife.' He said precisely those words without the slightest bit of reflection, and with the most simple, almost peaceful sort of conviction. Remarkable, really. Well, it was a great battle, but Friedrich has long since given me my freedom—or rather has stopped fighting to curtail it. And now—" Her eyes glister a little, newly moist. A blithesome smile. "Now we are almost like old friends."

Silence. Birds scuffle in the labyrinth of twigs under the bushes.

At last you say, "I understand."

"You'll like him, Rainer."

"When does he arrive?"

"Next week."

"Maybe I should go away."

"But this needn't end, Rainer."

"No. Of course."

"I mean you can come back."

She's in earnest.

"Back here?"

"Yes."

"While he's still here?"

"I can prepare him. It's important that he not feel like the guest, you see."

And so are *you* the guest?—have you dared to believe yourself entitled to something more?

"I see," you say. "*Ja.* I'll go."

As it happens, you've recently received word from Papa—a letter addressed to "René" in his Blütenstrasse room, forwarded from Munich yesterday. Papa wishes to visit. Now you write back that you will meet him at the Munich Hauptbahnhof. You will have just come off a train yourself, but Papa needn't know what is, anyway, impossible to explain. You'll take him to a restaurant and afterward, maybe, to the gardens. It's a ruse, yes, but what choice do you have? How could you express the way your life has opened, opened up like a face at morning time?

Rainer fashions a poem—maybe his first true poem. It will cause Lou to lose her breath. A quiet evening hour, and he writes alone in his Wolfratshausen room, but the walls around him have lost all meaning, just as the pronouns *I* and *you* have ceased to be distinct in this time with Lou, pronouns now facets of one undiluted source, as conjugal as water.

It's as if Lou herself has laid hold of his hand moving the pen. For in every line he now puts down, the letters take sight of each other for the first time: all his inner reweaving expressed in a sudden dramatic shift of his handwriting, almost calligraphic.

He leaves the poem on her pillow, printed on a pale blue sheet in his new artful script, and at the bottom of the sheet:—*Rainer.*

"Blot out my eyes: I can see you
Throw shut my ears: I can hear you,
and without feet I can yet go to you,
and without a mouth I can yet beseech you.
Break my arms off: I'll take hold of you
with my heart as with a hand.
Rip out my heart and my brain will beat.
Toss a fiery brand into my brain,
still I will bear you upon my blood."

*T*he young poet finds himself in the train station in Munich, having arrived two hours earlier and deposited his luggage in the Haberstock Hotel across the street. Absurd beginning to a day that shall remain absurd.

Papa arrives, and soon they are seated opposite one another at a restaurant table.

"Your mother tells me you've changed your name. What of that?"

"Not changed, Papa. Just adjusted."

But it *is* a change—why can't Rainer just say so? Why this feeling that he's dishonored his father by the act?

"And your cousins tell me you hope to unburden them of your allowance. Some talk of giving up university, they say."

Had Rainer written that to Jaroslav's daughters?—written it as boldly as that?

"I hope to make my own living, Papa." He can hear the cloying timbre in his voice. Watches his fingers absently pinching at breadcrumbs. They seem someone else's fingers, impassive, unattached, and he is thinking: *You don't even know, Papa! You don't know how far past all that I've already gone. Right now as we speak a woman waits for me in a cottage that is like our home together. Famous though she is, she waits for your son, Papa, your son whose name is Rainer and who is learning to speak simply. She has given her love to him, and every day he is a little farther along in his powers and one day yet he will say all these things—these mysterious things that comprise the world around us—will say them in a way that brings them to life. It is for him to do this, to give this task his all.*

But what use to speak such thoughts? For it would take but one mere question from Papa, one piece of fatherly logic, to confound all that Rainer might explain.

It hurts the young poet, has hurt him for some time, to look upon his father. Papa's thin, outmoded Bohemian manners. This man like a memory Prague has had: faded figure confabulated from the shadowy brain of that city. This man doesn't want his son's truth, only wants what a father should want. Nothing else.

The day draws to a close. The father goes away again. And instantly it seems to Rainer that Papa might never have come at all—the whole visit like something he merely imagined, a passing daydream.

Rainer loiters in Munich. All his thoughts become one thought. He dares not consider how altered everything will be in the presence of Lou's husband. Getting back is what matters.

First August, Rainer arrives again in Wolfratshausen.

Coming up the lane to the cottage he spots a figure hulking in the doorway. The figure's head grazes the lintel, both shoulders touching the jambs, the threshold filled entirely. It's the husband, standing there gazing down the village lane as if he's long since sensed the young lover's approach. So the husband is a door. No entry except through him.

Even from twenty meters off Rainer can see the man's brawny hands, great sledgelike things curled into slack fists and lodged casually at each jamb. And there's a penetrating, wolfish look to his face. Black hair combed up off the brow. Stern dark beard. But not for an instant, even confronted by such a figure, does it occur to Rainer to turn back. Onward up the dusty slope, up the steep ramp of the husband's stare.

At the picketed gate the poet raises a hand and calls out greetings, working down the quiver in his voice. For a second the husband does not react—is it malevolence or oblivion? Oblivion, it would seem, for now Friedrich Andreas seems to come awake, his eyes gliding over. So he wasn't watching Rainer's approach at all.

The man doesn't quickly come forward. His fists sink from the jambs and one hovers modestly near the hem of his waistcoat. With a twist of his neck he shoots an abortive glance back into the cottage. A long lock of his hair slips from place and hangs in a lank curl at his left temple. Then he steps down and starts across the big yard in a topheavy saunter, thick arms stiff at his sides as if something reins them in, some self-consciousness or gentility, the will of a smaller inner man encased in this outer one. He unlatches the gate.

"You must be the poet."

"*Ja.* How do you do?"

"Very well, *mein Freund.* I am Friedrich." His voice is as deep as his hard face suggests, though surprisingly tremulous. "Pleasant journey?"

The gate clatters back.

"Not too long from Munich, thankfully."

Andreas nods. Releases a serious kind of smile from the hackle of his beard. One hand comes up and scoops the lock of stray hair from his face. He's in shirtsleeves, cuffs turned back, collar aflare. His hands begin pinching at his waistcoat hems. His eyes drift down to the hedges at his side. He seems somehow embarrassed, like one blatantly underdressed for a guest's reception.

So the husband and the poet stand together in the path, mutually uncertain who should lead whom inside.

But before long Rainer's heart has warmed to Friedrich Andreas. Simply looking upon this gentle husband conjures torrents of pain within him. In the afternoons during the hours when the poet and Lou had lain in siesta together behind her closed shutters, Lou retires to the solitude of her room—to rest or to chip away at correspondence, she says—and Rainer is left alone with Andreas. Rainer knows the true reason Lou has withdrawn. Does Andreas sense it too?

"Can you bear it?" she whispered one morning when the poet stood alone with her in the garden. Her eyes wide and glimmering, lead-colored need rising there. Andreas had gone in to heat the kettle.

"You *know* I can't, Lou." And though Rainer's cautious glance skated away toward the cottage, he managed to spot the flush his answer caused in her.

So he sits with Friedrich Andreas in the afternoon hours. The husband's heavy, tired-looking hands rise and fall as words pour softly from his beard. Nothing pitiful about the man, but his deep eyes communicate a staid and tranquil distress. And how could one possibly blame this spurned suitor for continuing to love his wife as he does? In the young poet's crueler moments he equates Friedrich with himself: the husband and he locked in equally helpless orbits around her—but then Lou's pleasured birdcall rises in Rainer's memory and he sees the error of his equation, feels a splintering in his chest. Through Lou he has come to see the dark and trembling depths of Friedrich's placidity.

"This is the same man who tried to conquer you?" he whispers to Lou one evening while a summer rain rustles in the garden outside.

"No. That was a different man. Years ago. Even his face is different now."

"I can't imagine him any other way."

"It's hard," she says, "for me too. But I try to hold to those memories. There's such good balance between me and Friedrich now. Those memories help us keep the balance."

"I wish you wouldn't leave me with him."

"But he doesn't suspect you."

"I know. It's worse than that, Lou. He *trusts* me."

"Do you fear him?"

"No. It's impossible not to love him."

"I thought you'd feel that way. It's why I wasn't afraid for you to meet."

"But Lou"—something flings Rainer into motion and he seizes her hand. "How will we survive him?"

She puts his hand away from her. Calm commanding gesture. "Would you rather we told him?"

"*Ja,* maybe. To look at him, Lou—it's breaking my heart."

"Oh, Rainer," she says soothingly, "that will get easier. And maybe in time he'll accept what can't be denied. You'll be friends by then, you and he."

"But will we ever be *free,* Lou? *You and I?* What if we told him now?"

She stares at the ground in long silence. Then her voice comes up warm and maternal, as though she recounts an act of the greatest tenderness: "I once asked Friedrich if he'd let me tell him all the things I'd seen and done in my travels. I thought some peace might pass between us that way—there'd been so much struggle up till then. I'd won my freedom, you see, but it was just that: something *won.* The loss was *his* every time. Well, he answered me immediately: *No!* A single word as sudden as lightning. He was looking into my eyes as he said it, and there was such . . . such *resolve* in him, Rainer. We sat there without talking, and then something *did* pass between us. Not the peace I'd hoped for, but an understanding. A very clear understanding. For once, conclusively, Friedrich was *giving* me my freedom. Without losing."

The poet says nothing, but there is a terrible clenching inside him. Something stone-like, impregnable.

"You see, Rainer, he made himself clear."

"He loves you."

She purses her mouth—a wistful, buried smile. Resignation almost like that of her neutralized husband's. "I know."

"By *not* loving you," he says. "By granting your wish."

"Ja."

"So he already knows. About us."

"No. He'll never know. It's an impossibility to him, you see."

"But how can I be his *friend*, Lou? With all this going on?"

"Understand him," she says. Such clarity in her voice. And for a moment Rainer's thought drops away. Something clearing inside him, like steam wiped from a glass.

He says, "I will." Then, as if to himself: "It's all I can do, isn't it?"

Lou, inimitable Lou, perceiving his inner dialogue, doesn't even answer.

"You have to come to me. I can't wait anymore."

"I want to, Lou, but I'm afraid."

"Come late," she says. "We'll be quiet. We'll put a blanket on the floor."

So the night deepens and the cottage quietens and Rainer sits in his silent room with a book. The earth rolls in its gradual headlong dive away from the sun. He seems to feel it, and his skull fills up with blood. Pressure growing in his temples. The silence of the cottage increasing like rising danger. Deep nocturnal hours in which every rustle is a shattering.

At last he braves his way into the hall. The dark world on its head. Inversion of doors, and the ceiling below him like a floor, his feet clinging to upsoaring tile. His hair drifting away from his scalp and he's falling toward her door—then he has gentled the latch without a noise and stepped into that other darkness.

A whisper of blankets, bare feet sledding in the coarse fur of the bear rug. The very air now swerving as she comes toward him like something culled from the scattered nightspace. His blind hands suddenly sight-struck at the hollow of her sides. She has seized his fingers—molded his palms to nude hips—and the night has whirled endright again and she is blowing warm words into his mouth. Words he believed to be his own, for

195

the selfsame ones have beaten within him like a heart. *I know,* he says, *I know:* words breathed to her lapping tongue.

They struggle like combatants in a tangle of hands and breath. Fluttering across the floor together as though afloat. With every giving gesture of his body Rainer strives and strives to siphon the growing outcries into silence.

Then a final violent launch into her vastness, and he begins to weep uncontrollably. His coital nightfall, warm-blooded and penitent. She clasps him in the darkness, holding his skull in her hands, her fingers furred deep in his hair. *Shhhhhhhhhhhhhhh.*

He presses his face to her breast to stifle the noise. But with every sob he is drinking her indescribable musk and *every every every* blessing is the greater world's loss.

PARIS & FLIGHT :

1902–1903

And there came sickness as well . . . endless fever-nights and great fearfulness, and my power and my courage grew small, and with the last remnants I went away, went through many heavy mountains.

Letter to Lou, June 1903

A bright morning and Rainer Maria Rilke is walking along the boulevard Saint Michel. The street, unaccountably, gives off a peaceable garden-like hum. The poet can hardly believe his good fortune at having, perhaps, endured the bleak frenzy of Paris long enough to find a day so hospitable and full of color.

But then a man flounces around the corner from the rue de Medici, comes jittering past the glassy restaurants where workers in blinding white aprons are hoisting out tables. Immediately the workers take note of the man's lolloping gait. It's impossible to ignore. They begin pointing as he goes by, and now laughter ripples amongst them.

The spastic man seems not to notice—perhaps he's accustomed to such derision. But something within him, some network of thirsty spasmodic nerves, laps up their laughter like a tonic and sends him leaping, wild-limbed, his threadbare jacket bunching up about his shoulders as he flails along the boulevard toward the river. Outlandish doll plunked and yanked by a great invisible hand. He does not halt—perhaps it's beyond his powers.

The waiters continue to laugh, though the dance of nerves now looks like reckless rage. Bystanders stop and stare as though offended, as though it's a most egregious sort of impertinence for this man to suffer his torments so publicly. Still he goes on before their stares, spilling down the sidewalk.

Rainer, dumbfounded, follows all the way to the Pont Saint Michel, and there on the bridge, finally, the malady overflows and sends the man sprawling into the street. A throng of people swarm him as if to do him further injury—though it must be that they intend to help. Rainer stands back watching, jolted to realize that the man's every shudder has gone through him as he watched, has wrenched something loose inside. And why do the poet's own hands clutch his coat closed as they do? Why does he fear that a great orifice has opened in his breast like a second mouth?— that this shaken puppet of a person, struck down on the sunlit pavement before him, has come staggering out of that womb-hot hole?

A different November day. The poet returns to the zoo to find the panther still restlessly afoot behind its grill of bars. And this time Rainer stays and watches. He's beginning to grasp it. The panther's plight can become the poet's plight: seeing and seeing till nothing more can settle inside— choked witness to the tongue-broken barrage.

"His gaze, from the passing bars,
has grown so weary that it can hold nothing else.
To him there are a thousand bars
and beyond the thousand bars no world at all.

The soft drop of the dread sleek steps,
conscribed to a tight circle,
is like a dance of stamina around a center
in which a greater will stands stunned.

Yet sometimes the curtain of the pupil stirs,
opens itself soundlessly—then an image gets inside,
passes through the silent tension of the limbs and—
snared in the heart, ceases to be."

.   .   .

Snow begins to fall in Paris this month. It seems to lie with paralytic weight upon Rainer's days. On nineteenth November he writes in his diary:

"Oh, this longing to make a beginning, and always these blocked paths . . . Each morning I rise to this useless and frightful waiting, and go to sleep disappointed, distraught, and defeated by my incompetence. . . . Such waiting upon distant things—is it folly? . . . whomever's will is shaken, their world will shake as well. Oh, this winter cold. It is snowing. My stove is failing. I sit wrapped in my coat, freezing with stiffening hands indoors. . . . I am unspeakably afraid."

And the following day:

"I am like a lost thing. Like an animal that hears nothing. Like a flag over an empty house . . . It is cold. The snow falls heavily."

*T*he year 1903 arrives. By February the nagging yellowness of your health has become a total malaise. You're laid low with the grippe, inevitable upshot of all the distress this city has caused you. Feverish days and bouts of fitful sleep stretching out through one long ceilingward stare in which time seems paused. All clock hands inert. The shifting windowlight evokes nothing more than the fever's hopeless fluctuations.

Memories swarm you in these suspended hours—memories, from childhood days, of the many rooms in which this fever came. These memories reduce you to that child again—still that child despite your striving, still mired in the long labor of finishing the unfinished boyhood behind you. So as if it were happening just this morning:

. . . heavy-lidded eyes stare from chilled and wavy windowglass—a diaphanous child-face seized in deep solitude. The wide mouth ripples low near the chin. Face of a girlchild peering from the gray past, though the hair has been cropped to regulation, though the pale brow supports the Saint Pölten shako by day. How strange to have a face and rarely see it.

A moment ago René Maria lay on his back watching the high dark dormitory windows soften with dawn's approach, the huge lung of Kadettenschule sleep shuddering around him on all sides. But now he's crept from bed in stockings and slipped through big doors into this corridor by which he will march to breakfast in another two hours. Everything an ashen monochrome out here, toneless light falling in broad slats from the window arches. He sits curled on one of the concrete windowsills, embracing his knees. Dark pluming breath. His jaw juddering molar to molar. The blanched light has already crept toward color, and his face drifts backward in the riffled glass, like something sinking. Girl-face submerged in the cloudy waters of Then and Before and Once. Out there beyond the clearing glass: the insinuated world.

In the dank nip of many previous mornings, René Maria has stolen hours and hours alone by the window. So far frost has been his only danger. But now something whispers in the corridor: the groan of big hinges and the setting of a latch. A shadow steps from the dormitory and melts into the dark between casements. René Maria presses himself to the stone embrasure, stifles his quickening breath.

The figure flickers in the colorless pool of a window, vanishes. The flat whisper of feet like pages slowly aflutter. A noise of susurrus lungs. Then, into the close gray light comes Karl.

Remember: Karl standing before you, blue nightshift sagging from square shoulders, one hand clutching the cotton at his thigh, gathering it close around the backs of his legs. Karl's face is still bulging with sleep. He's eaten too many dreams; he is gorged with them.

—*You've been away,* Karl whispers, and sidles up onto the sill. His body gives off a subtle heat, though he's shivering already. *Were you really sick or just aping?*

Don't answer. The question stands in the space between. Say nothing. Just sit there. If he stays, then maybe you'll shout. The noncom sleeps down the hall.

Karl gazes. Strangely, he looks very sad.—*Tell me, René.* A request, like a gentle hand put forth.

—*I was sick,* ja.

Karl's mouth spreads back at the corners—a kind of grin, but of soberness more than pleasure.—*How bad was it?*

Why should Karl ask? Why should he come tiptoeing out here to sit by this window in the chill?

—*How bad was it?*

—*Very.* Your eyes are in a rapid flutter, starting to burn.

Karl stares. Silence. He leans close to the windowglass and exhales a puff of leaden steam. Watch his bitten fingernails, bedded with grime, as he begins tracing silvery lines on the pane.

—*You think you know a lot about me, don't you, René?*

Do not answer. Karl draws a five-pointed star.

—*What do you know, René? About me? Why don't you tell me?*

He waits. Listens. But you are silent.

—*What do you think you know?* Louder now, his words sibilating down the corridor.

—*Karl, the Slovenian's just down the hall—*

—*Tell me!*

—*I know you have bad dreams.*

But as though he hasn't heard, Karl blurts, *Have you ever looked at dead persons, René?*

—*No.*

—*So you can't know the first thing about me. Did your mama and papa send you here?* Ja? *Well, lucky you. Mine are dead. My uncle couldn't bear the sight of me. He's the one who shipped me to this place. And do you know how that happened, René—to my parents, I mean? Do you?*

Chipped wet teeth come out to chomp at Karl's bottom lip.

—*I killed them. You couldn't have known* that, *could you, René? Ja, and it was like I meant to do it.* His words warping now as he gnaws his own mouth. —*Killed them both with my fever—typhus—and then got better myself. Got better in time to watch their coffins go down.*

Karl leans forward. His breath upon your face. Venomous red smell. Press your spine to the icy stone. He's touching your knee, your thigh. Fingers clambering spider-like toward your hand. Like Jesus crawling atop your blankets, small and bloody. Pull away! But Karl has gripped you already—he's squeezing.

—*You see, René, you're just a sop. You think you know so much. But you don't. You don't. Because it's me who's suffered.*

Your fingers redden in Karl's grip. And now Karl lifts them to his mouth. His lips hot against your knuckles. Yank back!—but he holds you fast. Your free hand slaps and claws at his locked fingers.

Karl curses. Again the words clatter down the corridor. He clenches both your hands.—*Be gentle, René! Gentle!*

Then a brittle destructive noise, as of distant trees falling. Karl looks down—like one awakened by the sound. Stares at your hands clasped in his, your knuckles cracked. Something like pity coming over him. He hunches, presses his face to your hands. Slow devotional gesture. His breath on your fingers again. Thunder in your heart. And nothing to see but Karl's terrible scalp: the matted hair askew, obscene with sleep. And now his whole body slumps forward, the smell of him pouring down your throat and his hot cheek jammed against your own and his breath in your ear—breath of someone asleep—oh God he's asleep his dream is closing over you jerk back!—but you're pinned to the stone wall and as you thrash your forehead smashes at Karl's. Dull splintering noise. A cracking pain. Karl croaks and rears. Lets loose one of your hands and you begin jabbing.

—*Damn you*, he snorts. *Gentle!*—his restraining clutch again—*Gentle!*

It's his dream speaking. Unconscious lexicon choked with a single insensible word, and now the word—his word—is in your mouth as Karl's kiss comes hard against your lips and all your breath is shut off and his hand is clawing at your lap and now clutching you there, clutching you in that girl-place—but it has not been a girl-place since you were put into trousers and now you wear trousers daily, and deep in your stopped-up throat a bilious juice, the juice of a scream, begins to rise. You will scream.

Shake free and scream. But when Karl pulls away he bolts his arms straight, pins both your hands to your chest. And all your wind is lost.

He holds you that way till you stop resisting. Silence. Then with a horrible intricate slowness Karl's hard face opens and drains. As if he's emerged from his terrific dream. The brace of his arms relaxing now. His hands becoming timid, lifting away, sinking to his lap.

He sits there blinking, tufts of breath spurting wetly from his mouth.—*Have I hurt you, René?*

Be stone-still, silent.

—*How do you know my dreams?*

Silent.

—*How. How do you know my dreams, you shit.*

—*All the boys dream them, Karl.* A strangled whisper.—*Yours are loudest.*

Karl's eyes dart to the window. Out there, out of night, the morning is returning bluely. Like a memory of morning. In the frosted field a little creature lopes along: a pale hare with nose low to the ground. As though it senses someone watching, it stops and stands tall, its long ears tensed. But for the mild tan hue of the fur the creature is nearly invisible in the aqueous light.

Karl shivers, gathers his nightshift and hugs himself.—*It's cold. Too cold out here. We'll get sick.*

He slips from the window. Stands shoeless on the icy floor.

—*Don't you tell anyone, you shit.*

He jogs away high-shouldered toward the dormitory. Shadows engulf him. A latch clatters softly and he is gone.

Out in the cold, the hare slips into the brush at the field's edge. Once more there is nothing but field. Nothing but field, and silent insistent morning . . .

. . . and locked in the remote and feverish future of a Parisian bed, in the tight flannel twist of the headache, your grown body quivers and turns.

As if by these slight motions the body might unhitch these stalled hours, might impel you forward yet, out of that viscid past, back into your limbs. So did one ever become an adult through and through? The Saint Pölten morning remains seized in present tense, while somewhere very near a cathedral bell is tolling above city roofs. But did one grow up and become a husband? A father? All those things that make a man of a child? The cathedral bell intones a single word, insisting upon its relevance. Think hard. Through the hot murk of fever. Remember . . . wasn't one a lover? Didn't one have a home? Hadn't one broken free to reach all that? Or had all that broken free of the one who longed for it? Was one without all of it now because something from within had led one away? The cathedral bell insists and insists: *PA*-rissss, *PA*-rissss, *PA*-rissss. . . .

The fever retreats at last and you find yourself on your feet in time for Paula Becker's arrival in Paris. Paula *Modersohn*-Becker, rather. Remember. Two years ago, barely a month after your own wedding, the auburn-haired painter married Otto Modersohn. Their bond had come as a surprise to most everyone in Worpswede, for Otto was ten years older than Paula and still thought to be grieving the previous year's loss of his wife.

Eleventh February, you and Clara receive the auburn-haired painter in Clara's room. She stands by the window, small and slender in a beige dress, looking down through the shifting chestnut canopies. Her long hair is bundled at her nape.

"Things have changed," she says. "I see that now. Only three years since my first time in Paris—our time, Clara, remember? Only three years, but how different our lives are. All of us, yes Rainer?"

She turns and looks directly into your eyes. You say nothing. *She is in flight,* you think. *She is fleeing the heavy "Frau"—that house-like epithet which now arches itself over her art.* And you're remembering the things she told you in Worpswede three years ago while crossing the fog-steeped moors in the deepest hours of night. *In Paris I was like someone waking up.*

"Anyway," Paula says, "it's almost like old times, isn't it, to be together again—the three of us?"

There's a brief silence, a sober kind of joy passing between you all. The silence seems to speak of Otto Modersohn's absence, but nothing in Paula's manner suggests regret that Otto has not accompanied her to Paris. The husband's removed figure, and the fact of you and Clara now quartered separately—it *does* all seem, for an instant, like a reunion of sorts. Everything put back into order to allow for the old love of *the family.* Unimpeded love, as back in those days before it got parceled into marriage vows. But promptly the unchangeable facts of the present confront and defeat such a notion.

Paula says, "Your little Ruth. Is there a chance she'll come here?"

Clara glances at you, shakes her head. "We both fear the effect of the city. It's better that Ruth be at Oberneuland, hard as it is for us. We miss her terribly."

"Paris," you add, "is a heavy, difficult place."

Now Paula eyes you again. And that keen appraisal of hers has the effect of a mirror: somehow she reflects you to yourself. Your somewhat haggard face, your eyes still couched in the shadow of recent illness. No doubt you're a lean, shabby figure. You wonder what she makes of you. What she makes of you and Clara both, absentee parents that you are. Her sisterly friendship with Clara has dimmed considerably since your wedding.

"Otto dislikes Paris too," says Paula. "Finds it undignified. I don't see that myself, perhaps because I've been to England where everything is so much worse. No, I was very happy here before. I was full of anticipation. Already I feel it again—that sense of fulfillment ahead. In other places the fulfillment comes more easily, perhaps, but maybe it disappoints a little for that reason. Here in Paris fulfillment stays ahead of you. Stays ahead of *me,* at least. A wonderful feeling."

"No hope, then," says Clara, "that Otto will join you?"

Paula smiles—almost bitterly, it seems. "Oh dear, no. But that couldn't stop me from coming. And Otto knows how I cherish my work."

So you are right: she has fled here.

"Yes, Paula," you say. "Work. Work is the thing that makes it possible to stay in Paris, unbearable as this place can be. Do remember that, dear friend, if the city ever saddens you. If Clara and I look weary to you now, it's only because we've learnt it ourselves, what it means to be workers here."

"You must be nearly finished with your Rodin monograph."

"It's done, yes. It's brought us the gift of the Master's friendship; the Master himself has guided us both in our difficulties here—first me, now Clara. '*Il faut toujours travailler,*' he says. Says it wonderfully in that voice of his. '*Travailler et patience.*' I hope you can get to know him, Paula, so you can hear him yourself. He's a whole world, that man."

"You've had troubles here, have you?" says Paula. The old intimate, earnest concern in her eyes now. "But you're happy again, *ja?*"

This question a quick caesura to the flow of talk. You and Clara exchange doleful smiles. And neither of you speaks an answer; no doubt your faces give answer enough.

Clara says, "Rainer's health has flagged, I'm afraid."

"You must get out to the country," says Paula. "A retreat somewhere. Have you thought of that?"

"We've been so deep in our work," you tell her. "All our hope has been there. But you're right, of course. I see it now that I've worsened."

Paula's clear eyes are glinting in the windowlight. "You must take care of yourselves. Of each other too. Were he to learn of it, I fear Rodin might be shocked at how literally you've taken him." She seems, somehow, to have glimpsed the deliberate distance you and Clara have set between yourselves. And now her mouth lies shut upon some mild disappointment.

Something she would say aloud, perhaps, were you all as close now as you'd once been in Worpswede. You can tell that Clara sees this too.

Within days of Paula's arrival you receive a missive from an admiring young reader who wants your opinion on several immature poems. This reader notes that he's a cadet at the Military Academy of Wiener-Neustadt. He knows something of your own Kadettenschule history, he says, for one of the Neustadt instructors, Professor Horaček, formerly served as chaplain to the Academy of Saint Pölten.

Instantly that name brings a figure to mind: short round-shouldered fellow, Horaček still stands out of the old Saint Pölten horrors for his small gestures of kindness. Beyond this name, however, the young stranger's letter remains inexplicable—not to mention the enclosed verses. Why has this . . . this "Franz Xaver Kappus" bothered to implore such a poet as you? He says he's read a volume of your verse, but why should he entrust you with his poems? And so much conscientious care in their presentation too. Four verses copied neatly onto different sheets, a youthful hope painstakingly gathered into each penned line.

What if this Kappus only knew something of the person to whom he was writing: the lusterless nature of Rainer Maria Rilke's existence, the unenviable conditions in which the poet has come to find himself, the poet's defenselessness before all these troubles? How could one possibly reply honestly to a letter sent in such a trustful spirit?

You look the letter over a second time, then put it aside. For several days it lies consigned to purgatory on your corner table. All the time it weighs on your thoughts.

Later, sitting alone on your Paris balcony in an unseasonably warm gray afternoon, you read the young man's proffered work a third time, and now, shuffling the pages again, you know it's unavoidable: you must respond. For in truth this Kappus is no stranger at all—doubt-ridden poet caught in the miseries of regimental life. It's as though you've been pressed to send answers to your own former self. What would *you* have given, after all, to have been blessed by a letter of encouragement and counsel during your own days in that maelstrom of the academy?

The Paris bells begin to sound their vesper hours. Saint Séverin, then Saint Étienne du Mont and Saint Jacques du Haut-Pas. Each one near and brightly tuned. And but a little farther off, the stately low knells from Notre Dame.

Two hours ago you and Clara were with the auburn-haired painter again. She's found rooms in the quiet rue Cassette, across the Jardin Luxembourg. Together you all sat in her small apartment talking of art and this and that, the air between you taut all the while. It seems conclusive now that there can be no re-creating those memorable days passed in Paula's Worpswede atelier. Impossible. And perhaps it was an effort to acknowledge this awkwardness, to avow it and find some new common ground, that started you talking as you did: about the benedictions of solitude in marriage. About marriage between artists, and how it can be nothing but misunderstanding unless it consists of mutual consent to aloneness, and—what's more—a holy promise to guard the solitude of the spouse.

"But what about a time like this?" said Paula suddenly.

"Like what, Paula?"

"Like this time in Paris—this unhappy time for you both. Why shouldn't you come together and take comfort in each other?"

You reached for Clara's hand then, and felt her fingers in warm and lively response. "Our solitude *is* the comfort we give one another. It's through my love for Clara that I seek to help her keep and cherish her solitude. As long as we each have our solitude, and help each other to keep it, nothing can do harm to us or to our work."

"And yet you've both been unhappy," said Paula.

Clara stirred beside you. "But if I feel sad or lonely," she said, "the feeling itself becomes a kind of testament. For I see that I can bear it in the solitude Rainer helps me to build." She turned to you and her eyes were bright with belief. "In that way, no distance can really come between us."

Paula simply sat there blinking incredulous eyes, her mouth once again pursed upon withheld words.

Now, bending to your reply for Franz Xaver Kappus, all the pent-up energy come of being misunderstood spills forth in phrases blunt and biblical. And you are writing to yourself—to yourself amidst the impediments and unrelenting pressures encountered when one strives to live by an art born of the heart's deep and dumbfounded regions.

"Nobody can advise and help you," you write, *"nobody."*

". . . If your everyday life appears poor, don't complain to it. Complain to yourself. Say to yourself that you are not poet enough to call up its riches. . . . The creator must be a world unto himself and find everything in himself and in nature, to which he has connected himself. . . . Continue to grow quiet and serious through your development. You could not spoil it quite as violently as when you expect outward answers to questions which only your innermost feeling, in your softest hour, can perhaps answer."

The church bells have hummed to silence. You look up from the letter at the chilled blue dome of the Panthéon. And did one ever get free of the ensnaring past? Has one come anywhere near acquiring the strength to grasp and shape all that surrounds one?—to make of oneself a hand and mold it all to serve one's art?

. . .

Again the sickness rises within you and again you take to bed. Long fever-ish days prone in the gray bedsheets, the gray light of the outer world standing flat and impregnable in the windowpanes. Cement-colored Paris air in which bells clang out their warped tones as they have done for ages: indifferent, perversely regular.

Clara attends to you with great concern. And assents immediately to your talk of fleeing the city once you're somewhat improved. For there is no doubt inside you now—*was there ever?*—that the city is what causes you such grief. Yes, to depart will make all the difference. Clara also believes it. She too has come to suffer the impact of Paris.

And yet she has started working a great deal, and now commissions are coming in. The wife of a wealthy publisher will soon model for a minia-ture. So Clara will not accompany you, wherever you go—not with so much work just now beginning for her.

Clara's commissions, and her father's allowance, will keep her solvent while you're away. But as for you, how to finance your departure? The Rodin monograph equates to 150 marks earned, 200 francs. Barely enough to cover a month's frugal expenses. Beyond this, you've been reading man-uscript submissions for Axel Juncker, who published *The Book of Images* last year—all a frantic patchwork to keep at bay the notion to which Papa, back in Prague, continues to cling: that you will return to your wretched birth-city with the sensible aim of employ as a bank clerk.

Whenever possible you wave off Clara's concern, urge her back to her work, abide no talk of worries concerning money. A means will be found to get you out of Paris—at least for a while. Clara goes, however reluc-tantly, returning a few times a day. You remain convalescent as promised, though whenever you can bear to, you sit up and sort through Juncker's new stack of submissions.

You do not tell Clara you've written to your father, appealing for Papa's help in escaping Paris. This old ailment has stricken you down more than you care to admit, leveling your pride completely—and now nothing to do but to seek understanding from a source that has never offered it.

Still, you know this: Papa's love has always been deeper than Papa's understanding; his rigidity has never been for lack of gentleness. He is a simple softhearted father, even if he's incapable of expressing love. Even if he is fated to remain a stranger.

One day a noise stirs you from the depths of a senseless fever-dream and you open your eyes to the figure of Paula Modersohn-Becker standing at the window-table, her back turned. Her elbows shifting here and there, hands busy before her. Your vision funneling in a long cone of colorless light and she a distant apparition.

You remember then: a carriage ride from Worpswede to Hamburg with Paula Becker and Otto Modersohn. Late September 1900. You rode in the backward-facing seat. Autumn daylight in a low golden canopy above the moors. Before you sat Paula, her knees nearly touching yours. She wore a French hat of black straw, the brim adorned with two or three red roses. In the deep reflective brown of her eyes the flat country went scrolling like an inner terrain and you watched those pulsations unashamedly. Strands of clay-colored dust streamed past the carriage windows, kicked up by a second carriage clattering just ahead in which rode Vogeler and the others, the whole Worpswede *family* traveling to Hamburg for the premiere of Carl Hauptmann's new play. On your lap lay a large wreath of wild heather made by Clara Westhoff. A gift for Hauptmann. "But you should carry it," said the sculptress to you that morning. "It ought to be yours. For your reading last night." At the Barkenhoff the previous evening you had read aloud your short play *Beginners*. At the close, while *the family* trembled with warm applause, you saw the sculptress, with a look of breathlessness in her eyes, reaching to slip her hand into Paula's. Side by side in that moment they had seemed a masterpiece of composition. These sisterly girls who had managed in a matter of weeks to hold your heart off the earth. In the carriage your fingers grazed the braided moorland heather, that purple twist still endowed with the shape-giving strength of the sculptress's hands, and you felt yourself weightless with potentiality. Suspended. Clara Westhoff's work beneath your fingers, Paula Becker's brown eyes before you. There was no knowing then—and you wouldn't learn till two weeks hence—that the object of your enamored gaze was already betrothed to the man seated on the carriage bench beside you. How secretive Otto and Paula had been!

Specks of amoebic light swim through your Paris room. The auburn-haired painter, her back still turned, scatters to puzzle pieces, the light-spores dismantling her, growing, gaping to pools that blot out perception—and then nothing. . . .

Till you wake again and there is Paula looking down. How long has she been standing there? Shy and sweet in her plain dress.

By October you'd caught wind of the secret engagement, and early on the fifth you fled the familial embrace of all your Worpswede friends. An abrupt flight with no farewell but one: a notebook of poems left at Paula Becker's door, and a few lines scratched onto a slip of paper: *'Please keep this small book while I am away.'* Just days before, you had secured the lease of a Worpswede house, planning to spend the whole autumn there. . . .

"Brought you some tulips." Paula gestures toward the window. A vase of stupendous red flowers stands in the dimensionless light. Such color that all else in the room is rendered pale.

"Thank you." Your voice as remote as hers. Even sound is shrinking now, enfeebled by those fantastic bulbs. You don't try to lift your head from the pillow. Paula understands, pulls a chair over, sits. Immediately you and she seem more alone together. A heightened intimacy that might feel unnatural or forbidden were you well.

Still Paula looks small to you. Figure falling from your life. That won't be altered now, whatever closeness you contrive. Not that you would let it be altered were it possible. No, your time of possibility with Paula was no more than an intake of breath two years ago.

Not till mid-November, a full month after you'd flown Worpswede, did she write to tell you of her engagement. The letter found you in the Berlin suburb of Schmargendorf. You had escaped the bewildering magnetism of *the family* in order to return to Lou. Your one harbor, Lou. And yet you should have known things could not be so simple.

"I leave in a few days," says Paula now.

"Leave? For where?"

"Home. Worpswede. I'd stay in Paris longer were it possible, but it's not."

"I'm leaving too," you say.

"Are you well enough?"

"Getting better. There's no cure, anyway, but to go."

Paula stares, thoughtful. By something in her look she seems to deem it sadly appropriate, as you do, that your journey and hers shall coincide but not intersect.

"And Clara?" she says.

"She'll stay. She has her work. Anyway, I'll return."

"When?"

"A few weeks."

"Isn't it difficult?" Her head shaken in disbelief, an offended sort of awe.

"To be apart, you mean?"

"*Ja.*"

She's worried for Clara. You can see that.

"Paula," you say, "*everything* is difficult."

.   .   .

South, south, out of Paris to Santa Margherita on the Ligurian Sea. Your journey begins with an overnight train to Modane, then onward to connect at Torino for Genoa.

A bitter chill in the air all night. You slump sleeplessly in an upright seat, a camelhair blanket pulled to your throat. Despite the chill you keep your window cracked behind the curtain. The carriage is full and you cannot abide the enclosed air pregnant with strange breath. The train barrels through regions dark and slumberous, the wind whistling above you and Paris shrinking back by the minute. Worpswede in your thoughts. Schmargendorf in your thoughts: Paula, Clara, Lou . . .

. . . Fifth October 1900. You'd been away in Worpswede for less than two months when you returned to Schmargendorf. Lou seemed to chafe at your reappearance. But why shouldn't you think yourself welcome to come back to her—or back to your Russian work, which seemed destined to happen in no place but Schmargendorf? Just last year your first "Russian Prayers" had come forth in the solitude of your rooms there—sixty-six powerful poems in less than a month's time. How they had poured from your astonished pen. They'd been in Lou's keeping ever since. Even she— ever-so-discriminating Lou—had recognized the accomplishment those prayers were. Russia had made them possible, Schmargendorf had made them actual.

In the station at Modane the train sits and sits. Nobody seems to board or disembark. You stare through the warped window at the drab and soiled platform, the station's awning shadows stenciled there. Finally the train shifts sluggishly. The sad little station creeping backward out of sight. A conductor comes down the car. You wave him over.

The man already knows what you will ask. "Genoa, yes? Too late for early train. Late train from Torino now. Eight o'clock."

"And arrive at Genoa—"

"Midnight."

The conductor vanishes through the rear of the car.

Back in Schmargendorf you took lodging on Misdroyerstrasse, not far from Lou's house. You and she saw much of each other, but what a quiet torment that time became. And before long Lou managed to convey, with wordless clarity, her wish that you would leave. Leave, leave! Seek refuge somewhere other than at her threshold.

The route between Modane and Torino is a terror. Miles-long tunnels devour the bright daylight, the carriage screaming through impenetrable blackness as though the train itself is a great drill-head boring into layers of ancient stone. The clamor throws you side to side in your seat. The shut windowglass in a deafening chatter overhead. During the slow approach to the mountains the passengers were instructed to secure the windows, but still the car is filling with the odor of burnt coal. And still, not even the dimmest light. Nothing. You must mask your mouth with the blanket.

You saw your mistake. Lou made it impossible to *not* see: you had failed her by coming back. Failed all that she had hoped to nurture in you. You could not reclaim her approval now by any act but that of departure, striking out, forging your own path. And though you sensed all this, it seemed to clarify nothing, only caused you confusion. For where could you go while your heart drew you home to her presence, no place else? Why should she refuse—so adamantly refuse—to see that your path lay in *her? She* was your path. Hadn't you told her so on countless occasions? Worpswede, admittedly, was supposed to have been your commencement on a new path. And you had *tried,* oh, she could have little idea how *hard* you had tried or how defenseless you'd been against the allurement of the two sisterly girls in white—and your heart still harboring Lou all that time. Then, with a perplexing jolt, had come the knowledge of Paula's secret engagement. And you felt yourself snap to consciousness. As if you'd been dreaming and something heavy had dropped upon you where you lay. Nothing to do after such disorientation but correct your veering path. That meant Schmargendorf and Lou.

The train leaps back into day—a blinding dazzle of color—then blackness sucks the light away. Blackness, blackness, another brief blaze of light, blackness again. And now in that void it seems the train could be going nowhere at all. Seems the mountain's core has halted the train and these maddening fibrillations are no more than spasms of a violently failing machine.

But you go burrowing into the heart of the mountain, deeper. The mountain weighs upon you in stone, in dirt, the leaden abundance of minerals . . . *and I am a soft slow-moving boneless thing and I am ground between earth and stone.* . . . The long southbound journey entails a thousand such tunnels.

Finally: Torino. But the city is airless, unseasonable, dusty, as stifling as the carriage. You wander the parched streets in a daze and at last the great exhalation of twilight begins and it is eight o'clock. Time to rattle onward.

It wasn't that you'd expected, in returning to her, to find the Lou of Wolfratshausen. Not at all, for you'd not been lovers since Saint Petersburg, where with sudden severity she had denied you the warmth of her bed. But neither, in Schmargendorf, did you expect *that* Lou to greet you—that steely Saint Petersburg Lou who had left you to your bleak, city-locked solitude for nearly a month while she journeyed alone to Finland and back. And yet there you were in Schmargendorf, alurk once more at the outer limits of her affection. Loiterer between lives.

She was right to be disappointed in you. Of course. You had turned back from uncertainty for nothing more than the comforts of a past now inaccessible. And now work evaded you. With keepsakes from your travels you set up a modest Russian corner in your Misdroyerstrasse room, but still nothing. No steering landward once adrift. One forswore the harbor at one's first launch. Lou knew it to be so.

Onward through the endless tunneled night and then, at last—Genoa, where you will sleep before traveling further. And now you are shambling from the station through the midnight streets, no moon above to illumine the winding lanes. In the lobby of a little hotel, garish electric light sizzles on walls and tile floor. The people here can only offer you a very small room. "*Very* small," says the clerk, shrugging. "But it is a room. All the hotels are crowded like this."

A narrow Genoese cell. One tiny window sits high in the wall opposite the door. You must stand on the bed to get the window open. It resists, then groans free just enough to admit a minuscule breeze. Through the long night you toss on the tough mattress. Memory screams, sends you tearing backward. Still in a clamor of metal on metal, you are burrowing into some black core.

On a bitter Schmargendorf midnight, you wrote in your diary: *"Who knows how many such, afflicted with this in-between existence, live and perish in lunatic asylums?"*

And yet you'd not abandoned Worpswede entirely, not by any means, for you and Clara Westhoff had been corresponding fervidly since your departure from the moors. And though you could not foresee it, two months later Clara would arrive alone at your Schmargendorf door. Then another two months and you would find yourself standing in her family's dining room murmuring vows. Your seed already fertile within her.

A wake again and squinting at the light streaming through the high window. Where are you? . . . Ah yes, Genoa. Downstairs the breakfast room bristles with tourists—brightly dressed, ostentatious holidaymakers, every last one of them flagrantly imported from the north. Loud German speakers, all, locked in talk of business and other everyday matters. So you are but a drop in a stream of sightseers pouring toward the Italian Riviera. A waiter addresses you in German before you can utter a greeting.

It continues in the late-morning train toward the coastal villages: German boiling up and down the car. German gestures, German laughter, German cuffs and German brooches. You remain cloistered in a window seat with a big French newspaper spread before you. A porous barrier, for their natter bleeds through:

—Oh, Nervi is a charming little place. This will be our fourth year in a row. Won't it, dear? Our fourth! And isn't it strange to think how many people go there these days? We feel as if we discovered it first. Now it's so . . . so popularized, you know. But in spite of that—and in spite of the Italians, who can be horrendous—it's terribly pretty. . . .

Nervi—Rapallo—Sestri Levanti: the names of villages dropping with the utmost urbanity from mouth after mouth. Perhaps it signals some slim good fortune, however, that nobody has mentioned Santa Margherita. . . .

You arrive at noon. At first the village looks almost beautiful. But the one good hotel beside the sea—replete with a lush garden—is without vacancy, overrun by Germans. And no fleeing for friendlier climes today, not in this state of exhaustion. You've escaped Paris for your health, you remind yourself. Best to settle down a while, collect your energies. By relative luck you manage to find a room in a rather derelict hotel. Weird pyramidal chamber in what used to be the attic. A slack little bed, a lamp, a washstand, and that is all.

In the barren garden on the hotel's seaward side you claim a deck chair in full sunlight. All else must be put out of mind. You must *feel* the sun's warmth, smell the salt air, breathe the rhythmic lullaby of the sea.

An hour passes. The sensation of arrival does not arrive.

And now you can't help feeling dolorous. Can't help noticing how metallic the water looks, how wretchedly *scenic* everything is—as if this place has been fashioned in desperate mimicry of some Riviera postcard. A slight warm wind sends a number of fallen magnolia leaves rasping husklike over the gravel. Horribly hollow sound.

At dinner there are at least fifty in the dining room. And they want a piece of you, the ones seated closest.

"Where do you hail from?" asks a thin-chinned lady at your elbow.

"Paris," you answer. But what a mistake, for now she needs an explanation.

"But you are German, yes? Austrian, I see. And how did you come to live in Paris? A poet! Oh, what a delight! And might I have seen some of your books? And let me tell you about the books that I have recently read. And isn't Paris magnificent? And did you see Versailles? Did you see Chantilly? Did you see the Louvre?"

Gobble your food, excuse yourself, fly from the hotel into the evening. But after hurrying out to the seashore you merely suffer a sense of contamination, heavy and unshakable, as happens whenever circumstance compels you to prattle. And this night, while solitary, is hardly a comfort. In the gauzy moonlight the sea is coquettish, demeaned to harlotry by the day's long demands.

You already know you cannot stay in Santa Margherita, so here is what you will do: tomorrow morning write to the good Signora Malfatti at the Hotel Florence in Viareggio, remember yourself to her from your enjoyable tenancy a few years back, inquire about vacancies. Yes, good. Good to have a plan.

Next morning, up early with a chill. Best to get out for a walk, best to warm yourself in the Ligurian sun. You follow a road along the waterline. Dust and morning heat, the southern blaze already thickening. Every few minutes a carriage comes clapping past, burthened with German sunseekers, a swirl of road-powder lifted behind. Flurry of German jabber. On a railway running beside the road, two trains thunder along in less than half an hour. You must stop and plug your ears and turn your back to the tide of dust.

A surge with sudden action, you return to the hotel, pack your things, pay your bill, and find yourself on the one-thirty train for Viareggio. Flight within flight, as shall be your pattern for years to come. Yet somehow, on this particular journey, you know something lies ahead. Know yourself to be fleeing *toward* it . . .

The village is Sunday-bright as your cab rolls along the lanes from the station. Sunlight as pure and clean as milk. Sheer blue sky yawning above the countless red-tile roofs. Girls traipse the streets arm in arm. Fishermen warble age-old nautical songs. And beyond it all, the sea: blue-green horizon rising halfway up the firmament, alive in its soothing heave and sigh. The driver draws up before a newly built hotel.

"Hotel Florence, Signore."

"Florence?"

"*Sì,* you want Hotel Florence, *sì?*"

"Yes, but this is not—I mean the Hotel Florence I want is over—"

"Sold. That place sold."

"Sold?"

"*Sì.*"

"And what is it called now?"

"That other? Il Sirene."

"Il Sirene."

"*Sì.* If you will step down, Signore, I will give you your bag."

But you do not move.

"Signore?"

"Wait," you say. "I'm not certain I—please wait. *Un momento.*"

You sit very still in the cab. You see how clearly the images have formed in your mind already: the good balcony room that enabled so much when you were last here, the unique sea-view from that terrace, the hotel garden and its immense quietude. Always a mistake to begin hoping too hard about such things, allowing the memories to coalesce to firmness. Always a mistake. Yet you're lost to the hope already. And what disordered reality must be faced now? *But it's not all that strange,* you tell yourself, *a different room, yes, but it is still Viareggio, still the same sea.* . . .

Now a thin womanly figure comes doddering up the path from the hotel, one hand indicating the cab, a bevy of inquisitive Italian streaming forth. The driver explains the troubled caprice of his passenger. The lady puts her face into the car.

"The *signore* desires the Hotel Florence, *sì?*"

It is Signora Malfatti. In a reflex, you seize her hand, babbling to recall yourself to her.

She listens. Soon her eyes brighten. "Of course, now I'm remembering. The young writer, *sì?* Of course! It took me only a moment."

She is wonderful. So you pay the driver and allow the *signora* to lead you inside. The old hotel was too damp, she explains. Sold last year. This one has much better light, you will see. And you're in luck, she tells you, for a balcony room is ready now.

Within moments you're standing in a long chamber, chapel-like for its two close walls and vaulted ceiling. A marble veranda gives onto rolling green sea. Good simple furniture—no desk, but you intend to hire a beach hut and spend most days in the sandy warmth down at the shoreline.

"Dinner at seven in the dining room," says the good *signora*. "It is a pleasure to see you again, Herr Rilke." And in a slow flutter she is gone.

Almost immediately the exhaustion returns. Weariness of arrival— but somewhere beneath that: a good measure of hope.

> *"Dear Clara: For now . . . I will think on nothing, only catch my breath with a hundred mouths. . . . Already again I feel my solitude a little, and know that it will deny me nothing if I listen to it with new strength."*

The relief of arrival has not erased potential dangers from your thoughts. Coming down for dinner, then, you're not surprised to find the situation bad.

A dining room as packed as the one in Santa Margherita last night. Three round tables alive in a pandemonium of foreign chatter. The serving-boy seats you beside a red-complexioned lady with heavy jowls. Her roanish hair is done up in schoolgirl braids, though she looks to be at least seventy. She is prattling away to a gentleman at her side, but interrupts herself to swivel toward you with an appraising look. *"Guten Tag!"* she blurts—then shifts to an unaccountably accented stream of Italian. You can distinguish only a few words. The lady stops herself and begins again in French, phrases no less aslant, but intelligible enough: *"Excusez-mois, mais je ne parle pas Alle-*

mand—we have it that you are German, you see. I'm from Scotland myself, but perhaps French will prove mutual? *Oui? Vous comprenez?*"

"*Oui, je comprends.*"

"*Très bien.* We could speak English, I suppose, but it seems a dreadful bore when one is abroad."

She does not ask whether you speak English. Leaning close with a conspirator's tone, she murmurs, "These silly souls behind us are just the type I mean. Not to mention this fellow on my other side. Bores, aren't they? I'm sure they think us terrifically exotic, just flapping away *en Français*—one ought to tell them it's merely a matter of education, don't you think?"

The two other tables, you realize now, are roaring up a single horrendous conversation, bandying jokes about in their flat Germanic tongue. Ten or twelve in number, they appear to be the members of an English tour group.

"Don't you lump me as one of them, monsieur, don't you dare. It's said that my people and theirs keep a common language—I've never believed that myself. Anyway, Scotland is a glory to their drab little kingdom, no soul who's been both places would doubt it."

The lady goes on. Your mouth being full, she seems to judge herself at liberty to soliloquize. But at length she says, "Tell me, what part of Germany are you from?"

What complexity in the question. Better to deflect. "Munich," you answer, and take a quick bite before she can volley again.

"I'm from Edinburgh. It's the loveliest of cities, Edinburgh, and I've seen Paris, Venice, Seville, Constantinople—oh, I won't bore you with the names of all the wonderful places I've been. Barcelona. Kiev. New York. And are you making a holiday in Viareggio?"

You supply the affirmative, terse and blunt—but still she attends in mannerly supper-table style, and it seems inexcusably curt not to give her something more. "I've come for my health," you add.

"I could see it about you," the lady replies, sitting back a bit as if to view you better. "I hope it won't offend you, but as soon as you sat down I knew you had come south to *reconstitute,* as they say. You do look gray in the cheeks. But don't worry, this southern sun does wonders. Anyway, I know the signs because my late husband . . ."

So the dinner goes, and the Scotswoman cannot see what trouble she causes you, gray-faced traveler at her side, painfully eager for the silence of arrival.

"That was abominable," you write to Clara later that night.

". . . I constantly drew the thickest lines under my silence. It helped nothing. She always caught hold again and wouldn't stop to let me free."

Hereafter, you will take dinner in your room.

The days pass. The poet walks along a margin of tawny sand soft as cinnamon, his body no more than a ferule entubed in a rented bathing costume—cotton tank top and knee breeches patterned with bars of red and black. The whole stretch of beach lies remarkably clear of seaweed or other bracken. Clear of people too, the farther he goes beyond the fishermen hunched at their tangled nets.

At Rainer's back, on the higher sand above the tideline, stands his rented beach hut, tiny in the distance, its peaked straw roof improbably yellow against the green background of the village *pineta.* Beneath the straw awning, two books lie on a small table: the Bible and Jacobsen's *Niels Lyhne*—that prophetic novel the poet has loved for half a decade now.

Shunning propriety, Rainer peels his bathing tunic down to a flange of lifeless cotton about his waist. The bronzing touch of the sun on his chest is a blessing too great to resist for fear of scandalizing whatever English ladies may happen by.

Partly stripped, he appears a waif, a figure half eroded. His chest falls in steep concavity at the sternum, as though some drain has been unstoppered and his every part is whirling toward that center. The elbows erupt from his forearms like sheathed bolts. Knees like linchpins in the axles of his slight thighs.

Soon he's adopted a morning ritual of bathing nude from the farthest curve of the beach. Noontime, he shades up in the cool awning sand with Jacobsen or Job. A warm marine wind tousles the pages as it tousles his hair. Come dusk, the fierce southern sun drops straight into the sea and the countless fishing boats that have dotted the distant waters all day begin to swell closer, drifting shoreward like leaves in a tipped pool. With eventide, Rainer enjoys a silent supper on his terrace. Fruit and milk and, later, tea. Twilight songs float up from the lanes below him, sung by the village matrons and their daughters.

The solitary weeks unfurl. Day by day the instrument of loneliness gets purified in this metallurgy of sun and silence, and all the time Rainer feels his health improving. Feels himself extracted, degree by degree, from the frenzied dream of Paris.

On fifth April in Viareggio, he writes his second letter to the earnest young Franz Xaver Kappus. *"In the deepest and most important things,"* the letter avows, *"we are namelessly alone."*

Still, a strange friction remains inside him; he is not wholly recovered. But perhaps a knife, when laid to its whetstone, feels the same. For there's something *positive* in the friction now. Discomfort of an additive sort and no longer that feeling of abrasion, deterioration.

"Dear Clara: Quietly, utterly quietly, a feeling of wholeness already sometimes attaches itself—like I have not known for years. . . . I feel that I must draw my strength up from the ground anew, but I feel also that this labor is possible here, if I have patience and believe."

Not since writing those second "Russian Prayers" a year and a half ago at Westerwede has Rainer felt so inexplicably uplifted. And before that, when? Oh, yes: the day Clara arrived at his Schmargendorf rooms. February 1901, the world still seized in frost. But the sun lay like hot milk on the civic lawns. The grass blades steamed. He had weathered the whole of the dismal winter. Had weathered Lou's disaffection. And there stood Clara Westhoff in the light of his window. Her sculptress hands were moving with great attention from one to another of his Russian trinkets.

She was talking in her modest way, her voice vivid with something more than words. The small room turning redolent as if she emitted some alluring balm. Then, inexplicably, though her back was turned, something had pulled him across the carpeted floor and he was engulfing her from behind. His nose burrowing at that narrow nape where her upgathered hair lay wispy and dark—the spot from which that sweet scent originated.

How Clara trembled, he remembers. It was more ardency than surprise. And how quickly she clutched his hands and pulled his arms tighter around her.

With collisional violence, a noise of fury, the weather changes in Viareggio. The blue fleece of Ligurian sky is suddenly metalized. An El Greco horizon comes down like a falling ax blade, all color cut away and the boiling swarth of offshore storms darkening everything with a premature dusk. Light streams its exit through the shutters of the clouds—the sun occluded with great nocturnal plumes, sinister forms vulturine and skeletal. A clattering wind. The waters leaping up. Fistfuls of sand flung like fear.

Rainer flees to the sanctuary of his room and there becomes captive to a storm-locked loneliness, drear encores in his theater of memory: February 1901. He and Clara clung fast to each other like swimmers finally avowing the water they'd been treading for months. Their four-month letters, tumbling back and forth between Schmargendorf and Worpswede, had carried them toward those moments, but only now, perhaps, did they both understand the longing that had welled. It was overspilling them. The poet's room, with its candlelit Russian shrine, wrapped itself around their shape-shifting figures. Young friends quietly becoming lovers. Inevitable metamorphosis. Before long, in that hinged space where their bodies now silently met, a daughter would crystallize. . . .

Five days after Clara's Schmargendorf visit Rainer was packing his things. Dismantling his Russian shrine with a feeling of ceremony, conscious of the greater dismantling denoted by the act. Then he called on Lou.

"I'm leaving tomorrow," he told her, and gave the news of his new love. "I mean to marry her."

And he stood watching the color drain from Lou's face. It was something like the fearful look she'd shown in Wolfratshausen on the day he refused to walk by the acacia.

Silence between them.

Lou stepped closer. Her scent embraced him. Her dark look seemed to dive into his eyes. She said, "You're making this choice."

The words scraped down across him: the blade-teeth of her anger, her horror. *What did she feel?* It seemed she was speaking to someone else. For all the moment's pain, he was not surprised that she should fail to understand. She'd helped him to such pure independence that perhaps he could only become strange to her in the end.

"We should destroy our letters," she said.

This startled him. For a moment he was at a loss to respond. Then quietly he concurred.

Two full days battened down in his room and still the storm does not abate. Rainer's claustrophobia drives him out of doors. He walks through a tattered drizzle to the *pineta,* takes refuge in the cathedraled glades where the high tapering trunks clash and creak.

The rain lets up for a while, but an unnerving wind whistles warm and electric through the forest. Somehow the carpet of yellow pine needles is not ruffled. The poet wanders barefoot in that midday twilight—tranquil pocket of the storm's heart. Humidity high and febrile. A shadowless atmosphere. He plants his feet and gazes upward into the tossing heights of the pines and his earth is but a vessel skating side to side on a sea of hours. He but a passenger.

Lou had pressed a narrow slip of paper into his hand. And suddenly he was outside. He had left her. Had left *her!*—yes, but her gestures of months before had brought it to this. *She* was the banisher yet. Her door clicked shut behind him and he was walking back through the Schmargendorf streets to the rooms he would vacate come morning. He was staring at the paper in his palm. An old milk bill. On the back: her cold comfort scribbled down.

> *'If some time, much later, you are in a very bad way, there's a home with us for your grimmest hour.'*

He would burn all her letters. As she'd asked him to. But this scrap of paper he knew he'd keep.

Next morning he left Schmargendorf for the second and final time.

He has asked that Signora Malfatti have a small table brought to his room. Now he sits with the double doors open to his terrace and the rage of the storm outside, and something, perhaps some dark storm-like blood, is pumping inward. Inward. He is pounding pounding pounding through mountain rock, clenched in the steely canister of a train car as it burrows through blackness. And how much ancient rock stands piled upon the frangible sense-heavy heart inside his chest? How can such a heart hold? How? And how break?

He writes:

"I am still inexperienced in the pains of labor,—
so this great darkness makes me small;
if it is You, though: be heavy upon me, break in:
that I might experience your whole hand on me
and you the wholeness of my cries."

Sheltered there with the village of Viareggio battened and ravaged below him, Rainer gives release to the rage of new work. The sea rising up in turmoil whenever he looks out. And though he writes of Paris terrors, he is caroming backward past the furious city streets, past Rodin and past Clara, past his daughter and Worpswede and Paula—back to his bright storm of a time with Lou: in Russia, in early Schmargendorf, and in those first strange and potent "Russian Prayers." Rainer the twenty-four-year-old poet garbed in blue Russian tunic at Lou's kitchen table in Schmargendorf where he and she bent their heads together in a marvelous foment of study, full of plans and anticipations for their second Russian journey. In the parlor beyond the kitchen door, Friedrich Andreas was absorbed in his own silent work. His wife's coveted attention lay with Rainer alone, and soon Rainer would show her the first upswelling of his "Russian Prayers." No frigid Saint Petersburg had yet come between them, no Worpswede spells bewitched his heart. There was just Lou and work and nothing else.

Only with Lou was a time like that possible. And the chance of such a time lies lost behind him now. Rainer's months in Paris, adrift on the hard terrain of the city as on some desperate plateau of his heart, have driven home this loss. Henceforth work shall be his sole protection. But he knows work, *real work* of the kind he's accomplishing now, to come only rarely. . . .

Seven days at your table in Viareggio and thirty-four poems arise in that same monkish voice that spoke in Schmargendorf and later Westerwede. But now the voice is astray in rampant fear as in a flood. The voice speaks of city squalor, ignorant death, children sallow as sapped flowers, beggars and skeleton-folk and broken bits of humanity strewn amongst garbage and gnawed bones. And you seem to feel yourself listening as a novitiate would. For this is the voice of something beyond you.

To create is to hearken; perhaps that's true after all, perhaps one must *wait* for whatever will arrive, despite the stern edict of perpetual work gleaned from your days in Rodin's presence.

All the time during this frenzied discharge, Lou's last words are redoubling themselves in your heart and head. The words of that *"Letzter Zuruf,"* that "Last Shout" of hers, dashed out in a spill of ink across two disheveled pages. You held the pages in your hands just weeks after your engagement to Clara. It was a letter, and yet there was no "Dear Rainer" and no farewell at the paper's bottom edge, no "Love, Lou." Nothing. Just the ominous heading: "Last Shout," and then that scarring of words. Lou ripping herself free. Confessing how you'd weighed her down.

'I . . . *went along next to you only automatically, mechanically, could no longer spare my full warmth. . . . After Wolfratshausen I had still to grow, to grow further and further until . . . strange as it sounds: I had come into my youth! For the first time now, I am young; for the first time now I'm allowed to be what others become at eighteen: completely myself. . . . To you*

I say: go the same way toward your dark God! he can do for you what I can do no longer . . . he can bless you with light and maturity. Over vast, vast distances I send this shout your way: I can do nothing more than this to guard you from the most grim and testing hour. . . . That's why I was so moved when we said goodbye that I wrote those last words down . . . because I could not speak them out. I meant all those words.'

Thirty-four poems written and the rain still pounding Viareggio. From the terrace threshold you watch the thrashing curtains, the cadmium spray on the darkened tile roofs.

And nothing like relief inside you, though this work is done. No, for this storm of work has somehow punctured the patch of health these recent weeks had furnished you. Fear again—as though you'd never left Paris at all . . .

Your hands begin moving amongst your paper now. Slowly, with an automatic air, the hands spread out a fresh sheaf. You watch them. They seem to have a will of their own. Your writing hand tapping the excess ink from your nib. It moves to the page and begins:

Dear Lou,

—a year and a half since you've written such words, but now in a torrent the others follow:

I've come back to Viareggio. Back to this place which proved such a reprieve from the staggering riches of Florence five years ago. Florence, which quickly became too resplendent, too much like a fugue, while my young heart wanted to hearken to just one thing: your voice, Lou, solitary and pure. I found it here, your voice. I remember that: how I lived with it in a new and richer silence. . . . I say my heart was young then. You might think that strange, but I say it with great sincerity. For in the time since we last spoke, Lou, my heart has out-aged me. . . .

Stop now. Sit back. Lay your pen down beside the paper. Wait . . . but wait for what? You needn't send the letter after all. You'll read it over first, then decide. And if you do determine to send it, you'll recopy it before.

So you lift the pen, start again:

Dear Lou,

I am laid low—after months of lassitude and quailing health—laid low again, this time by the folly of all I hoped for in my hurried travels south. You see, I must have believed a younger man, a younger self, to be lingering here in this village. Must have told myself I could journey backward to a different life in which I was heartsick for but one thing only and not for a thousand things. For but one thing that I knew with utter clarity (you must see, even now, what I mean by this)—and not for a thousand things I can perhaps never know. . . .

And now I see you shaking your head, Lou. And I know what you are thinking. You are right as always. It should be no wonder we have not met again, that younger man and I. His heart bore blessings I can barely recall. . . .

Dear Lou,

My road is winding as never before. How can I explain the way Paris displaced me? For a time, alone in the city, I clung to the thought that all would be better once my wife arrived. But when she arrived I saw only what a stranger Paris had made of me. . . .

Can it surprise you that I am writing to you once more—after such long silence between us? Can you blame me for my need to draw the letters of your name in the sand of this desert stretching before me?

The younger man is gone. A different man speaks to you now. You will forgive him for coming to you if it seems premature. You must forgive him, Lou. He remembers a vow you once wrote on a scrap of paper. During his recent troubles it was those words (on that paper he still keeps) that stood out for him, stood out as though from the surface of his heart in which they've long been etched. . . . And somehow, some-

how, Lou, this man—despite the strange cankers that disfigure his spirit—this man knows *you. Perhaps you are the* only *thing he knows. . . .*

Dear Lou . . .

Now the letter leaves you crumpled in its fist. Something has dropped away, and you see there's no saying these things to her. Not yet. But still it's clear to you, somehow, that in this whispering attempt you have commenced upon a new path, new work, for which your final monkish prayers, just written, are mere preparation. Yes, for you will *make* something of Paris for Lou, will take those long bleak months and craft from them moments that will awe her: moments sublime with misery or fright, but sublime all the same. *Sublime.* She can't be approached in any lesser way.

Crumple the letter. The hour hasn't come, but you will return to her in time, for it's from *her* that all your future paths shall branch. The proper account will burgeon darkly within you by the day. You will wait.

From Viareggio Rainer writes his third letter to Franz Xaver Kappus. A message of new jubilation:

"Everything *is germination and then bearing forth. . . . To wait, with deep humility, for the arrival-hour of new clarity: this alone is called artistic life: in understanding as in creating. . . . I learn it daily, learn it in pain to which I am thankful.* Patience *is everything!"*

A brief letter arrives from Paris. Auguste Rodin offers the poet staid and cordial thanks for the copy of the Rodin book Clara has presented on her husband's behalf. It's clear to Rainer that mere etiquette has prompted this gesture, and it saddens him to be reminded that the monograph's profound understanding, bedded in German as it is, will remain inaccessible to the Master.

"Dear Clara: This much is certain, that I will first of all return to Paris . . . it seems to me, always, as though Paris must still give me a work. . . . Each must find the center of his life in his work, and grow outward from there in radial manner, as far as the work will go."

First May 1903, Rainer arrives again in the tangled streets of the Quartier Latin. Again Paris oppresses him. The tenuous health regained in Italy quickly feels jeopardized in the city. The grippe symptoms begin to resurface. Back there, in the last bright Viareggio days, he was sure of his recovery, his new resolve, the steadfast work that awaited him here, but now the weeks drag past and very little seems to be happening.

Neither can Clara bear the city much longer. Together they begin making plans. The sculptress may win a grant enabling her to work and study antiquity in Rome as Rodin has advised. The Master himself has written a letter recommending her. But even if the grant should not be won, she will go. And Rainer will accompany her.

First: a summer together in Worpswede, a season spent close to little Ruth, long overdue. Then, come September: south again . . .

two

ROOTLESS:

1903–1904

Try it. Go away and think nothing of a homecoming. Go as one likes to go by the sea in the night, farther and farther out under the many silent stars. Try it.

Florence Diary, 1898

A damp back room of Heinrich Vogeler's Barkenhoff. The little chamber can boast but one narrow window, panes of old leaden glass depleting the daylight to a watery yellow. And the trunk of a massive tree further obscures all but a patch of that outer world. Hunched at a desk before the casement, a lamp lit beside him though it's barely past noon, Rainer finds himself in the midst of correspondence with Lou. Two years of silence becoming gradually erased.

Back in Paris in the late spring, while the trees along the Seine embankments swelled green and whisperous, Rainer had stood in a crowded art house, mystified by an ancient Italian painting. In antique pigments the painting showed a man and a woman in audience. The woman sat poised in folds of regal drapery, her chin uplifted, her noble mouth closed in hearkening. The man stood before her in frayed traveling garments, his sandals bleached with highway dust, hands folded atop a pilgrim staff. By his posture it was clear that the man had come to this lady with purpose, in order to speak the things he now spoke. To tell her of his journeys. But he was not there to stay. He would continue onward. This lady was a destination, yes—but not a destiny, for this traveler had long since surrendered the notion of arrival. He would tell his tale and be gone again, maybe he didn't know where.

For weeks afterward, Rainer carried that image inside him, resisting and delaying though the image bespoke so much—and finally toward the close of June he dispatched a missive to Lou from Paris, a few timid lines hazarding his ardent request:

> *"During July and August this summer I will be in Germany. . . . If only once during this time, for a single day, I should be permitted to take refuge near you! I don't know if that is possible."*

Now beyond the closed door at the poet's back the Barkenhoff fairly shudders with the ululations of Vogeler's firstborn daughter. No longer the placid household that had once sheltered Rainer. Hard to believe in those harmonious Sunday gatherings of three years ago: the Worpswede *family* convening in the white-walled parlor downstairs. They seem a congress of ghosts, something imagined, something that never was. Is every chapter of life destined to become inscrutable once a person leafs forward through the days? But now Rainer recalls the fracas of carousal, the smoke-palled Barkenhoff dances that had caused him alienation even back then. So maybe this house was always somewhat foreign to him, maybe its master was ever a stranger, as Vogeler bewilderingly seems these days: once-promising painter diverted by domestic trifles, stealing a few moments here or there to dash off his fairy-tale pictures, all of them the same.

Rainer had felt his heart beating at the backs of his eyes as he sent his tentative plea to Lou from Paris. Was it still too soon to entreat permission to come to her? He couldn't quite know. Too much had happened. Harder, by the day, to be sure of anything at all—but perhaps that alone was the reason the entreaty must be sent. For there *was* the danger he might wait too *long,* his troubles intensifying to the point of paralysis. So the letter went drifting toward Schmargendorf, and Rainer, in hand-clamping distraction, waited. Then promptly (thank God!) came Lou's reply: a very short note. Rainer was of course welcome to come to her, she assured him. But wouldn't it be better if they first wrote to one another for a while?

So for hours now, while the gloomy Barkenhoff reverberates with the terrors of a thunderous barefoot child, Rainer has bent across this sheaf of blue letter paper, striving to fashion his recent anguish into equivalencies of language.

"I'd like to say to you, dear Lou, that Paris was for me an experience like the military school. Just as a huge fright astonished me back then, so now again I was gripped by that sense of horror before everything which, in unsayable confusion, is called life."

Rainer pours out Paris to her; pours out the hospitals and the sick people and the wandering harridans who carried in their hands the sordid things they hoped to sell, never realizing that nobody would want such things. He pours out the man on the boulevard Saint Michel, that spasmodic figure whose own fierce nerves chucked him along and then threw him down on the bridge.

"Had I been able to make those fears which I so experienced, had I been able to form things out of them . . . But they stood up within me and carried themselves against me, and I could not get around them. . . . Instead of using my willpower to make them into things, *I just gave them their own separate life which they turned against me and with which they chased me far into the night . . . Had all been better, quieter and friendlier, had my room been loyal to me and had I stayed healthy, perhaps I would have been able, then, to make things out of fear."*

But already, as these recent troubles wring him out into words, Rainer senses a seed of some kind nestling into rich soil. Senses it very dimly and cannot say what it means. Something in the making . . . Are they seeds then, these words that drop from him after so much squeezing? And what will grow of such seeds?

.   .   .

With Clara the poet travels the few miles from Worpswede to Oberneu-land to see Ruth. Under the thatched roof of the Westhoff family's large country manor the little daughter lives in the care of her grandparents.

Rainer and Clara, after some discussion, have deemed it best not to thrust themselves upon the child, not to overtake her with tenderness, for they'll no doubt seem strangers to her at first. So they come slowly into the parlor where Ruth awaits them, seat themselves side by side on the sofa, remain very still and quiet while their daughter subjects them to her steady gaze.

At a year and eight months, she's a wholly different child than the one Rainer last laid eyes upon. And yet she's wholly familiar too: large-eyed and low-mouthed, reflecting to him the daughterly René Maria. Mirror-child, she seems to have stepped from some mysterious chamber of Rainer's soul, and it moves him powerfully to look upon her. She has long dark locks which her grandmother has adorned with yellow ribbons. Eyes blue and beautiful. She hangs back in a swaying bowlegged stance, half en-gulfed in Grandmother's skirts, circumspect as a judge. She cannot yet converse, but with soft slurred musicality she seems to be reasoning aloud about the trustworthiness of these visitors before her.

"She might as well have never seen you before," says Papa Westhoff, standing by in the parlor door. Comment blunt and accusatory. He appears to realize his unsubtle subtext, murmurs, "But she'll warm to you."

A long half hour of silence. The awe pulls tight behind Rainer's breast-bone. This delicate creature a powerful part of him, a vibrant tone in the humming chord of his body. He wants to take her up and cradle her fast. But he knows he mustn't cheat her of the life she's come to assume here, with all its unspoken loyalties.

Ruth's babble gradually brightens. At length she unclutches her grandmother's skirts to dawdle here and there upon the carpet, safely distant yet. Closer. And finally she approaches. She drums an exuberant palm at Clara's knee, turns to look up at Rainer, lets her mouth drop hugely and sends him the lively salutation of her squeal. Everybody laughs their relief. This startles the child. She takes on a look of suspicion. Only when the grown-ups have suppressed the laughter does she gain back her confidence; then she gives them all a crushing smile.

Rainer reaches to touch her hair. A strand of it silking across two fingers, weightless and fine. He believes he can feel, for a moment then, his fatherhood. A thing within him, put there by some great and governing hand. It's that tightening in his chest, a kind of breathlessness. Ruth turns her big gaze upward and locks her blue eyes on his and makes a crooning dovelike sound.

"Did you hear her?" says Clara. "She sees herself."

"What?"

"In your eyes. She sees herself."

Rainer listens as the child makes the sound again. "Roooz," she intones. "Roooz." Her tiny hands stretching out, fingers spread to graze his beard, her awestruck stare diving up into his eyes.

"Yes," he tells her. "That's you. That's little Ruth in my eyes."

For the rest of the day Rainer and Clara are the girl's sole distractions. She has a great many things she wants to show them and leads them trotting about the lush grounds that border the house. By evening she's taken to calling Clara "Muzzer." Rainer, for some virtue unknown to himself, earns his own endearment a few mornings later, waking to the child's voice, her small stout face very close at his bedside, blue eyes afire.

"Man!" she blurts, and fists a parcel of his hair as though to mimic his own fatherly gesture on the day of their reacquaintance. "Gooth Man!"

She presses her face to his scalp. Rainer lifts his head and her soft cheek brushes his jaw. The smell of her childish breath rich with buttermilk or porridge, and beneath that the more general fragrance of her childhood, her fresh limbs well browned from the hours upon hours she spends outdoors in good weather. Inexpressible, the blessing of having his daughter close like this, of being recognized by her. She gives him something like a home-feeling. So remote from him, in Paris, have such feelings been. Come September, though, he and Clara will take their leave. Life has ordered it of them.

At the far perimeter of the Westhoff acreage the full-throttled Hamburg trains screech past with rhythmic regularity. Deep in the black morning hours Rainer lies listening to their transit. Rome awaits. And something more: new work, of which he can dimly perceive the first thread; far out in some unlit grotto of his being its frayed end is waving. He cannot know yet what sort of work it will be, but he knows he must reach it, knows the reaching of it is all he can do in this world, and knows he cannot reach it from where he lies. No, the going will engender everything—for out there, abroad, he will have surrendered all that belongs to him, will have so steepened the pitch of his own destiny that it would be impossible for *nothing* to happen.

Yet can one move on past need of a home?

Another morning little Ruth comes to him in the breezy garden, sent to deliver the sealed letter clutched in her fist. He takes her into his lap. "And what is this?"

A Berlin postmark. His name in Lou's hand.

"Man!" says Ruth. "Man!"—watching from his embrace as he unseals the envelope, unfolds the two thin sheets. Her hands beat gently at the paper as he reads in silence.

All will be well, Lou writes. His recent letter communicated such powerful impressions of Paris that she found herself forgetting him entirely as she read, lost to his images. Already, she tells him, he's begun to master the fears he faced in that great city—his letter was his own unwitting testament to this triumph. And so he was mistaken to think that nothing had come of these fears. They were there in the letter, already transformed into art. Does Rainer remember, Lou wonders, how she told him during their Wolfratshausen days that his work would emerge from all the dark residue of his time at the Kadettenschule and before? Now, at last, it's begun. Paris has stirred it up. *'The poet in you writes poems of mankind's fears.'*

Rainer sits gazing at the bottom of the second sheet where she has signed herself. That blessed name, *Lou*.

He's like someone awakening now. He looks about. Somehow Ruth has wriggled free of his arms. She's gone.

You pass your weeks in this north German countryside as in the landscape of a former life. Your letters to Lou continue, and with each one you build something for her; each one gives voice to an undercurrent of your soul, returns you to yourself. And out of Lou branches your pathway back from the place where you've been lost.

Meanwhile, this whole moorland world seems altered around you. You feel yourself a sleeper dizzied with a long dream in which memories shift shape, distort, refuse to function accurately. All this was really your home for a time? The land, two-voiced, shouts *Yes!* and *No!* at once.

"O Lou," you write on eighth August, *"in a single poem that seems to me successful there is much more reality than in any relationship or affection I feel. Where I create, I am real, and I want to find the strength to ground my life wholly upon this truth."*

And for Franz Xaver Kappus, whose latest anxious letter you received in Paris upon your return from Italy, you again assume the role of counselor, even as you administer with every written sentence a stern edict to *yourself*:

*"Have patience toward everything unresolved in your heart. . . .
Don't search to draw near to answers now, which could not be given you*

because you cannot live them. . . . Love your solitude, and bear the pain it causes you by making beautiful sounds of your complaint."

Following a few glorious sunlit days the broad moorland sky holds itself closed in a grizzle of humid cloud. The country air crumples, as though jammed into some narrow bag and knotted tight. You feel you must breathe very shallowly, taking care not to exhaust the supply.

In Papa Westhoff's study one afternoon you drink tea with your mother-in-law, Johanna. Sipping compliantly from delicate saucers the serving girl brought in on a tray five minutes ago. Mother Westhoff sits ensconced behind her husband's massive desk, and you before her in a purple Empire chair, awkward and shy as an applicant at his first vetting. Somewhere outside the shut study door, in a realm of the house beyond earshot, Clara and Ruth play one of the child's fantastic games.

"You've noticed," says Johanna, "Father Westhoff is not in the best of health, or he'd speak to you directly." There's an embarrassed quaver in her voice. "You'll forgive him if he's brusque these days. The condition in his blood, you understand, changes his temper a great deal."

"Yes, Mother Westhoff. Though I pray he improves before long."

"Thank you, dear." A plaintive smile flits across her mouth, vanishes. "In any event, the matter at hand concerns me every bit as much as my husband." With an air of great thoughtfulness she lifts her teacup and drinks.

You sit very still, wordless. Wait. In a wavering bush just outside the study window a number of tiny birds huddle together, deep in the shrubbery, holding fast to small tremulous branches as the wind tosses them up and down.

"Rainer, Father Westhoff and I wish—very *earnestly* wish—to understand the course you and Clara are taking up."

"Yes, Mother Westhoff, I—"

"You know, of course, that our daughter has had our support from the beginning. My husband and I have never been the kind to look askance at a life devoted to art. Father Westhoff himself is something of a painter, after all. He can well remember a time when he weighed the prospect of an artist's vocation. That he thought better of it back then is perhaps the reason Clara's situation . . . well, *worries* him now."

"Of course, Mother."

Her careful preface ended, Johanna seems to gain a little comfort. Eases forward in her chair and sets her cup and saucer on the desktop. "I knew I needn't spell it out for you, my dear. And now I think we can leave the question of Ruth as it stands. She's cared for here, and comfortable—and a treasure to her *Großeltern,* as you know."

"We're very thankful to you and Father Westhoff, Mother."

"Of course, dear. Now the main question pertains to you and Clara. I know you won't be unsympathetic to our wish for . . . for assurances."

And so Johanna sits and awaits your word, your assurance. Yes, but how can one give assurance while suffering such a deficit of assurances himself? Were circumstances different, perhaps, you would recount the fortuities lately come to Clara: regular commissions, however small—and now her stipend from the city of Bremen, the encouragement of Rodin, the promise of advancement in Rome—all the things you constantly recount to yourself to twist assurance from your most worrisome hours, but you know these things will not address the parents' main concern. For it's not assurance regarding *Clara* that Mother and Father Westhoff seek.

You could, perhaps, mention Papa's long-standing proposition from Prague: the bank clerkship ever dangling beside you like a safety rope—but you know this would be tantamount to deception, for that rope has long been a noose in your mind.

Johanna says, "Are there prospects of a particular kind awaiting you in Rome, dear?"

"Not just now, I'm afraid."

Your glance demurs to the saucer in your hands: the teaspoon banked at the saucer's edge and your own inverted image elasticized in silver. You mean to say something more, but it escapes you. For suddenly you are remembering those weeks in this house before your wedding: feverish and supine and the ceiling plaster an edgeless blank to your eyes . . .

"That must be dismaying, mustn't it?" says Johanna. And now she looks much smaller, shrunken—the great bulwark of the desk bizarrely enlarged and its edges warping up like fins before her. She leans one thin elbow upon the massive blotter, a kind of hesitant hope in her eyes. "And so difficult too," she says, "to be away from Ruth for so long. Is it really necessary, do you think, to endure these anxieties?"

"It *will* be difficult, of course. It's brought us such happiness to see Ruth. . . ." The tea is trembling in your cup, shrunken swells attending every syllable. "And yet this happiness, I pray, will help us while we're in Rome. We'll hold to the happiness, both of us. Then too, my father . . . my father gives his great assistance now and then. . . ." But now you cannot tell where the thought was headed. Papa's intermittent help is rarely enough for both you *and* Clara.

Johanna still cranes at the desk, listening a long moment, though you've fallen silent. She will not, of course, bring you to suffer the indignity of self-defense, but she needs something more.

"No doubt you can imagine, dear Rainer, how hard it must have been for Father Westhoff to make the choice he did, electing to become a merchant and not a painter. The wisest path is rarely the easiest, as I'm sure you understand. Of course it's not for me to suggest—"

"I've been unwell," you stammer—and again appear those long tangible bars of April daylight pouring in above you as you lay gray-faced and spoon-fed in these rooms. This woman herself coming up from her bent knees with your loaded chamber pot in her hands. "Unwell for some time.

The grippe. And Rome, you see, holds for the moment the hope of better health."

You've had a thousand talks with your own conscience already, but none of them can be repeated here. Some things, deeply true while held within, can only be incomprehensible to people who hear them spoken aloud. Still these truths never change for you, not through thunderous doubt or the warring of the earthly loyalties within you.

"With health comes work," you say. "I made great progress in Italy this spring. I only need a while longer, you see. I intend to accomplish a great deal in Rome."

No, the unutterable truths do not change. In Rome will arrive all that has been imminent for some time now. After the cataclysm of Paris it will surely be work of the greatest kind—what with so much shaken loose inside you, ripe for creation. It is the going that will engender everything. And as you stammer away, you feel yourself blessed to know that Clara understands you at least; yes, so you need not emasculate yourself here. Therefore you look your good Mother Westhoff in the eyes.

"You and Father Westhoff needn't worry, Mother."

"No?" Johanna's chin skewed in the palm of her hand.

"No," you say, for you know this will finish it. Merely a little time and in the course of things they will all find you redeemed. Your work will redeem you. Because it *must*.

Yet who can conceive of the doubts suffered daily by a poet such as you? His silent rages in which hope does war with happenstance? Isn't the truth of the matter just this: that for all his dutiful self-subjection to the path of art, he may fail to attain the necessary command? He may be cursed with a vision far surpassing anything he's been granted the powers to fulfill. He may consecrate himself to a task and pour every strength into an image of eventual attainment and, in spite of devotion, humility, or discipline, meet with the ultimate reproof of his own insufficiency. Oh yes, but always the unshakable conviction remains: you must *say* the world. For if you are not a poet, what *are* you? *Nothing!* comes the booming rebuke— and again and again the world will disappear within you, festering there in nothingness, unexpressed. No choice, then, but to steepen the pitch of your own destiny. No choice but to cast yourself out beyond return—and yes, beyond the warmth of a daughter's nearness—to a place where failure becomes impossible.

In your mind the ardent prayer of Baudelaire is tolling: *Lord God, grant me the grace to produce a few beautiful lines. . . .* You shall understand now and forever the level of despair, the level of danger, from which that prayer is made. It is a daily prayer.

ROME: APRIL 1904. AGE
TWENTY-EIGHT . . .

*N*ine months later now. The city of Rome, which must have been monumentally unreal to its first subjects, is unreal still. It seems to Rainer as though history stumbles to a halt in these swarming streets cluttered with ruins. He finds the Roman atmosphere too deliberately impressive, too photogenic. A world embalmed for the sake of postcards.

For three autumn months he lived alone in the frenzied Via del Compidoglio, neighbor to the Forum. Clara had found her own lodgings in the Villa Strohl-Fern across the city. The famous rubble of the Forum, held sacrosanct though it might be, was yet rubble to Rainer, little more—new kingdoms forbidden forever after to germinate there, all things stymied in homage to an irrelevant past.

So here he is in different lodgings now, a modest garden house in the same park where Clara's been living, near the Villa Borghese. Cottage all his own: a single spartan room serviceable in work, sleep and repast. All through the barren winter he's dwelt in hermitage here, disposed entirely to work and rarely venturing into the city. His cottage stands atop the arch of a small bridge beneath which a pedestrian path runs through the gardens of the Villa Strohl-Fern. In three of Rainer's four walls high windows admit a flood of southern light, and his roof is a broad terrace where he stands by morning, by evening, looking out over the gardens around him to the Roman *campagna,* the horizon a faint ripple of distant mountains.

A humid April day, and Rainer stands barefoot on cool tile, watching a cord of ants erupt black and hard and gleaming from a crack in the plaster of his wall. Beaded bodies fat and frantic. At the peripheries hundreds of others wander in great sprays clear to the ceiling. A moment ago, while sitting at his desk immersed in the furnace of his thoughts, he had felt something bristling beneath his Russian tunic. Then he noticed, in a ray of windowlight, the seething crack.

He tugs at his collar. Down on the floor: a spiraling commotion. Looking closer he finds the tiles boiling, frenzied soldier ants scattered from a column his feet have disturbed. At the front of the column a rank of thousands teems single-mindedly across the tile to the edge of his bookcase. And already the broken regiments have begun to muster forces again, a thick line of them coursing over his foot. They're desperate for water, no doubt—the earth outside prematurely parched, the Roman spring jarred to early summer in recent weeks.

Rainer gets a towel and begins slapping at the floor, the wall. Watches the formations scatter across the plaster in whirling adumbration like the blooming of a huge black bud. These ants are not his first interruption. He's been slapping at distractions small and large for more than a month. His Roman February, immensely fertile time that it was, stands immeasurably distant now, gauzed in lifeless winter colors. His recent weeks sterile, this barren spring swelter so unlike that month of gray abundance, his February of steam baths and shuttered silence and most of all: work. How can such a great shift occur with not even the slightest alteration in lifestyle? Shouldn't that month of solid progress have resulted in *roots* of some kind, something to anchor and stimulate further progress, regardless of distractions to come?

Till February the winter had been a hard unfocused listless time. He'd written numerous letters to Lou at her new home in the German university town of Göttingen and had received one or two in reply. She has christened her new house "Loufried," like their Wolfratshausen cottage of several summers ago. To learn this caused Rainer many strong pangs of remembrance, and in his letters he told her again what a profound event she'd been to him in his younger days. Told her that she still remained his help and harbor. Told her, even, that during his recent struggles in Paris it was his awareness of *her* that had carried him through.

"I held to this: that I could still recognize you in my inner self, that your image had not grown strange to me, that it had not abandoned me like everything else."

Meanwhile the Roman winter moved sluggishly along, fruitless, lonesome. Rainer told himself it was merely a transitional spell. He would just suffer its frustrations, persevere. But the blockage would not ease. Work refused to come.

On a scrap of paper he wrote out a single Russian word that he and Lou had learned together. The word lay there on his desk, a powerful command to himself. *"Break it open!"* it meant. He felt it helped him. And at last came a feeling of conduciveness, confidence. February arrived and Rainer sensed he had surmounted the worst of the winter—yes, but the *best* of winter would remain for some time yet. The trees stood enormous and still all across the vast green stretches of the Villa Borghese, their high limbs lustrous in the steely light, their leafless canopies contriving intricate gothic patterns. Rainer's creative zeal grew stronger by the day. Come the eighth of February he could begin to see the lineaments of what was coming, so he started that morning. Shut himself away in his cottage and served himself up to work.

What he had seen was something like a dark mirror-plain: a room of indeterminate depth reflected there. In that space a figure stood, shadowed and faceless but familiar. The figure's shoulders sloped away like Rainer's own, but this was not the poet himself. Not entirely. It was a different poet. A troubled young soul. Franz Xaver Kappus came to mind, yet this imagined figure would be a Dane, in homage to Jacobsen and *Niels Lyhne:* a penniless poet prone to nightmare and uncertain health. And this poet had come to Paris to live, or so he himself had hoped . . . but maybe it was really to die. He was called . . . Malte.

For the entire day Rainer bent heavily over his notebook, held himself curled into that dim mirror-space; got up and stood at his standing desk, remaining in the mirror all the while; sat again; rose again. Only late in the afternoon, as if with a lightning flash, did he feel himself awaken to the little Roman house around him. Feel himself, peculiarly, a fragment projected from some separate world into this one. This pleased him very much; it meant he had gone deep and far in the previous hours, it meant the work had rooted itself, the work would remain with him. Yet this figure, Malte, would want more and more of him. More time, more focus, more precision. Rainer could feel that already: the bewitchment Malte effected. This hungry poet who had set up house within him some time before but had only now begun to speak—clearly Malte was here to stay. Could months—months on end, even—be enough to heed and record all that Malte would slowly reveal? And what to make of one's other allegiances in life, were it not so?

For the rest of February Rainer clung to his day labor, working, working, an anchorite in his garden cottage, preparing his own meager meals of groats and vegetables but nourished entirely in another way. Come March, though, he was hit with the surreal dismay of one confronted by something dimly presaged. His mother appeared in Rome.

Phia Rilke's narrow heels, puncturing Rainer's quietude as she descended upon him, seemed to puncture his winter too. All shape suddenly went out of the world around him. A devitalizing heat beset Rome, and then within a week this distraught and blundering spring had collapsed to unmistakable summer. There in his steaming cottage Rainer found himself looking at his mother: black-bedecked woman surfaced from his deeply embedded dreams, her silhouette kinked in the blinding light from his windows behind, her enormous green paper fan flapping and flapping beside her face.

At his doorstep she had flaunted an incredible panther-black sunhat—headgear as wide as most church doors, its scalloped ribbon secured in a bow beneath her chin. Now she sat primly in a chair, holding the accoutrement like a large tamed pet upon her knees. Visitor from some less sensible world.

And with Mama as always came everything, everything out of Rainer's disordered past. So much remembered now not with the brain but with the belly. A chilling swirl inside, something like shame. And surely there was nothing to be ashamed of, yet always in Mama's presence, as by some irreversible years-long sorcery, the shame returned. She clearly had no idea of all that she summoned up. And surely Rainer could not blame her. And because this was so he suffered in her presence all the more.

Sucked backward into his old bafflement, he sat before her in his cottage atop the bridge. And Clara had come from her own garden cottage nearby.

The air lay sun-heavy and stagnant, but the threesome dutifully sipped hot cups of tea.

Slow scrape of stirring spoons. Slow clink of porcelain.

Soon Phia commenced in her discursive, rapid-fire way. "Did you say he's Austrian—the gentleman to whom this property belongs? Might I have heard his name before?"

"Perhaps, Mama. It's Strohl-Fern. Alfred Strohl-Fern. I believe he's Alsatian, in fact."

"Oh, is he?" Phia leaned to Clara with a proud little smile. As though to someone hard of hearing she said with immoderate enunciation, "You've an Alsatian mother-in-law, my dear. Has René told you? This husband of yours, you ought to know, is not of that mongrel Teutonic-Czech stock that clutters Prague. Indeed not."

Clara said, "Yes, I believe you told me so when we saw you last, Mother."

"Did I? Well, it's worth remembering, my dear. Did you know that René, for a time, believed himself a Czech?"

"Not believed, Mama—"

"Belittled himself a Czech, one should say. You really ought to thank God, René, that your Uncle Jaroslav set the Rilke name apart as he did. Sad or no, the man's title is the best thing in your patrimony. But I've no doubt that the Alsatian runs strong in you yet. Surely it's what drew you to Paris."

"Auguste Rodin was in Paris, Mama. The sculptor. I went there to meet him."

"Yes, of course, but you didn't even know, did you, that your own French spirit was also drawing you there."

The light had grown scorching behind her. Rainer rose to let down the blind.

"Oh, René, can you guess what I saw as I was coming across the park?"

Rainer was struggling with the window-cord and did not answer.

Clara said, "What did you see, Mother?"

"A fair-haired little girl out with her governess. A lovely thing running about in pinafore and ankle boots. Ribbons in her hair. And she had a gray squirrel on a leash. Does that bring back a memory or two, René?"

"*Ja,* Mama, of course."

"You used to love your squirrels, remember?"

"Of course, Mama."

"Every summer, Clara dear, we holidayed in Arco and René Maria would keep a pet squirrel. Most of the children did, you know, just for the summer weeks. But René Maria was different as always. For the other children, you see, liked to keep their creatures very close, but *my* boy would fashion the longest of leashes. Twenty, thirty feet. He wanted the squirrels to climb as high as they liked. He was the gentlest child. You were the gentlest child, René. Still gentle, isn't he, Clara? Still delicate. It's why he's a poet no doubt."

Clara smiled softly.

"And do you remember little Amélie, René? Oh, but that's a different story altogether. Unless of course our dear Clara wants to know of her husband's first romance?"

Rainer turned a blank look to his wife. Clara, indulgent daughter-in-law, begged the mother to tell.

Phia gave a curious slight jump in her seat. "Well"—set her saucer on the table and drew herself up with an air of preliminary delight. "On those southern holidays René would play for hours with his cousin whose parents kept a big house in Friuli. Amélie was the girl's name. Precious little thing. Next to René Maria she's the most God-fearing child I've ever laid eyes upon. Like an angel incarnate. Every year she would announce herself at our door with flowers for her cousin. My, how she made him blush! Really, Clara, he was smitten.

"One summer René Maria gave Amélie the gift of a tiny ring. As it happened, it was the last time he ever saw her. You couldn't have known then, René, that you were really bidding your cousin farewell, but I believe, very truly believe, that by some spiritual insight you *sensed* it was so. You were always such a devout child. Well, for quite a long time after, Amélie's mother wrote me by the month. Letter upon letter I had it that the girl still wore her cousin's ring devotedly. Oh, but real love, as everything does, lies in God's hands and can never blossom without the Lord's blessing. You see, Clara, what René Maria had understood on that day long before was that God's designs had already set him and his cousin apart. Sure enough, during my boy's first year at the Kadettenschule I received word that his Amélie had gone to a nunnery."

Phia paused to shape her lips in a whimsical pout. With deep melodrama she concluded, "It fell to me to inform my sweet René Maria of his first heartbreak."

"How very sad," said Clara with equal mellowness.

Rainer sat stiffly in his chair, his mouth mannered in a flat grin, his stare fixed upon Phia's wraithlike fingers stroking and stroking the silver cross lying low on her blouse.

Spindly little Amélie moving backward, sucked away or falling through blurred and colorless ether, her blond hair in a crazed cascade before her face, her outstretched arms two darkening streams and that tarnished ring he had given her speeding toward him deadly as a musket ball . . . a recurring dream he'd once had, forgotten till now. How unnerving to peer back into that ineffectual nightmare from this future of his, to know the dream for the lugubrious thing it had always been: something he himself had never authored. Something his mother had set to seed within him.

"This Alsatian proprietor must be terribly well-to-do. There are a number of cottages like this one?"

"Twenty-five," answered Clara. "All let to artists. Strohl-Fern is an artist himself. Extremely successful."

"I see. And this cottage provides space enough for both of you?"

"Clara lets an additional studio," said Rainer. "That's more than enough room."

No reason, of course, to correct his mother's impression, or mention how seldom he and Clara had seen one another in recent weeks.

.   .   .

Later they walked through the park together, poet and sculptress and mother. Phia's black dirndl in a gossipy rustle all the way, the wings of her hat stroking hugely. At a junction of paths she jerked to a halt and pointed. "Look, look, René! That small girl I told you about. Can you see her over there with her squirrel?"

"Ah. Yes."

"She reminds me so much of you, my dear, in her ribbons and skirts. You see her?"

"*Ja,* Mama, I see her."

Three weeks Phia Rilke was in Rome. Unreal lady aflutter in the unreal city. All the while the sham Roman summer deadened the fresh flowers around Rainer's cottage and he felt the ground he'd gained slipping away beneath him. Work refused to come again, though he waited, though he practiced patience as well as he knew how. And finally, inevitably, all prospects dropped away as the old grippe touched him once more.

So transpired March and most of this month too, the poet locked out of the world of his work.

He moves back and forth across the cottage now, doing battle with his army of tiny invaders. Day and night Rome's refulgent spring continues to drain itself of color, and while Rainer fights off infestations of one kind or another he feels his heart haunted by unreachable figures. Figures pushed into the outermost halls of the mansion within him where they lurk like revenants. Pale shy shapes construed amidst sheeted furniture.

They are figures of Paris, each one still in need of a face. They are part of Malte's tale. Malte shall speak faces onto all of them. They're sad slumped figures, but not just the city's destitute ones, not just the lees of society—no, they are *all* those who lack wealth, all those who have failed as perhaps Malte the penniless Dane is failing, in the perilous game of as-

cendancy played perpetually by everyone. And now if only Rainer could
forestall such failure himself, in order to render it. In order to show how
things stand when one is eternally a beginner.

On his desk lies that scrap of paper with its Russian characters in dark
admonishment: *Break it open!*

Oh, but distractions! A letter, a request, an incessant noise, mercurial health,
the machinations of weather, a date that must be kept, a gregarious or in-
somniac neighbor who wants conversation or paces through the night, or—
worst of all—a face appearing at your door, unannounced. It's this last that
befalls you one afternoon when the sky above the parkland sags in a gray
weave of cloud. Atmosphere of saturation, as though the very air exudes oil
and unguent. At your threshold hovers a stranger's face: freckled vulpine visage glistering wet, hairline dark red and sweat-rimmed. He says his name
and gives a courteous smile, but even while you are shaking his hand the significance of the name escapes you. He seems to note your puzzlement.

"Forgive me," he says. "I'm the previous tenant here."

And now the name rings familiar. You'd seen it written down. He's the
young painter whose sublease you've assumed.

Still he stands there on your step, something apparently unclarified.
He tilts his head and looks past your shoulder into the cottage.

"You've been borrowing my furniture," he says with a remindful air.

"*Ja.*"

His eyes skim to the ground, only to rise again with a confounded
look. "Perhaps there's a misunderstanding. . . . Might I come in? I've been
walking, you see."

"Of course. Pardon me. Would you like a drink of water?"

"I'd be very grateful."

And now he's in your quarters. He's finessed his way through the door and stands there in this space over which, through winter and spring, your fragile solitude has grown degree by arduous degree.

The painter gulps from the glass, gives a sated sigh, presses a cuff to his wet mouth. "An early summer down here, is it? Strange how everything changes when you take yourself away but the shortest time. Well, I'm in Rome for just two days and I'm afraid I must collect my furniture."

"Furniture?" You flinch. "But our agreement was—was something else, was it not?"

"No, it—"

"The furniture was loaned, yes, but with the option to purchase."

"Indeed it was not," says the painter, chin thrust high. Something fearsome within him, quick to flail at the slightest whiff of slander. "It's *my* furniture and was never for sale." Then, just as promptly, he softens. At seeing your face perhaps. He looks about at your neatly made palliasse, your desk, your papers and pens. "Look, I wish I needn't barge in like this, but the agreement stands as always. I'm sorry."

"I see." You receive the returned glass. "And so the furniture will go—"

"Tomorrow."

"Tomorrow. Very well."

At the threshold the painter turns. "This must seem a rotten surprise. Best thing, I suppose, would be to make your agreements in writing from now on, wouldn't you say. That way there's no . . . *confusion.*" With a sober grin he is gone.

The following evening you find yourself alone in the cleared cottage. All the more a monkish chamber now. The palliasse and a bookcase have been left at least. And the standing desk, because that is yours.

So goes your time in the southern capital. Everything, by the week, seems to be falling away from you. And it seems clear that some insuperable centrifugal force means to dislodge you from Rome. In the morning hours now, the year's first scorpions begin to throng your door. Brittle hairless creatures plump and pink, their stingers armed.

And a deep unavoidable pause has taken hold of you. A kind of lethargy, spiritual and physical at once.

So it's decided. You will not summer here. It will be Phia Rilke's summer now anyway. Not yours, not Rome's. Somehow, by her mere three-week presence, Mama managed to make it something false, something garish. No, no staying now. But onward already? And where?

The loss of this cottage will cause you pain of the keenest kind, for you've had solitude here, and quietude—weeks upon weeks of both, and with those things in place, at least, there is always the chance of solid work. A *chance* is the most important thing. What other tools is a poet ever given?

To Lou in Göttingen you write a long, long letter over the course of two full days, describing this peculiar lassitude that has seized you, reiterating your determination to live fully in your work and to thereby become more anchored in the world. There is so much you have yet to learn, you tell her, and you must find a place conducive to your aims. Wouldn't a small university town somewhere in Germany be best? And delicately, with a slight flurry in your stomach, you add:

> *"I'm not asking whether the place with everything I'm seeking could be Göttingen?"*

Seven or eight days letter a postcard arrives from Venice: the Grand Canal in its elegant clutter. On the back a few short words from Lou. She's been staying at a Venetian spa and will return soon to Göttingen.

You sit turning the card over and over in your hands, dumbfounded. Venice! She's been this close for several weeks and not till now does she write to you. Meanwhile your letter of pages upon pages has gone beseeching her at home, its timid question irrelevant to her state of mind—for she does not ask, with this postcard, that you come see her in Venice. Why, then, would she welcome you in Göttingen?

A photograph is taken in your Strohl-Fern cottage this spring or summer of 1904. It captures you seated at the desk with papers and books. You look left toward the camera, unexpectant. A harsh glare spills in through the window before you and bleaches your face to white particles at the edges. The blue Russian smock sags from your shoulders, its sleeves falling long and flaccid to your fingertips. Boy in a man's shirt.

In a letter to Lou you will enclose this picture, and in response she will ask, '*Are you really that thin?*'

So you are shrinking in these days. Your face lean and furrowed, tall pockets of shadow in the cheeks. You are hollowing. As though you would make of yourself an instrument. Fears arrive, fevers arrive, as frequent as in boyhood, but now you've begun to make use of them, despite your complaints. Like the luthier's plane, they begin to lend you shape and resonance. Repeatedly you strike your own side and listen close. Something deep and discordant in that stir of awakened notes. And what if you fail to give everything to this hearkening task?—or cannot tell just what that sound denotes, let alone transcribe it? . . . Can you think of the depth of failure that would signify?—how completely cancelled your existence would be?—what shoddy work the first luthier, back in the beginning, must have done on you?

MALTE COUNTRY:

1904

"*Ich weiß nicht, was ich werde,*
was ich zu sein versprach,
ich ahme nur der Erde
ernste Gebärden nach."

I know not what I am becoming,
what I promise to be,
I can only emulate the earth's
earnest gestures.

Schmargendorf Diary, 1900

An answer always comes. It matters not how impossible the question may be or how much discomfort one must first endure: an answer always comes simply because one stays alive. In Rome the question was: Whither now?

So you stand on the leeward deck of a steamer in the dark of night, wind-whipped and hugging fast to a rusted cleat as the boat labors through waters hugely restless and a surly rain veers down. Ragged tongues of sea-wave, lit to a queer golden-green by the tossing gaslamps on deck, come licking through the scuppers and slather your shoes.

You're alone up here, every other passenger tucked away in the berths below. Two hours ago a scrawny boatswain came squelching up, soaked clothing sucked tight to his every limb. "Should get below, perhaps, before you freeze." A glint of baleful amusement in his sailor's eyes.

You gave him a grim smile and told him you'd be all right. The boatswain shrugged, staggered artfully along the pitching deck without even reaching for a handhold.

You were already drenched, which seemed reason enough to remain above. Upon boarding the steamer earlier this afternoon you had clambered below and found you could barely stay under as long as it took to locate and inspect your cabin. And then the cabin's meanness was itself sufficient to commit you to a topside journey. Up here, at least you needn't go scrambling if your gorge refuses to settle, and the open air is preferable by far to the staleness of that closed-in berth, even if this tempestuous dark affords no horizon.

The swirling weather has so blurred your senses, in fact, that it would come as no surprise to be told the steamer is heeling and yawing in circles.

Somewhere out there beyond the black torrential waters is the harbor at Kiel from which you departed five, six, seven hours ago. It brings a profound sense of displacement, already, to think how smoothly the boat set out: the dropping sun swabbed in feathery orange, its color enormously cloned as it kissed the water's surface.

You had stood at the gunwale with all the other passengers. A quality of festive commencement had stirred in the crowd. Then the ship was rolling along and the chill salt wind was touching your lips, the boilers blackly fuming overhead, the steamer gaining speed and slapping toward Denmark. *Denmark!* Home of Jacobsen—and now, too, of Malte Laurids Brigge.

You, of course, are ultimately headed for Sweden, but this boat will land you in Denmark by morning, and then just a few hours via train will bring you to Copenhagen—*Copenhagen!*—where you'll find yourself blessed to enjoy two full days alone. Sweden will follow directly, and Sweden is still Scandinavia—still, in a sense, Jacobsen country. Malte country.

You're simply glad to be gone. How providential it had seemed, as the dread Italian summer encroached and brought with it such misery of uncertainty, to receive the invitation as from some divine intermediary, to be granted escape from Rome and its stagnation for the surely more dignified, more conducive northern climes.

Everything is arranged: you are to be welcomed at a rural estate called Borgeby-gård near Lund. A fellow named Ernst Norlind, your hostess's fiancé and a painter of some esteem, will meet you at the Malmö pier on the twenty-fifth and conduct you to the country manor. Before leaving Rome you received a most affable letter, in very precise German, from Norlind himself. And the painter's fiancée, Hanna Laarsen, mistress of Borgeby-gård, had also written—in French. Two warm epistles extending welcome, apparently for no special reason save the couple's wish to host a poet of whom they'd heard a good deal.

Ellen Key is the woman to thank for that. A noted author (and a friend of Lou's), Key has been singing your praises in her native Sweden and throughout Scandinavia since reading your *Stories of God* a few years back. For some time already you and the lady have maintained an eloquent correspondence, and last year, during a successful lecture tour dedicated to your work, Key made the acquaintance of Norlind.

But Ellen Key is not alone to thank. No invitation would ever have been secured without Clara.

In Rome on the day you received Ellen's news confirming your Borgeby-gård visit, you crossed the dry and tangled Strohl-Fern grounds to Clara's studio.

"You did this?" you said, showing her the letter.

Clara looked the letter over. Smiled. "Not I. Our good Ellen."

"Yes, but Ellen says here that you wrote to her."

"I did."

"About me?"

"*Ja.* Is that all right?"

You fell still then, astonished by that gentle generosity in the dear woman before you. You tilted your head and made a tiny sound like a sigh, then took Clara's hands and held them. Your glance in dumbfounded delay at her fingers and wrists coated in plaster dust. "Of course, my dear. Of course it's all right. It's wonderful."

"She adores you, you know. Ellen. I merely mentioned your health and made a suggestion. That was all."

"Clara . . . Clara"—but you did not know the words to follow. You felt your eyes welling.

The sculptress smiled again, so perceptively. Reached and touched your lips with her rough warm plaster-coated fingers. "*Ja,* darling, I know."

Now you cling to this cleat in the dim vertiginous deck-light while the wind plucks at rearing waves and splashes you with brine and rain. The steamer lurching into deeper darkness, deeper waters, the great machinery of the engines groaning underfoot—wheezing, groaning, wheezing—as the vessel plunges up the swells, drops, plunges again. It's your first sea voyage. A threshold of kinds—and the crossing made with Clara's forthright blessing, her smile of understanding. Indeed then, it must be possible: the life that you and she have fumbled toward. Separate solitudes guarding one another.

Morning arrives at last. Pallid sodden morning with a bloodless sun rubbing blindly behind the sheet of gray sky. A lighter drizzle now, and the green harbor water here and there hollowed in gentle pockets that vanish as fast as they've come. No reflections in that pulsating surface, only shadows.

Soaked, you stand at the gunwale, pressed upon by all those who stowed themselves through the night, and stare at your first Denmark, the Korsor pier: barnacled pylons black and sinewy in the drenched air.

A two-hour train ride delivers you, still wet, to Copenhagen.

But for your vivid forty-eight hours in the Danish capital, it could be that your first crossing had never ended. Toward Sweden now. Rough waters again, and again you stand braced at the gunwale of a boat, slashed by rain and leaping waves. But this journey, thank God, takes just an hour and a half, and with reasonable grace the steamer slides in to the rainy Malmö pier. Then you find yourself standing on the warped dock-slats at the bottom of the gangplank, a puddle forming at your heels as Ernst Norlind, a small man with a long red beard and kindly face, smiles into your eyes and presses your frigid hand with great warmth.

"Good Lord, my friend!" he says in German. "Let's find a hotel where you can dry off."

Through the thrashing rain together into the town, Norlind extremely affable, talking a great deal. He says he was in Munich in '97, which accounts for his expert German. You will love Borgeby-gård, he assures you. The best of the Swedish countryside is to be found there. And he's cleared his room for you, as it's the most comfortable guest-room in the house. He talks of Munich and German literature, of Ellen Key, of Jacobsen, of life and of art and of their points of intersection, their points of divergence.

In the snug compartment on the northbound train out of Malmö, you grow drowsy. With some embarrassment Norlind stops himself midsentence, says, "Forgive me for pressing conversation. You must be terribly tired."

"I'm sorry. I've had very little sleep."

"Don't feel obliged, *mein Freund,* to keep awake on my account. It's a long trip to Flädie, another long ride by landau after that."

"I just might doze a bit," you say. "Please don't be offended."

"Not at all, *mein Freund.* I've made that crossing from Kiel myself. We'll have plenty of time to talk at Borgeby-gård."

And so the journey's remainder passes in silence, the train charging ahead with soporific beat. But you do not sleep, merely watch the drops of rain stretched to silver streams across the windowglass. A flat green country flashing by out there. Norlind thoughtful and silent beside you all the while.

At last, after several hours traveling in a rattling landau through the rainy country of pasturelands, Norlind taps the back of his hand at your knee. *"Mein Freund."* He points a finger out his window. *"Wir sind angekommen."* *We've arrived.*

Bend your neck, peer past him through the bleary glass. The shapes of cattle scattered over rain-soaked fields out there, a number of the animals clumped around huge and solitary trees rising intermittently from the pastures, ancient-looking trees with corded trunks as thick as bell towers. A cream-colored farm building stands back across the fields. And just off the road, another: steeply gabled roof and heavy barn doors of dark wood. On a shingled ledge above one of its eaves sits a massive ragged wreath.

"*Was ist das?*"

"*Das? Storch,*" says Norlind with a smile. *Stork's nest.*

The road curves broadly and then three fanciful towers rise up across it, the arch of the central one straddling the way. Homely towers, salutary rather than defensive, weathered to the yellow of old book pages. The landau passes through and rolls along a lane lined high with chestnut trees in abundant leafage. Across an expansive lawn a country manor rises into view. The main house. Old agrarian estate constructed of yellow brick. Tendrils of ivy climb hungrily to the top of every wall, lending the place an unkempt kind of elegance.

The lady of the manor, Hanna Laarsen, appears in the drive as soon as the landau draws to a halt. You climb down with Norlind into a late-day drizzle, the air rich and fructuous. Fragrance of farmed earth and wet soil, cattle and manure. Fräulein Laarsen is broad-jawed with a long ridged nose, low-set mouth and tall eyelids like hoods. Handsome earthborne sort of woman, she manages, so Norlind has told you, the whole Borgeby-gård farm and its two hundred head of cattle. She draws up to you, smiles, spreads her palms before her, and says, "*Willkommen.*" And rather than venturing further German, she turns and murmurs Swedish to her fiancé.

"Fräulein Laarsen," says Norlind, "wants you to know how glad she is that you have come."

Once the painter has translated your rejoinder of thanks, he leads you inside to your room. Set apart from the main house by a deep landing, it's a simple room, modest in size, somewhat dim in this sunless afternoon. It contains a bed, bureau drawers, a few chairs, and a long slender desk before a big window covered partly in vines. Beyond the vines: fields and fields, with more of those ancient trees surging here and there out of greenest grass, their canopies darkly cluttered with rooks.

"I hope it will serve you well," says Norlind.

You turn to him with a smile. Clasp his hand in a surge of warmth. "It will indeed."

"We'll take dinner at five," he says, and leaves you.

The dining table stands in a vast high-ceilinged room that the people of the house call a "salon." The far corners, at this hour of day, are already turgid with shadow.

The main meal is preceded by small cakes of different types eaten with butter and cheese. Most delectable is a soft sweet patty of corn kernels. Then comes a tureen of steaming asparagus soup and an earthenware platter bearing a substantial joint of meat garlanded with potatoes and cauliflower. A lone maid, apparently the only servant retained, brings out all the dishes in turn.

For propriety's sake you sample a bit of the meat, but the abundant vegetables are your main delight. At table are Fräulein Laarsen, Ernst Norlind, and the steward of the farm, a willowy little man in a high-buttoned shirt. The steward can't celebrate enough the bounteous rain, as Norlind translates for your benefit.

The mealtime passes slowly, everything said twice—once in Swedish, once by Norlind in German. Hanna Laarsen attempts to draw you out in French, but you find that after a year with no practice that recalcitrant tongue will not return beyond a stammer. For dessert the maid brings out fresh strawberries and milk. The tastes evoke abundantly these arable northern fields.

Later Norlind leads you out of doors to the cow barns. The young night now rainless and still but for the guttural cluck of roaming fowl or the flap and scrabble of rooks swooping tree to tree overhead. Twilight air sweet and mild. This whole vivid northern world saturated with transformation and the talismanic light that attends it: blue heat-lavish light, incipient even in the deepest corners of blackness. And out there past the high walnut trees: the scrim of sky seized smoke-blue in its last illuminations.

Soon you are standing in a long hay-strewn passage with cattle heavily breathing, half-a-dozen deep, in the stalls to your right and left. Norlind goes before you with lamp raised shoulder-high and the tawny backs flow past in the rays of light, here and there a bloodshot eyeball rolling in its wallet of hide, a wet muzzle lifted, a pink knife-tip tongue testing the slack corner of a mouth, bolts of bovine breath discharged from the nostrils into clouds of cooling steam. Two hundred cows. Also some calves. And further on: twenty-four horses. In a remote pen: a sober bull tied up alone. You stand a while with Norlind at the pen's gate, admiring the colossal form. The creature lifts his horns and lows hugely at the barn wall before him. At a rude beam above him a net of straw-flecked cobwebs shudders membranously.

Two months the poet shall spend at Borgeby-gård. Early in July Ernst Norlind departs on a journey to Russia, and thereafter Rainer is left almost entirely to himself. Even daily meals, though taken in the company of Hanna Laarsen and the farm steward, are solitary affairs, the conversation conducted entirely in Swedish. Now and then the hostess good-naturedly turns to the guest and broaches a topic in French. To the best of his ability Rainer stutters out a reply, adds a few gesticulations for good measure, smiles, receives a gracious smile in response, then the table returns to Swedish again. Day by day he takes great pains to indicate, as clearly as he can through sheer deportment, his contentedness with his mute position in the house. In all truth Rainer feels as though he's enjoying a cure in some blissful country sanatorium. Everything about the place is recuperative—and to such a degree that it must all, at some point hence, become *creative* as well. How long has it been since the world has given him so effulgent a welcome? He wants to receive the gift of these months completely, to remain wholly present, to miss nothing.

Mornings the maid brings cinnamon cakes and a pitcher of warm milk to his room. He sits before the window with his breakfast at hand, reading a book or a letter by the pale natural light, or writing to Clara. And since his time in Rome he's been engaged in heavy study of Danish, determined to read Jacobsen in the original. This, no doubt, accounts for the decline in his elementary grasp of French.

After breakfast, if the day is clear, Rainer walks barefoot across the wide back lawn to the edge of a rain-swollen stream. He stands at the water watching the horses and cattle in the opposite pastures, the low distant hills out beyond them, the blue-gray sky rolling and rolling in great surfs of cloud. He feels himself intimately enfolded by this northern world, its wind and weather and soil and the pure food that comes of such fertile country: gooseberries, strawberries, currants and cherries and plums. Also: buttermilk, eggs, asparagus, barley, corn, rice. Amidst his meditative strolls about the grounds every day he fairly hums the names of abundance—names Clara once taught him at Westerwede: lime tree, beech tree, chestnut, walnut, jasmine, mallow, dahlia, lilac, laburnum, thistle, hawthorn, violet . . .

He writes to his wife by the day, and sometimes both morning and evening.

"Dear Clara: Everything, at bottom, merely assumes the shape of a wide circle: all strength we've given forth returns to us enriched and transformed. So it is in prayer. And what is there, really and truly accomplished, that is not prayer?"

Scandinavia is granting him image, solitude, time—all in bounty, all unalloyed. Rainer understands and avows it now: these are the things he most needs. These are the things he must seek henceforth and always, no matter where they take him.

Out in the fields, here and there beneath the glide of his gaze, dark swatches of turned earth lie unhusbanded, ditches dug along their sides. Stands of corn rise tall beside them. He wonders what purpose these fallow sections serve. At dinner one evening he puts the question to his hostess in careful, preformulated French. The lady's gray-haired steward, soupspoon paused aloft, takes an interest and begs to know the guest's query in Swedish, canting his thin face as Hanna Laarsen translates. Then the steward draws himself up in his chair, touches a napkin corner to his lips, and gives Rainer an answer in most melodious Swedish, eyes glittering beneath the wispy bushels of his brow, as though he can foretell the pleasure a poet should take in such an explanation. Hanna Laarsen renders the answer into French: *"C'est de la terre en repos"*—and the steward sits very still with head cocked and jaw agape, intent to witness his answer's delayed effect.

It is the earth at rest, hears Rainer. He nods to the steward with deep understanding. The steward nods back, and Rainer sees a grave poetical smile submerged in the man's scraggy face as he returns to his soup.

In the dim library at Borgeby-gård the poet sits poring through old ledger books and family papers. Outside, the day is restless. Intermittent wind gusts inland from the Sund, chill marine wind that cuts the warmer country air to strips, boding rain. Though the great library curtains stand open at every window, daylight comes meager through the leaded glass and Rainer has lit the desktop lamp at his arm.

Yellowed sheaves riffle between his thumbs, blurred or faded penwork fluttering past his eyes and a yellow scent breathed in: the parchment odor of this ancient estate's peculiar, unuttered history. Beginning already to shuffle through the poet's mind are musty figures summoned by little more than names or the uncommon flourishes of an old soul's antique script: *Spegel, Lindenow, von Ramel, von Hastfer, de Greer, von Wachtmeister, Bergenstrahle.* Family names scratched quill to parchment by candlelight some evening ages past—in this very library, no doubt. All the documents, of course, were set down in Swedish, but by virtue of a bit of context and a good deal of fancy, much can be gleaned from their accounts.

Late in the afternoon the papers lead Rainer out to the small retired church at the edge of the estate. His shoes plashing over the shallow flood-plain of the lawns, the wind whipping at his coat, setting his hair on end. Then he stands before the eerie chapel. Hushed and stalwart structure, its old immobility weirdly intensified in this gale.

The gambrel roof is rotted, the belfry drabbled by decades of hard weather. Plaster crumbles from every wall and in the moss-eaten eaves great testiculate wasp-hives cling bloated and colorless. From one bottom hinge the church door tilts out, arrested in its fall, the opening thickly cobwebbed. Rainer finds a fallen walnut branch and cuts the webs away and slips inside.

Smell of must and mildew and dirt. Stone floor encrusted with bird guano, bat dung, and a reddish alluvium sluiced in during past storms and long since dried to pools of marbled powder. A slick coffee-colored sala-mander curls away to the corner to hide its head amongst chunks of plas-ter and ancient nails.

The shallow nave, cleared of furniture, is dappled with gray light from the torn-away roof. A lancet of stained glass stands high in the front wall, every panel intact. Daylight sets the upper colors in a jaundiced glow: old family insignia worked in green and yellow and red, topped with a blue Latin cross, but the window's whole bottom half is grimed black on its

exterior. Upon the stone platform beneath the lancet slouches a wooden altar, rain-mottled and sun-bleached and heaped with debris from the caved-
in roof. Against the base of the north wall a church kneeler lies tipped on
its side, faded cushion furred in mold.

From somewhere overhead comes a sudden blasting noise, rapid as rifle
fire. Rainer flinches back as a giant stork descends in a concussive clatter of
wings. Wizened legs dangling down from the white spool of the body, the
atavistic feet gaining purchase, the creature alights at the ragged lip of the
roof. Fanning its huge wings back, furling them, it roosts there all preemi-
nence, half the size of a man, the enormous shears of its beak held in close
profile against its breast. One red primeval eye fixes the poet below.

Rainer stands dwarfed like prey. He waits. But the avian eye does not
wander. The bird will remain.

Rainer turns about and something brittle grazes his cheek. The old
belfry rope, strung down from an aperture overhead. His lifted eyes halt
upon a human form. A large triptych mounted on the wall above the door.
He steps back to see it better.

Three portraits of the sixteenth century, the edges blistered and the
images themselves chalking away in long streaks. What paint remains has
already darkened to near obscurity. The central figure's face is eroding in
curls of pulp, but clearly it's a man. He wears a tricornered hat. A sash. His
phantom hand palms a rapier hilt, one finger bearing an enormous courtly
ring. Beyond the anemic peach tone of his coat all the portrait's color has
been leached away. Figure once moneyed, once mannered, but honor and
affluence however old are finally subdued to long inexorable corrosion,
every regal face at last withering to a blur of paste like this one. At the
man's breast, though, a handsome astral device still accredits him, and the
piecemeal image conjures dark faraway days. Duels fought with slaughter-
ous civility. Deaths died in rages of excellence now long forgotten.

Rainer stands staring. Feels the sanguine eye of the stork staring too.

This portrait doubly recognized, perhaps. Yes: the old Lord Chamberlain. Faceless now, but his name still bristles from the crackling estate papers of Borgeby-gård: Hans Spegel, vassal to Frederick the Second. The two faded panels flanking Spegel depict his two wives. White-wigged ladies with bare larval-complexioned arms.

Rainer turns to start across the nave, eyes lifted to the watchful stork above. The long scissor-head turning to follow him, sharp birdfeet gripping the perch with impassive strength. Then the poet's shoes send a scrap of nailed shingles clattering and in a flurry of stretched wings the stork swoops back as though lifted by an ineluctable updraft and with a whisperous sound is gone.

Wind pours down through that hole in the roof, sings a hushed song through the leaded gaps of the broken windows. A fragrance of ozone swirls in the open church.

At the far corner of the south wall Rainer finds the dim threshold. An opening hardly wider than his own shoulders. Two stone steps descend. He bends, sees a stream of light coming in under there: a big chink in the decayed crypt wall. He steps down. Beneath him something rustles away over the gloom of the cluttered floor. He stops at the base of the steps, waist-deep in darkness, head bent beneath the coved stone ceiling. Listens to the wind whistling along the sides of the church. Beyond the broken wall the grass is stirring, murmurous and furtive. He realizes he's still gripping the gnarled walnut branch but does not throw it away.

The crypt is no more than a tiny room. No space for walking about. The poet squats beneath the bar of colorless light, soaks himself in under-darkness. A blind moment. His eyes recalibrate. Then he makes out a long lank shape on the stone floor. Deformed figure mantled in gossamer. A bulge of naked joint abuts the blackness: the bare scalloped seat of a pelvis. And lower: a curving shank. The poet is close enough to smell the moldering wood: crumpled coffin kept wet by years and years of seepage. The walls of the thing long ago fell away, the lid dropping to compress the skeleton, scatter the dry joints. And then came rats, mice, foxes, cats, to nose by turn through the pile of odorless bones. Old elegant Lord Chamberlain, perhaps, dismembered by scavenger teeth, sprawling on a dank phreatic floor, grayed by generations of Borgeby-gård dust and unfit to fortify the smallest of beasts.

"How would the chamberlain have looked, had someone demanded that he should die a different death than this? He was dying his own difficult death."

The skull, as faceless as the portrait upstairs, lies here against one wall. Swollen sphere of bone in its own taut spider's shroud, cold cheek tossed to the cold chamber floor. And two other skulls as well, rolled by chance to random pockets in the flagstone: the nobleman's wives.

A sudden scissoring noise now. The violent rattle of feet overhead. Someone running, someone tearing through the church toward the crypt. It sucks Rainer back up the steps. And then he stands in the church watching fat cords of rain coming down to slash at the raw stone floor with a noise like an army at charge. This nave given up to nature now.

Rainer hunches and makes an awning of his coat and heads for the door but stops beneath the belfry to look once more at the painting. The mulched face and figure of the Lord Chamberlain. The poet will not forget it.

He ducks through the door and starts his jog toward the house.

The summer storm has raised a thick ribbon of vapor from the lawns. Beyond, the stately roofs of Borgeby-gård seem to hover with a staid and ancient knowledge.

"The long, old manor house was too small for this death; it seemed that a wing must be added on, for the body of the chamberlain kept getting bigger."

Rainer's quiet Borgeby-gård room. A single candle burning on a stand behind him. The whole house sleeps. Beyond his window the cloudy moonlight lies blue on the fields, glancing to ivory in moments when the brisking cloud cover opens. Swedish moon like an upturned cup of milk with the sable cloth of night behind—then grayness again as the clouds shuttle over.

He remembers a Schmargendorf night like this one. The whole of that earliest Schmargendorf time was as vivid as these recent days have been. His eyes so enlivened and nothing to keep him from inhaling the world through them, tasting the world in all the chambers of his heart, breathing the world forth again. Five years ago, between his Russian journeys with Lou, he stared from his Schmargendorf window into a plain of soundless night such as this, the moon outsized and brilliant in its icy glaze and clouds veering over it with a speed that seemed to conjure the whisper of fan blades. That night he took paper from his drawer and wrote, start to finish with incantatory prose that never faltered, a tale of age-old heraldry and heroism. By then it was a story he'd carried with him for years—or rather an anecdote, for its source amounted to no more than that: a tangential paragraph in Uncle Jaroslav's ancestral papers. Not even a hundred words glossing the fate of an eighteen-year-old standard-bearer called Cristoph Rilke, fallen to enemy Turks in a Hungarian battle of 1664.

Rainer thumbs through his notebooks now, finds the old Schmargendorf prose, rereads with fresh interest. "The Cornet" it is called. A very short piece. And more like a poem than a story. But the language is strong and sure of itself, and the weaker moments are certainly salvageable. He begins right away to revise it.

A clear morning at Borgeby-gård, the early sky a soft blue, and wind spilling over the lawns with a watery noise. Rainer paces barefoot through fibrous grass blades toward the stream, his trouser cuffs turned to his shins and the dawn wind chilling his ankles. From the stream bank, broad farm fields lie before him green and glowing.

Out there amongst the grazing horses a small gangling thing staggers, falls. A dark mare stands motionless nearby, head sloped, watching her foal quiver to its feet again. One try, two, and with a toss of its tumid head the little creature stands, stands, all knobby-kneed and splayfooted, withers steep and bony above the bent neck. A few jouncing paces, an attempted turn, then the foal flops to the pasture again in a splash of yellow feet.

The mare walks over, nuzzles the long loaf of the face, the damp and tangled forelock, the side of protuberant ribs. She seems to bestow confidence, for the foal sucks breath and tries again, this time capering a bit—ten sprightly steps—before dropping at the mother's feet. Ungainly little life begun with a hundred beginnings, happy to fall and fall and fall . . .

After dinner one evening the serving girl taps at the door to Rainer's room, bringing the day's post as usual.

"Copenhagen," she says as she tenders a single postcard.

"Copenhagen?" He turns the card to his lamp. An elaborate ink drawing of several buildings and storefronts in the old city, and across the front of one a bold lavender X has been made. The Hotel Bellevue. The back of the card is blank, save for yesterday's postmark.

Lou!

Rainer shoots to his feet, starts through the dim house in search of Fräulein Laarsen. His pulse is surging in his temples and ears. He finds his hostess in the library, stands before her somewhat breathless, the postcard fluttering in one unsteady hand as he strives to stutter out the French.

"To Copenhagen. I must go there. A train to Malmö. Do you know . . . a train tonight perhaps?"

Hanna Laarsen, apologetic and pitying his alarmed state, informs him the last train has long since gone. *"Mais demain, le premier train. C'est possible. Vous allez bien, monsieur?"*

"Oui," he says. *"Oui. Pardon. Le premier train. Très important."*

The lady assures him she'll have a landau ready come dawn.

Back in his room Rainer folds a change of clothes into his valise, wondering how he'll ever get to sleep tonight. So much to wonder now. Lou is in Copenhagen!

From beneath the front cover of the Jacobsen on his desk he withdraws his photographs of little Ruth. Images captured in Oberneuland with the Westhoffs' camera. Here the child stands barefoot and skirted in the garden, one hand waving a blur above her own shoulder, her small shadow pooling before her. He slides the photo into the valise. He wants Lou to see this daughter of his. Somehow his life's divergent parts will be brought together then. A sort of healing will happen, won't it? Somehow . . .

The night sails dark and slow through some sleepless oblivion. By first light Rainer is rattling through the pasturelands in Hanna Laarsen's landau, the green Swedish country ribboning past and a chill wind humming through the cracks at the sides of the window. He holds Lou's postcard before him on his knees. Nothing but a lavender X, yet so much bespoken in that, so clear a message. Lou might have scented the card with her rosewater and given it similar clarity.

In fact, this gesture harks back to one he himself made during their Wolfratshausen summer. To fulfill a number of earlier plans and appointments, Lou had been compelled to travel. From his lonely Loufried room Rainer sent one and another letter chasing after her. All the letters dripped with excess. And when Lou's replies came late and tepid he was made to see his mistake. Then a simple idea touched him. He bought a postcard and blackened it thickly with ink, blotting out all but a tiny celestial spot at the upper corner: white polestar meant to represent the chink of confidential daylight he and Lou had shared on their afternoons in her shuttered bedroom. Unsigned, the card went winging toward her. Later she told him what pleasure it gave her, that gesture, its secret significance not lost. Now this Copenhagen card of hers avows those old days together. What better message could invoke their reunion after three years apart?

The landau delivers Rainer to the station at Flädie. By the day's first train he arrives, several hours later, at Malmö, where he boards a boat for his crossing and soon after, by some dreamlike displacement, finds himself walking the streets of Copenhagen in the late-morning light. Lou's postcard still in his hand.

And here you come now, weary and red-eyed, striding through the polished lobby of the Hotel Bellevue up to the desk where you lay Lou's postcard like a discreet credential of kinds.

"*Deutsch?*" you say.

The clerk nods.

"Frau Lou Andreas-Salomé if you please."

"Of course." The clerk bends to consult his ledger, shuffles the pages. He straightens and frowns. "I'm sorry, but it appears that Frau Andreas-Salomé has left the hotel."

"I see. Did she give any word of her return?"

"I cannot say, I'm sorry."

"I see. Well, as she's expecting me I believe I'll wait here in the lobby."

The clerk's brow puckers. "I'm sorry, Herr—"

"Rilke."

"Herr Rilke. Forgive me, my German is perhaps not so good, but I mean to say that Frau Andreas-Salomé has . . . checked out."

Something staggers inside you at the words—a sudden plummeting sensation. You clutch the edge of the counter. "But perhaps . . ." you say, "perhaps she left a message of some kind?"

The clerk consults a second man, a balding fellow with a cropped reddish beard. The bearded clerk comes forward.

"I'm sorry, Herr Rilke, Frau Andreas-Salomé left no messages. If you'd care to leave a message for her, however—"

"Ah, she intends to return then."

"I believe she may have said something of the kind. Or perhaps it was the gentleman who said it."

"Gentleman?"

"Yes, the gentleman with whom she was traveling. Of course, this hotel is not privy to the plans of its guests."

"Of course, no." A dusky look in your pale eyes. *The gentleman with whom she was traveling*—a phrase to throw relentless light on your mistake in coming here. Who is this gentleman? It requires but a moment of thought. Friedrich Pineles, no doubt. The Viennese doctor she calls "Zemek" in her letters. She's been constantly in his company since last summer at least, and who knows how long before that? In her terrible *Letzter Zuruf* three years ago she mentioned Zemek, having talked with him at length about your struggles in body and mind. And last summer Zemek insisted they take an excursion together through the mountains of Bohemia. He was treating her—has been treating her all this year—for an infirmity of some sort, her letters have made only vague reference to it.

What does she suffer? Why won't she tell you? It's as though she refuses to cultivate anything beyond the most remote connection. Your letters, for instance: How many of *yours* exist to a single one of *hers?*

Oh, but now you're sliding backward, aren't you? Yes, these grudging thoughts are the stuff of a younger self, a younger self and his grim time alone in Saint Petersburg. Or the young lover of those last bitter days in Schmargendorf, Lou's expulsion so terrible, so inevitable. Mustn't beat your fists now, mustn't spoil. Surely this is just the shock of disappointment. To have arrived here and to find yourself standing at this counter, rebuffed. Why would Lou have sent you such a postcard? Could she have expected you to receive it in any other manner? How far her thoughts must be from yours. How great your mistake. And now, suddenly, it occurs to you how *thankful* you should feel at having missed her, having missed *them,* avoiding the humiliation of an encounter with Zemek under such false assumptions—that man who no doubt knows too much about you already.

But really, did you travel here assuming anything beyond the renewal of friendship, the resumption of old eye-to-eye understanding? Doesn't this shock, this profound disappointment, come rather of seeing all too clearly the gulf that gapes between you and this woman to whom you've recently written:

> *"I speak to you like children speak in the night: my face buried against yours, with eyes closed to feel your nearness."*

Lou goes on without seeing what a singular soul she is for you—or does she merely pretend ignorance of your reliance upon her?—pretend, perhaps, for your own sake?

"— — —"

—a voice now, the bearded clerk's lips issuing slots of inscrutable sound. You raise your head a little. "Pardon?"

"I was asking Herr Rilke if I could be of any further service?"

"Ah. Perhaps. Do you have a room available?"

So a night in Copenhagen.

The following day you are rolling aboard a boat again. Behind at the hotel you've left a brief letter to Lou, written in great restraint and, you hope, great maturity:

> *"If you arrive to find this letter and want to say something to me, it must be by telegram to Borgeby-gård. How I wait: R."*

And now you recall some words you wrote just a few days ago from your quiet room at Borgeby-gård, the latest in your series of letters to Franz Xaver Kappus:

> *"We are solitary. One can delude oneself about this and act as if it were not so. That is all. But how much better it is to grasp that we are this way, yes, to start off from this point of acceptance."*

Days later in Borgeby-gård a second postcard arrives, this one also blank save a date written in Lou's hand. The frontside depicts the Christiania province of Norway.

Another few days, then a third postcard, also from Norway, with a brief line to say she plans to reach Saint Petersburg soon.

Two weeks more and at last a proper letter comes, postmarked Saint Petersburg. Returning to Copenhagen to catch her ship to Russia, Lou says, she found your note and realized what a blunder her first postcard had been. The rest of the letter is mostly reportage. The Danes she did not like. Stockholm reminded her of Russia. And she is at a loss to think of any German university towns to meet your needs—Göttingen particularly would be impossible because Zemek means to prescribe a few months of bedrest upon her return there. The missive closes with the request that you not hold her thoughtless postcard gesture against her.

 Sweden: November 1904 . . .

*B*leached earth and smoke-gray sky, and you are reclining in the plush depths of a sleigh with stands of trees filing past in garlands of snow all pinked by the gloaming. Your Scandinavian days have fluttered by with similar swiftness, seasons seized in transition. Winter now, already, and you are in Sweden yet.

You'd intended, after Borgeby-gård, to take up residence for a time in Copenhagen and lend yourself entirely to the pressing world of Malte Laurids Brigge. For the blackish figure of Malte loomed within you all through your time in Borgeby-gård, his fate pressing at yours, impossible to ignore. And how to go on shaping that fate?—how render its feeling into form? You remained at a loss. If the novel would not take shape in Copenhagen, you thought, you would devote your energies to a monograph about the great Jacobsen. Then too, a new endeavor had stemmed from your study of Danish: a translation from the correspondence of Kierkegaard. So you'd gone to Copenhagen in search of rooms—a move that found you wandering the streets for days, determined to secure a hotel better than the one you could afford. Strange muddled attempt to take footing in a new kind of life, for you felt you mustn't suffer a relapse there of your first Paris days. For Malte's sake, you mustn't. As things happened, Ellen Key secured you a second Swedish invitation in the midst of your wandering—this one to an estate in Jonsered called Furuborg.

Ahead of you now the bridle bells jangle breathlessly, the blades of the sleigh rustling after. Noise like a dancing girl's dress. At your side sits your

Furuborg host, James Gibson, a man of soft manners and agreeable elegance somewhat unexpected of an industrialist. Together you've traveled seven long hours from Furuborg, first by train to Småland, now onward through the hushed winter country in this sleigh, the late daylight stippled with flurries of drifting snow. You are bent upon arrival by nightfall at the country home of Ellen Key.

At length, just as the day begins to dim, the sleigh lists into the long curve of a drive, slowing as the good woman's house rises before you. A big farmhouse, stately enough, though obviously built not long ago.

Neighbor to the house and set back a small distance is a wide open area where a series of stacked stones runs here and there like hedgerows. These, apparently, are the foundations of a former manor, all charred black. The empty spaces between the rows—where the many rooms once stood—are piled thick with white drifts. A wall of forest rises behind, but somehow the dusky air above those foundations does not give over into the trees; instead the air hangs there as though caught, contained, still molded to the shapes of rooms. In front rises an ancient stairwell with four steps leading up to where the landing ought to be, now nothing but air in its place.

The old house, though vanished, remains an insistent presence, so overawing in all that vesseled space that you can't help but wonder whether those stone steps exist at all, whether you're suffering a vision none other can see. Meticulous persistence of the invisible. These months in Sweden, despite their lack of formidable work, have made this moment of pure seeing possible. Much has been cultivated. *La terre en repos.* So much power to such spacious times. The vanished house stands there yet, its defiant spirit unsubdued by the laws of weather or time.

And immediately the thought arrives that here is the structure of an old relationship. For are your present encounters with Lou any different than this?—the impossible persistence of things burned to cinder long ago. She told you flatly in that most recent letter from Saint Petersburg that you cannot come to Göttingen. And yet in your pocketbook, since Schmargendorf, you've carried her promise, her words scratched across a milk bill. Lou has made herself invisible to you but remains before you always and always.

"But you are very tired, yes?"

A voice in your stunned mind. The sleigh has drawn to a halt. And here is Ellen Key, come from the new house to greet you. Her matronly face is smiling up from the drive. Back-pinned white hair and large welcoming eyes. She is laughing in a soothing kind of way, those eyes glinting.

"A long journey, wasn't it?"

She holds out her hand.

COPENHAGEN: DECEMBER 1904 . . .

Fourth December. Rainer's letter to Lou from Copenhagen. His twenty-ninth birthday and he writes while sitting by the window of a Danish hotel room. He will disembark in a matter of days—across the waters again, to Germany. For weeks he has wanted to set down the words in this letter. With the ardency of a lover ready to profess himself, he's longed to tell Lou of the burnt-down house on Ellen Key's estate. He has waited for the image to raise itself up inside him, that he might build it properly for her. He is learning, more and more, to have patience. To transmute the fervent and fleeting into slowness, into image pure and cool. For image alone is his lot; he's begun to see this now—the onetime lover in him turns to Lou, but now he's a lover of a different kind altogether.

Here before him the invisible house seems to stand up again. And now he writes it for Lou, for Lou who ever helps him, by her remoteness, to new and clearer depths of seeing:

> "One had to say to oneself: no, there is no mansion there, but nevertheless one did feel that something was there; one felt, somehow, that the air beyond that terrace had still not become one with the other air, that it was still healing from its division into corridors and rooms, and that in the middle it still formed a hall—an empty, high, desolate, dusky hall."

.　　.　　.

Five days Rainer is alone in Copenhagen, the green resplendence of Borgeby-gård and Furuborg behind him. In the cluttered shops of the Havnegad he buys presents for his wife and daughter. For Clara: a jacket bodice of lace. For Ruth: a pair of soft-soled shoes, a doll with a mouth of red yarn, and a small furry cow that makes a phlegmatic lowing noise when tipped just so.

On eleventh December the poet arrives in Oberneuland for Christmas. Again little Ruth is a different creature altogether. A wonder. Her powers of speech surprise him. And yet she's the same, at first, in her apprehensions. This time, though, the child clings not to her grandmother's skirts but to Clara's.

"It's Papa, my sweet," Clara tells her. "You remember Papa."

But Ruth remains timid, and now with a stab Rainer feels it's not for lack of recognition that the child shies away. Something in her sober un-wavering gaze tells him this. She does not judge him, but that look of hers—thrown up at him from so deep a place . . . unsettling how that look conjures his own small face of years ago: implacable girlchild face fringed with ribbons, staring from photographs.

He shows Ruth the soft cow he's brought. Watches her gaze take hold of it as it moos, her small hands hungrily rising toward the softness. It grieves him sorely to feel the gift is a kind of ransom. This toy that had caused him an irresistibly full smile when he first saw it and thought of her.

"She'll be all right in time," Clara murmurs to him later. She gives him her warm kiss in thanks for the garment of lace.

But still, with his daughter's uncanny likeness there before him he is left to wonder: Must that afflicted specter, that girlchild showing itself now in Ruth's eyes as it had shown itself in his own, go on drifting down the generations, imbruing youth with all its adult-sized troubles? *Ismene-Ismene Ismene . . .*

A MASTER, A MUSE:

1905–1906

We must become human beings. We need eternity, because it alone gives our gestures room; and yet we know ourselves to be bounded in by tight borders. We must, therefore, create an infinity within these limits—even here, where we no longer believe in boundlessness.

Florence Diary, 1898

 WORPSWEDE: SPRING 1905.
AGE TWENTY-NINE . . .

*T*he poet is steeped for weeks in the work of ordering and revising his three-part cycle of "Russian Prayers." They will be published come winter by the Insel Verlag of Leipzig under the title he's proposed: *Das Stundenbuch. The Book of Hours.* With Ruth well cared for in nearby Oberneuland, Clara has once again taken a workshop in Worpswede. Rainer has joined her, bearing in hand his old black Schmargendorf notebook restored to him by post from Lou's keeping. Its pages hold the first "Prayers" from his distant Schmargendorf life of five years before. By late May his work is done. With yet another anguished letter he dispatches the notebook back to Lou in Göttingen. In prompt return he receives an unexpected gift: her welcome.

And Rainer's surge of joy, he knows, is instantly clear to Clara when he shares this news. Behind her dark eyes glimmers the trouble it causes her. He stands with his wife in her bright atelier, his hands cupped to her shoulders.

"It makes me very happy to think you'll meet Lou yourself someday, Clara. I think you *must* meet her before long."

"I'd like that," she answers, even-voiced.

"She's meant such a great deal to my development."

"I know it, Rainer."

"I can see, already, how she'll mean just as much to you, darling. Before long."

"Perhaps, Rainer, *ja*. From everything you've told me it seems possible."

"Before long," he says again, and squeezes her shoulders. In response comes Clara's cool smile.

"The reunion with you," he'd written to Lou not long ago, *"is the single bridge to all that is yet to come,—you know it, Lou."*

And so simply does it happen, as though no great chasm of years had to be crossed for this to become possible. Somehow Rainer Maria Rilke finds himself in Göttingen, sitting in the sunlit garden at the back of Lou's house with Lou herself beside him. Four full years gone since they last saw each other.

A notebook lies open upon his knees. He's just read aloud the poem from the Paris *Menagerie*—of the caged panther and all his imprisoned strength. These verses written three years ago already. Lou listened, listened with that old infinite listening manner of hers, though the poem concluded in less than a minute. And now that Rainer has read, now that he's laid himself open in this way and given her something of the person his recent letters have striven to show, now he feels he may tell her of other things.

Before he realizes, several minutes have soared past, his voice streaming forth in full release. And he's talking to Lou as he talks to her in his letters. His hands gesticulating above his open notebook. He hears his own voice, the undammed words somehow heavy, somehow hollow. They flow long. They frighten him. . . .

". . . I could not love, Lou. That's how it was. Even at Christmastime I was incapable, and for these last six months I've been so troubled by this. I came home from my solitude in the north and suddenly—very suddenly it seemed—there was Oberneuland and there was the old Westhoff family home where my daughter has been raised these last two years, and there were Clara's mother and father, and all their eyes were turned upon me. I'd given them my promise, you see. More than a year before, I'd looked in Johanna Westhoff's eyes and given my promise. And then I'd gone with Clara to Rome, and afterward to Scandinavia alone, and now here I was again, a guest in that house. A stranger, really, though of course none of them could see that. Well, I think little Ruth could see it. She stood back from me, Lou. And why shouldn't she, after all?

"And all through Christmas, Lou, I felt the good mother's eyes turned upon me. Felt the father's eyes, God knows! And I knew what they were seeing, knew it very well, and it was *not me,* not *me* that they looked upon, Lou, but someone *else,* and yet *I* was the one to blame for the fact that they should see this *other* person. I was to blame because I had promised. And it's not that I failed in my promises, no—but how could I explain all the work I'd accomplished in the last year? How justify myself, in their eyes, with the very thing that had made me a stranger amongst them? This work of mine . . . it's such slow, invisible work—especially this prose work—and it seems to take me so far away. How can they understand that? They can't. Of course not.

"Well, the whole situation, Lou, instead of shaming me, instead of bringing me to beg forgiveness and commit myself to another course—I think it all just made my heart . . . close up. *Ja,* just like a fist it closed up and . . . made love so hard. And *should* I have been ashamed? There I was, surrounded by love, for really love was the motive behind their concerned looks—but of *me particularly* this love seemed to require too much strength, strength that would have to be stolen from the very pursuits that might, perhaps one day, restore my worth in their eyes. You see, I wanted to love, Lou. How I wanted it! But something . . . something prohibited me.

"I think Clara understands. Yes, I *know* she does—bless her. And yet I can also see what a test it's becoming for her, a test intensified by all those eyes turned upon us, and I wonder if she'll bear it much longer. I won't blame her if she can't, of course. But still I cannot redirect my strength. *Cannot.*

"For other people it would be simple, if moderately painful: other people need merely elect to change course, to devote their energy elsewhere—to a family, to a home, to a profession. My father did so. Clara's father did so. But with me, Lou, it's as though—and this is the frightful thing—it's as though *it lies beyond my power* to choose another way. It's as though this *tenacity,* this *pursuit,* this long heavy *work* will fulfill itself. Whatever the cost. Despite whatever wishes I may make. Else how could I possibly be surrounded by the warmth of Christmas, the embrace of my daughter, however timid, of my wife, and find my heart so stunted, so . . . so disobedient?

"I love Clara, Lou, as I love our Ruth. I want to help them both as much as I am able. But only now have I begun to understand how right you were in your warnings four years ago. How you prophesied all this, Lou. Back then all I could feel was my love for Clara, and it was a *real* love. We made our little house together, Clara and I, and that whole time my heart was completely involved—yes, I had a *stake* in that life. But you were far ahead of me already, weren't you Lou? You saw, from the beginning, how all of that would only result in a world I'd built outside myself. *Ja,* you saw it. And just as you foretold, there I was: trying to live a *real* life amidst things that were real, and yet all my actual growth was happening in a place far from that life.

"But am I to cause injury to those I would love? Am I to dispose of everyone who lends me their affections?

"Before, I couldn't see your reasons for warning me as you did. But now I know and understand everything. Everything. And this is why I've been trying to get back to you, Lou.

"I think I can see now that the best answer is my education. I must pursue that unfinished business to its end and then, perhaps, there will be something of a bridge back over the abyss. With an education, at least, I won't be completely without prospects while this work proceeds in its slow, heavy way.

"Our good Ellen Key has translated the essay concerning my work into German, did you know? She sent it along for me to look over. Well, I found myself—it surprised me, Lou, but I found myself drawing lines through her sentences, and when I looked back at what my pen had done, do you know what I saw? Every sentence concerning my marriage, my family, my time in Paris even . . . had been scratched out. Every sentence. All I'd left her was my art. No doubt she had trouble understanding that. Because *none* of this can ever be understood by anyone—*anyone* but you, Lou. I believe that. It's so perfectly right that you should love my Rodin book as you've told me you do, because that book is so much the work of my heart in these days of . . . these days of learning."

Rainer falls silent. He slumps back into his chair like one winded. He would be mortified, gut-sick at all he's just spoken aloud, he knows, had he spoken it to anyone other than this woman beside him. But in Lou's presence his testimony is what it is. Frightful, of course. But frightfully *true*.

She sits impassive at his side, as grand and unjudging as an oracle. She is still listening, seeming to await his further outpouring. And her face is like it was in their first days together. She's changed not at all.

Rainer closes his notebook. He raises himself in the chair and presses the heels of his hands to his eyes, breathes deep. "It's taken a very long time, Lou, but I must say it all, mustn't I?"

He feels his gorge rising in the anguish, stiffening to a fist at the base of his throat. All these truths still rising hard within him. To say them is to suffer his aloneness knowingly, incontrovertibly. To say them is to see, in hard, harsh clarity, all that he is espoused to.

He hugs the notebook to his chest, sits back, and begins again. . . .

Hours upon hours are spent in talk of this kind. Rainer tells Lou much, also, of his stay in Sweden and Denmark, of the novel that's been growing tenderly and fitfully since Rome, of Malte and how that figure sits with strange and needful weight upon his heart.

In the parlor one evening Rainer reads aloud a tight fragment of the book: Malte's boyhood memory of the ghost of Mathilde Brahe as she manifested herself at dinner in the Urnekloster dining room. Lou and Friedrich Andreas sit before the poet in dark stupefaction, ten lit candles insinuating ghosts on the walls all around.

During Rainer's visit Lou spends a good many days bedridden. A heart condition, she's told him. And how strange this seems in a woman of such strength. The condition began to exhibit itself, apparently, in the Schmargendorf days not long after she and Rainer last saw one another.

While Lou convalesces, the poet walks alone in her garden, stalks barefoot through the meadow below her house, amongst the fragrant fruit-bearing trees. Stands gazing over the valley of the River Leine, rimmed with small mountains. By and by comes his day of departure and as he bids Lou farewell Rainer feels a sudden conviction astir in his blood: the powerful sense that his whole visit has been a long gentle goodbye.

Staring up at him from her sickbed, her face bereft of its usual color, Lou says, "I'm sorry, Rainer."

"Sorry?"

"*Ja*, for causing you to come to Copenhagen last year."

"Still sorry for that?" he says.

"I just hope you'll forgive me."

But he sees he's far past need of forgiving her. He touches the back of her hand where it lies at the blanket's edge. "I'll write to you."

She smiles. "*Ja*, do."

Lou will never again be a stranger to him, and yet he knows now that she does not sit in state upon his heart. No: with a fatal kind of calm, Rainer perceives the truth. The truth is that no one does. . . . Or is Malte the sole presence there? Yes, hasn't Malte begun to displace everything?

.   .   .

"All the vast
images within me: in that far-away, intensely experienced landscape,
cities and towers and bridges and
unsuspected changes of direction,
and a godlike immensity
pulsing through certain lands—
all this climbs within me to mean you, you who escape me."

Meudon-Val-Fleury: September 1905 . . .

Fifteenth September, Rainer finds himself at Meudon-Val-Fleury. A peculiar sensation of doubleness within him as he comes walking again down the chestnut-lined drive toward Auguste Rodin's tiny chateau. It almost seems that this is but another day in the poet's first airless Parisian September. Yet he feels some disorienting difference of temperature or light. And there's a sense too that something inside him has stretched to a state of new delicacy, new hardness. Age, he supposes. Three full years have burnt past since that first arrival in Paris. Three years already, despite the unfinished business of Malte, which ought to have brought him back sooner. But now, just after he'd resolved to pursue his incomplete education and commit himself to an autumn of intensive study, Rodin's marvelous letter of invitation came fluttering down upon him in Germany. What a letter to drop from the blue, utterly unprompted, with its words of huge kindness! The Master had read the poet's monograph, which had finally been translated into French.

"Mon cher ami!" Here comes Rodin himself, rounding the corner of the house to greet him. "How very good that you've come!"

And so Rainer is standing before the Villa des Brillants with the Master clasping his hand in great affection and the estate's two big dogs gamboling in breathless circles nearby.

The Master looks the same: somewhat grayer, somewhat wan in the face, but not extremely older.

"We have so much to talk about," he says, his eyes aglimmer with friendship. "Your book is a work of great completeness, *mon ami,* great strength. Come, let me show you where you will stay."

The poet follows him across the grounds behind the house. On the slope before the grand Pavillon de l'Alma several small structures have been built where there was previously nothing but lawn and trees.

"We've been making many changes since you were last here. It has been a time of tremendous work, a heavy time—but I will tell you about that. Here, this will be your house while you stay at Meudon."

Rodin leads him across the threshold of a little outbuilding into a small, well-appointed room complete with bookshelves and desk and a window giving onto the garden slope and the expansive Sèvres Valley below. A short hall leads back to two other rooms, as Rodin demonstrates with great ebullience. All these rooms Rainer shall have to himself, the Master informs him. "One for sleeping, one for dressing, and one devoted to nothing but your work."

Rainer walks about in disbelief, comes back to find the great old man standing in the doorway. This legend with his big legend-making hands, so actual in his magnanimity. "You will like this, yes?" Rodin holds the poet's eyes with his bright beneficent look, a look of such pleasurable knowing that Rainer need hardly answer.

But he answers, "Abundantly, *mon maître.*" And cannot contain a smile.

Following a homely supper with the Master and Madame in their pale-green dining room, the poet strolls through the Pavillon de l'Alma at Rodin's side. The hall bristles as always with the Master's vigorous work—countless plaster figures solitary or grouped, miniature or life-sized or monumental.

Rodin speaks in soft and rapid cadence with that old contained force of his. That familiar fashioning energy which hasn't diminished in the least, for it stands evidenced in the teeming new work all around. And the substance of his talk is much the same as three years ago: just as massive, just as visionary, except that now, very pointedly, he makes note of more intimate things. His loneliness, his vulnerability before the many dangers he feels to be facing him. The burden of his correspondence. His constant stream of callers, of collectors and antique dealers and interviewers.

Rainer, still struggling with his own submerged French, tautens to listen, eager that nothing should be lost upon him, for even when the Master speaks of troubles he does so in a manner sagacious and instructive.

Rodin says, "This one here," and draws him toward a small plaster figure. "She's an example of what I'd like to tell you. She is . . . *misunderstood,* you see."

The Master's big hand rests gently upon the spine of his *Old Courtesan,* the figure Rainer studied in an expanded arrangement on his very first visit to Meudon. Ancient shriveled woman hunched nude beneath the curling shell of a grotto with her twin beside her. Here she hunches alone.

"She's an example, *mon ami,* of the problem of one's success in the world. Can you imagine that for nearly every person who looks upon her she inspires little but revulsion? *Oui,* revulsion because she is *ugly,* I'm told. But you see—and I know you will understand me—the very meaning of this figure is to show her fuller nature. To show what ugliness becomes when lent to the purpose of art. To show that nothing is ugly except what is false, except what is pranced around and called by the name of beauty simply because someone has decked it in ribbons of ease or fancy, without seriousness, without *real* joy or *real* suffering. Do you see? *Mais oui,* I know you do."

The Master squares himself before the poet. His hand comes off the figure and touches Rainer's arm in a loving, brotherly manner. A deep warm earnestness in the Master's eyes.

"As soon as I started reading your book I could see that you were writing about yourself as much as about me. And then I knew you had done something extraordinary, *mon ami,* something wonderful. You'd found out the only way a book of that sort could be written—*oui,* by writing of *one-self* as one stands before an artist's work. And then I thought, *I am very fortunate to know this man. He understands me, understands my work, because he understands himself!* Now you see my reasons for wanting to tell you how this figure has been received. I tell you because . . . because your own work will have great influence, and you will find you have to endure misunderstanding. These are very strange times for me, *mon ami.* Times crowded with dangers and distractions. Fame, you understand, fame is a great peril to the work we hope to do, people like you and me."

People like you and me. Words to set Rainer aglow inside. What greater sentiment than fraternity could one hope to hear expressed by this Master amongst men? The Master counts Rainer a friend. Indeed, he has *besought* Rainer's friendship.

Starting forward again amongst his creations, Rodin elaborates on this notion of ugliness and the artist, on the dissipating effects of notoriety. His masterful thought opens up, widens, flows to depth upon depth, and then he is talking of Baudelaire's supreme example. Here Rainer ventures a number of his own observations, his troublesome French stopping him short more than once. Patiently the Master listens. Then again his gray beard pours forth his paternal counsel. And Rainer sees what a blessing it is that he cannot reply at length. All he really wants is to hearken to this greatness.

Later they've quietened, and it seems to Rainer that at any moment the Master will take his leave for the night—but then Rodin seems to gain new vibrancy, clutches Rainer's arm and starts once more down the long display. "This one here," he says, halting. "What would you call it?"

"This one? But it already has a name, *mon maître.*"

"Maybe not, how do we know? I think perhaps someone of your understanding ought to name it anew." Such bright pleasure in the Master's eyes. "Please, tell me what you would call it."

Clearly he's in earnest, so they linger together while Rainer studies the piece, silent in his considerations.

Rodin stands off somewhat, intent. Three minutes, four, and still he awaits the poet's word.

At last Rainer produces a name. Then he looks on in alarm as the Master bends with a pencil and scratches the name down on the pedestal.

"Now this one," says Rodin, steering eagerly to another.

And on they go, here to there through the pavilion for an hour or more.

So it happens that several weeks later Rainer sits at his cottage window trying to fathom his great fortune while the lights of the Sèvres Valley twinkle in the September darkness below. It's no use: there's no fathoming it. His thoughts merely come to a blessed bafflement.

To think that Rodin should *need* him—*him* of all people, the Master's own most earnest disciple!—but yes, this is the message so clearly conveyed when the great man looks him in the eyes. The Master deems him, as that beautiful letter of invitation proclaimed, an important *friend,* a person of *great influence, a worker*—and however it has happened, Rainer now finds himself, after three years abroad, at home in the Master's presence with Malte's Paris in reach and a cottage completely at his disposal. Really, now that weeks have passed this way, he wonders how he ever expected to depart from Meudon after a mere visit—to cut himself loose from such sustaining company in order to go chasing the trifle of a degree. Impossible. For he's been delivered back into the one presence he regards more highly—he sees this now—than any other presence on earth. He shall be near the Master day after day; they shall talk and be silent together and understand each other.

This evening, while they sat together at the edge of the small pond watching three swans glide round and round, Rodin made his proposal. And something in the Master's deportment gave Rainer to see that he'd had the arrangement in mind for a great while.

"Since you have been here, *mon ami,* I've felt a joy that only comes to me rarely beyond my work. *Oui,* and now I do not like the thought of you going away very soon. From what you've told me, I understand that you have no certain destination after you leave Meudon. So."

Rodin paused. Touched his beard. Put his head back and gazed up into darkness.

"If you would like to remain at home in Meudon, in the cottage as you are, and help me to gain control of my correspondence, we would not have to part ways soon. As you know, I am without a secretary. I believe I can foresee the question this proposal will bring to mind—you needn't even ask it, *mon ami,* I'll give you the answer now, which is that these duties would require no more than two hours or so each morning. A simple secretarial job, with the rest of your days given over to your work. And so that you cannot possibly refuse I must tell you that these few hours would bring a sum of two hundred francs monthly."

Rodin fell silent. And as *everything* with the Master carries great expressiveness, so his silence gave Rainer to understand the awkwardness the Master had suffered to present the idea, the profound delicacy with which his suggestion was made.

Rainer thanked him and said he would like to think it over a while. The Master nodded. Yet already, by some strange current between them, they both sensed the arrangement was virtually sealed.

Another cottage, then. Westerwede was first, the Roman cottage followed, and now with a sharp shudder Rainer sees it clearly: with each little house he's gone farther out and away from the notion of home, farther along toward work and nothing besides. If that must be the order of things, though, then how significant it is to have *this* little house, standing in the immediate shadow of Auguste Rodin who every day embodies with grace and power his grand *toujours travailler, rien que travailler!* Not only has Rainer received the huge blessing of the Master's welcome, but now Papa, back in Prague, need no longer dispense his ungrudging allotments to a son who never means to come home. And for Rainer to gain this measure of security, to win bread and shelter and the friendship of a Master— does this not incline him back, somehow, toward a life as husband and father? Toward a life that might somehow hold it all—work and love, everything, everything?

The Master is all fruitfulness, all patience. He breakfasts at dawn, then receives the village barber for the daily house call. While his great beard is fluffed and singed, Rodin discusses matters of correspondence with the poet, afterward going to work about the various studios of the Villa des Brillants, addressing a number of sculptures in turn throughout the morning. Early afternoon he travels into the city to his atelier in the rue de l'Université.

By then Rainer has been long alone in his cottage, sometimes with his secretarial duties already dispatched, usually not. A good number of letters must be written, and he's finding that his slow French prolongs the task. But Rainer is glad to be of help in these days when the old man stands in need of sympathy and friendship.

In the latter part of the day, the poet's own work consists entirely of preparing an address to be delivered next month in Prague. An old acquaintance from his university years has read the Rodin monograph and solicited a lecture on further aspects of the Master's work.

The autumn weeks stream by, disposed wholly to Auguste Rodin and his great example. And while the nascent world of Malte Laurids Brigge remains untended, Rainer does not suffer by it but takes heart from the sureness of his shelter, trustful that much is being inwardly cultivated yet. He's learning to bear Malte's presence, to appease the waiting figure. By sheer proximity to Rodin some immense creative tilling is surely taking effect; if the Master teaches anything, after all, it is patience, *patience*. His stern exemplum of *Toujours travailler* acquires a deeper, more pervasive significance by the day. Instead of the ideal of work at every hour, the phrase now bespeaks a spacious life, a life unhurried and imperturbable because it is disposed to nothing, *nothing* but work and the vast life-silences against which work glimmers like stars in the empty depths of night. All this Rainer tells himself, and all the time he feels Malte listening.

At the end of the garden path that runs before Rainer's cottage the Master has set out an ancient stone Buddha. Time and time again throughout the day, the poet looks up from his desk to find that small figure empedestaled against the garden greenery, enthroned upon the lotus blossom, alone in his world-sized equanimity.

Come evening Rodin returns to Meudon and Rainer takes supper with him and Madame in the dining room. Afterward he and the Master stroll the grounds together, or sit side by side at the swan pool. In such hours they give each other much of themselves, together with quantities of companionable silence.

The trees of the Villa des Brillants relinquish pears in plenty. Fifty or more stand piled at one end of the dining room table. From a single pear Madame's kitchen knife makes ten large wedges, and now in the after-dinner hour Rainer and the Master walk through the garden, plucking by turn the glistening wedges clumped atop a handkerchief in Rodin's outstretched palm.

The talk has turned to Clara. She's remained much in Rainer's thoughts throughout his tenure here. He's encouraged her to send Rodin a few photographs of her newest work. They arrived this afternoon.

"It is very fine what she does," says Rodin. "Only a small number of sculptors, really, are able to accomplish such things. She was wise to study under Klinger."

"And under you, *mon maître,* of course."

"Well." Rodin's beard moves gravely as he jaws a slice of pear. "Klinger always said she was a good worker."

"Did she ever tell you the story, *maître,* of her first lesson with him?"

The Master does not recall, so the poet recounts it as Clara once told him.

Known to harbor misgivings regarding female artists, Max Klinger had nevertheless personally invited Clara for six weeks of intensive study in Leipzig. Upon her arrival, Klinger showed the sculptress directly to a tiny rear studio where a hunk of raw marble stood waiting beside a hand modeled in clay.

"Make a marble of that hand," Klinger said. And leaving Clara to the work, he promptly forgot all about her.

The day had darkened before Klinger recalled depositing his student in that back room. Returning, he found Clara asleep on the powdery floor. But on the table above her the marble hand lay finished.

The story elicits the Master's admiring chuckle.

"Clara is a hard worker," says Rainer. "But I worry for her these days. Her father passed on last summer, you see, and she lost a whole allowance. And the number of models available in Worpswede is far from sufficient. I want to help her, *mon maître.* I want to help her as much as possible."

With hardly a thought, Rodin replies, "She should come here."

"To Meudon?"

"*Bien sûr! Oui,* tell her to come. Tell her to come for several weeks. A month. I'll see she has a studio to herself."

"*Mon maître,* you are too generous."

"One *must* have a woman, *mon ami*. This I know only too well!"

By way of the garden path they've come upon the clearing where Rodin's Buddha statue reposes day and night. Figure touched bluely with moonlight now. Some residue in the stone catches that soft light and flares in a mellow spangle of silver.

"This great figure here," says Rainer, "is an example of my own mind on the matter. Every time I look at him he seems more lonely. But this is not the loneliness we usually mean by the word. This, *mon maître,* is a loneliness we should reach for, don't you think?—the artists among us most of all. *C'est le centre du monde, n'est-ce pas?*"

Rodin says nothing for a moment, merely holds the poet's eyes and smiles. And what does that wry, enigmatic look signify? The Master is amongst the most solitary of souls; why should he appear so bemused by Rainer's words?

He lays a consoling hand to Rainer's shoulder and says, "But one must have a woman."

Clara's Meudon tenure is confirmed for late October. The poet will be away for his Prague lecture when she arrives.

 PRAGUE: OCTOBER 1905 . . .

*P*rague again: city of progenitors. Out of the station as on so many occasions before, across the lawns of the Stadtpark, into that time-locked world. World of the past—again it superimposes itself as it has done for years. Labyrinthine streets like a childhood dream from which a boy should have awakened long ago. Affixed like parasites at the elaborate fronts of buildings, countless walleyed faces still leer in faded baroque plasterwork or stone, sidewalk sentries seeing all.

You secure a room in the Hotel Goldener Engel. Then walk to Heinrichsgasse to find Papa at home. Ah, the old house with its door like an orifice into which one crawls darkly, holding one's breath. The steep stairwell rises before you, its close air pregnant as always with the old smell of neighbors and of food one never sees.

Soon you are standing in the apartment. The several once-immense rooms seem to have shrunken since you were last here. For some weeks Papa has not been well. In the rear chamber you find him: a long gray shape, hollow-cheeked, confined to his narrow bed. This man who once stood by mantels. This father whose voice will always be strength, guilt, conscience. This edifice from which the son was chipped. He lies here gaunt and gangling.

He turns his head on the pillow to smile and his face looks weirdly reduced. His greeting is a groggy whisper.

"Hello Papa."

"Sit down by me," he says. "Do you need a chair? Tell the girl to bring in a chair."

"There's one just here, Papa. See?"

His blue eyes roll in vague notice as you drag the chair near. A sand-gray tongue prods with lank curiosity at the corners of his mouth.

"Are you thirsty, Papa? Would you like a drink of water?"

He doesn't answer, but you take up the glass pitcher from the bedside table and pour. Tip the cup gingerly to his lips. He gulps the water down, then lies back eyeing the ceiling, gently gasping, seeming to catch his breath.

"I'm sorry son. I just awoke. It takes a few moments, you see, after a sleep like that, to get back. . . ."

"Of course, Papa. It's good you've slept."

"*Ja.* And now it's good that you're here. I'm very happy to see you, my boy." His unshaven cheeks again stretch back in a smile. His eyes very bright and soft. A strange new light in them, as they never had in your boyhood. He says, "Of course I won't be able to attend tonight, as you know."

"Of course, Papa. You shouldn't. I just want you to get better. You are getting better, yes?"

"Yes, this is the end of it. Sleeping through the nights again at last. I've needed that a good while now. It's the pleurisy, they tell me." He looks past you to the bedroom door. "Has Clara come with you?"

"No, Papa. It's just a brief trip."

"Ah, *ja.*" For a long moment he holds you with a dreamy stare. "So you'll be talking of the sculptor tonight, then."

"Of Rodin, yes. It makes me very happy to tell people about him. He's been so good to us. To me and Clara both." And with an inward shock of tenderness you fear such words may injure this sickly father—for do you travel abroad to tell the world of *him?*

The words hang upon the silence. Then Papa says, "No doubt he sees a great deal in you."

"What, Papa?"

"The sculptor. No doubt he sees much in you."

"I think we understand one another, the Master and I."

"I'm very glad for you, my boy."

"Thank you, Papa."

"I had a caller, René, back in the spring—a lady called Ellen Key. Exceedingly kind. She'd come to Prague to speak of you in public."

"*Ja,* Papa. I remember your letter."

"An exceedingly kind lady, René. We spent an hour together and do you know what she said to me? I recall her words exactly. She said, 'Your son, Herr Rilke, is a consummate artist.'"

"She is a very good woman, Papa."

"But that wasn't the end of it, René. I recall her words completely. She said to me, 'Your son's work, Herr Rilke, is destined to be long remembered.' What do you think of that, my boy? 'Destined to be long remembered,' she said."

"Well, Ellen Key has done much to help me and Clara both." You've said this with great delicacy, but again you balk at the seeming bias of your words.

With new wakefulness Papa wriggles up and plants his elbows beneath him, raises himself against the pillows. His lean fingers pull at the blankets, the sharp nails in sore need of clipping. "Would you open the curtains, my boy?"

"Of course."

"More than a few people saw the notices for her talk, René. Frau Key's talk back in the spring. I couldn't attend, but for weeks afterward one and another person wanted to call my attention to my son's name as they'd seen it in the papers. What joy for a father."

"I'm glad, Papa."

"There, I thought I saw the light pressing through those curtains. Thank you, René. Wonderful, isn't it, the way the sun touches this side of the building?"

"Wonderful, *ja*."

Illumined now, Papa's face seems to show better coloring. Or is that a trick of the light? He sits silent a moment, head cast back and lolling, blue eyes in a contented squint. At length his voice comes low and supple, its intonations weakly musical, such as you've never heard from him.

"I've wanted . . . I've wanted to be the best kind of father to you, René. To see you . . . *succeed* in life."

"*Ja,* Papa." Something scoops ruthlessly through the fibrous tissue of your chest. Sensation of disgorgement, ice-burn.

"You can well imagine, then, what it meant to me, all that . . ."

Papa drifts. Does he mean, by these words of his, to render some apology or recompense? No saying. A father's secrets are inviolable. Meanwhile the son is dismantled by his own secret tenderness.

Papa's gaze returns from its inward place—outward again, the blue eyes opening. He seems weirdly strengthened, as if years have ticked backward. "And you take care about your health, don't you, René?"

"I try, Papa, *ja*."

"That's good, my boy. You must try. You know how it runs in our family—these . . ." One long-nailed hand makes a frail sweeping gesture over his blanketed legs. ". . . these indispositions." It seems that by noting his condition in this way he would remove himself from it. And whence comes such quickly summoned hope?

"And how is Ruth?" he asks with inquisitive brightness.

"She's well, Papa. A sturdy little girl."

This news he receives in thoughtful silence.

"You know, Papa, you're looking much better already."

"Pardon?"

"I say you're looking better already, just in the few moments I've been sitting here." And you must believe this now, for you have said it aloud. For disbelief annuls every comfort.

"Am I?" In a wondering manner Papa stares down his own bedded length. Then his near hand floats up from the edge of the blanket, touches your fingers, squeezes cool and lank. "No surprise at all, eh my boy? None at all."

Your lecture that evening is sparsely attended. Afterward, though, while the indifferent numbers shamble noiselessly from the hall, a few young people—a girl, another, and then three boys in turn—come to smile and press your hand and thank you with great heart for all you've told them of the Master and his work. Their eyes all bright and indelible. And so the evening was not for nothing. . . .

When the poet returns to the Villa des Brillants, Clara is there to welcome him. Rodin has designated one of the small workshops for her use. Rainer finds her hunched in labor, gowned with her plastery smock. For a moment or more she doesn't notice him and he's able to hold her in his vision: the artful silence enwrapping her as she works. Something so dear in that lovely profile, something in the fall of the dark locks across her temple.

Then she hears the rustle of his shoes upon the stone floor and looks up. Smiles sweetly. "Why, hello."

"Hello."

He kisses her: a brief, gentle touch of the lips. She would prolong the moment but he doesn't want to disturb her, steps back that he might look at her in full again.

Though she smiles, a sunken shadow remains at the back of her eyes. This look arrived in August with the death of her father and shows no sign yet of receding. Natural enough, but Rainer and she both know the look signifies something more than daughterly grief. The loss of Father Westhoff has induced the loss of Clara's longtime allowance. It was never an immense amount but always enough that she needn't founder. And now, though the Master has welcomed her to Meudon, though a month in this place is a treasure, still it is only a month, after which she'll return to Worpswede while Rainer stays on here without term. All this remains unspoken. This shadow persistent and silent.

"I've just had word from Ellen Key," Clara says. "Her essay concerning your work will appear in the *Prague Review* and she's forwarded the honorarium. She told me you insisted that I have it. Thank you for that, Rainer."

"Well, I want to bring bread however I can."

"It does help."

A clear affection in her look, together with the shadow.

She says, "You've a few letters, according to Madame. Mountains of letters actually, if you count the Master's—but a few addressed to you."

Rainer leaves her to her work and in his cottage finds a missive from Axel Juncker, expressing the hope that the poet will resume his reading duties at the former agreeable salary. But what's more, Juncker wants to publish a new expanded edition of *The Book of Images,* along with the prose poem *Cornet* in its own edition, as revised by Rainer in Sweden last year.

Meudon is quiet this month, the Master away in Spain since Clara's arrival.

One mellow evening following dinner with Madame Rodin, Rainer and Clara retire together to the Pavillon de l'Alma. The panels of the high windows look blindstruck in the bluish glare of the electric lights. On a bench beside one of the windows the poet and sculptress sit talking, voices hushed as though in deference to the Master's figures before them. Clara will return to Worpswede in a few days.

"We can't know, can we," she says, "how much longer you'll be here?"

"No. Most likely for some time yet. He's so lonely, the Master."

A silent assent from the sculptress.

They sit, wordless. High above them the light fixtures hum with rigid constancy.

"Did I tell you," says Rainer, "about Madame and the doll? No? We were together one evening after dinner, she and the Master and I, when suddenly—I don't know how she managed to produce it—Madame was showing me a doll she's kept for several years. A heavy-headed cotton thing with a skull of painted porcelain and real human hair glued on very painstakingly and delicate eyelids that close when you tip her to sleep. Madame explained she keeps the doll as a kind of heirloom. But by the way she handled it—so tenderly, so girl-like—you could see it means much more to her than that. Her hands, as she held it, looked the way children's hands look when they are walking their dolls about or holding them up and speaking to them like people. Once she'd thoroughly introduced me to the doll she sat back and hugged it in her arms, and then the Master spoke up. 'You know, you could make a gift of this doll to the Rilkes' daughter.' He didn't mean anything by it but kindness, of course. He'd suggested it very gently. But you couldn't imagine the change that passed over Madame's face. Rodin might as well have torn the thing out of her hands. It was frightful. The moment I saw her shock, I refused the Master's suggestion with as much forwardness as possible. But one could see how hurt she was already."

Clara sits motionless, her glazed listening look fixed on a spot of air beyond Rainer's shoulder. From somewhere low in her throat comes a quiet contemplative noise like a sigh.

Slowly she stands up. She moves a few paces down the hall toward the hulking *Balzac Monument.* Stops before the figure, shrunken. The rugged demigod standing over her encased in his long robe, his rude chin upraised. His horned and haughty stare soars far above the head of any onlooker. Clara lifts a hand and touches the plaster pleat of the robe.

Rainer rises, moves near to her.

"It means so much, doesn't it," he says, "to spend time in here?" He stops short, abruptly aware of Clara's dark state.

She hardly moves, posed there with hand outstretched. It seems she cannot suffer to look at that relentless roughcast face above. Her eyes cling instead to *Balzac*'s giant toe jutting from his bottom hem. In a low fretful tone she begins to speak.

"One of his assistants told me that they're not even married—Madame and the Master. Not even proper man and wife, though everyone calls her Madame Rodin."

"I know it," says Rainer.

And he gives Clara the silence, watching her troubled profile. Waiting.

At length he touches her shoulder. Speaks quietly into her ear. "In this figure of *Balzac* I see it all clearly, Clara. Rodin's most representative work this is, yet it was refused by the people who begged him to make it. It's never had a home beyond the Master's presence. And look around here. Most of these figures are destined to homelessness. That's how he works, in great patience with all that. And even his nearest relationships are cultivated in this detachment. Without hope and without despair."

"And should it be so?" says Clara quickly. "*Must* it be so?"—her words stiff and breathless, carved close at every edge. "How long can that go on? How does he know that's what life really wants of him? Sometime we must learn what life wants of us, Rainer, mustn't we? How do *we* know?"

"You and I, Clara?"

"*Ja.* You and I."

So now, the shadow. The shadow she's carried in her gaze for months emerges between them, as Rainer knew it must. Clara, dear heart, bore it alone as long as she was able.

He closes his eyes, breathes slow. Her scent so close beside him: that fragrance whose source is the back of her neck. Soft smell of time passed and passing. Of a world they share and of worlds between them. Despite his intractable resolve, Rainer suffers depths of gentleness toward her. So many warring things within him, each so fervid, yet each so gentle. He whispers, "Those are my very questions, Clara—mine as much as yours. You know that, don't you?"

Her downcast stare does not shift, but she nods with a very natural certainty. "Of course, darling." And now she sounds immensely sad to him. "I'm not accusing. I don't mean it that way, Rainer. Please don't think that. They're real questions, all."

He feels her sadness, deep and indubitable. Bears it as she does. "I think—" he says, halting somewhat as he sees the inarguable answer before him, "I think the most we can do is keep working."

Silence between them. Rainer's words sifting down, settling. Clara will not object. She knew the truth of the matter before he spoke it, but they must say it aloud together. They must say this truth and see it and in this way converge within it before the inevitable course of things sends them apart again.

But how many such frightened recapitulations, how many new divergences, can a love countenance? And what scars, all the while, are being notched upon the future?

"Do you know, my dear," Rainer says, "sometimes the Master looks at me for no apparent reason and smiles a sad little smile and says to me, '*Bon courage.*' Isn't that marvelous? '*Bon courage,*' he says, when I've hardly said a thing myself. As if he knows exactly the nature of my doubts, my fears. And look, Clara, how this man works and works and all these things grow up around him. All unhurried. All unforced. Despite the demands of circumstance. They have no regard for time, none of these things—and *that* is how they are able to mount again and again to greatness. 'I become at one with everything around me,' Rodin tells me. And *that* is what *I* must be able to attain, Clara: the ability to work like that. Because my work too must be *built,* just as this work has been built. And that freedom has been given to me here, Clara. I have the Master's example, all his great achievements around me all the time. For now at least. And you understand, I know you do, my dear, that it's my duty now to live in this example while I can. To let my work come as it must and perhaps bring its own rightful answer to these questions of ours. We *both* must do this, Clara, in our own way. It's difficult, of course, but we must see that this is possible for one another."

His words are whispers now. Utterance of his somber certainty, his pledge to this life they've both believed in and struggled toward.

Finally Clara lifts her hand from the sculpture. She turns to him and touches that hand to his chest: warm sculptress palm pressed flat to Rainer's heart. His own hands rise to cover it.

And she looks as she looked that day in her parents' dining room: *facing him in her simple white dress, spotless organdy aglow in the windowlight and her bell-shaped sleeves coming to her knuckles as he held her hands in his, her moist eyes moving up and down from that handclasp to his face, her glance with its dread and breathless joy.*

But now her eyes have gone gray. She too is whispering, her words drifting up slow and explorative: "Can we know what's right? Maybe not, Rainer. Maybe there is no right. But we must do what we feel. In that you *are* right. And we're learning, aren't we, darling? And for now we have shelter. . . ."

She falls silent. Somehow her thought, though unconcluded, is finished.

They stand there. The *Balzac* towers over them, immense and inscrutable. At last they return to their bench and sit close, clasping hands.

Distantly Clara says, "I've decided to bring Ruth to Worpswede."

"To live with you?"

"*Ja.*"

"When?"

"As soon as I get back."

Rainer looks at her deeply. Lays the backs of his fingers to her magnificent cheek. "That will be marvelous, Clara."

"It will be better to have her with me. For her and me, both."

"I'm very glad, Clara."

"It's difficult, you know, for *everyone*. How to live, how to work. Paula, for instance. Her marriage is none too joyful, she tells me. And I can see it. She seems terribly discontented when she talks of Otto. She wants to come to Paris. I think she's planning on it, though he objects."

"They're unhappy together?"

"The unhappiness is *hers* mostly. Otto does seem a bore when you hold him up to her liveliness."

"She's always loved Paris, I remember."

"*Ja.* Her work will flourish here, she's sure of it. You must see her paintings when you come for Christmas, Rainer. Startling, the things she's doing. Worpswede really is much too small for Paula."

"She should do what's best for her work. We must help her if we can, Clara."

"*Ja.* We must, of course."

A few days later in Meudon, while Clara labors in her workshop a hundred paces across the grounds, the poet writes to Lou with a new hardened resolve:

> *"Only the entirely great ones are artists in that most strict but only real sense, that art has become a way of life for them."*

.   .   .

Clara departs back to Worpswede. In the following days a copious snow falls over Meudon, whitening everything. For the better part of a week the whole world stands at a pause. . . .

*D*ark when you arrive, and Worpswede's dun fog sits thickly upon the moors. Walking the highway, you are a black figure in great-coat and hemisphere hat, your collar high and your long goatee buried in a muffler.

A half decade ago you walked this road with Heinrich Vogeler, Russia rife within you, and found yourself talking with a young sculptress in her darkened yard. How clear those hours seem, even for that darkness. Now your way is engulfed in cloud: nothing to see beyond the small circle of packed highway dirt underfoot. As if both future and past meet with obliteration in weather of this kind.

Even the lights of the nearby houses do not disclose themselves till one stands at the very porch steps. So you turn at random to pursue your dim estimations. And find yourself twenty paces into a vacant field . . . or a half step short of tottering into a ditch . . . or in near collision with a neighbor's front hedge. And despite these several miscalculations it feels somehow sudden when you come to stand at the dark stoop of the cottage Clara has let.

Scrape your shoes at the mat. Then pause there in the shadows with the front window gleaming soft to one side. Pale golden glow diffused weirdly in the fog curling noiseless against the house. Light of these lives glassed-in from the cloud in which you wander.

Listen now. Are they about just beyond the door? . . . Nothing.

Put your hand to the knob—but wait. It requires a long moment's thought to know whether you will simply make your entry or knock. Finally you press the door, rapping it firmly as it swings, and you're standing in the small house where you are neither at home nor merely a visitor.

There seems to be no one about. In the empty front room a lamp stands lit upon a table, three chairs pushed in around it. A doorway behind leads into a dark hall. You start toward the hall but stop near the table's end. Two big sheaves of paper lie there on the floor. Screw your head downward to see the childish sketches cluttering the paper from top to bottom. Your daughter's dainty handiwork.

Squat and take up one of the sheaves, tilt it to the lamplight. Rich brown odor of pulp, of pencil. Various scenes scratched boldly in restless leaden lines. You believe you can make out a bicycle, riderless, adrift in an otherwise empty corner. And here is a house: a triangle roof and a chimney rendered with confident precision, mullions across each of the two front windows. The house stands on a flat meridian with nothing about, no family. Or are they cozied up inside?

Now a door clatters at the rear of the hall. You rise and see Clara's shape approaching.

"Ah, good," says her voice with a pleased sort of sigh.

"Hello, Clara."

She draws up just within the lamplight. Leans at the doorjamb with darkness behind her and smiles her lovely calm closed-mouth smile. "I thought I heard you come in. Ruth will be so glad."

"Is she here now?"

"*Ja,* she's back in the studio. I've been modeling her."

"Have you? She sits still?"

"Dear no, she sits still for nothing. But it will be a fine model, I think. You were able to find us despite the fog."

"Just a few near misses, but yes."

"And you've found her work, I see. That's what she calls it, did I tell you? Calls it work, just like her mama's."

"She's taken to life here, has she?"

"Terribly well. Now and then she complains she misses Grandmama, but there's easy remedy for that with Oberneuland so close. She's extremely excited to see you though, Rainer. She's talked of hardly anything else since Thursday. I wish you'd heard it. Come see her."

"Clara." Before she can turn, your hand goes out to seize her wrist. She falls still at the lightness of your grip. You stand and give her a long trustful look. You have not kissed her hello. A full month apart since she left Meudon, and yet you've stood several feet back, still in your coat, talking of Ruth—little vehicle of affection between the restrained parents. "It makes me very happy," you say, "Ruth being with you here. I want you to know."

"Of course, Rainer." A placid smile. "As long as I can work here, it seemed the happiest arrangement. And now we're so glad you've come."

"I wanted to show you, Clara"—already your hand has drawn back to bring the book from your valise. Small embossed volume. Her hands receive it with slow care, her fingers coming over as though to bless it.

"*Das Stundenbuch.*" Her eyes lifting, moved and bright. "Oh Rainer!"

"It owes a great deal to Westerwede, you know."

"I know it does, dear, of course."

Her touch runs lovingly over the cover, the monastic design embedded there: a three-headed fountain with gothic lettering above and beneath.

Then she opens the book. And with a jolt of clarity you can see everything halting in her. Her eyes have found the printed dedication.

Laid in the hands of Lou.

Clara's glance dulling to defeat as she looks upon it. And now you're ashamed. For what did you think her feelings would be? Oh, but Clara, in her great dignity, is already mastering the shock. Her falter only momentary. The warmth returns to her eyes.

"And now it's finished, isn't it, dear?" Words very gentle, almost brittle.

"I've inscribed it," you say and show her the other page.

She reads.

"Ja," you say. "Finished."

And only now does she come forward to embrace you.

It seems impossible that your daughter should be four, yet it can't be denied. Clara has tied the child's dark hair back, enunciating Ruth's big soft eyes. She's wearing a blue dress with pinafore, white shin-high stockings and black buckle-overs. She moves about in these ladylike clothes with incredible confidence, sits down, springs up, flounces and struts and jumps.

Her small mouth much resembles your own—even you can see it—and you watch as she spouts words with her breathtaking childish eloquence. You can see, also, your shallow chin in hers, the dimpled shadow bred down from Josef Rilke. But it's Ruth's special four-year-old dominion that causes you the greatest awe. That your own daughter should hold this fantastic sovereignty of the four-year human soul, this dominion very few remember later in life (will she remember?). Where does she learn it, everyone else in the world having long forgotten? It's a whole universe all her own; anything she wishes becomes possible in it, her hands endowing dolls with a life she'd never think to doubt. And what a wonder the way she flies to your open arms and right off wants to give you little parts of this world of hers, things you could never importune her for. She seems to possess none of that troubled hesitancy that overcame her just a year ago. She calls you "Väterchen" now.

In the studio while Clara works, Ruth sits bandied upon your knee, her immaculate small fingers plucking at your coat hem, your collar, your beard, as she tells you all about what a good model she is. She knows how to model so well, she says, because she watched Mama doing it for Paula last month.

"Kopf oben, ja Mama?" Ruth's chin juts high.

"That's right, my sweet. Head up."

"And does it look like Mama, Ruth? Paula's painting?"

"But Väterchen, I have not seen it!"

"It's not finished yet?"

"No, Väterchen, not finished!" she falls against you, forgetting her poise, buries her face in your waistcoat only to discover the watch tucked there. Her fingers tug at the silver fob.

Clara lifts high the child's clay likeness, looking past it to the living daughter. "Paula was to be finished a few days ago. We should walk over tomorrow and see."

So here, on this fog-rich Worpswede day in your fourth year of marriage, is Paula's portrait of your wife:

Clara's slender fawn throat bared above the white décolletage of her dress, a scoop of shadow in the triangular divot of the collarbone. Her head tilted back and her face nimbused by darkly gathered hair. The clay-colored leaf of her mouth cambers tautly, drawn down at the corners, somehow evincing the rich quietness of her voice, that modest élan so completely Clara's own. Here in this picture is all the harbored power that so struck you five years ago, the night you first met her by the light of her raised lamp.

—*I thought you were German. Or Austrian, perhaps. But you are not?*

She had seen it about you immediately: no proper home, no country of your own, though Russia had meant so much. Russia, the vast homeland beyond whose borders you've lurked for years. No proper home even yet— and mustn't Clara see *that* just as clearly now? Do you even seek your home now as you sought it then, in those days when you first thought you'd found it in this face? This soulful face which Paula has conveyed with amazing fidelity. Something catches in your throat.

.　　.　　.

"It does look like her, doesn't it, Väterchen?"

Ruth tugs at Rainer's coattails, but he is lost in the painting, so the child moves to her mother. "It looks like you, Mama, do you agree?"

"*Ja,* my sweet. Paula made it very well, didn't she?"

"Very well!" crows Ruth, and leaning deeply into Clara's skirts she calls out across the studio, "Very well, Paula!—that's what Mama says of it!—did you hear?"

From across the atelier, stooped at the waist and gurgling like a predator, Paula comes racing to engulf the child with feigned violence, a kissing embrace. "Is that what Mama says of it, little one?—is that what she says? And what say *you* what say *you* what say *you?*"

Ruth shrieks and squirms in her arms. They tussle till she is breathless with laughter, then Paula frees her. The child darts away to a small table where the painter has set a cup of milk.

"And what is the papa's word?" Paula says, standing to smooth her skirts.

But Rainer finds himself mute. Her soft smiling eyes, glistening brown as moorland soil, awaiting answer.

"There is . . . there is nothing I can say, Paula. It is wonderful."

"Wonderful." Paula murmurs the word toward the canvas with something like disbelief. Then sidles over to Clara, throws her arms around her neck, kisses her. "She's a *wonderful* friend anyway."

Clara blushes, laughs, pushes her off.

"Wonderful is a good word," says Paula. "Thank you for using it, Rainer. I'm glad you like the painting. I am. I was standing all the way over there for fear you wouldn't."

"It's extraordinary, Paula. Truly. And these others as well. Such colors! None of the Worpswede painters are doing such things. None that I've seen. But this—" he gestures to a still life—"this is like what Van Gogh has done. You're working hard, one can see that."

"Harder than ever—even with these moors burning at my feet. Or maybe because of that. It's very hard to stay still in this place. Some time ago I set my thirtieth birthday for a threshold. I'll either be somebody by then or not, I told myself. The day is fast approaching now, but I'm becoming somebody after all. Big or small, there's no saying just yet—but somebody. And somebody *outside* Worpswede's boundaries."

"It's already so," says Clara.

"But I must still learn to draw. That's what Otto tells me. And for that I must go to Paris."

With a small noise like a hiccup, a strange glazed look overcomes Paula now. She lifts a tentative palm to her throat.

"No, not just for that," she says, fingering her beaded necklace. A sudden levelness in her voice. "But because I *must* go. Because it's *Paris*. That's all."

Walking back from Paula's atelier, Clara tells Rainer, "She has fifty marks saved already. All for Paris. And Otto doesn't know a thing about it."

"She'll be right to leave. Worpswede can't keep her. Her paintings testify to that."

Ahead in the glaring blur of the afternoon fog, Ruth is cantering along in two-step imitation of a horse, her blue skirts and blue woolen cloak swaying brightly. Her enthusiasm sends her wheeling into the moor. She begins to vanish in the white. But Clara calls and the child turns back to the highway with hardly a hitch in her pace. Her breath fans above her, diffusing in the fog.

"Last week," says Clara, "we were together in her atelier a whole evening long. She wept for more than an hour, the poor dear. Just sat at her stove door breaking peat between her hands and throwing it into the flames and talking all the time about Paris. She said it's become the whole world to her. She can't understand why she shouldn't be there. It's like her heart is crumbling here."

"Let's help her, Clara. Fifty marks is a start, but she'll need a great deal more. Let's buy a painting. We can do that, can't we?"

"If we buy it together, yes."

They saunter a while. Then: "Yes"—Clara clutching Rainer's hand in quick ebullience—"Yes, let's buy one!"

The poet smiles, nods his concurrence. And for several sure moments feels a happy silence aglow between himself and his wife. That feeling they knew for days at a time once. And around them the silence of the fog, the lovely light-steeped world it contrives. Here and there in the tufts of grass that fringe the road, tiny conical spiderwebs sprout like shrunken cyclones.

Clara says, "I will miss her though."

Rainer hears clearly the selfless joy in her voice. His sweet wife who wants so much for those she loves.

In the evening they raise a Christmas tree in Clara's studio, a lush young fir with boughs fine as fleece, its resinous scent as strong as something cooked. Ruth beams in four-year-old ravishment while the three of them deck the branches with candles and plaster snowflakes of Clara's design.

Rainer lifts his daughter in his hands that she may set the crowning star in place. Her frame small and solid in his grasp and Ruth hushed to an attitude nearly prayerful as he sends her gliding upward, her fingers clutching the bright heather star she's crafted to her mother's instructions. Breathless silence as the child's arms stretch out, stretch out . . . and finally leave the star in place. Then an exhalation of awe from all three.

When the poet moves to set Ruth down she clings to his neck. "Not yet, Väterchen. Keep me a little while."

Rainer flushes. So much uncomplicated affection in his daughter's tight encircling arms. How willing a child can be, how ready always to receive another's love, in a manner to put any elder to shame. Something swells his heart, a dangerous tumescence. A feeling of strange ennoblement. He knows himself unentitled to it. And yet his daughter clings with uninjured trust.

Clara, on her knees beside the tree, tinsel in her hands, looks on. Watching him in that fatherly embrace. And Rainer sees his wife smile. Small self-possessed smile that sits like sadness in Clara's deep compassionate eyes.

*I*n the first chill days of the New Year, by foggy dawn light, Rainer kisses Clara, kisses Ruth, and climbs aboard a waiting landau.

"You should go back inside," he says. "The frost is too much."

Clara huddles in her cloak before the gate. "In a moment. What good are we for farewells if we can't even see you off?" Then she chuckles to find that Ruth has stepped away.

The blindered horse has drawn the child's interest and she wants to question the driver. "Can he see his way? Isn't he cold? Do you suppose he likes to pull this carriage?"

Rainer smiles. His daughter's dulcet voice ringing in this dead drear morning where nothing else stirs to intimate waking life, not even the chitter of a bird. Ruth's blue cloak strangely bright in the drab Worpswede fog below him.

Soon the landau rattles forth along the frosted highway. And Rainer finds he cannot look behind to the place where Clara and Ruth stand watching. Cannot bear to see the retreat of their colorful figures in that pall of gray. This Worpswede streaming away from him, and he knows he'll never have native eyes for it, though it be forever home to his wife and child both. While they remain here, sensing always the receiving nature of this place, what will Worpswede become to *him?*—to him whose birthplace, even, has forever seemed a mischance of kinds?

By the seventeen-hour train from Bremen Rainer will betake himself back to Paris. To Meudon. And what has Paris, city that so displaced him once, become to him after all? It seems he must remind himself now, for he feels like one emerging from a deep and pleasurable dream, implicated all these weeks in the all-consuming warmth of family. And yet there was a whole other life before. In Paris. In Meudon.

Paris has granted him the last of his "Russian Prayers"—what is now *Das Stundenbuch*. Has granted him the beginning of *Malte*. Malte. Yes, and there's a whole world still parceled in that dark insistent figure who took lodgings within him two years ago.

Thus the poet—who has long suffered the mischance of his origins, who once suffered Paris as torment and terror—has by some impossible transmutation made the city itself his work, even made it—dare he believe?—his home. But still Rainer remembers when it was not so. All those bleak days in which he would never have supposed the city itself could become the salvation. And has Paris really become just that? Or mustn't he first learn the fate faced by Malte in Paris?—young poet alone in the clench of the Latin Quarter. Mustn't Rainer stay with Malte's figure, shepherding Malte clear to whatever vast threshold he will cross in solitary and fulsome silence? Perhaps only then, finally, once Malte has made that passage, can Rainer's freedom be absolute. Then he will have Paris at his feet, all its dismantling powers reversed—his life no longer a miscellany of fragmentary images. Ah, but what is the nature of that ultimate threshold Malte must travel over? And can Malte be taken across, ushered toward his dark fate, without drawing Rainer through after him?

And what is the world to do with one such as you? What are friends and loved ones to do?—with one who travels endlessly and sleeps in an unshared bed and takes long walks alone and sits at a desk and works and waits in order to simply *say something,* not even to name something but just to take the name already possessed and say it over again, to show it, *show it,* hold it up in two devout hands in all its beauty or splendor or fright, and in this way give back to maybe one person (maybe no more than one) the wondrous disquiet this person once knew as a child when first faced by the thing they're now seeing again.

> *"But to say—understand this now—*
> *oh to say these things*
> *in such a way*
> *that the things themselves would never*
> *have thought to exist so earnestly."*

Partings:

1906

Sei allem Abschied voran, als ware er hinter
dir, wie der Winter, der eben geht.
Denn unter Wintern ist einer so endlos Winter,
das, überwinternd, dein Herz überhaupt übersteht.

Be ahead of every farewell, as though it were behind
you, like the winter just gone.
For among winters is one so endlessly winter
that wintering-through, your heart will at last withstand it.

Sonnets to Orpheus; II,13

 PARIS: 1906. AGE THIRTY . . .

$\mathcal{A}$ month of gray sky and sleet and you are stowed away in the stove-warmth of your Meudon cottage writing Rodin's letters by the hundreds and longing for work of your own while the Master's great shadow courses this way and that, his shaman-spell unbroken.

Then at the Master's side you walk in the Versailles gardens, stand here and there amongst the high hedges at garden pools overgrown with weeds. Timeworn fountain figures carved of marble leap up or repose atop the algal waters, faces of moss-eaten stone frozen to grim green smiles. Rodin in his stovepipe hat circles the pools.

"Do you know what I love about this place? The inner life of an age is everywhere given form here. Nothing like this happens anymore. Not in our time."

At a crossing of paths you watch him halt and bend to pluck up from the gravel a fallen twig. He turns the twig in his fingers, lifts it against the gray sky, lays it across his palm as if testing its weight, finally tosses it away.

"I understand it forever now," he says.

Weeks later you stand with the Master before the ancient cathedral at Chartres, its huge stone face soaring up from your feet into dizzying towers, and at one corner a Romanesque angel in long chiseled robe is mounted to the stone, bearing a half-moon sundial to the heavens and smiling a grave and placid smile.

A freezing wind howls down the hard flank of the cathedral, lifting thin cyclones of dust that coil about your legs and whip at your face till you must shield your eyes from the sting.

With a mild dispassionate voice the Master says, "It is always like this. These cathedrals anger the wind with their greatness."

And then: February. Rodin away in London. You are standing on a swirling platform of the Gare du Nord with a bundle of lilies and freesia in one hand, your packed valise in the other, two fifty-franc notes in your coat pocket, watching passengers spill from the doors of a steaming train.

For the heavy tide flowing past, you do not catch sight of Paula till she's just beyond arm's reach, and not till she's uttered a quiet *"Bonjour."* There before you, then, is the painter's fair face peering up from beneath the brim of a lank gray hat.

Something in your chest makes a surprised little leap. You suck a draught of breath. Paula's brown eyes tired but bright, her mouth fixed in a wary smile. Smile of cautious arrival after her incautious flight.

"Paula. *Bienvenue.*" You hold forth the torch of aromatic flowers. "These are for you. *Parce que nous sommes étrangers les deux en cet lieu, vous et moi." Because we are both strangers in this place, you and I.*

With a fluttery noise she accepts the bouquet. And garbed in her yellow dress and traveling hat, one hand clutching a small trunk and these flowers now sprouting from her other fist, she resembles a woman come to Paris on a honeymoon. This matrimony, though, is husbandless, solitary, for Otto Modersohn has been left behind in Worpswede.

"I'm here," she says. Her eyes casting about in wonder. "In spite of the odds, I've done it. I've come back." She laughs a shy, quiet laugh, then her mouth flattens to a sober line. "I emptied all my drawers last week. Otto didn't notice. It will be an awful surprise to him. That's why I waited for his birthday to pass. But I had to come. He'll see now. It will cost him some pain, but he'll understand in time. Won't he? *My* birthday too has just gone by, and if I'm ever to begin my life it must happen now. My thirtieth year or never."

Two weeks ago, on the day following Paula's birthday, had come a letter from Clara, shocking in its disclosures. She had called on Paula with birthday blessings. The two had passed the afternoon in the painter's studio, and Paula, disconsolate and eventually reduced to weeping, had confided the secret she'd lugged about for five years of marriage: Otto Modersohn had never in his half decade as her husband taken her to the bridal bed.

Staring at Clara's letter had caused a blazing ache in your limbs. And now the auburn-haired painter stands here before you. Gentle Paula Modersohn-Becker, five years spurned, the platform thrumming around her in the flurry of a thousand feet, her own feet firmly planted in brave rebeginning.

From your pocket you withdraw the two fifty-franc notes, hold them out flattened and furled. "I want you take this, Paula. It's a loan. Not very much, but you will need it."

She sets down her trunk, plucks the tendered cash, tucks it away. Gone. No insistence required. "Thank you, Rainer."

Her eyes alive with unashamed gratitude. She knows what she's facing by coming here alone. No illusions. Behind the soft gleam of her glance you see her coiled fierceness. The strength of her resolve.

"Clara has written you a little letter of welcome. She sent it to the rue Cassette already. You will find it waiting. We both wish you every strength, Paula. Every success."

"I'm very grateful." Now she notes your valise, says, "And you're going away for your lectures?"

"*Ja*. A few weeks. First to Berlin."

Paula hoists her trunk again. Stands with gaze cast abstractedly above your head. "I've been given a new life," she says. "It's going to be beauti-ful." Her voice drifts into a faraway timbre. "It's awful, isn't it, how we hu-man beings cause each other such pain? But one must trust others to understand in time."

She looks slender and small as you watch her shamble away, tugged to one side by the weight of her luggage. You *feel* yourself into that com-mencing walk of hers—the vast and unforgiving city before you, and be-hind you, laid by: the broken things your departure necessitated, fragile things rent gently and unmaliciously by your own hands.

. . . *I'm sorry, Clara. And give my apology to Ruth in the tenderest kiss.* . . .

You and Paula and how many like you describe your webbing paths alone across the surface of Europe? These paths somehow bind you all to-gether, despite your loneliness. You many solitary souls whom nothing can bind.

The swirl of travelers flows thick over the platform and Paula is gone.

Berlin now, and the city is repugnant as always. Streets piled together like discarded ribbons awaiting the dustpan. A mishmash of buildings—copper-roofed, tile-roofed—plunked down indifferently, without plan, like cap-tured game pieces removed from some immense playing board where the greater attention remains fixed. The place is unseasonable with a stagnant colorless warmth, storm winds astir beneath the leaden lid of the sky.

Berlin, quite naturally, signified pain to you once, back in your last Schmargendorf days—and again two years ago for reasons wholly differ-ent. Several long weeks here with Clara then, in that time fast upon your return from Sweden. Airless summer weeks that found you conscripted to the dentist's chair day after day, your teeth in a terror of pain, jaw swollen from the gawping forceps, blood at the sides of your tongue and your brain swimming through foul webs of ether. Strange now to return to this city that always took, took, and never gave, but to *feel* its pain no longer—not the pain come of Lou or that of the dentist's blade—while yet everything around retains the *look* of the pain. Numbed and numbing city, Berlin.

As it happens, you and Lou shall meet again in the coming days. She's to travel from Göttingen to review the premiere of a play by Gerhart Hauptmann, and you've arranged a rendezvous. What's more, Clara has come from Worpswede.

It makes me very happy to think you'll meet Lou yourself someday, Clara— those tense moments before your visit to Göttingen last summer, you the husband fleeing to the presence of another woman. It's a wonder that so much time has elapsed before things could come to this: Clara and Lou face to face before you at last. Your life, for so long now, has seemed to call for this encounter.

At the Hospiz des Westens you find Clara already settled in a room of her own, her tall familiar figure revealed at the opening door a moment after your knock. A bright window glowing in the room behind her, so at first she's a silhouette. But as you reach for her hands and raise them in your own to kiss she comes forward into the light and she is svelte and elegant as ever.

Almost three months already since you last laid eyes upon her. Ah, this uncommon marriage that makes a spectacle of the spouse's face, a reunion most every time your glances meet. And ever this contained surge of affection between you—but always bridled back to no more than a kiss, an embrace, a clasping of hands. Clasping her hands now, it somehow unsettles you to discover that the old hammer-wound across her knuckles is faded to near disappearance. Effacement of a memory once made together. How long since that memory healed so cleanly?

Clara says, "You found your room?"

"Yes, thank you. It's fine. Shall we dine downstairs?"

"You're not too tired?"

"I'll need to rest before tonight, but no."

"I'll put on my shoes. Come in."

In your wife's lilac-scented room you stand at the window. Across the lane: nothing more than the high brick wall of the next building. An enormous notice in faded colors reads KURTZWEILS SHUHGESCHÄFT. A rayless light scintillates in the windowglass, where it comes from hard to tell.

"Do you remember, Clara, that difficult time we had here? What was it, two years ago?"

"Of course. Agonizing for you, as I recall. At the mercy of the surgeon, weren't you? Poor dear. But being here reminds me also"—her voice softer now—"of our time in Schmargendorf. Different days altogether, those."

"Ja," you say. *Her figure in your Schmargendorf rooms—and without a word or gesture, her back still turned, she drew you across the carpet toward her.* "That was a February like this one, wasn't it?" *And your mouth burrowed into that dark scent at the nape of her neck. . . .* Despite the ardor that has cooled since then, despite the agreed-upon separate quarters now, this memory remains a blessing. Moments of profound clarity those were. Have you known any such moments since?

"Oh, Rainer, I meant to tell you. Lou and Friedrich arrived yesterday afternoon, the same time I did as luck would have it."

You turn, startled. "They're here? You mean you've met?"

"Ja."

"You and Lou?"

"Me and Lou and Friedrich, yes. We had the most lovely little talk, Lou and I."

"Did you."

In the bureau mirror to your right you see your poet-figure. Turned to his wife, all attention, hands hanging dumb at his sides.

Silence in the room, though someone passes whistling down the hall.

"Rainer?" Clara falls still at the look of you. "Rainer, what is it, dear?"

"I don't know." The mirrored figure's fingers in a slow distracted flutter along the hem of his coat. "I'm a bit surprised, I suppose."

"That they're here already? Surprised that we met?"

"That you met, *ja*. I mean that you met without *me*. I wanted to be there. When you met. I wanted to see it."

Clara nearer now. She lays a light hand on your shoulder. "Oh darling. I know it meant a lot to you. I could tell you what was said if that would help, I'm sure I could remember."

"No, no, but if I'd *been* there, Clara. To *see* it. Somehow—" Your eyes are welling. Yet it seems inexpressible, this feeling.

"Somehow what?" Her doctoring voice. Her deep, indulgent eyes. "What is it, dear?"

How to say the significance of seeing it—this meeting? How to say the good it would have done you, after so much time adrift between this sweet wife and that woman who was the beginning of everything?

"Nothing. Nothing. You'll love one another, I'm sure of it. She's wonderful, isn't she?"

"She's lovely, yes. I think we both felt we had a great deal more to talk about."

"She'll love you, Clara. No doubt she does already."

Tenderly Clara takes your hand. "Come, let's go to lunch."

For his first Berlin appearance, the poet speaks before the Art Society. His subsequent Berlin engagement shall take for its topic Rodin and his work, but tonight Rainer reads from his own poetry. In the audience before him, in surreal array, sit Friedrich Andreas, Lou, and Clara.

·　　·　　·

It is surely a sign; yes, surely—that these two women should look each other in the eyes at last, that such harmony should permeate the moment and that Rainer should sit here as witness.

Tea in the lobby of the Hospiz des Westens. Their foursome encircles a small white-clothed table laid with saucers and cakes. Lou and Clara talk at great length, Rainer and Friedrich Andreas merely listen. And sitting back with that long-since gentled husband, Rainer believes himself to share something of the man's equanimity now. Andreas's gray beard and mellow eyes remind him, strangely, of Rodin. Not of the Rodin whose glance so sharply glimmers when he proclaims, "One must have a woman!"—no, but of Rodin the worker, the Master, that true and final Rodin.

The disparate elements of Rainer's life, at last, are coming together. Both these women, whom he has loved and loves yet, remain unpossessed by him, held dear to his heart but not grafted there. And so this life he strives for daily—of a love that leaves the lovers free to lift their longing into art, into work—is not impossible after all. This is surely a sign.

A telegram arrives from Prague. A blue envelope handed to you during dinner in the hotel dining room. Set down your fork, open the envelope, read. Clara at your side, Lou and Friedrich before you.

And now there's a blinding glare in your head and heart. A moment of sheer white sightlessness. The words of the telegram come charring through, stark and still.

Fold the paper over. Tuck it away in your coat pocket.

"What is it?" says Clara.

"My father."

Take up your water glass, drink, a tremor in your hand.

"Is all well?"

"I thought it was, but no."

Silence. Begin to eat again. But now the others have fallen still, the silver idled at their plates.

Lou says, "Is he ill, Rainer?"

"*Ja.* So his doctors say."

"The doctors sent the wire?" says Clara.

Nod your head, sit back, swallow. "*Ja.*" Clear your throat. A blue thread of paint rims the curve of your white plate. Your hand rises to trace the blue line. But there's that tremor in the hand. "*Ja,* his condition is quite grave, they say."

Your voice very quiet. Hollow words meant for no one in particular, yet they seem to require utterance. You feel Clara's touch settling at your arm as you speak.

"He was getting better when I saw him last. He'd had the pleurisy—that's what they'd told him. I thought he looked quite older, but then I hadn't seen him for a great while. He seemed to reawaken in the time I spent with him. He's alone, though, that's what's the matter. There was a girl there, a housekeeper, but really he has no one to look after him."

Lift your eyes to Lou, her hands still paused at the edge of her plate. *Her hands coming up from the dark banister and her strong fingers plunging deep into your hair . . .*

"He's been so patient with me. So patient in a way that just saddens me. He postponed his retirement, you see. . . ."

Lou's blue gaze locked upon you, bewilderingly familiar. "Will you go to Prague?"

And it seems you are suddenly alone with her. Everything around you reduced. Erased. Some great original silence supervening.

"Rainer? Rainer, will you go to Prague?"

—the question again, but now Lou's mouth does not move. Voice close in your ears, rich and intimate.

You are staring at Lou's full, soft, motionless lips.

Rainer? . . .

Later Lou Andreas-Salomé recalled an air of distressed avoidance surrounding the poet in these Berlin days, while his father faded away in
Prague. . . .

 PRAGUE: MARCH 1906.
AGE THIRTY . . .

*Y*ou find Papa in the hollow flat. He lies in the bed where you saw
him last, but now the drab blanket has been pulled atop his face.
At the window the curtain is drawn, its loose orange knit soaked with
subdued sunlight. In this false amber dusk nothing moves. Nothing moves.

Beneath the shroud Papa's feet lie splayed, divergent, things fallen
over and not set aright again. The death-tent of the smartly tucked blanket betrays the body's impossible flatness. Even the reposeful head lends
hardly a bulge to the covering.

Clara stands beside you just within the bedroom door, her hands
cupped with quiet self-consciousness at her womb. Hands warding, perhaps, that place of engenderment. Yes, for this father's death took seed in
such a place as all deaths do. This death began as the membrane the womb-
small child ensheathed. Father's infant form enfolded this death in Grandmother's dim womb, back in the very first days. You've never seen Clara
stand quite this way. As though in submission to the will of her hands. She
remains motionless at the door as you step further into the room.

Those motiveless feet draw you first. What seems immediately necessary is that someone take note of their collapse and raise them up again.

Upon the varnished floor on all sides of the bed a pale scented powder
has been sprinkled like decorative snow. Balmy fragrance of aged women,
of church chancels, of hospital lavatories. The powder whisks beneath your
shoe soles, drifting up into tiny plumes.

You turn back the blanket and Papa's long feet, shrunken in sagging stockings, sprawl at your knees. Shift the feet upright onto their heels. Gently. Cold bony things. Behind you a small breath of air comes purling through the window. You hadn't noticed it was open—but of course it should be. The curtains stir, the room's burnt light brightens a little.

Papa's face, when you undrape it, lies pronounced on the flat pillow, seeming to listen to something yet. A look of total self-forgetfulness. Some wisps of his hair have been disheveled by the blanket's sweep. You brush them back from his brow. But this face is a change. Yes, indeed. And what a profound change: the features so long familiar now slack and pooling in the osseous cavities of the skull.

Clara comes closer. She stands at your side in the room's great bottom-less silence while the curtain stirs and the emberous light riffles very faintly.

Bend and press your lips to Papa's blanched temple.

Chill flesh. A subtle pungency from his white beard. Beard of a grand-father. This man you've loved all these years while hardly even realizing. Is it so with every person one loves?

"More and more," you whisper, "he became my father."

And you stand by as Clara, dear soul, holding back her hair at one ear, stoops to your dead father's temple.

Until tomorrow the body will stay where it lies. Then the final rite will be performed, the coffin will come, and the corpse of Josef Rilke will travel to its interment at the Rilke grave in Olšany. For now, while Papa lies in the bedroom in his imperishable silence, you must deal with his effects— possessions to sort and dispense with, payments to be settled, accounts closed, papers burned. Clara, steadfast, remains close at your side, helping with everything. Methodically, patiently, she conscribes bundles of docu-ments to the flames, sheaf by sheaf. Again and again scoops the grate clear of the growing mountains of ash.

·   ·   ·

The doctors are the first to arrive in the morning. Returning to the apartment from your brief night of slumber at the hotel, you find them busy
about their preparations. They have been given the key for just this reason.

"Herr Rilke." The superior doctor approaches with a humorless clinical grin. "You will see we're ready now. And we've understood correctly—
have we not, sir—that you wish to bear witness?"

"Most certainly, Doctor."

"Very good. Well, as I say, all is in order."

"Yes, very good."

But the doctor stands there, unmoving. A quizzical look flickers across
his face. He touches two fingers to his chin. "Forgive me, sir, the only
thing we should like to know now is whether *you* are ready?"

"I believe I am, Doctor, yes."

But this answer, apparently, does not suffice. The doctor says, "One expects the near relations to need a few moments to prepare."

"I believe I'm prepared."

The doctor's glance falls to the floor. He shakes his head slightly.
"What I mean to say is . . ."—he now appears touched by some painful bewilderment. "What I'm referring to, Herr Rilke—and please don't take
me to be speaking out of turn here—is what one might call the . . ."—his
voice drops into breathy confidentiality—"the *ceremonial* aspect of our
business today. No doubt you think me presumptuous, sir, but the bereaved
often face a great many matters all at once. A great *too* many, really—so
you'll forgive me if I call your attention to the true and solemn nature of
today's . . . You see, Herr Rilke, my commission this morning lies more in
the priest's domain than in that of the doctor. I knew your father fairly
well, sir. A good man . . . he saw this morning's business as the grave and
venerable tradition it once was and requested it specifically. Not a great

many souls, I can tell you, observe such an old tradition nowadays, not a great many. Ours being a scientific age. But as your father's doctor and respectful acquaintance, I might assure you now, sir, that the bereaved—in this case yourself, of course—will find great comfort in the presence of certain . . . *sacral* elements during the procedure."

The doctor's round face floats before you expectantly, inordinately near and outsized, his open mouth a slack dark rectangle.

"*Candles,* for instance." He verily bites the noun from the air.

"Candles?"

"*Candles,* sir."

"Oh, I see!" And now your hands rise to your coat pockets, as though the truant items might somehow be found there. "Candles. Of course, Doctor. I'm sure you're right. I'll be along with them shortly."

So you go looking for candles, berating yourself for your neglect. From the parlor mantel you procure two large copper shafts with tapers. Carry them into the darkened bedroom and position one at each bedside table. Within moments they are alight, their thin blue fire framing Papa's head. The doctor and his assistant, having retreated to the far corner of the room, stand by with hands neatly folded.

Befitting the doctor's assurance, all is indeed in order. The deathbed lies stripped but for the bottom sheet. Papa's lifeless pillow has been doubled into a cylinder and squeezed beneath his neck, his head pitched sharply backward. The steep arch of his Adam's apple juts at the candlelit air, his mouth open to the ceiling, the tips of the front teeth a flat glitter of white. His beard, bristling upward, appears at that peculiar angle to be standing on end. The doctors, or someone—who but the doctors?—have sheathed Papa's legs in trousers. His feet have spilled outward again. Papa's nightshirt lies open from the collar to the waist, scissored through and pulled clear to each shoulder.

"— — —, Herr Rilke?"

—a voice like a face interposed before you. It is the doctor. He has stepped forward from the corner shadows. The trim assistant has already fluttered around to the bed's other side.

"I beg your pardon, Doctor?"

"I was asking if Herr Rilke would like another moment."

Your eyes coast down Herr Rilke's lean immobile length. His bared torso thrust taut and high. The dead Papa is entirely readiness; he will not answer. Nevermore. But of course it's *you* the doctor addresses: the son and survivor. Yes, of course: under the Papa's name all the hard, long-suffered questions will press for progeny's answer.

With a strange womanish voice the assistant speaks up. Words like dark velveteen. "You need not stay after all, sir, if you'd prefer not."

Needn't you? Oh, no: but you must. Papa and progeny *both* must stay. And can the son aspire to match the papa's peerless readiness?—Papa's exposed and nerveless breast? To bear witness is the honor now called for. Witness, nothing more, and yet witness seems so tremendous a duty when one's chest is aching as yours aches now.

No leaving the room, no question of that. The duty is to stand by and watch. Anyway, the room's door seems to have vanished—nothing but wall and wall and wall. So when one stepped into the papa's death-chamber one contrived an irreversible and fearless fidelity. Every wall healed closed behind. This, then, is the meaning of grief. One stays in the painful room and endures it all for love of the departed. And one loves through one's furious grief, meanwhile mustering bravery for the sake of decorum.

Step back now, give a deferential wave. "If you please, Doctor."

Decorum is a series of simple motions, little more; one maintains it by recalling the motions. But decorum and the painful room are impossibly at odds. And yet someone must remain in the room—and who will that be if not you?

The men, given your leave, stand with legs pressed against the bedsides. The bedframe quivers, headboard clicking at the wall, the lank flesh of Papa's face ashiver. From nowhere at all the long silver lance appears.

In smooth hushed voices the doctors confer: *Hold the shoulders. The breastplate . . . here . . . Ja, just here . . . All right, on my command . . . slowly . . .*

The instrument stands at Papa's chest: stream of absurdly bright silver, as though these doctor-savants draw sterling thread from the precious spindle of his heart-bone.

—*For certainty, you see.*

Papa's voice. Papa thrusting himself before you in Uncle Jaroslav's drawing room aglitter with candles.

—*René, you're not alarmed, are you?*

And Papa's eyes wide awake now, the whites agleam as they dart from the dead pillowed face!—*René!*

But with a small shake of your head the father's body lies motionless again, his bluish unpalpitating temple bared like a watching eye.

Who would it be if not me, Papa? I'm staying, do you see? I will bear witness. Because I've loved you. My grief proclaims it now.

That blanched temple watching you. That place where yesterday you laid your kiss. It sees you now. The dead see everything, and worst of all, they cannot speak their judgment. They hold us to account, and it's for us to draw upon our deepest dignity, to maintain decorum. Where they could teach us so much, we are left to teach ourselves. Would it be any easier to do if they did not watch?

Between the bedsheet and the torso, during their earlier preparations, the doctors inserted a firm flat square of wood. Now without warning the silver instrument falls—*bludgeons-drops-slick*—and stops with a fatal tap. Tap of pen to paper, but tenfold as loud.

"There," says the doctor under his breath, and he makes a relieved little grunting noise. "There."

A matter of inches and the body is run through from front to back.

Upon the instrument's removal follows the blood. Blood sudden but slow like foam, and equally inert. It oozes to a head and sits there black in the candlelight. The assistant swabs it away.

Like that it has come and gone, your Papa's inky blood which you've never seen till now. Blood which you helplessly *are*. He's contained it so well; all your life he's contained it without complaint; now the vessel that he was lies here emptied, the air let in, the old red river stilled and drying already. And René Maria the son must carry to sea what the papa could not. . . .

The doctors have vanished. They are gone. How long, already, have they been gone? And here you stand, alone in candlelight beside the drilled body. This room, for its fragrantly powdered floor, smells of a nursery.

The doctors covered the hole in the chest before they went. But now the white nightshirt grows wet at the spot. Some clear watery seepage, not blood. The body's last expressiveness. Tears drained from the heart itself, perhaps—but no, nothing so interpretable; the living cannot know what such pooling stuff divines, not by any augury. The living can merely describe, perhaps, the dead heart's gestures—and even then, barely so. You stand and watch that seepage bloom.

The undertaker appears at length. Clara too arrives, bearing violets for the coffin and a telegram from Rodin. It reads: *'Do you have enough money?'*

"How kind of the Master," you say. You'd wired him the news as soon as you'd heard it yourself. You feel yourself asurge with love for the gray sculptor in Meudon—but just as fast a darkening abashment rolls heavily in your breast. Something like shame. Why should that be? Why shame now? You've loved Papa all along, whether conscious or not of just how deeply. And to have loved, in the meantime, this second father in Meudon—what treachery is that? Still, the abashment will not go.

Papa is arranged and clothed. You do not watch. Then he's laid away in the bare stately box, his bloodless hands composed, violets dropped about his head. Ruth fashioned him a heather funeral wreath. Her mother's art adopted by her light small hands. Clara carried the wreath from Worpswede, where the mortal news reached you both two days ago. Your lecture date in Weimar had been unexpectedly cancelled, so you'd reconnoitered to the moors together for a few days of rest.

"I want to make him something," said Ruth, of her own bright volition, once you'd told her. "Something pretty that he will like very much."

Clara sets the wreath upon Papa's breast and the coffin is closed.

At three o'clock in Olšany you watch the loaded coffin creak to its earthen depths on the slowly paid ropes of the gravetenders. Declivitous spring sun beams down through the trees: heat-starved sun that hurts the head, hurts the eyes.

Your breath, as you walk from the grave, smokes hugely in the bitter air. Clara walks beside you. Your two shadows slink away ahead, supple and black across the serried grave markers.

"You're wondering why we waited," you say.

"Waited?"

"*Ja,* waited to come to Prague. After the doctors' first telegram two weeks ago."

For a moment Clara doesn't answer. Then, delicately: "Perhaps I am. But I trust there was reason."

"And what if there wasn't, Clara? What if there was no good reason at all?" A quiver in your voice now—you cannot master it. You clear your throat but it does not go. "What if I was waiting for him to die?"

"Were you? Is that what it was?"

"I . . . don't know."

"Still," she says—again gently, "that's possible." Clearly she means it without judgment. Means it with marvelous understanding.

And now you are silent. Aquiver inside. So much choked back within you. Do you wish, somehow, that Clara *would* judge you?—would thereby sharpen the edges around this inexplicable act of yours, your having come so late to your father's lonely death? Perhaps. But what seems worst of all is that the dead do not utter judgment.

Saturday, seventeenth March, Josef Rilke's Holy Requiem mass is said in the church of Maria of the Snows in Prague. The black-clad congregants come afterward to squeeze your hand and smile their grief, their quiet condolences, their fondness for your lost father. "You're the poet, aren't you?" they say in turn.

"I am," you answer. I am. I am. I am.

From Worpswede on the death-day, you wired the mournful news to Mama. She was on holiday in Arco and replied that she would not make the journey.

Upon returning to Berlin, you write to her of the funereal week, beg her in so many words to deal gently with her estranged husband's memory.

Rainer Maria Rilke delivers his Rodin lecture to a large audience assembled in a Berlin art gallery. The poet's unchosen father lately laid to rest, he is tonight the gospeler of his chosen one. And again that abashment clouds his breast, impossible to ignore.

From the podium he spots a person entering at the rear of the hall. The man stops just inside the door and for several minutes does not doff his bowler. Finally he remembers himself, and the hat comes down with a flutter to bob along his fingers.

But he does not move to take a seat. He hangs back, perusing the rows and rows of listeners. And now in the chandelier light Rainer catches the familiar glister of those eyes. He keeps speaking, but he's suddenly deaf to his own address. There's a deep red flower pinned to the figure's breast—something like the stigmatic blossoms of the old kitchen crucifix. And Rainer loves him for coming: this man who never came in life. Their eyes meet and the poet notes the startled tautness in the pale cheeks. The bearded mouth is carefully closed, but behind it the jaw hangs slack in surprise. It's a look of guarded appraisal—but that's merely custom; his pride and pleasure are clear enough, his tender awe at the sight of these rows of people come to hear his son.

All this in a mere moment, then Papa's eyes drop away. He casts a cursory glance to his right, his left, flips the bowler to his head again, and goes out. Gone forever.

 PARIS: 1906 . . .

*T*he city has come completely into the grip of spring in Rainer's time away. His gray, grief-stricken days in Berlin and Prague seem, against such brightness, like another existence entirely. In the restaurant Jouven's in the boulevard Montparnasse, the poet sits to breakfast with Paula Modersohn-Becker. From their window-side table they watch the bright Sunday-people streaming past on the sidewalks.

"I'm sorry about your father," says Paula.

"There's no need to talk about that. But thank you."

Still she seems to hold back somewhat, loath to take up lighter subjects. Only after several moments does she begin telling him, delicately, of her life in Paris. She is studying at the Académie Julian and the École des Beaux-Arts. Her drawing skills improve by the day, and she's exhilarated by her new command of anatomy. Every morning she greets her new life with strengthened certainty. "None of this was possible in Worpswede," she says. "I suppose you heard of the awful scandal Otto and I caused last year. No? Clara didn't write of it? Or are you just pretending for modesty?"

"Modesty?"

"You really haven't heard!"

"I have not."

Paula smiles a coy, guilty smile, flares her fingers and flattens her palm atop the table. "Let me tell you then!" A derisive tone: "One glorious summer day Otto and I went out to the Weyerburg that he might paint me in *plein aire*. We found a little copse of trees and I posed there—*au naturale*,

as they say. We used every possible prudence, but somehow we were spotted. We couldn't have done a more harmless thing, of course, yet by the
furor it caused when word got round you'd have thought we'd murdered
someone. Heinrich Vogeler quite reasonably expressed no alarm about the
matter and found himself vilified! Even one of our local painters, an absolute boor, demanded that Vogeler give us up completely. Naturally, he
would not oblige, at which point he was challenged to a duel!"

"A duel?"

"*Ja!*" Paula convulses in laughter. She must muffle her mouth with her
hands. Her face flushing dark above the high blue collar of her blouse.

She catches her breath, dabs her napkin to her eyes.

"I laugh now. I'm at *liberty* to laugh, being *here*—but at the time the
whole thing was absolute misery. You'll understand how I longed for Paris
after that."

"I understood it already, Paula. But yes."

They nibble at their *pâtisseries,* sip the coffee from their tiny cups. A con-
fraternal silence settling between them, moments floating by, pleasurable
and unselfconscious. Then Paula's eyes take on a look of pensive distance.

"Here . . . here I can become more and more the person I am. That
wasn't possible in Worpswede. And yet even my sister's against me. My
sister Herma. She's lived here in Paris for some time. She's an *au pair*. Despite our love for one another, even she disapproves of me. Everybody pities
Otto, you see. They all take me to be the most wicked wife. And Otto *has*
had a miserable time without me this last month. He's sent me so many
letters, so many pleas. I've had to stand very firm with him. But then, just
last week came a letter of real friendship, of real selflessness and good
hopes. So I think he may begin to understand me soon. I don't know that
he's accepted the truth, but understanding is a start."

She stares down at the table. Her paint-stained fingers are plucking
idly at the crumbs in her plate.

"It was a torment is what it was, life with Otto. Not every day, not every minute, but *cumulatively,* you see, it became unbearable. I know Clara's told you how he held me off."

Her glance remains diverted. Thank God, for Rainer feels fiercely the blush she's just caused him.

Paula leans chin in hand and stares mournfully across the boulevard. "It's not Otto's fault, poor dear. But we couldn't be happy like that. And the fact is, Rainer, that certain souls live for others and certain souls live for something . . . something more impersonal. Live for beauty, perhaps."

And suddenly tears are rising to the poet's eyes. Suddenly he wishes to press Paula's hand.

"Dear friend," he says, twisting his napkin beneath the table, "you've put it perfectly. Perfectly."

Back in Meudon, the Villa des Brillants is teeming and anxious. The Master's *Le Penseur* is to be unveiled before the Panthéon in three weeks' time. The event will be of great significance to Rodin, but a bad case of the grippe has just laid siege to him. Mountains of letters await Rainer's attention, accrued during his month-long absence. And now more than ever, though he has only just returned, and though he would not dare to leave the good Master in the lurch, the poet feels a good many things arising within him, convergences of the most unmistakable and pressing kind. Given leave now, he could work with rarest power. The vision of Paula Becker's brave, luminous face haunts his thoughts. *I've been given a new life. It's going to be beautiful.*

Rainer has felt this terrific readiness once before—back in his stormy Viareggio days—and then it had surged forth in fulfillment of *Das Stundenbuch.* Something wants to surge now, yes, and were it possible to give it passage, he would leap aboard a train to Viareggio without a second thought. But of course it is not possible. He's been back for a mere few hours. And now he mustn't think—*absolutely mustn't*—of all that might stream irretrievably through his fingers in coming days. He must set himself to the Master's paperwork, think of nothing but the Master's need of him in these crucial weeks. Later, later, work will be summoned deliberately. Unsuperstitiously. *Toujours travailler . . . travailler et patience!*

The poet hears a noise from the garden—a voice. He steps to the front window and looks out and there, strikingly clear in the blue blur of the dusk, is the Master himself in his heavy house-robe.

"Ah," says Rodin. *"Le voilà."* His hoarse voice is gentled and soft.

"Bonsoir, mon maître."

"I am sorry, *cher ami,* for the loss of your father."

"Thank you, *maître.*"

"Everything is settled for the poor gentleman, *oui?*"

"Oui. Everything's done."

"C'est bon."

Rodin remains standing there on the sloping grass, hands buried in his large robe-pockets. Despite the current frenzy of his estate, he possesses, just now, the slow focused silence of the convalescent.

"And your health, *mon maître?*"

"Improving." One of the Master's hands floats up beneath his beard, moving at his throat. He gives a slight sigh. *"Alors,* I am again very sorry." And with a small nod he turns and shuffles back across the lawn to the house.

The next morning the Master is not at breakfast. Madame herself brings the poet's plate to the table.

"I'll have the coffee up in a moment," she says, sitting down at her usual place.

"Is Madeleine unwell, Madame?"

"Madeleine is gone."

"On holiday?"

"No." Madame waves her fork as if to scratch something out. "Gone. Dismissed, I'm afraid."

"Dismissed?"

"*Oui.*" A pert affirmative, the lady's gray brow rising nonchalantly.

Dismissed. Such a trusted servant. Rainer begins to eat.

Silence a moment, then: "Forgive me, Madame, did Madeleine offend?"

"Offended *le Monsieur, oui.*"

"I see."

In spite of his wonderment, Rainer deems it best to beg no further answers. It seems he's already overstepped propriety. So they breakfast in silence. The morning light moves obliquely across the slender dining-room windows, over the tiny marble torso at the table's center.

Madame disappears and returns after a moment with the cups of promised coffee.

Rainer cannot quash his astonishment longer. With a tone of careful idleness he asks, "Madeleine was with the Master and you for a great many years, was she not?"

"*Oui,* more than thirty." And now Madame's head quivers somewhat, as though she fights to keep from wagging it in disgust. "He does not think sometimes of the messes he makes. It's best that other people remind him how to keep hold of his happiness. Usually that's sufficient, but sometimes his temper wins out. His nerves have been high, and so now—" she shows Rainer the back of one upflung hand, a gesture of futility, "now we are one more servant short when we need the help most extremely." She purses her lips in a grim stolid look. "So be it, *non?*"

At Meudon, the Master's will is all.

·   ·   ·

In spite of everything else presently demanding his attention, Rodin has agreed to model a bust of the famous foreign writer George Bernard Shaw. The Master's health still tenuous, he requests that Shaw come to Meudon for the sittings. Rainer drafts and dispatches the letter and then, in the first weeks of April, watches as the blond-bearded Irishman and his wife alight from their cabriolet before the Villa des Brillants.

Clasping the Master's hand with great admiration, Shaw appears to Rainer a trimmer light-footed version of Rodin himself. A bulky black camera dangles from a strap around the visitor's neck, and in barely comprehensible French aided by jovial pantomime, he begs to take the Master's picture. Rodin consents with great forbearance, standing there in the gravel drive while the sprightly Shaw, quite particular regarding the angles of his portraiture, darts this way and that, pressing his face down into the camera and fumbling at the dials and fluttering English. So the Master is rendered by the model.

In the drafty glassed-in atelier at the side of the main house, the writer poses for Rodin, standing to attention beside the Master's working table. Rainer and Madame Shaw stand by in audience as the Master takes three precise measurements of Shaw's head with a set of long calipers, marking each in turn onto a big sphere of wet clay. Chin held high, Shaw's face professes new depths of seriousness. But the ironic glimmer has not left his eyes and he continues to expectorate his bizarre French, stopping up its gaps with crisp oddments of his native tongue. The elegant Madame Shaw lends vocabulary now and then. And though her occasional murmurs to Rainer are wholly unintelligible, clearly the lady is engrossed by the Master's work. Every few minutes Rodin leans forth and presses the back of one clay-wet hand to Shaw's shoulder, compelling him to turn a few degrees.

The modeling stretches to two hours before the Shaws take their leave.

The Master swaddles the unfinished head in wet cloth and there it rests, like a burn patient in an attitude of silent and healing erasure.

At Shaw's third modeling, a few days later, Rodin asks him to sit, drags from the corner a shrunken armchair proportioned for a child and with a shy little laugh makes a flourish above the seat as though it's a throne.

Shaw draws back, feigning royal offense, spouting his high Anglo-Saxon indignation. Laughter all around, then the writer squeezes himself into the low chair.

Rodin has unwrapped the nearly finished bust. The clay already bears an uncanny resemblance. Gripping a taut length of wire between his fists, he declares, "Let this be a warning, monsieur," and in one fleet motion passes the wire blade-wise through the clay neck. Shaw gapes in sardonic delight as the Master lifts the severed likeness from its mount and lays it down against a brace.

From his place behind, Rainer feels a strange shudder within him to see the writer's two faces, agebound and ageless, both, tilting there before Rodin's godlike countenance.

Twenty-first April 1906. Under the doubled vault of gray sky and gray iron dome the poet sits with the Master, the Shaws, and Paula Modersohn-Becker before the Panthéon in a row of chairs arranged across the broad stones of the Place du Panthéon. Onlookers spill up the steps to both sides, furled umbrellas depending from countless arms.

Monsieur Dujardin-Beaumetz, the Undersecretary of Parisian fine arts, stands at the center of the steps, orating from a big sheaf in hand. Small white-bearded hatless man pronouncing with panegyric flair the triumph of *Le Penseur* by Auguste Rodin. On an inscribed marble plinth at the base of the steps stands the sculpture, massive figure muscled and nude, his unreckonable power coiled, his wordless mouth couched heavily upon his knuckles. A potent answer to Michelangelo's *David*.

Rainer leans and whispers to Paula, "Look at the Master. This means everything to him."

Against the black of the onlookers' coats, Rodin's profile itself appears as sure and immovable as any great monument. Today at last the Master's art comes home to this city so long home to the man. His noble *Balzac* was refused by Paris years ago, and neither would Paris accept his *Monument to Victor Hugo*. And even this ceremony has been forestalled more than a year as a result of last January's shock, when the first installation of *Le Penseur* lay decimated here in this spot, cleft to plaster shards by the hatchet of a midnight vandal. But since the Master's boyhood in these very streets, this Panthéon has represented the stupendous heart of his birth-city. So now the native son, gray with long labor, brings his treasure home again, and finally it shall stand in bronze before the country's most important mausoleum.

For Rainer too this day is a powerful landmark, for not three blocks behind him in the squalid cul-de-sac of the rue Toullier is the blue door marked number 11 at which he stood drenched and knocking four years ago. Malte's door now. Malte, already a life unto himself, a willful shadow-form drawn from the poet's limbs. And Rainer sits now beside the world's great Rodin—something like a son, perhaps, to a Master.

The ceremony concludes and the many onlookers flare up in applause. Instantly Rodin becomes a magnet at the center of the swarming crowd.

Rainer touches Paula's sleeve. "May I show you something?"

They disentangle themselves from the noise and whirl of the mob. Together they float briskly down the rue Soufflot toward the Jardin Luxembourg, the garden gates gleaming dully ahead, tipped in gold.

"Here," says Rainer at the Toullier corner.

Paula follows into the cul-de-sac. Little lane as dim as ever in the day's cloudy light.

"Number 11," he tells her, stopping on the sidewalk opposite the door to point it out.

It is unchanged. Crude blue door that creaked to receive him in his soaked clothes, in his presentiments of loss. Thresholds are forever. But is he the same displaced soul who stood there knocking four years back, he who sat a moment ago in the company of Europe's celebrated few?

Rainer seems, somehow, to see himself from above: he and the auburn-haired painter standing there at Malte's curb. And from that height he sees a second self as well. It's the poet of that first Parisian hour. That poet stands there yet, still knocking at the door while the dismal rain pours down.

So, Rainer thinks, that day of arrival, remote as it seems, lies not at all distant from this present moment. Yes, for every moment is a layer of eternity. Nothing that has happened ceases to happen; none of it goes away; we are but leached through one and another translucency as through planes of thinnest glass till at last we come out on a different side. It's merely a process of long transference, nothing more, and all along the way we bleed off our temporality. This moment with Paula is but superimposed upon those storied moments beneath. By some law of eternal recurrence the poet shall forever stand there knocking, forever escape to better quarters shared with his wife, forever stand here with Paula at his side.

And most mystifying, most remarkable now, is the diaphanous figure Rainer can already make out in the clear dark plain above him. There, looking down, is Malte Laurids Brigge. Malte is unmistakably *there;* his fate and Rainer's lie stratified one upon the other. Malte sees it from that future of his. Fates glazing one another.

And now Rainer begins to tell Paula of Malte; of the things Malte sees in Paris, of Malte's memories and the bits of his destiny these memories clutch; of the work Malte does to pry back the fingers of each memory in turn, to assemble all the pieces as one would mend a torn-up letter; of Malte's growing astonishment as his destiny becomes clear.

Paula stands there gazing up at the garret window. "I feel as though we could walk in and meet him."

Rainer smiles darkly. "Ah, but he has such work to do. We'd disturb him. Better to write before we come."

"He sounds lonely though, from what you say."

"Of course, Paula. He's vastly lonely. But that's the price, you see. That's the toll. And that's precisely the work Malte faces. The work of expanding his loneliness across vast stretches."

Still she stands watching the upper windows as though expecting the figure to appear. "I hope sometime you'll convince him to have visitors."

"It would be awfully untoward of me, Paula. But you'll meet him one day."

She turns and smiles into Rainer's eyes. "I hope so."

But of course neither he nor Paula can yet know that she will not.

This same afternoon, as if to repay him for sharing Malte, Paula has Rainer into her atelier. A drear gray high-ceilinged apartment in the avenue du Maine, sparsely furnished with handmade shelves and tables of raw pine. An old wardrobe stands against one wall, a narrow cot is pushed up against another. At the center of the unvarnished floor lies a small threadbare rug of exhausted red. But here and there the room's crudeness has been brightened with colored cloths. And Paula's paintings alone provide remarkable vibrancy. They look to be great in number, scattered about as they are, leaning at random against the walls or hung up together in marvelously conversant ways. Amongst them are a few self-portraits, multiple rough sketches, some still lifes. It's the boldness of Paula's color, though, that

Rainer finds most affecting—color she seems to fling fearlessly against the drabness of her impecunious state.

"Here's what I wanted to show you," she says.

On the wall above her cot hangs a large horizontal composition. Rainer steps closer. It's still unfinished and unframed. A full-bodied woman asleep on her side, nude, her languid bare arms stretched out before her. Pillowed at her lower arm, the woman's naked infant curls against her breast, also asleep.

Rainer stares. Feels himself, despite its incompleteness, to be staring through the canvas as through a window into that intimate world. The paint-created bodies, unrealistic and entirely expressive, are drawing deep serene slumberous breaths.

Several moments drift by as he looks; he does not sense them passing. Then he seems to feel himself awakening and realizes the painter has vanished from his side. There's a soft clattering noise across the room. She has stepped away to warm the stove.

"I hope the colors are clear enough," she says. "The light in here is completely deficient. Such murky glass in these windows."

He does not want to tear his eyes from that tenderness of form. "But you make your own light, Paula. I should think these works glow in the dark."

And strangely, for all the vivid grace of the picture, he can't ignore the low unsettling shiver it has caused him. He stares, stares at the mother and infant asleep, wondering what this shiver could be.

*I*n the black Meudon hours you wake to a voice. Shrill soul's noise from the darkness of the Sèvres Valley below your cottage. A mournful call owning and disowning the sleep-carved emptiness of that world down there. The voice brings no picture: it is not bird or dog or child, neither earthborne nor airborne. What is it? *Voice* and nothing else. But what does it portend?

It calls, and again the uncreated night opens, opens like water around something submerging, a surface healing seamlessly as the sound seeps away. Then again it calls, again the night wavers.

You lie listening, your own sleep-vast self aqueous, invisible in the dark. You cannot decode the call, and yet in some deep way you already know its message. For it is a *de profundis* as old and distinctive as your very heart: child's heart, lover's heart, father's heart, friend's . . .

Morning, there's a quiet tapping at the cottage door. You open it to Madame Rodin standing in her rumpled floral dress. She keeps her eyes at your top waistcoat button as in a kind of wounded deference. Her mouth is trembling slightly.

"Madame?"

You are about to stretch out your hand, to lay a comforting touch upon her arm, but she blurts, "Monsieur Rodin wants you to go."

With your whole body you hear her words, soft and sharp. Behind her the sunlit garden shrinks in rapid parallax.

"To go?" you say dumbly.

She lifts her eyes. Her wide gaze fixes upon you. Still that shuddering modesty in her look—and now you understand: she is the gentle envoy of the Master's decree.

"*Oui*," she says. "You are dismissed."

You find yourself stuttering to know the reason.

Madame answers in tones of rote recital, "You've taken liberties with the Master's correspondence in your letters to Thyssen and to Monsieur Rothenstein. Monsieur Rodin was not consulted about these letters."

"Madame—forgive me, but might I speak to *le maître* himself?"

"I wouldn't. He's in a rage. And he's leaving for the city."

"A rage?"

"*Oui*, terrible. He dropped a glass in the dining room. I insisted he let me come down here to tell you. It would be very bad to speak to him just now. Very bad."

"I see," you say—nearly a whisper. And a sudden slackness overcomes you. Motionless, you remain holding the door.

"It's very unfortunate," Madame is saying. "More than that, really. An awful shame is what it is."

Your eyes sink vaguely to her hands: her soft and knobby fingers hold back a slip of paper.

"Is that my dismissal there?"

She turns the paper toward you. "Your final payment." It glides into your dumbstruck hands. Its figures inscrutable.

"How long do I have?"

"You are to go immediately."

You have not lifted your eyes, but Madame's quavering voice evokes her disturbed gray face as though you've looked directly at her.

"I see." Your own voice sounds very small to you now.

"I can promise you he'll regret it," Madame says. "He may never say it, but he will. I hope that's a comfort."

Seized in your strange torpor before her, you can feel words beginning to drift upward from somewhere deep, words like your gorge rising. What words? You cannot know till they've come whispering out.

"My father, Madame, has recently died. Did the Master tell you?"

"He did. I'm very sorry."

"Yes, he's gone, you see. And now . . ."—but your voice fails. The words drift away entirely. Lost. No articulating such a thing.

Madame, with the stately slowness of a dancer, declines closer and takes delicate hold of your wrist. "I know," she says. Soft warm fingers. A tender resignation in her voice. "For everyone who loves him it is like this. Don't worry."

Instantly it's over. The Master's expulsion, severe and surgical, sends you adrift again. No farewell. What words could possibly pass between you now? And did you believe that he loved you?—that his vast work left any space for such requital?

> "Dear Clara: I have rented a room in the small hotel in the rue Cassette (—No. 29—), in which we once visited Paula Becker. I will now be there by myself to think, and will be alone a little with what is in me. . . . Don't be worried about what is to come. There are ways, and we'll surely find them."

THE AUBURN-HAIRED PAINTER :

1906–1907

What if we go ahead and become beginners now, since so much is changing?

The Notebooks of Malte Laurids Brigge

our letter to Rodin of twelfth May, written immediately upon your move to Paris:

> *"So, great Master, you become invisible to me, as if by ascension car-*
> *ried into skies all your own. . . . Life begins for me, a life which shall cel-*
> *ebrate your high example and which shall find in you its consolation, its*
> *rightness, and its power."*

The previous evening Auguste Rodin had written to a correspondent with words that would remain unbeknownst to you forever: *'Something is wrong with me, I don't know how to keep hold of happiness.'* He'd evicted you just hours earlier.

Adrift again. Alone in Paris. Quartered in a small and musty room at 29 rue Cassette. The edges of the desk are worn smooth, lacquer dulled to the grain at the sides of the blotter. The papered walls zoom with vertiginous fleur-de-lys. Where it meets the ceiling the paper bears a wavering trim of brown—smoke damage accrued imperceptibly over many years: candle smoke, lamp smoke, cigarette smoke. The old odors imbue the stale and faded furniture. So many pasts never set free.

The vista from your narrow window is the notice-plastered wall of

Saint Joseph des Carmes and the cropped trees in the churchyard. Cheerless Paris, but not the city as you first knew it. That city is Malte's now. As you sit at your desk the church bells toll close and coppery by the hour.

The day before your expulsion by Rodin, an exuberant note from Paula Modersohn-Becker had reached you in Meudon. The esteemed sculptor Bernhard Hoetger, Paula wrote, called on her in the avenue du Maine and, astonished by his first glimpse of her canvases, overwhelmed her with encouragement. He'd even goaded her to give up her academy courses and focus exclusively on work. Paula's note read like an ecstatic testament to the certainty of her aims in Paris. She was accomplishing all she had set for herself. She would live fully and fearlessly in her art, however poor she remained in the meanwhile.

Now she wants to paint your portrait. So you find yourself, in the middle days of May, seated motionless in Paula's shabby atelier. The glow of Hoetger's encouragement, you can see, will not fade soon. Paula is a whirl of new confidence. She's hungered for confidence till now, that's clear.

"I rise and sleep with my paintings," she tells you. "And sometimes in the middle of the night, I wake up with no other wish but to stand and stare at my work. Would you believe I do just that? Stand right here with a candle in my hand, in the deadest hours, for an hour or more."

The canvas board upon which she's painting you is very small, no larger than a sheet of letter paper. The long-legged easel holds it like an afterthought.

At Paula's back as she works, a number of new and partially finished canvases hang in brilliant array across the wall. Amongst the several self-portraits is one of startling uniqueness. The painter is shown from the waist up, nude. A big-beaded necklace falls almost to her breasts. In each upraised hand she holds a small pink flower. Another three flowers adorn the gathered hair at the back of her head. Hovering in the background greenery are heart-like dabs of most brilliant fuchsia—little butterflies or blossoms, no saying. Her mouth is painted in that same crimson-pink. She looks out from the canvas with remarkable self-assurance or self-possession—or rather *self-inevitability*. For somehow this self-portrait has been created not as a likeness, not as a contextual image of a personality, but as a still life, a thing seen—*ein Ding*—a radiant mélange of surface and contour. Her hands, hinged at each wrist to hold the flowers, are like elegant soft-surfaced clams.

Immobile in your pose by the window, you stare past the living painter to this rendered one behind. Stare long till you understand what makes the work magnificent: it's the fact that this painted woman meets no viewer's eyes but her own. Her gaze is closed completely. The canvas is a transformative mirror, reflecting no one but the painter. Though others may look, the mirror will not hold *them*. This image begins and ends entirely within in its own borders, seamless.

"That one's magnificent, Paula."

She lifts her brush from the board and stands back somewhat, her face becoming itself again.

"Pardon?" A softly startled tone.

"The piece with the necklace. It's really magnificent."

Her eyes skim back that way, over her shoulder.

"Oh, that one's very recent."

There's a peculiar lightness in her voice, almost like indifference. And you can see that your compliment will not settle in her eyes, not for a moment—and now she's back to the work at hand.

What seems very clear is that she and this self-portrait have made inviolate peace with each other; neither painter nor canvas requires approbation, for they see *one another*—portrait and painter—and *nothing else*. World unto themselves. Were it not so, you realize now, you wouldn't even have known how to look at the painting, let alone speak of it. No, instead you would have blushed helplessly at the sight of her bared body.

Several mornings in May Rainer sits for his portrait in Paula's studio. Summery light sifts down through her tall atelier windows, the dull glass blunting the sunrays to swaths of muslin gray.

"Otto's letters keep coming," Paula tells him. "It will never get better. And then I have to ask him for money, which so complicates things. He sends it, poor dear, without fail. My mother says he's hung my paintings on every wall of his studio. The Vogelers want to buy one, but they're almost afraid to ask him. 'Paula can have whatever she wants,' he tells my mother, 'Paris or anything, if only she'll take me back.' But I can't stop working now, not with everything beginning at last."

"You're very brave, Paula. And with good reason."

"They think me foolish. Spiteful."

"They haven't seen all this." Rainer gestures to the colorful walls.

She glances across the paintings behind her, seeming almost surprised to be reminded of their presence. "No they haven't, that's true. Except for her." She points out a new portrait, a small canvas leaning at the baseboard beside her wardrobe. "That's Herma. My sister. She was here during Hoetger's glorious visit. She saw what happened in his eyes when he looked at the things I'd done. And she told me she now knows I'm right to have come here, alone or not."

"Maybe Otto will come to Paris and see for himself. Maybe that's what it will take."

"I don't want him here," Paula says. "Not now. Now would be an awful time."

She falls silent. There's a grave concentration in her face as her brush whispers at the board. At last she lifts her eyes.

"It's difficult, *n'est-ce pas? Everything is difficult.* You once said that to me, as I recall."

Rainer smiles softly. "I remember."

Back in number 29 rue Cassette the poet sits at his desk with the pages of the *Cornet* fanned out before him. His window, behind, gives onto the bright Paris day. The susurrous city in its afternoon distractions. Sheer uncluttered sunlight falling in the narrow lane and in the walled churchyard across the way. Sunlight somehow vacant, swept out, somber in its quality of hollowness. It falls and falls while he works, pushing its slow shadows eastward. The window glass is a flat cool blue already. The world's day rolling by. Rainer rises and steps to the washstand and takes up the small shaving mirror.

His face professed there in his hands, reduced in the silver square. His hair cropped short. Wispy blond mustache above the parceled flesh of his mouth, thong of beard dropping to his shirt collar.

He sits again and tilts the mirror against a book, turns it till it holds him, takes a fresh sheaf of paper from the drawer and writes across the top: *"Selbstbildnis aus dem Jahre 1906."* Self-Portrait from the Year 1906.

Paula's necklaced self-portrait haunts his memory. Her body bared to no one but herself—that closed mirror of the canvas untroubled by judgments or doubts.

Rainer's fair eyes look back at him from the tilted glass. They seem to spill forth all they've beheld: Madame Rodin's sad smile at his dismissal. *For everyone who loves him it is like this. Don't worry.* And Paula's brave face in the Gare du Nord. *I've been given a new life.* And the delicate dark sadness of Clara's eyes; and Ruth in her Christmas dress, clinging fast to his neck; and the watery seepage from the dead father's breast . . .

Rainer writes: *"In the gaze still: the blueness and fear of childhood."*

． ． ．

On a different day, as he arrives to sit for Paula again, the poet's glance snags at yet another self-portrait propped against the wall. Before he can perceive the danger, he has stepped closer to look.

And there she is: nude again, save for that same amber necklace falling to her breasts and a worn blue cloth pinched about her waist with one languid hand. But she has not closed the space around this image as in that other more vibrant self-portrait. Instead, her figure stands bared to the world, intentionally subjected to the viewer's judgment.

She's as pale as life here, her flesh a tepid white, her breasts no more than two loveless satchels. Only her cheeks burn with color—a fierce red modesty, for she *feels* the eyes that look upon her. Feels *his* eyes. She is standing in quarter profile. Her womanly belly bulges as though betraying a fertile fullness.

"I painted that yesterday."

Paula's voice behind him now, but Rainer sees he cannot possibly turn around.

"It was my fifth wedding anniversary."

He cannot turn around, cannot know how to look at her after this.

"Oh, not to worry," she says with a laugh, "It's not a literal portrait. I'm not expecting. Not in the physical way, no, but I wanted to show my fruitfulness somehow."

The canvas *sees* him—that is the matter. His face, he can feel, is as fiery red as her painted one. And was there a time, far away now, when he would have gazed with unconstrained pleasure upon this body, had she shown it to him? He stands there in silent distress, unable to move.

A letter arrives from Clara. She's eager to know for certain when they'll be together again. She's deep in her own work in Worpswede, but she feels a great many questions pressing in. Does Rainer feel them too? she seems to wonder.

With a clinch in his brain and breast, he writes back: *"I understood your letter as if I had written it myself."* But though nothing more of Malte has come to him, he finds he cannot yet pull himself from these days of long labor in Paris. He wants to feel these days yielding something, for when was his work last so unobstructed? He adds the words: *"I believe we must still have patience for a while."*

*Y*our final sitting occurs on second June and ends—not with Paula's completion of the portrait but with a knock at her door.

She steps back from the easel, brush and palette aloft. Fixes you with a blank unknowing look as though perhaps the caller knocks for you. Finally she says, "My sister," and swivels to put down her things.

"Shall I?" you say, half rising. But she shakes her head, already flowing past, her painted hands worrying a cloth. She parts the thin curtain beside the door, glances out, then rebounds across the studio. "It's Otto!"

Instantly you find yourself on your feet. The act of rising happens unaware, as if the chair has been sucked from under you and dragged several paces off. Otto here from Worpswede?

You stand by—what to do but stand by?—as Paula scuttles her palette and brush and comes back to swipe the portrait from the easel. "Better put this away." She slides it behind the wardrobe.

Her alarm is no less disturbing for being subdued.

"Paula?"

She's heading to the door again. At the unnerved note in your voice she throws back a fretful grin. "Don't worry."

All this in no more than a minute, and then she's pulling the door ajar.

You retreat deeper out of eyeshot, listening.

Tense cordialities exchanged at the threshold.

Only when the warm stove touches your hip do you realize you've backed up clear to the wall. You stare down at the kettle atop the dusty burner, consider lifting it and making a noise and in that way pretending busyness—but for the fear that this would only worsen your case. So instead you come stepping forward into plain view, your hands dangling at your sides with terrible self-consciousness. Huge heavy things.

At Paula's threshold stands Otto Modersohn, hat in hand. Dark thin hair a bit askew across his pate. Dark beard cocked in his soft staid appeal to the absentee wife.

At the sight of you, Otto pauses. His head ticks up. A frightful opacity frosts the glass lunettes in his spectacles. As if touched by some unexpected spasm of pain, he emits a small "Ah."

Step forward now. "Otto"—hand held forth—"how do you do, my friend."

He clasps your hand limply. A distracted smile. His palm is clammy. "Yes, yes, hello."

Now the glare has passed from his lenses and you can see—clearly, clearly—his worried husband-eyes tergiversating, rushing to take account. Will you become his rival? Must he take action for honor's sake?

No, no, Modersohn, let me be clear!

"What funny timing," you blurt. "I just stopped in to say hello."

"Ah. Well," Modersohn's eyes frosting again—or rather his lenses, and now he fashions his words with slowness and weight, not to be played a fool, not to conclude too much. "I'm glad to know Paula is looked after."

"I'm sure it's nothing like that," you say lightly. "I just like to get a glimpse of her work when I can. Marvelous what she's done lately."

"I've no doubt." Again Otto's dark little beard-smile, his bespectacled glance truly joyless.

And you all stand, while a weird moment drags by. Paula in the middle holding the door, her displeasure plain in her face.

Tonelessly Paula says to her husband, "You should come in."

With a slow guilty lope Otto crosses the threshold, stands just within the door looking abstractedly about.

Hold now, you tell yourself. *Mustn't leap to the escape.*

Put out your hand again—"I should be going." And strive, strive most earnestly to smile assurance into this husband's fearful eyes. "Will you be in Paris long, my friend?" A question no doubt like a thumb to a bruise, yet affability requires you to ask.

"Not very long, I expect."

"Well, safe journey then. Goodbye. Goodbye, Paula."

"Goodbye."

Looking back as you move to the stairs, you meet Paula's unsettled glance in the gap of her closing door. Then the latch falls to and she is alone in her resistance.

Stay the course, Paula. The thought is a shout, and pray God your eyes have expressed it to her clearly just now.

Descend the stairs. Nothing else to do but descend the stairs. Paula can profit from no intercession in these moments—*but may she stay the course, for oh those paintings of hers!* Yes, her paintings will plead her cause inarguably. And that's a comfort. Surely Modersohn, standing in that atelier so profuse with canvases, will see his wife's reasons at last. Surely he'll understand and free her, or at least not try to restrain her. You must believe it.

The poet sees nothing of Paula now. In his lonely quarters at 29 rue Cassette he finds himself immersed in fresh progress. His work steadily drawing him back from the diverting tensions of human entanglement. *The Book of Images* moves toward completion, and then too a number of individual poems begin to pour forth.

In these days hard upon the unexpected arrival of his self-portrait in verse, Rainer takes down the small gilt-framed picture of Papa. It belongs to him now, collected from the dead man's hutch in Prague three months ago. He props the frame before him on the desk. There, bordered in red velvet, stands the youthful Josef Rilke. Shrunken and drained of all brightness in the old hand-colored plate, he is outfitted in his artillery uniform, his saber drawn, its point set to the floor and his young hands composed upon the hilt.

Faded as the image is, this young Josef seems a figure fit for willing death, consenting already to the peril of battle. Dreaming of it. The hero's death, perhaps, was always his greatest wish. And did he die it in the end?—laid flat upon the doctor's wooden board, his bourgeois breast bared to the ceiling and his feet splayed at the end of the stripped bed?

Perhaps that's the reason Rainer didn't rush to him in those last days. Papa needed his *own* death after so many years spread thin. Couldn't that be it? There was no way to understand it just three months ago, but now this seems the truth. Seems . . .

At the top of the sheet Rainer has written: "Youthful Portrait of My Father." And in a quick whisper of the pen, he concludes the verses:

"You quick-fading daguerreotype
in my more slowly fading hands."

In the small shaving mirror again lurks his face: bearded apprentice's image, selfsame countenance that reflected his first impressions of Paris in those sultry days four years ago. Face lately rendered in the tan-gray velvet of Paula Becker's oils. But Paris is no longer what it once was to him; Paris means much more now, and Rainer is not the recoiling apprentice. So by the late-morning windowlight the poet stands before the basin with mirror in one hand and straight razor in the other and scrapes away his beard.

Coarse blond fleece falls to the gray water, stray wisps drifting here and there about the washstand.

When the job is done he holds the mirror at arm's length, meets his own new gaze. This bare face looks older, it's true, than it did when last he saw it beardless—but perhaps not as much older as he expected.

He touches his fresh shallow chin, smiles.

Still the work pours forth, and Rainer's days are becoming entirely work. He cannot bear to be of any lesser use than this—for in everything but *this* he is something lesser, something incomplete.

In these bounteous days he betakes himself to the Bibliothèque Nationale. There in the high hush of the great reading room, while recalling the trepid thankfulness with which he first came here four years ago, he finds that Malte deigns to render up a little more of himself. Astonished, Rainer hunches at his notebook and records the murmurings. Malte cannot be pressed for them; they arrive like this, by Malte's good graces, as wonders. But one must be ready all the time. That's the most important thing. One must create the conditions for such murmurings. And look: they come!

The days glide forward and the weather in Paris shifts to a greening blaze. Vigorous, fresh, young-summer heat.

Thirty-seven poems are added to the new *Book of Images,* and by thirteenth June that volume and the *Cornet* are both complete. With a triumphant surge, Rainer sends the manuscripts off to Axel Juncker.

Another letter from Clara arrives the same day, its wishes much like those of her missive a few weeks ago. He understands completely the bewilderment, the uncertainty and loneliness with which she writes. But he is too much in his labors to take himself away just now, and once more he tells her so, gently, buoyantly.

"Let us perhaps keep doing as we are, each in his place, so long as work continues and circumstances allow it, without thinking of anything out beyond."

Included in Clara's letter is the news that Otto Modersohn has returned to Worpswede from Paris—without Paula. Rainer immediately dispatches a note to the auburn-haired painter in the avenue du Maine. He apologizes for his weeks-long absence and sends his wish that she may now enjoy a full return to the fruitfulness she'd known before her husband's arrival.

Paula replies with appreciation. And soon begins sending him a number of friendly—even pressing—entreaties. But he's not prepared to see her again either.

June wheels past and is gone. Still the poet holds himself off from the auburn-haired painter, meeting her but once, and only then in company, their relation cordial.

At the end of July Rainer departs Paris for Belgium. Rootless again, he shall not return for an entire ten months. Paula will be gone by then.

 FURNES, BELGIUM:
SUMMER 1906 . . .

*Y*ou await your wife and daughter in Furnes. Bright coastal town aswarm with sunseekers garbed in holiday colors. The beachfront is a teeming promenade of parasols and sunhats and dandy walking sticks, plump snowy-complexioned children doddering dizzily in bathing attire, itinerant musicians and trinket vendors and loitering socialites, every visitor's scenery comprised as much of the passersby as the postcard vistas all around. Amongst the crush come aged slow moving pensioners and their wives; they must pause in the paltry shade of every palm tree and put their withered hands to their hips and cast their squinting eyes about in a sort of sluggish alarm, as if some unforeseen fate has transported them here from their more moderate native climes and they expect, at any moment, the arrival of an omnibus back home.

Till evening you remain sequestered unhappily in your none-too-distinctive room at the Hôtel de la Noble Rose. Outside, the seawater is a field of glaring steel, serrated with combers like knife-teeth.

Clara and Ruth will arrive tomorrow, this rendezvous at Clara's instigation, her wish for companionship having grown more and more ardent through her lonely Worpswede spring. You finally agreed to the plan, and a coastal holiday was decided upon, so the small Rilke family geared toward convergence again.

Though you forced yourself to postpone acceptance of the notion, a family sojourn had struck you with immediate allure even amidst your good work in Paris. For why shouldn't convergence come, every so often, to your little familial unit? Why shouldn't you give yourself leave to live, at least for a while, as others lived? Alone in your cheerless rue Cassette quarters, you felt a veritable uplift at the thought of seeing Clara and Ruth. In fact you grew so joyfully anxious about the approaching reunion that when Paula Becker's last letter reached you with its touching request, your reply shot out by pure reflex.

Paula wrote that she hoped to flee the oppressive Paris heat for some coast or other—and couldn't she join her good friends and their sweet Ruth on their summer getaway in Belgium?

You answered with a flat "No." For you wanted your summer energies, given that you were bound to expend them, to amount to something happy and free for your small family. With Paula along, your meager talent for effecting such an atmosphere would be spread one person too thin; yes, you had to be truthful with yourself about that. Reading your letter over, though, you saw that your refusal was curt, so you amended it with recommendations for desirable retreats in Brittany. Paula would understand your position. She knew, didn't she, of the delicate balance your family must seek to strike, of the quiet dangers that attended every reunion?

But now, sequestered in your mean room at the Hôtel de la Noble Rose, not wanting to expose yourself to the thronging holidayers outside, you feel the slap—already—of a dejection all too familiar. This same funk has attended how many of your countless arrivals after how many high-spirited journeys? Always it's your errors of expectation that bring it on. Met by anything less than the most propitious conditions, any contingency not foreseen (contingencies should always, of course, be foreseen), and you feel yourself wheeling off balance; any deflation at the prick of reality and you feel yourself lost, dissipated, aimless, while your heavy work accretes within you and no foreseeable outlet reveals itself. Always and always these hazards confront your hopes—so why in this case didn't you anticipate the possibility of dejection in Belgium? The balance of your family unit was one thing, the hospitality of new surroundings something different altogether. Always unpredictable. Just a little foresight and you might have relented to Paula's wish, might have made the more human gesture that in hindsight seems called for: supply of a few easy words to the effect of *Yes, Paula, do come, and here is where you will find us.* . . .

But you'd been dull and unfeeling and had failed to see how untenable your original designs were. You'd hoped too hard, that's all. It had ever been your error, one you must resolve to never make again.

But now it's far too late, you know, to revise your position for Paula—maybe she's gone already to Brittany or someplace else. Still, with an awful, nauseating clench inside, you can't help picturing her in that drab atelier in the avenue du Maine. Alone, exposed to the remonstrations of husband and family and friends alike, she strives to shut out the clamor and realize her ideals.

Whatever color surrounds her in those rude quarters is color of her own creation. Her achievement itself would render null the censure of friends and family—yet how much does that censure scatter her power to achieve? Thus far she has stood firm even against her husband. Otto has gone home without her and now Paris is hers to keep for a while, but in the meantime she will wear herself down in work, and who will hold her up while she collects her scattered strength in the slow intervening hours?

. . .

Clara and Ruth arrive in Furnes, shining and youthful and happy. Rainer embraces them in turn. His daughter sinewy in his arms. Her small hot hands graze his shaven chin and she giggles fearfully at his new face.

The unlikely family idyll begins, amidst and in spite of the holiday hordes. All summer long the poet shall strive to shape himself to the role of husband and father.

 CAPRI: DECEMBER 1906.
AGE THIRTY-ONE . . .

"And even still to depart,

hand torn from hand,

as one tears anew at a healing wound,

and to depart: whither? Into the unknown,

far into a warm country, a land detached and all its own . . .

and to depart: why? Out of an urge as of thirst,

out of impatience, out of dark expectation,

out of incomprehension and lack of judgment:

to take all these requirements on, perhaps

in vain. To let everything else fall away around oneself,

to let it go, to die alone, not knowing why—

is this the way to a new life?"

Four months later now. And you would have preferred a return to Paris, naturally, after the long dissipating summer. But as ever, money—or rather its lack—has rendered the pursuit of preference impossible. And what is now important above all—above *all*—is *solitude. That* has surely become clear. Clear, anyway, that there will be no chance of you and Clara working side by side as you did in Rome two years past. Let that picture go.

Following its awkward season of unity, your little family has dispersed again. Ruth to Oberneuland, Clara to Berlin, and you to this remote and islanded south.

You arrived on your thirty-first birthday, the steep primeval line of Vesuvius rising up at your back as the boat slapped across the waters from the Naples pier. The Italian sun fell in a glaring canopy of warmth. A thin salt-breeze fluttered your jacket. Weather briefly clement after the previous day's *sirocco* and pounding swells and restless chiaroscuro sky. The barber in Naples had predicted the storm as you lay tipped back in his chair.

"Sì, sì, Signore, sirocco, sirocco!" His baleful little whistles intimating the fury as the straight razor went waving above your lathered face. And despite your genteel denials the barber's storm had come by nightfall, a squall as fleet and fierce as those you'd seen in Viareggio three years ago. You watched from your hotel window as the waters began to shiver beneath the first encroaching clouds. Soon huge mallets of wind were driving hollows into the ragged surface. The ships that had not come to harbor toggled and dove on the rolling horizon like fallen acorns.

But the following morning brought a different world entirely. Your boat to Capri slipped out upon a bay of leaded glass. Every sight—water, rock, foliage—lay awash in the elemental tones of southern dawn: gold and blue, everything everywhere an elaboration on these twin tinctures, the two-part flush of antiquity itself. The boat skimmed forward and you stood with your hands at the rail and felt, with peculiar poignancy like never before, exiled. Willingly exiled, yes, self-conscribed to your remote island of work—and yet the longing for Paris remained sharp within you.

Your thoughts inevitably flitted to Paula, herself an exile of sorts. In a letter to Clara just before your departure south, the painter had imparted the news that she was returning to her life with Otto Modersohn. Whether this meant she would return to Worpswede remained unclear, but one could guess; it was well known that Otto detested Paris.

Alighting at Capri you found yourself received with great warmth. Alice Faehndrich, the good lady of the Villa Discopoli, showed you to this small Italianate cottage overspread with Mediterranean ivy. It stands in Frau Faehndrich's garden, fifty steps below her villa, and has been appointed for your use alone as long as you should stay on the island. She calls it her "Rosenhäusl" for the enormous blossoms that thrive in this garden even in the winter months.

Something like your Roman cottage, this Rosenhäusl has a rooftop terrace, but instead of arid *campagna,* the vista afforded here is of hillsides bright with mustard grass, and farther below, in the sea just offshore, terrific bone-colored rocks where gulls perch by the hundreds.

It's all much too picturesque, and you felt immediately that this scenery would be no help to you: more of the tourist-treasured views that you'd endured the whole summer long. Wistfully you thought of your crude quarters in the rue Cassette, but the overwhelming sense of displacement stirred up by that image made you put it out of mind at once.

You've now been here several nights. Despite its unsubtle beauty, this place is not lacking in graces after all. At evening the terrain around the Rosenhäusl assumes a votive hush, and you may stand barefoot at the terrace with no lights about save those of the stars and a few windows aglow in households nearby. Nothing to hear in that hour but the sea's weird whisper and boom. A pelagic wind carries its salt-savor across the island, and under the immense stars, for moments at a time, you have the illusion of headlong suspension over some phosphorous black abyss.

And so far, despite your misgivings regarding the scenery, despite your status as visitor, your solitude is mostly safe here. That had been your greatest apprehension: the demands of sociability inherent in this arrangement— but Frau Faehndrich, whose late sister greatly admired your work, is a dear and sympathetic soul and has clearly taken pains to provide an atmosphere of privacy. There's a strong quality of asylum in your monkish cottage, recessed from the main house as it is. And your small high-ceilinged room seems extremely conducive to all that you hope to cultivate in the months ahead. The room has everything you require but nothing extraneous: a narrow divan, a few chairs painted sea-blue, twin lancet windows fringed with ivy, and a wooden writing desk. This airy Rosen-häusl will hold you very kindly, yes, and help you to atone for your recent fruitless months. The whole of every day shall be yours, devoted as you deem fit.

So if manners demand that you repay your hostess's extreme kindness with an appearance at dinner every night and conversation in the drawing room afterward, it is not so inequitable an exchange. True, your talent for recreational conversation is very meager; sociability often costs you, in good part, the energy and attentiveness you'd rather reserve for your work—yet you must bear in mind that this is nobody's fault but your own; it would be very unjust to resent the generous Frau's native gregariousness merely because you yourself feel so deficient in that realm.

Your new fruitfulness begins with a prodigious outflow of letters from the Rosenhäusl, one and another account of your current position in the world and of your progress in work. In this way you take stock of all that has accrued within you, the unnumbered images still sifting down through the roving months since leaving Paris last summer.

It is a quiet sort of ingathering, this letter-writing. You will write without pause until at length you find yourself properly oriented, and then you will set out upon the real work at hand. This at least is your design—until, like a squall from the very waters beyond your window, comes your wife's jarring letter from Berlin.

Clara reports that Lou Andreas-Salomé recently stopped in the city and paid her a visit. Inevitably their conversation touched upon you and your absence, at which point Lou began to impart her intimate knowledge of your dilemmas and obsessions and finally, after some very frank and fretful interchange, denounced you to your wife's face, showering Clara in sympathy. Naturally, stunned as she was, Clara found herself unable to refute Lou's sharp assessments. As Lou saw it, Rainer Maria Rilke was an apostate father and husband and would well deserve to be turned over to the police if he did not soon answer to his duties in life.

You run your fingers over Clara's careful cursive. In that embossment you can feel her distress surfacing, sentiments she has expressed only indirectly till now. A flush of white pain comes on—yet it's no surprise, is it, that all this which has simmered so long should finally bubble up into such grievous utterance?

Clara does not denounce or assault, in spite of her troubles. It's like her, poor dear, to be so gentle in her crisis of faith. She merely passes Lou's words along with the hope that you will give convincing rebuttal. But that Lou of all people should occasion this crisis! Lou, who sat beside you in her Göttingen garden and let you spill yourself out to her and listened with unjudging closeness.

—*I love Clara, Lou, as I love our Ruth.* That's what you had told her, and you thought you had said it in a manner she could understand, with all its complexities clear.

—*It's as though this long heavy work will fulfill itself whatever the cost. Despite whatever wishes I may make. But am I to injure those I would love?*

Clara's pages fall in your sinking hands. You stare away into the blue marine distance beyond the terrace. You're trying to envision Lou and your wife, these two magnetic poles of your existence, alone together in such a conversation. But the most you can see is what you saw when the women met at tea in Berlin last spring. They wear the same clothes, even. They are genial, at ease, and at the periphery sits Friedrich Andreas. No, you cannot picture it.

You move to the desk and withdraw your letter paper, settle down to an immediate reply. But anguish is the only immediate thing. In anguish, then, you will write what must be written.

So the day rolls by with a slow grinding motion. Then dinnertime arrives and you must set down your pen and go up to the house.

Later, after the evening's parlor hours, you return down the dark slope of the island estate and the lonely stillness of the Rosenhäusl absorbs you again. As the island takes on its nocturnal chill and the sleepless sea hums below, you continue writing. The letter itself is a work, as all your best letters are. And just as it's addressed to your wife, so also you know it to be addressed to yourself, to Rainer Maria Rilke and all that he has become at this grand and grievous outset of his thirty-first year. The letter, as you write, holds you up against your own beginnings. *Dear Clara . . .*

"To me it's like this: I am absolutely determined to miss none of these voices which are to come. I want to hear each one."

And you see before you the boy René Maria, wandering the lanes of Prague's Lesser Town while icons of plaster or stone peer from high niches carved at most every corner, each statue seeming to mutter inscrutable words as he goes by. And here is René alone in the Saint Pölten graveyard amongst the unweeded headstones. And here is the young man in his shabby Munich quarters, in flight from the labyrinth of Prague. And here sits the famous Lou Andreas-Salomé in a chair beside a window, her hair effulging in the light and his hand going toward her, meeting the warm clasp of her fingers.—*You say you've written me?*

"Lou thinks a person has no right to choose amongst duties and to withdraw from the nearest and most natural ones—but my nearest and most natural ones were always, as early as my boyhood, these ones here, upon whose side I again and again try to stand."

—Here is young Rainer arriving in the north-German moors and talking to a sculptress, in her darkened yard, of Russia, whence he's just returned.

"And have I withdrawn from this responsibility? Don't I try, as well as I ever could, to bear it, and on the other hand don't my longings, in the largest sense, meet with infinite fulfillment?"

—With the storm-gripped Ligurian Sea thrashing before him, the poet, having fled the oppressive atmosphere of Paris, completes *The Book of Hours,* the work that has germinated for four long years—and this so soon after his magnificent Rodin book. And not far ahead of him now, in Rome, a whole new world shall open to him through the figure of Malte Laurids Brigge.

"If we are therefore living separated from each other by days of travel, in order to do what our hearts demand of us day and night, don't we turn ourselves away from the difficult in order to welcome the difficult? Don't I have this consciousness myself, at least, as I try to live this lonely life?"

—Soaked to the skin and bearing a suitcase of books, the poet knocks at a Paris door while the rain beats down and church bells clang their stark music above him.

"Tell me: is there not still a house around us, a real one for which only the visible symbol is missing, so that others don't see it? . . . Ah, you can grasp that I'd like to make my strength and standard hold up against great things."

Is there not still a house around us?

Stretched out on his divan in the later, blacker penetralia of the island night, Rainer does not sleep but hovers in a limbless displacement just be-

yond the margin of slumber. Hovers as once the boy would feel himself
hover whenever the fever arrived to extract him from his body.

Is there not still a house?

He isn't sick tonight, but this uncoupling, this weird lucidity, is the
same.

Is there not still a house?

Hovering, hovering in the vaulted chamber, watching the body as it
shifts about below. Outside, the surrounding sea breathes its hush, hush,
hush: *Is there not is there not is there not . . .*

His will be a lonely Christmas this year—the first without Clara or Ruth.
On nineteenth December, two days after his defense in the face of Lou's at-
tack, Rainer writes a long Christmas Eve letter for Clara: *"Nothing, indeed
nothing can hinder me from being about you so that you feel me."*

And with delicate truthfulness he shares the sensations he has suffered
on every Christmas they've spent together, all but their first at Westerwede
so soon after Ruth's birth. This, he sees, has been his mistake: not impart-
ing to Clara, much sooner, these gravest truths of his heart. He will tell her
now the things he told Lou in Göttingen. It was a mistake, yes, to impart
all that to Lou alone.

On every Christmas but their first one together, Rainer writes, he has
felt himself divided inside, some recessed piece of him watching without
involvement and prepared, prepared even in the height of joy, to depart.
For it always seemed to him that the face he turned to his family was only
half a face, that this face must yet accomplish itself, must become complete. Still he feels this, even now, as he warmly recollects their Christmas-
times together, even as he remembers the outflung love with which his
daughter clung to his neck.

And now he tells Clara of the joy with which he remembers Ruth's birth, tells how vividly he relived it on Ruth's fifth birthday a week ago as he sat alone with his thoughts in the quiet Rosenhäusl. How in those wintry midday moments of the child's arrival he had stood by, a young man in awe, gazing with profound attention. Now he can see what a resurrection the child's birth effected within him. How the miracle of a daughter rooted him, that younger man, in life.

Yes, and then had come that first Westerwede Christmas, which would remain for so long unparalleled amongst his small family's Christmases. And because of that sacral evening beside the illumined tree, because of the manner in which Clara held their daughter's warm face against her own while Rainer looked on in wonder at those two beloved faces mysteriously enriching one another, because of such a Christmas he may now be alone in this one on Capri. Such past joy makes it possible. Gives him strength. Grounds him in life. Even as he continues laboring on his unfinished face. *"This face must be in solitude, much behind its hands, much in the dark,"* he writes.

> *"You have never seen in it the greatness of your trust and the wholeness of your love, which it was incapable of receiving. . . . It was a face scattered apart in its unfinishedness. . . . But if sometime it should be given back to you better, it must still be worked on, night and day. For a long time."*

On twenty-third December the poet receives his first published copies of the new *Book of Images* and *The Lay of the Love and Death of Cornet Cristoph Rilke*. In calm amazement he turns them over and over in his hands, sets them by only to pick them up again. *The Cornet,* on its cover, bears an embossed reproduction of the Rilke family device. With a good deal of apprehension he'd entrusted Jaroslav's old medallion to the publisher, half afraid he'd never see it again, imploring Juncker to give it his greatest care. The medallion came back, in the end, unharmed, and now the book will bear it forever.

After he's leafed repeatedly through both of them, the volumes lie on his desk, silent and solid, proclaiming accomplishment.

Just before the New Year word arrives from the Insel Verlag in Leipzig that the first print run of *Das Stundenbuch* has been exhausted. A full five hundred copies sold! Anton Kippenberg, chief editor at the Insel Verlag, makes clear his eagerness for new work, and Rainer responds that he foresees a book of poems being ready within the year. His "Panther" shall be amongst them. Yes, the two fresh volumes on his Rosenhäusl desk seem to emanate good prophecy now. Something, *something* has been granted him in recompense for the sacrifices he's made. And much is yet to come. He feels it.

*I*n Rainer's bright frigid January days Clara comes to Capri. A patrician family has given her a commission, meanwhile inviting her on a sojourn of several months to Egypt. She will depart by ocean liner from the Naples pier. Ruth is safe in the care of Clara's mother in Oberneuland.

On Capri the sculptress quarters herself alone. No need even to discuss this arrangement. By morning Rainer walks the short distance from the Villa Discopoli to meet his wife at the door of her hotel in the Villa Pagano. Together they ramble about the rugged slopes. A sort of dispassionate kindness courses between them all the while. Rainer takes it for a new expansiveness come to their long friendship, and Clara, as far as he can tell, regards it similarly. It's as though all expectations have been excised at last and now, unbound from one another thus, they've achieved a serene companionship, entitled to affection of the most weightless sort. And yet this is clearly not a reunion, not a renewal, for though Clara breaks her journey on the island, still she is journeying, and still Rainer is more intensely islanded than his proximity can suggest.

After a few days the poet and Clara make the crossing together to Naples and visit Pompeii, where they purchase a number of fine photographs of the city's antique paintings. Art that does not age, though born of that ancient ashen world. These photographs will be sent to Paula Becker for her birthday in the first week of February, a joint gift from her old friends.

Later, at the Naples pier, Rainer stands with his wife, holding both her hands in his. Passengers stream past them and climb the gangplank to the ocean liner that will carry Clara to Egypt. Rainer stares into her dark sea-deep eyes. He leans to graze her cheek with a farewell kiss, then steps back and watches her mount the gangplank, her white dress clutched in both fists.

Near the top she turns. "I talked with Ruth before I left. She understood I had to go. She didn't even shed a tear."

A look like bewilderment or fright moves quickly across Clara's face. Barely there at all, it pulsates and vanishes, but Rainer sees it.

"Isn't that astonishing?" Clara says. "Ruth's so young, but she already understands. Do you remember, Rainer, how we wondered if we'd ever get used to this life?"

"I remember, yes."

"It's as if Ruth's already managed it. As if it's for *her* to have that. Not for us."

Rainer merely meets her eyes. He cannot answer. By her soft look he can see that she doesn't expect an answer.

She says, "You'll stay on Capri for some time still?"

"There's no telling, really. A while yet. Then perhaps Venice. Safe journey, Clara."

She turns. Already the file of passengers begins to hide her from sight.

"Clara!"

She doesn't hear.

"Clara!"

She disappears. A moment passes. Then, amidst the flurry on deck, he sees her again. She is turning back, edging toward the rail, her eyes upon him.

"I'll watch you go!" he calls and points to Capri out in the bay. "From the Tiberio, atop the island. I'll see the ship for a long time from up there!"

He thinks he notes a smile on her face. Then she is crowded from the rail again. Vanishes.

And there stands Rainer, alone in bleak January sunlight, the ship gently rolling in its moorings before him. For a long time he stands there, unready to turn away. Hard to shake the sense of conclusion in this parting, though he and Clara have parted a thousand times already.

I'm sorry, Clara. And give Ruth my apology in the tenderest kiss. It was a poor man that made you his wife. Ruth's father is a poor man. Has he made strangers of you both? Don't blame him, please, for believing he could have a home. For wanting just what everyone wants.

Out in the sheer blue foil of the sea far off the pier stands the dark hump of Capri, necklaced with blinding sunlit waves. He'll return across the bay this afternoon.

—*We must never be like the hammer. . . .*

The poet's own voice in his ears now, years younger. A voice quiet beside the pain of a young woman's hammer wound.

—*Like the hammer?*

—*Invulnerable.*

And how he believed it then. And does this pained life of his not testify, still, to that old pledge?

By noiseless evening a chaise carries Rainer up the island road from Capri's Grande Marina back to the Villa Discopoli. He is tired. He has sat for several hours at the Naples harbor watching Clara's ship creep away on the waters, the large black letters across the stern blurring slowly: OCEANA. He'd felt it a kind of commission to remain there. It seemed that by witnessing the ship's retreat he would do honor to something. And he'd still thought he would climb the Tiberio upon his return to Capri, but now he knows he's too exhausted. So much sapped from him in these comings and goings, these dear light-filled days concluding in such swift farewells. He needs a quiet hour or two in his Rosenhäusl, then a night of peaceable sleep with the sea waves whispering beyond his window. Selfsame currents that carry Clara's ship horizonward.

Arriving back at the villa, Rainer brings a great atlas down from the main house and sits with it open before him to pages depicting the River Nile. The faint blue course his wife will follow. He wants to imagine all she will see in Egypt. The many undreamt images that will bless her there . . .

In the morning the poet finds himself still suffused with yesterday's parting, a sense of incompletion tugging inside him. Haunted thoughts of Clara's seaward journey. So he sets out from the Rosenhäusl up the rocky paths to the crest of the Tiberio.

On that barren summit the January sun seems to squat in relentless and brooding brilliance. And away to the south the water stretches, a hard and scintillating surface, illimitable.

Up here in a plaster-walled hut lives a young monk who serves as steward to a tiny sanctuary and an icon of the Virgin. The monk emerges in his black frock, genuflects before the Madonna. Shuffles over to stand at Rainer's side. Soft of voice, the monk murmurs something Italian. Then he turns a look of puzzlement upon the poet. *"Italiano?"*

Rainer shakes his head.

"Tedesco? No? Francese? Austrìaco?"

Rainer disavows them all. The monk gives a moment of thought. Smiles. Lays a hand at Rainer's shoulder and with deep understanding says, *"Un bambino di Dio."* A child of God.

"Sì," says the poet. *"Sì."*

They stand a while, the planet's boundless waters surging away before them.

The monk sweeps his arm across the waters and begins to soliloquize in a lilting voice. Rainer, catching a word here and there, makes out that he's describing a sight beheld from this summit last night. The lights of a great ship receding forever in the blackness of water and sky. The poet's imagination supplies the rest: how those lights, the longer the monk looked, seemed to become but stars amongst the many millions twinkling out there, and at last merged entirely with the night heavens.

"*Sì, sì,*" says Rainer, listening. He keeps his eyes fixed on that glare of sun against the horizon and seems, even yet, to see the twinkling ship.

The monk stops and considers him again. Poses another question in rich Italian.

His gestures make the question clear. *Do you know someone on this ship?*

"*Sì, mia . . .*" The poet does not know the word. "*Mia . . . femme. Épouse. Mia . . . Frau.*"

"Aaah," says the monk with great pleasure. By the shine of his eyes it's plain he understands. "*Moglie,*" he says. "*Moglie.*"

"*Sì, mia moglie.*"

"*Moglie.*"

The monk's brown hand settles at Rainer's shoulder again, remains there with uninhibited warmth. And something in the poet stirs to see the young friar's bright and guileless face, that smiling mouth enunciating brotherly words now—a benediction uttered with faith beyond the bounds of language.

Rainer *senses* the meaning in doubtless clarity: *May she be given safe passage.*

"*Grazie,*" he tells the monk. "*Grazie.*"

And though he's just failed to summon the Italian word for "wife," now from some dim treasury within him Rainer withdraws the word for "brother."

"*Grazie, mio fratello.*"

three

THE UNFINISHED PORTRAIT:

1907–1912

If it is good, one can't quite live to recognize it as such—or it's still just half good and not reckless enough . . .

letter to Clara, 1907

# CAPRI: 1907. AGE THIRTY-ONE . . .

*I*n March of this year, more than a month since Rainer sent the gift of the Pompeii pictures, Paula Modersohn-Becker writes from Paris with the news that she and Otto are returning together—*together*—to Worpswede. A laconic little letter. Her last few lines convey humble abstractions: the hope that everyone will reach heaven, then the somehow dissonant assertion that she's pleased with the life she is living.

A week later the poet replies. His letter begins gently, acknowledging the disservice he did to Paula's friendship by refusing her company in Belgium last summer. He ends with assurances. All will be well, he writes, even though circumstances require her to give up Paris for Worpswede. He has nothing but confidence, he says, in all she'll continue to accomplish.

Through the spring on Capri, Rainer's restlessness gradually grows and his thoughts move toward a return to Paris. Small as his means remain, he knows he must get back there.

Come the end of May he's made his departure, and soon finds himself setting up quarters again at number 29 rue Cassette. Again he feels his solitude enfolding him. Through the Paris summer he labors steadily. The new volume of poetry is completed and dispatched to the publisher, seventy-two pieces collected under the modest title *New Poems*. Amongst the works are "The Panther," his "Self-Portrait from the Year 1906," and "Youthful Portrait of My Father." Here also are a number of Paris impressions: the unicorn from the ancient tapestries of the Musée de Cluny, the children's carousel in the Jardin Luxembourg, and that bewitching statue of the Buddha which stood before his cottage in Meudon.

"He may leave behind all that we strive to discover,
and he discovers all that which spurns us."

In August comes a flood of further poems, similar in spirit to those in the volume just finished. And now too the poet is tugged back into the fervent and frightened world of Malte Laurids Brigge.

Come October, though, Rainer uproots himself once again. A three-city reading tour, the immediate solution to his moneyless state, necessitates travel. Prague, Breslau, Vienna. Once more his belongings are stored away, once more he is drawn from Paris.

On first November, by this whirling turn of events, he arrives in the city of his birth. All Souls' Day, and here to greet him, like a phantom of the past come sweeping from the shadowed tableau of memory, is Phia Rilke.

Leaning forth with a kiss, she smells the same as ever. From no other woman come these old scents of night and Christ and candlewick, of dimly spiced perfume and black-dyed lace—scents pasty and somehow lactic.

"Mama," he says softly in greeting. More bizarre all the time that this queer figure should be called such a thing. And yet not bizarre at all.

She clutches his shoulders to look at him and her eyes are jeweled with tears. Her thin face incised with lines since he saw it last, and nothing but this clear unconfused affection welling up in her glance. And why, with such a doting face before him, should so much contempt overtake him? The contempt arrives almost without reason. And already he suffers the hurt of his own hatefulness—suffers it in order that Mama, in her innocence, need not. Might one ever encounter one's mother without this age-old vexation seeping up?

"Are you well, my boy?"

"*Ja,* Mama. A little tired."

"And hungry too, no doubt. Are you hungry?"

"Not terribly, no."

But she is deaf to this and begins, like a guide to a tourist, to rattle off the names of various restaurants.

"Perhaps, Mama, we might go to my hotel first."

"Oh, of course, dear. You must set down that suitcase. Where is the hotel?"

"In the Wenzelsplatz."

"The Wenzelsplatz? So close to your mother and you didn't think to stay with her?"

To this there seems no possible answer. Silently, then, he walks the old streets with Mama at his arm. Twenty minutes later they are sitting together at a table in the hotel restaurant.

"Is it nice to be home, René, after all this time?"

Again he is without an answer. He studies her and wonders: What rendition of his childhood years does she treasure away behind that sweet narrow-mouthed smile, that she can ask him such a question?

She says, "Prague is no Paris, of course." And sighs and turns her glance out the window. "But it's home as no place else could be."

"I was here last year, Mama. Not all that long ago."

"Oh, of course . . . your poor father." She blushes, looks immediately girl-like.

Why can he not muster mercy toward this overdelicate dame? She understands nothing, that's all. Everything escapes her. Need she be castigated for it? Quickly now his horded memories begin to mellow, melt away. Memories etched of sickness and shame that have stood starkly forth at every encounter, so much so stupefying for so long—it's all draining off, inexplicably.

"Mama." His hand goes out across the table. She catches it up and squeezes.

And now to speak tenderly to this mother, to let soft but forthright words pass between them as has never happened. To ask the question he's carried over all the trying terrain of this year. How heavily he's carried it, he sees that now. He strives to stare love into the lady's eyes as he asks it. "Mama, why . . . why did you not come to Papa's funeral?"

A shudder in her glance. Her eyes, suddenly pink-rimmed, skating off in befuddlement. "I was . . . I was on holiday, René, didn't I tell you? I was away in Arco. . . ."

He waits, pressing her thin hand. Waits for more.

But the moments pass and this, apparently, is the whole of her answer. The sole answer she possesses, he can see it by that look of hers. Clearly she's perplexed to feel, for the first time, required to give further reason.

I was on holiday.

Everything is changing now, everything that surrounds and has surrounded this woman all these years. She's becoming less and less complicated as he looks upon her, as if her figure shrinks before him. No special motives lurk in this lady's reasoning. Perhaps that's been the truth these many years. Yes, that seems possible now. Mama has at least understood *herself* all this time, this small woman unsuspectingly aging in her frilled black ensemble.

"I said a prayer for him," she says, sitting forward with a look of bright satisfaction. "In the church at Arco. I lit a candle and prayed for your father's soul."

She means it generously. So the most that seems possible now is for Rainer to return the lady's loving smile and allow her to keep pressing his hand.

"Thank you, Mama."

It need hardly matter if she thinks these tears in his eyes are tears of gratitude.

Your reading at Prague's Concordia Society is fairly well attended, though it seems the listeners are all of that old grim Prague stock that so somberly peopled your young years in this place. No saying whether they're receiving anything you bestow.

You give them some poems from the *Book of Images,* then a section of *Malte:* the death of the chamberlain. A few newer poems follow, amongst them *"Das Kind."* The Child.

> *"When it grows tired in its small dress*
> *it will sit aside as in a waiting room*
> *sit and wait upon a time all its own."*

—and while concluding this last stanza, something shakes loose within you. Something drops warm and thick upon the back of your hand. A stream come burbling out of you—*as in the fog-heavy field of Saint Pölten on that winter morning not long ago.*

Not long? How long? Yesterday? The day before?

A crimson face shrinks back and turns away—but that's not the main thing. The main thing is the fog's absorption—fog enfolding and erasing you and your blood bled alone in secret and nothing to stanch this bright current but the press of one's own mittens to one's own face . . .

Out of the fog comes a startled rustle. A rustle in the seats you've ceased to see. Your hands are rising to your face, palms cupped to catch the ponderous droplets—they are falling faster now. Past your hands the papers are already splattered red. Into your hands you muffle a slurred word or two, already stepping back from the podium to turn with red-slathered fingers cupped at nose and mouth, to fumble through the curtains to the stall behind.

Within seconds someone is there in the darkness: a voice, unnerved but eager to soothe. And someone is fetching a bowl of water, a cloth. And now you must sit and put back your head. But no, if you put back your head it will just flow down your throat and then that rime of dried blood will destroy your voice. So when the bowl of water arrives (instantaneously it seems) you sit above it, silent in the dark, and patiently bleed. As ever, one must do that alone.

*T*en days and nine nights in Venice. What a respite the floating city seems after Rainer's tour, the surprisingly frenzied reception in Vienna, the flurry of introductions, young strangers praising him to his face, his hotel room flooded with flowers.

A pleasurable but taxing time that was. And in the midst of it had come, unexpectedly, a letter in the careful script of Auguste Rodin's new secretary, bearing the Master's own signature at the bottom. The Master had been working on a series of drawings inspired by the story of Psyche, that womanly figure of the soul roaming the world and its nether regions in search of her destined. The legend had brought the poet to mind, said Rodin, for surely Rainer should rewrite it sometime. And whenever the poet was next in Paris he must come to Meudon for a visit. *'We have need of truth, of poetry, both of us, and of friendship.'* What pure amity from that great and once-furious old man! Rainer immediately wrote to Clara of this renewal. And now he feels Venice receiving him with a quiet amity of its own, the city shrouded in subtle winter pallor. He means to savor his solitude here, however brief its term may be. When one is poor one is made to work against time. Ten days and nine nights.

He stirs awake to the gonging of bells. Blackness in the room but for the wavering canal-light from beyond his window. And he is hovering, hovering, semiconscious, his heftless body pulled from the bed as from the floor of sleep and held, held, held. . . . Those bells somehow bearing him up off the bed, two inches aloft into watery music.

It's a sensation something like hovering over a high precipice. And there seems a heavy message in the beating of those iron tongues. Some premonitory sentence uttered over and over. He turns in his weightless state, his senses awake while his body sleeps. The utterance of the bells outlasts their ringing and resonates. . . .

Morning, even before he's dressed, the terrible telegram from Clara reaches him in Venice. Paula Modersohn-Becker is dead.

*R*ainer travels to Oberneuland. Old northward country swathed in fog. The flat moors themselves dunned in funeral dress. How unshined it all looks after Venice. How unwatered, this world skinned in frost like plates of bone.

The poet sits in his late father-in-law's study with his wife. A fire crackles in the hearth. Clara in black, her eyes themselves rimmed black. She sits before him and describes with halting voice the auburn-haired painter's final moments, as learned in the days after the death.

She'd been abed for more than two weeks following the birth of her daughter, Mathilde. But at last Paula wished to rise and sit up in the parlor a while. She was in no hurry. She seemed very refreshed, seemed intent on taking great care with each passing moment.

Before leaving the bed, Paula asked for a cheval glass. It was carried from another room and placed beside her footboard. She sat up and began to comb her hair. She took her time, combing and combing with a rapt and placid mien. A ceremony of sorts. She parceled the auburn hair into four thin panels and braided them and coiled them up around her head and pinned them in place, affixing here and there a few of the small red roses she'd received that morning, a gift from somebody. Then she was ready, her mirror-portrait complete.

Garlanded, she got up and moved in her gaunt nightshift to the parlor. They helped her, her family, draping the still-warm coverlet across the chair so that she needn't feel the shiver of rising. She sank slowly to the chair and drew the coverlet close about her, breathing a tired sigh and smiling. She said she'd like to hold her daughter in her arms. Her care-givers, eager to assist, all turned about, one went away to fetch the child, and now Paula raised her legs to the ottoman—and in the small effort of that one mundane motion something leapt to a halt within her. From a sudden silent collision of amnion and vessel the painter's death had blos-somed inside. Elision of all the futures she'd supposed. She must have felt it, though it was nearly instantaneous, for she lay back in the chair and with a bright harrowed look almost like joy said, "A shame!"

Clara's eyes are fierce with glistening grief.

Rainer feels her grief hard upon him. "That's what she said? *A shame?*"

Clara nods, coughs out a sob.

"My God," says Rainer. "My God." And it seems to him that every-thing has halted now. The day's moments themselves stunned from their account.

His limbs are humming, hollow. He's been emptied of everything.

In her lifetime Paula Modersohn-Becker had painted nearly six hundred pictures. She had sold but four or five, all but one to friends.

Paula's portrait of Rainer, unfinished: he gazes to great depths from the painting's shallow plain. It seems that no one can join him in that taut solitude. Paula, even, is no presence there; she merely perceives him from afar. His eyes, as she has seen them, receive and receive, while his mouth, like a dark low-slung nerve, wants to give back all that it has tasted and breathed. To return it all unalloyed, newly complete.

He appears remote, alone, a beginner. And in truth he'll stand forever at beginnings, will *begin* his way into everything—*begin* his way, even, into death itself. This portrait will remain the most faithful of the many that seek to capture him, even the countless photographs. Paula has stretched tight, in her soft colors, the bare infallible membrane of Rainer's poet-feeling. It vibrates across the canvas. In this face that strives to judge nevermore. Haunted, lonely, mournful face, its sad receptive eyes swallowing everything, yet fixed upon a faraway goal. How well the painter understood such endless beginnings.

In this grievous December Rainer receives from the Insel Verlag his finished copies of the *Neue Gedichte*. *New Poems*. He inscribes and dispatches a copy to Rodin in Meudon. The Master is the source from which, in patience and slowness, this strong work has come. A copy goes off to Göttingen as well, to Lou, with Christmas salutations inscribed in Russian.

Soon, as a crust of Christmas ice seizes the country beyond the windows, the old insistent sickness levels Rainer yet again. Bedstricken for weeks in Oberneuland, clutched by the savage headache and fever as on how many occasions before? Only this time it all seems to him the cold slow panic of grief.

Paula's fate is written out inexorably now. Written out written out written out—he feels himself writhing as if to erase it, but its ciphers only darken, life-black, death-black. Its ciphers will not be censored. No. For who is he to scrub at fate?

 PARIS: AUTUMN 1908 . . .

*E*leven months later. Paris again, and for eight weeks Rainer has been installed in the cavernous Hôtel Biron at 77 rue Varenne, a derelict eighteenth-century château. Some years ago, following innumerable transfers of ownership, the French government disbanded a resident order of nuns, the sisters of the Sacré Coeur, and opened the rooms for lease to artists. The poet's ground-floor corner room has served recently as Clara's studio, but she's gone away to Germany.

He is photographed during his residence here. Thirty-two years old, he sits at a great wooden galleon of a desk in the milky light of a window. No other visible furnishings, just a bare expanse of wall looming up in front of him. The images radiate hollowness, solitude, the vast airiness of this once-grand house. The poet is shrunken in the picture-plain, engulfed in a thick duffelcloth coat, for he suffers a constant draft in these autumn days. This unsealed house in which spirits stir.

He's deep in the fourth year of his struggle with Malte when quite suddenly on All Soul's Day, almost a full year after Paula's death, her requiem arrives:

> *"I've had dead ones, and I've released them. . . .*
> *Only you, you turn*
> *back; you graze against me, you move about*
> *in order to unsettle something, so that it will ring with you*
> *and betray you to me."*

And there she is. She stands in the gray corner before his desk. Paula Modersohn-Becker, an apparition, small-shouldered and shy in her lank dress. Her long hair is braided in a coronet about her skull, affixed with roses. Auburn hair which looks nearly white in the autumnal glow of the room. And it is not strange to him that this dead woman should manifest herself. Not strange at all.

So to Paula's ghost he says, "I didn't even know you'd been pregnant."

She gives a somber smile. Her voice is a limp trill of kinds. "Otto came back to Paris. He realized at last, you see, that I couldn't give up this city. He agreed to live with me here if I'd have him."

"And you did. You took him back."

"*Ja.*"

"And . . . then—"

"Then it happened. Simply, quickly. I was with child. After all those years of married chastity . . ."

"And then you died, Paula."

"*Ja.*"

She looks away. She looks out the window into the tangled garden. The light shines in her clear eyes like tears. But the dead don't cry.

She says, "You blame me for it. For dying."

"It's not blame, Paula, no. But . . . but dying in the manner you did . . . Dying the death of *childbirth* when . . ."

"When what?"

"When so much else was set to blossom through you."

She keeps staring into the garden. Her pale profile limned sharply against that world beyond the glass. World remote from her forever now.

"Really, Paula, I blame the *others*—the people around you who failed . . . failed to keep you free."

"You were always like that," she says. "Weren't you?"

"Like what?"

He can see that she's receding already. Some far-off realm is drawing her back.

"Paula?"

But she hasn't moved. She stands there, still turned away. "Why should you accuse on my behalf, Rainer?"

"Because I'm alive. Because for anyone striving in the way I strive daily, it must be said. It must be shown. What a danger being loved can be. How it can pull us back from where we ought to be going, spirits like you and me. While for us, really, to be loved . . . to be loved means to be alone. We all must find, in our time, someone who understands these things about us."

Paula is silent. What seems worst of all is that the dead do not utter judgment. Oh, but where they could teach us so much, we are left to teach ourselves.

"I had a sister, Paula, did I ever tell you? I had a sister and she died before I was born."

"What was her name?"

"Ismene. I was friendless for so long because of that, friendless from the beginning. And my later friends, one by one, have fallen away. Not all of their own choice. I've let them, you see. Sometimes I've begged it of them, in my way. I've made clear that I've had no choice but to fail them. A few have understood. I've loved them all, helpless as I am. . . . Anyway, there was failure and because of it they cannot reach me anymore. All except you, Paula! You were different because you died. And I mustn't fail you now."

She stands there.

The low November clouds sweep by beyond the glass and in their transit cause the daylight to waver, flatten, effulge again. Skyscape reflected upon her, as her brown eyes once reflected the moors rolling past the cab that had carried her and the poet together to Hamburg. Far back in the days when it seemed they might love one another. Pasts and futures wheeling upon her ghostly surface. The dead possess no present.

Paula turns. Her eyes opaque and bright, two luminous points like starlight streaming away into her skull. She speaks with a distant, aimless air. "The bedbugs," she says. "Here in Paris. Weren't they terrible?"

"Bedbugs?"

"Yes, being poor the way we were, you and I."

"Ah." She is fading. "*Ja,* Paula."

"Terrible," she says. "And yet I'll miss them forever, I think. Bedbugs . . ."

The churning sea of windowlight begins to settle. A surface closing. Soon Paula will be gone. For the moment, though, she seems to let Rainer look upon her. Merely look upon her, in silence.

This haunted night, in her requiem, he writes:

"See how we glide back
without realizing
out of our progress
into something we never intended. . . .
For somewhere there is an old hostility
between life and the great work."

The auburn-haired painter is not the first ghost he's encountered in this ancient *hôtel.* The place seems to surge with figures out of Rainer's past. Back in September, just as soon as Rainer had set up quarters, Rodin had called on him here, had sat down opposite the poet's desk, and together they'd talked at great length like old friends. The talk had come round to men and women and the different manners of love that draw them toward one another, from one another. Such things have been much on Rodin's mind of late, for he's deep in a romance with a mistress who has tempted his affections for several years, the Duchesse de Choiseul. She's considerably younger than he, and it saddens Rainer to see him blundering in this manner. That day, the poet read aloud to the Master the words of Beethoven:

No friend have I. I must live with myself alone. But I know well that in my art God is nearer to me than to others.

Rodin said he'd heard the words before and believed in them, but he also believed that the pull of female affections was a perpetual and unavoidable hazard for the artist. Because a man, by virtue of his nature, absolutely must have a woman—any man, at least, who is not a monk.

Rainer told the Master that he believed another kind of love, a higher unconstraining love, could exist between the sexes. And though Rodin would not let himself be convinced of this, Rainer felt he'd somehow gained new ground with him. Two years since Rodin had so injured his love, and now they came to a new understanding—but it was clear too that they would never again love one another the way they once had.

The very next day Rodin arranged to rent half of the château's ground floor for use as his atelier. That afternoon, in gladness, Rainer brought him a gift: a wooden statue of Saint Christopher. The saint carried the Christ-child on his shoulders, and the Christ-child's small hands clutched the orb of the world. To the poet's eyes this particular Christopher, long-bearded and French, bore an uncanny resemblance to the Master.

"This is Rodin carrying his work," Rainer said. "The work grows always heavier, but it holds the world."

And the Master smiled his great pleasure.

In those same first days here the poet received a copy of *The Sermons of the Buddha,* sent by Clara from Hanover. A beautiful volume bound in buckskin. At first he turned it lovingly in his hands. But opening to the first pages, he saw it would be impossible to read. For Malte's sake he mustn't read it. This much he wrote to Clara:

"I mustn't go too far out over his suffering, else I won't understand him anymore, else I'll go past him and he'll be gone from me and I can no longer give him the whole fullness of his death. . . . Help me, as far as you are able, to quiet time, that I may make my Malte Laurids. I can only progress through him, he lies in my way."

Now the chill and laborious months go sailing by, and Lou Andreas-Salomé comes to the Hôtel Biron to hear you speak in a manner much the same. May of 1909 and here she is, this priestess of your past, sitting at your side before the open window.

She looks the same as ever. She stares with you into the untended garden rampant with summer and the knotted fragrance of the season's overgrowth. Small cottontails scamper in and out of view.

"I often feel," you say to her, "that my childhood still waits for completion. All this time has gone by, Lou, and still my childhood remains unfinished. Unaccomplished. And how long ago you told me my work would come from all that. You were right, Lou. But I've avoided it, you see. Somehow, in all these years, I've avoided it. It has yet to be completed, that past with its many darknesses."

You tell her that in the meantime you've found yourself completely taken up with other figures, other personas. And these figures—though they live only in your imagination—often *make* themselves real to you, make themselves into *life-presences,* such that at certain hours you feel you've lost hold of what is life, what is mind, or the intangible boundary that separates the two.

"I'm taken over. That's how it is. And all the time my childhood stands waiting. Waiting for this spell to break."

Lou is silent, contemplative. She urges you to say more.

You sit up and lay your hands flat on the arms of your chair. Stare deeply through the dusk into the graying garden. Stare to the depths of this strange sense that has haunted you for years.

"It's as if I've stumbled into a well. Down in that watery darkness my limbs brush something again and again, something that will save me. A rope, perhaps. But it slips from my hands. Always it is there. I feel it. Always that shape in the darkness suggests salvation—yet I'm never saved. I'm never saved, Lou, so how do I keep my courage?"

But Lou does not answer.

Turning, you find her gaze fixed fast upon you. Those blue sky-vast eyes of hers, so clear. And there is that gothic sweetness in her face, the look that first received you in your brave youthful gesture the day you made yourself known to her.

—I have read you. I have written you.

She *sees* you now, you know it. Sees you and approves you with all the prophetic power of her vision. Her full, soft face conforming absolutely to the face you've carried in your heart for years. Lover, mother, sister, friend: she has become everything, and being *everything,* she too is but an element of your soul, absorbed entirely.

Still she does not answer you—need she answer at all, being within you as she is?

A warmth comes surging through your limbs. Sensation like you've not known for a great while. You look down to discover Lou's hand clasping yours. Those two hands each older now by years. But vividly the hands remember this, they fit together even yet. So you and Lou sit joined in silence while dusk draws down in the rustling garden.

. . .

Come December Rainer Maria Rilke is deep in the final throes of the heavy book he started in Rome years ago. On the thirteenth of the month he walks from the Hôtel Biron down the Esplanade and across the Seine and through the Tuilleries to the dining room of the Hôtel Liverpool in the rue Castiglione. There for the first time he presses the hand of Princess Marie von Thurn und Taxis, the noble lady who has recently written in hopes of making his acquaintance.

"After Malte," he tells her wearily, "I may have nothing left to say."

And means it. For a book, he's learned, can sometimes be a fatal thing. And he's amazed to feel that this princess, listening in her thin matronly equipoise, understands this truth. To feel, by the look in her shrewd empathetic eyes, that she knows him. Even, perhaps, that she foresees something he cannot . . .

But of course there is no knowing yet how the Elegies await him at Princess Marie's Castle Duino. How they will announce themselves, a voice in the storm-waves, as Rainer paces the high Duino cliffs above the gulf . . .

Until 1911, in spite of lengthy absences, the Hôtel Biron remains your home. Till the Duino Elegies take you and fling you back into your wanderings. It's the longest you've lived in any one place. Only the tower of Muzot will keep you longer. So this old Parisian château is a final waystation at the edge of your future, and when you emerge at last from the Hôtel Biron your ultimate fate rises up before you. Paula's death behind you, Malte behind you, and you are moving toward your own story's conclusion, nothing ahead but the days and days that will build the way to Muzot. In December 1911, a year beyond Malte's publication, you will write to Lou in terror:

"After this book I am just like a survivor, stymied in mind and body, helpless inside, inactive, never to be active again. . . . It's the dread truth of art that as one keeps going further into it, one becomes more and more bound to the extreme, the almost impossible."

Oh, but the Elegies, once they've arrived, become an impossibility of a whole new kind. Ten silent years must pass before they can be finished.

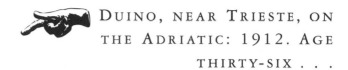 DUINO, NEAR TRIESTE, ON
THE ADRIATIC: 1912. AGE
THIRTY-SIX . . .

*P*rincess Marie's remote seaside castle. Rambling white structure stalwart atop its cliff, the Gulf of Trieste a leaden blue below. You find yourself alone here through most of that first long winter and spring of the Elegies, writing the initial Elegy and part of the second.

> *"It appears that everything*
> *keeps us secret. See, the trees are;*
> *the houses in which we live still exist. Only we*
> *file past everything like a swapping-out of air.*
> *And everything agrees to conceal us,*
> *Half out of disgrace, perhaps,*
> *And half out of unsayable hope."*

In February comes word from Clara that she wants a divorce. You take her letter out to the clifftop garden where hedge and lawn lie coated in a half-thawed, ruinous kind of snow. Lean lonesome figure walking there, small atop the escarpment, treading barefoot along the paths till your feet have lost their feeling. Rereading her words, it becomes clear to you that Clara's request is sensible and right, that you may receive it with calm acceptance. For the better part of a year she's been taking psychoanalytic treatment with a doctor in Weimar, and surely a proper severance of the marriage would do measures to assist in her treatment. Not that this marriage has ever become hostile or anything like. No, but it would surely be

best if Clara could get somewhere beyond you, beyond her pattern of endlessly absorbing and expelling you, beyond the constraining label of
"Frau" which affixes itself even as her life transpires at such a distance from
yours. Really, you and the sculptress have been effectively divorced, as you
both understand it, since those strange January days together in Capri, and
were it not for the byzantine nature of the legal process you might have
made the situation official much sooner. Anyway, it can begin now. And
may she be at peace, this woman who has grown stranger and stranger to
you through the years. May she finally expel you altogether and be in good
health.

With these feelings of goodwill you give Clara your consent and continue your remote and silent existence at Duino. But in the course of the
following weeks an alteration creeps in upon you, slight but staggering.

It begins one evening in March. In the castle library you discover a
volume of correspondence by Montaigne. Retiring to your bedchamber
with the book, you sit up reading and chance upon a letter in which Montaigne describes the slow death of his beloved friend Etienne de la Boetie
in 1563.

At the letter's end a fit of uncontrollable tears takes hold of you. You
must set the book aside. Something is welling up convulsive and violent,
and as you lie in the silence of your darkened room, you can do nothing to
stop it. Some part of you has seized upon the fit, determined to make it
count for something. So you spasm and cough and cry, shivering in your
snug four-post bed in that old castle atop the cliff, helpless to fall asleep
and sorrowing alone, child-like, into the deep morning hours.

"A shame it was," you write to Lou, *"how this crying returned the following
evenings without clear reason."*

.   .   .

"Like dew from the early grass," says the Second Elegy:

> *"that which is ours rises from us . . . like the heat from a*
> *hot dish. O smile, where do you go? O expression in the eyes:*
> *new warm escaping wave of the heart—;*
> *how it hurts me: we* are *these very things. So does the world-space,*
> *in which we come loose, taste of us?"*

It will be ten years from these wretched nights till that glorious February evening in Muzot when the poet will step from his tower, the ten Elegies at last complete, and stroke the bastion's stone wall in thanks.

In the years between comes the creative nightfall of war.

ENDNOTES & ELEGIES:

1914–1917

So all this comes and comes, and one has only to be there with a whole heart.

Letter to Clara, 1907

*L*ate in your life you would recall the fateful departure from Paris that led you to your uniformed days. That July of 1914, at the threshold of war. July at which your future first stumbled. Your Paris land-lady, you would say, seemed to bestow a strange prophecy as you left.

That recent winter in Paris had blessed you with the Third Duino El-egy—two long footloose years having dragged past since the completion of the second, you traveling all that time like one close on a scent: Venice-Madrid-Cordoba-Seville-Ronda—finally back to Paris. To a one-room apartment in the rue Campagne-Première. There, at last, the third:

"Oh softly, softly
place a love in front of him, a lonely, reliable day's work,—
take him
lead him right up to the garden,
give him the overwhelming
nights."

The new Elegy finished, the months swept by and then you found the sweltering city summer rising up around you. In that oppressive weather it seemed nothing more could happen for another great while. Lou Andreas-Salomé invited you to Göttingen. So you packed some clothing, a few books, and locked up your tiny Paris apartment. . . .

PARIS: JULY 1914. AGE
THIRTY-EIGHT . . .

*T*he concierge is knocking about the landing with mop and bucket as
you come out and set down your valise and turn to lock the door.

"Ah, Monsieur Rilke, so you are still going as planned?" The lady
stands back behind the iron banister, in the narrow triangular space where
dust collects. She hugs the mop handle to her armpit with both fisted
hands. Her gray hair grazes the slanting garret wall.

"*Oui,* Madame Suzette, back in a few weeks."

"To Germany, monsieur?"

"*Oui.* Göttingen and Leipzig. Munich perhaps."

Her face seems to fall, something almost ominous in the wrinkled
eyes. She steps forward into the warm yellow of the landing window. Beside her, beneath the banister, the stairs descend steeply, curving out of
sight ten steps below. "You will take care, won't you, Monsieur Rilke?"

She is a gracious lady. She has the hard-worn, maternal, selfless air of
certain aged women. A gray face quick to smile, a bleached apron and
pushed-up sleeves. She seems to deem herself, in the kindest way, a mother
to everyone around her. "Call me Suzette," she insisted on the day you
moved in, "promise you will call me Suzette!" But you've never managed
to drop the "Madame." You stand there at the top of the stairs, valise in
hand, your shadow spilling away down the steps to splash in black contor-
tion at the spiral below. She seems to want to say something more to you.

"Is all well, Madame Suzette?"

She gives a slow shrug. *"Je ne sais pas.* Nous *ne savons pas."* A distant,

uncertain look in her face. Things foretold or things remembered, no saying. "The world is anxious, Monsieur Rilke. We cannot tell what will happen. You've read the papers, *non?*"

"No, I don't read the papers."

She sucks breath through her teeth. *"Non?"* Her mouth in a wince, her
head shaken. "So many things, Monsieur Rilke, are out of joint. There
could be a war, they say. *Oui,* if some little thing should happen—just
some small thing . . ."

With your free hand you touch the smoothworn banister. It's meant to
be an intimate, comforting gesture; you would lay that hand on the lady's
slack shoulder were it not improper. "It will not be *our* war, Madame. Even
if it happens, it will not be *ours.*"

But Madame Suzette looks as though she might cry. Watching you
start down the stairs, she beams an uncanny sad smile. As though she can
see how your brief descent of only a few moments portends the greater one,
years long, also commencing here. Your Paris home receding already to a
rare and unattainable distance above you.

—*Not our war,* you say. But within the hour you present your passport
to the ticketing agent at the Gare du Nord. In plain lettering it reads: AUS-
TRIAN. Just days later, in Germany, comes the news of Austria's war on Ser-
bia, followed fast by Germany's declaration against France. All at once
you're forbidden to return to Paris bearing such a passport. Your tiny flat
stands locked at the head of Madame Suzette's stairs, awaiting you. All
your belongings in place, paused as you left them, stored away in that
chamber outside time. No saying when you'll return there, to that city
you've come to love like no other.

GERMANY: AUTUMN 1915 . . .

*e*xiled in Germany since the declaration of war, more than a year. Now, by way of a letter postmarked Paris, you learn that since spring you've had no home in that city. No possessions either, for nearly six months ago your flat in the rue Campagne-Première was unlocked and cleared out, all your worldly belongings put up for auction.

You'd made arrangements, back in the New Year, for your rent to be paid from abroad—but something happened, or failed to. Something inexplicable. And now all the little things you'd thought safe in your Parisian harbor at the top of Madame Suzette's stairs have been scattered to the winds.

Even your papers are gone. Your manuscripts. Your hundreds upon hundreds of letters and copies of letters. Your own published volumes: *The Book of Hours, The New Poems, The Notebooks of Malte Laurids Brigge.* Uncle Jaroslav's old Rilke family crest. The small silver-framed photograph of your young Papa, decked smartly in the uniform of an Austrian officer candidate.

From Munich you write to Princess Marie:

> *"I was long disposed to see everything that had accumulated around me during those twelve years in Paris as the estate of M. L. Brigge. And perhaps with all these accessories and books and the few heirlooms, the obsession of this figure, whom I was still utterly determined to banish from my vision, has been taken from me. And yet . . . since that news from*

Paris, I've been going about with a peculiar feeling, something like one who has taken a fall and gotten up again unbruised and still, somehow, cannot lose the suspicion that a late-coming pain may suddenly break out in his entrails and bring him to cry aloud. . . . Once again, my heart has fallen out."

A great many years gone since your passage through the high iron gates of Saint Pölten, your terrors in the throng of jostling bodies, and yet today the bodies still jostle. A swarming multitude in this clotted artery of Munich. Hundreds? Thousands?—amassed beneath the high soot-blackened facades enclosing the Marienplatz. At the center on her tall column stands the Virgin Mother herself, holding the blessed infant in her arms. She is fashioned of gold, gleaming against this frozen day.

Someone climbs atop a table to be seen above the countless heads. A man in uniform shouting instructions. His arm sweeps up and down, bladelike, hacking the mob into neatly parceled lines, double file.

You have your doctor's papers in hand. Someone is shoving from the back, bodies piling up, your papers crumpling against the sharp shoulder blades of the man ahead. Twist of his grizzled cheek as he turns to look, dark tobacco-yellow gums, grit-encrusted teeth.

—*Scheiße*!—A spray of his rancid breath.

You beg his pardon and avert your eyes to the backs of his knees.

An hour or more skulks by. At last the line relaxes, quietens. Nothing to do but wait: a kind of mass slumber, every man swaying on his feet. Delirium of the long, objectiveless endeavor. At last you are called forth from the wavering white line ruled crudely across the cobblestones in chalk.

An officer rigid in his chair behind the table, pens and inks and forms in orderly arrangement at his wrists. He receives your papers, glances them over.

—*Was ist das?*

—My bill of health from my doctor. Doctor Stauffenberg.

The officer's wry, thin smile, a row of tiny teeth beneath a fleshless upper lip.

—Herr . . . (He must riffle the papers in his hands) . . . Herr Rilke, this will not do at all.

—No?

—Not at all.

—But you've noted, haven't you, the deficiency in my lungs as shown there?

—Won't do, *mein Freund*. Not at all.

A rubber stamp beats down on a sheet of thin paper. The table quivers. The officer rips away the sheet, snaps it toward you. The discarded stamp wobbles, topples, its flared handle hitting the tabletop with ominous noise. A fallen structure.

—To the examination hall please.

—Now?

—Immediately.

You stare at the stamped character. Smear of fresh black ink wetting the paper through, darkening your fingers behind: a great E aslant, spilling from the edges of the printed box.

In through the leaden doors of the Austrian Consulate, the double-headed eagle affixed there in fearsome bronze. Do not look behind to see whether Mama holds the crucifix high or chokes into her kerchief as she turns from the gate.

Somebody directs you down a corridor. Another points the way through a dim passage. You come out into a cavernous hall, a field of pink flesh, hundreds of naked men in a dizzying file. Pungency of bodies disrobed and hairy.

An officer materializes before you, takes your papers, thrusts them back.

—Quadrant E. Remove your clothes over there.

A wooden chair at the end of a line of chairs against the wall. Shed clothing is piled on every seat. You sit down and remove your shoes, your stockings. Stand and turn to face the wall. Begin unslipping buttons, your abashed eyes held low.

Moments later, barefoot on the cold floor, face aflame despite the hall's chill, you hold your papers in clasped hands before you, shuffling in another slow queue. Papers held to cover your girl-place, that locus of shame, that region you have never but in reddening modesty bared amongst men.

Just ahead: a small man. The slack skin of his sides droops away at the waist, a reddish margin in the flesh where his belt cinched all day. The skin of the buttocks a deathly white beneath.

The queue is alive with murmurous anticipation. Words to cover nakedness. The riddle of the day's curt instructions decoded:

—It's done. It's settled. They assign us from here and that's that.

—The exam don't mean a thing. We're going, you know. *Ja,* else they'd have turned us home back there.

Late afternoon. The sun in bleak obliquity, fierce rays glancing down the cornices of the buildings outside, jetting inward through the high glassless windows of the hall. Light shaved and sharpened and magnified to nauseating brightness by a screen of cloud like sand-blown glass. No warmth to such light. You bristle from neck to heel.

Examination in the atrium. Your body prodded and poked, your eyes pried between finger and thumb. If there's a queue for the unfit it doesn't branch from here.

Finally, in the worst of the window glare, you stand naked before another table, blinking. Bolts of piercing pain in your scalp and skull. Another officer here, this one portly. Wrists pressing at his sleeves like tubes of wrapped dough. He doesn't even look at your face, snatches your papers down in the blur and shuffles them this way and that, their crispness utterly lost.

—Birthplace Prague?

—*Ja.*

Thank God he doesn't look at your face. In the glare your eyes are beginning to stream.

Another stack of papers shuffled. The officer's head bent steeply, a sore line across the back of his neck where the high woolen collar rubs.

A huge stamp-handle fills his clutch. The Austrian eagle pounds down like a fallen hammer, hammers its black shadow across the paper.

—These are your orders. Fourth January, Turnau Bohemia, Territorial Reserve, enlistment conclusive. Move aside now.

—The *Landsturm?*

—*Ja.* Move aside.

Clutching the orders, you weave your blind way back to your clothing. Dress again. Drift sightlessly down the stone passages and through the massive doors and out beneath the *Liebfrau's* golden figure toward the Odeonsplatz. Mother of Gold, Mother on High, Mother Maria your namesake, never to be anything but neutral while your earthly mama brandishes the crucifix at the gate of your lifelong loneliness, sobbing into the kerchief clutched to her mouth. And now you're to be the soldier Mama would have watched you become those many muddled years ago, soldier with the face of a girlchild back then, now called to wield a rifle, his valor the valor of a man amongst men. Yet this soldier's slim hands—holding his orders before him as he walks—are undeniably a *woman's* hands, as they've remained these long years.

Down the long imperial boulevard into Schwabing. The world teems in uncertain color and noise on all sides. Your way shaded now and the water in the corners of your eyes stinging cold.

Through this city that once liberated you, this city that gave you Lou—and it was back then, almost, that you moved toward manhood, toward destiny. But Lou would not mother you, and surely she shouldn't have served as a surrogate—and yet to have *dropped* you as she did . . . oh, but she is long since forgiven, and you walk, years older now, your inexorable orders in hand. Beneath them Doctor Stauffenberg's diagnosis, ignored.

Only yesterday, four full years since the grand moment of their conception, you wrote the fourth of your great Elegies. The fourth! In four years! So far along in that harrowing war of your own—but now this *other* war, this *nothing war,* this *war toward nothing,* has sucked you into itself. Into its nothingness. Nothingness you thought you'd long since defeated—but here it is again it has returned it is rearing up large in your face and you are alone as ever in the war against *this war* and your allegiances mean nothing for you must don the uniform of the *enemy* now. Even now, with four Elegies complete!

 HUTTELDORF, VIENNA:
JANUARY 1916 . . .

—*Walsch! Walsch, help our ladyfriend Maria off her knees!*

Blackness and voices. Then the frosted grass shudders into vision. A stiff hand hooked roughly under your arm, hauling you to your feet. The ice-hard field heaves below. Something rattles to the ground, a dead heavy weight lashing your thigh.

—*Dammit, Maria, hold your weapon, will you!*

—*I . . . believe I fainted.*

—*Damn right, man! Dropped like a fuckin puppet. Nearly sent the rest of us falling over you! Come on now, stay along for godsake!*

Clatter of boots and breech and bayonet—a giant's feet pounding away. Gray bulk hurtling to overtake the regiment far ahead. The shape blears away in the wall of winter fog. The wall bulges at that place where the body is curled.

—*What is it Mama?*

—*I've told you. Don't you remember?*

Somewhere the whistle shrills.

Your name launched from the ragged clamor of a throat.

Gather your swirling senses, clutch the weapon and rise, slap your frayed sleeves clean, heave the heavy pack, plunge forward again, lungs afire in the bitter air. Forward into that glare, that wall of hard white. Frost and fury and nothing else . . .

. · . · . ·

"A revenant is nourished by the number of those who perceive it. This one has become everything. It has climbed out of every grave. Everything has become it. Yet who recognizes it?—No. You should not claim acquaintance with it. You should not attach to it the equipment nor the titles of earlier wars, for whether it is a comparable war you still do not know."

Is there comfort in knowing that the Fourth Elegy is done?—does that bring solace while you lie in your numbered bed in the hurtful blackness at day's end, the barracks ashudder with so much sleep? Think on that. Hold it close. It keeps you here in this age to which you've mounted through thick protracted years. Four Elegies done. That won't be changed now, no matter what should happen. And so you are not a boy. Not a boy, alone in his cot in the great unsolitary hall impacted with sleep and bloated nightmare. No, you have traveled long. You have stood at the ramparts above the Gulf of Trieste and have heard what the storm-waves said. Princess Marie's old Castle Duino rose up behind you, venerable, unshaken. It had been Dante's brief hostelry some several hundred years ago, or so you'd been told.

Four full Januaries gone since that stormy day above the sea, and an Elegy for each. That is not so paltry. Not at all. Say to yourself now the words of the first:

"Strange
those wishes no longer wished.
Strange,
to see everything, all reference points, fluttering loose
in the room.
And this being-dead is arduous

and full of getting-near-again,
that one may catch scent, gradually,
of a little eternity."

Say them, for you are not the boy who lies prostrate in the dark Kadet-tenschule dormitory. No: your feet now reach to the end of the numbered bed. You have grown. You have grown through years of work and you are a poet to whom a princess attends—*Doctor Serafico,* she has dubbed you—and four marvelous Elegies are finished already. Say the words and roll to sleep now. In but a few hours the *réveille* will arrive to decimate slumber. After that there will be nothing but marching.

Nothing.

Do not think of what you may be marching toward.

$\mathcal{G}$ hree long weeks in the rigors of basic training, but at last the intercession of friends effects your deliverance. Princess Marie, most namely, is your savior. The Empire honors, if not its poets, then the wishes of those nobles who cherish them. That you cannot be extricated entirely from the web of enlistment now seems a small complaint, as long as you needn't bear a rifle and pack any longer. You will still serve, yes, but in a capacity more suitable to your talents, or so the Empire sees it. Thus you find yourself detailed to the Imperial War Archives in Vienna, passing again through a deep stony threshold with the frightful dual-headed eagle of the Empire eyeing you from its mount above the doors. The gothic vaults of this immense imperial complex called the Stiftskaserne will ensnare you for six hours daily.

Lieutenant-Colonel Veltzé leads you down a chill interminable corridor, his heels clapping smartly all the way.

"We have very high report of your character, Herr Rilke. And I suppose I needn't tell you that your fine works precede you in reputation."

"Do they, sir."

"Oh yes, my good fellow, I'd wager that most of the men in this sector have read your admirable *Lay of the Cornet*. You'll find them a very affable lot, these men—no need to worry about that. They count a few rather distinguished writers amongst themselves even, though of course nothing to match your achievements."

"You're very kind."

"Not at all. I count *myself* rather cognizant of the pains required to produce a commendable work. I'm something of a literary man, in whatever small way."

"Are you, sir."

"Indeed, Herr Rilke. You see, you'll find you're not completely out of your element here. And no doubt your duties will outrank the infantry by miles and miles."

"No doubt, sir."

"It's work of a rather transparent kind, I'd say. Most the men call it hero-tailoring, which to be truthful is not far off the mark. Ah, now here we are."

Veltzé pushes a lancet door of heavy wood. It opens to a spacious chamber with gothic ceilings. At one side runs a long wall of frosted windows. Three-tiered shelves beneath are filled end to end with neatly ordered files and bulging document bundles.

Veltzé steps away toward a partition, stands there in the sterile electric glow of a desklamp, speaking to someone out of sight. A uniformed figure rises, a youthful face turns toward you.

The two come over and Veltzé says, "Herr Rilke, this is our man Wenzel. He will acquaint you with your duties here."

Wenzel gives a stately nod and draws you to his desk. Veltzé's heels are already clapping away to the door. A lancet of feeble light projects across the wall of windows, then the door shuts to.

"He's a good fellow, Veltzé," says Wenzel at the sound of the falling latch. "Very gentlemanly. Runs this place like a fraternal organization nearly. He says you've come from the infantry."

"*Ja.*"

"Good God, man, aren't you lucky! You've heard, I trust, of the writers we've lost out there. Georg Trakl and others."

"I have, yes."

Wenzel sucks a self-conscious breath, drops his chin against his tough collar and with a slight wave of his hand says, "Before we get started I might tell you, Herr Rilke—to clear the air, you know—that I've greatly admired your work."

"Have you? That's very kind."

"Most recently those 'War Cantos.' Where did I read those?"

"The *Insel Almanac.*"

"That's it, yes. And then, of course, there is your marvelous *Cornet.*" Wenzel stands there smiling a wistful young smile, seeming to await some gesture. At last his eyes drift down to the desk beside him. He clears his throat. "Well, as to the matter at hand, you'll find it's rather uninspired work, I'm afraid, but here's the gist of it: these are the reports from the front. They come in regularly and are filed by date in those baskets there. It's up to us to take these and shake from them whatever heroism we can."

He stops himself with a little laugh.

"I'm speaking very generally, you'll understand. The main objective is to supply the Glorious Empire a bill of good health. Save the morale of our compatriots, you see."

He stoops to a drawer and brings out a thick folder of papers. "Here are some bills of health I've produced. I suppose the most efficient thing would be if you looked these over yourself."

Wenzel shows you to a desk a few paces from his own, a shallow wooden cubicle built into the stone wall. He flips a switch and a cylinder of hot light beams down from a buzzing lamp fixture.

"Do let me know when you've got the drift of it, and I'll show you our catalog system."

Wenzel claps away to his desk behind. His desklamp sends his shadow in huge adumbration across the wall. Black figure swelling, swelling, distorting as he hunches down into his chair. The chair squeals and then there is silence, the shadow curling over, headless.

You open the folder and begin reading.

In a moment Wenzel's chair squalls again, his shadow expanding, shrinking, and he stands close at your arm. In low, flat voice he says, "Look, Herr Rilke, I hope you will bear in mind—I mean, I hope you will not think, as you read, that this work"—an ashamed little wave at the folder before you—"represents in any manner my natural gifts."

"Oh, not at all, my friend—"

"The fact is, you see, I had published some things here and there, and by some stroke of luck they came to the attention of General Baron Höhn and—"

"I'm sure," you say, "that a whole different standard must be applied to work of this kind."

Wenzel breathes his great relief. "Precisely. Precisely, Herr Rilke. You see, I've really got such good stuff in me, and it will just be a matter of time until it can be . . . given expression."

"I've no doubt," you tell him. And you feel his eyes upon you, wide and hopeful, as though he awaits a word or two more. But what more could you possibly offer him in days as dim as these?

*T*hree photographs. Rainer Maria Rilke in the drab uniform of the Austrian infantry. In each photo he wears the gray woolen field jacket, buttoned high, belted at the waist, the flaps of its breast pockets deeply scalloped.

Here: he's capped in the regulation kepi, one arm hugging a slim leather briefcase to his side. Here: he stands against garden shrubbery, the doffed kepi held in his right hand as it falls along his thigh. Thinning hair recedes high on his brow, his mustache enunciates a dark frown. This full-figured shot betrays the poet's thinness, his narrow unsoldierly shoulders. And here, in close-up: the poet's shallow chin rides high above the dark collar, his face half shadowed, wide eyes looking askance at the lens, fixed in bleak and numb alarm. Face like a glove turned inside out, a soul invaginated and rammed worldward before its time. Lips clamped shut, tumescent, almost ulcerous with shame. This uniform, tattered in several places, had already seen combat by the time he'd received it. A dead man's woolen shell. He was not issued another when his transfer was approved. *I am here to say life,* says the poet's exploited face, *but they've garbed me in the getup of death.*

And this raw face knows that war can exist nowhere but within the individual. That war is nothing but a creature comprised of singulars: one finger trembling at a trigger, one sword brandished in one fist, one conscience consenting to its own suppression. This consent is given a million times over, in a million different souls, but in the singular each time. So what comes of one who seeks to be conscience and consciousness through and through? How does the Colossus of War make use of such a soul?

I am a soft slow-moving boneless thing. I am inching along the earth my mouth is clotted with humus that tastes of blood and down from above comes a great stone. I am ground between earth and stone I am crushed. It always comes. . . .

Sitting by day at your shallow desk in the Stiftskaserne. On countless crisp and civil sheets piled before you, in lines of neat print, the so-called progress of the war is conveyed with antiseptic clarity.

Draw the sheets toward you by turn, bend your head above them, read. In the shallow desk drawer a stack of official composition paper awaits. You've withdrawn a few pieces already. They lie beneath your hands, the pencil atop them.

Set the war report by, take up the pencil, scratch a few laggard lines. Pause. Take up the report and study it again, pencil another line. Two. Now stop. Stop and set the pencil down at the paper's top edge, as if to put it as far away as possible.

Take up the paper, read over what you've written. Now slowly, from top to bottom, tear the paper in two. Lay the halves together and tear again. And again.

Tuck the scraps silently away into the deep breast pockets of your uniform.

Days pass. Perhaps weeks. Still the light from the frosted windows spills its sick bluish tones inward over the desks, the two desklamps blaze obscenely, and there you are, bent in the gray uniform, your hunched shadow stretching away.

You stir in your chair, glance about, turn to Wenzel behind. "I don't know, Wenzel," you say, "what one can do."

Wenzel swivels. "Pardon?"

"What *I* should do. I simply don't know."

Words halting out of you into the barren room, slack and ragged like something coughed. "I feel . . . it's so strange, Wenzel, but I feel sometimes as if I could accomplish good work in this room. In this quietness. If there were not a war. If the world were more at peace. If I somehow found myself here. . . . I would work, yes. I've written four Elegies already, you see. . . . Maybe I would do great things. That's all I wanted to do, you know. Since the beginning, Wenzel. I've given myself to that. Utterly. And I am not the only one. What does any artist try to do if not open a path to change . . . to change, and maybe ennoblement . . . in people's hearts? Have I failed to do it well, Wenzel? Has *every* artist failed, so that now this war can do it on so large a scale and in such a backward way? How can one be so nerveless, so hollowed-out, and remain an artist now, still carry on that work of the heart? No, now . . . with everything so out of joint, one must think seriously of giving it up."

A long motionless silence. Then Wenzel rises and crosses the cold floor to your desk, coming close as if to lay a hand on your shoulder, but he doesn't lift his hand. He just draws near and stops short.

You begin again: "But the problem remains, what would one do? Where would one go? . . . I was in Russia on two occasions. I was young. I was traveling with the woman I loved. Russia was my destiny. I felt it, Wenzel. And yet I never returned. All these years and still I haven't returned. . . . But that was a homeland, that place. I've never been a *member,* you see. . . . I mean to say I've never been a citizen of anywhere, Wenzel. You can understand that, yes?"

Wenzel does not answer. Merely remains at your side in that scorch of fake light. His long knifeblade shadow burns away across the room, clear to the wall. He is listening.

Another day. Seated to your reports again, your gray cap atop the desk before you. Lieutenant-Colonel Veltzé enters and sweeps to your cubicle.

"Herr Rilke, your duties have been revised, sir." He places a thick roll of paper in front of you. "This paper needs to be ruled for our ledgers. Do you have a straight-rule there, Wenzel?"

"*Ja,* just here, sir."

"Very good. Columns and rows, Herr Rilke, if you please. Columns and rows."

With a hurried air the Lieutenant-Colonel vanishes out the door.

Wenzel comes over, smiling small.

"Did you do this, Wenzel?"

"I did, my friend. Veltzé was very understanding when I conveyed your difficulties. But did you see how he rushed out of here just now? It shames the poor man to give you such a duty. He's been reading your novel, he told me. Anyway, work of this sort will prove better, won't it? Not enjoyable, of course, but better. Let me show you the previous ledger."

So you set to work at once, pulling a pencil along a straight rule with assiduous care, drawing line after empty line. And this, you find, is not so undignified a commission at all. Not at all.

A morning in Vienna, 1916. Narrow-shouldered in Austro-Hungarian gray, capped in the flat unflattering kepi, Rainer Maria Rilke steps from the streetcar in an outpouring of passengers. Thin briefcase in hand, he walks to the corner, stops and turns his head to watch the traffic flow past. His breath plumes in the chill morning air.

Not yet spring, though the sun is almost festive in the colors it contrives. At a gap in the traffic he steps from the curb and brisks across the busy street, down the length of the next block, and then his body moves as if to round the corner—but his legs suddenly lock in their trim black trousers.

He halts. Turns to face the way he just came. Pedestrians stream past.

He stands there turning about, hands held slightly away from his sides. Like one plucked up from some entirely different spot of earth and dropped here without warning. Any onlooker would know he is lost. But he feels that no one sees him now. Pedestrians stream past, their eyes all white and slick and sightless. And as they pass they seem to snag at something within him—his memories ripped away in that incessant flood of figures. And the castle at Duino destroyed! Bombed to rubble just this month. Princess Marie, with the most dismal eyes he's yet seen from her, informed him personally.

But how can that be? Where is she? Where is *he,* that he saw her? Where *is* he? All recognition abandons him. The city sprawls in all directions. Nothing to do but cast his glance about.

Ah, but finally something returns. Association however arbitrary. Scattered reference points brought together again—and with a weird tautening of his neck Rainer draws himself up, tugs his jacket hem smart, and starts forward once more.

MUNICH: NOVEMBER 1917 . . .

*M*idday in Munich. You are seated on a wooden bench in the Hauptbahnhoff, awaiting the arrival of your daughter's train. A numbing, sunless November day outside. Even here in the station's marbled concourse the chill makes smoke of every breath. You keep your coat collar high, throat bundled snugly in a cotton muffler, your broad fedora pulled down to the tops of your ears.

The concourse is patrolled heavily by indolent gray-garbed figures in kepis and overcoats, rifles slung from their shoulders, bayonets aglimmer with dull malice. Wartime in this Bavarian capital as in Europe everywhere. Wartime even yet. America declared the German state its enemy several months ago. One can hardly recall a time when the streets of every city did not sag under the heavy bootheels of these war-bored minions in gray, bayonets bared at all hours.

Since June of last year you've been free of the uniform yourself—untethered at last from your untenable post in Vienna thanks to the good word of friends and the recommendations of your superiors in the Stiftskaserne, all of whom remained perplexed till the end by the question of what use you could possibly serve.

Ruth's train is an hour delayed. But at last the letters of the schedule board flutter with transformation. The eleven o'clock Bremen has arrived. You rise and pass through that stolid company of gray to the platform. Within moments your daughter is off the carriage, coming toward you with a smile.

"Väterchen," she says—that term of affection she's favored for how long now?—since well before school age, wasn't it? And always, at the very first, this devastating smile of hers. Smile that recognizes you with an authority only a daughter can possess.

After your traded kisses and the negotiation of her luggage, you stand together outside the Hauptbahnhoff. Ruth at your arm. A lady she is, almost sixteen, her clasp so sure upon your sleeve. And she comes to your shoulder in height, this womanly creature who once soared weightlessly between your hands to set the Christmas star in place. From her hair now: a scent of lavender or lily.

To your concerned questions over the comforts of her journey Ruth is imperturbably mature, as though she travels alone every day amongst those made restless by war. The conductor was most attentive, she says. As the sun came up above the fleeting country outside her window, he gave her coffee. She hadn't even been required to ask for it. "And I thought how very nice it is that everything needn't be meager just because one must be alone for a while."

Together you remain waiting at the station curb. A half hour goes by and no cab presents itself. On Höhenfeldstrasse an auto now and then snuffles past, each one about its own business and not to be beckoned. This slow-making war like a weight at the ankle of everything.

Now the day's drab atmosphere rends itself apart. Slugs of limp wet snow begin to fall with a humorless sloshing noise. In minutes you and Ruth are soaked. She sidles closer.

"I'm sorry, dear," you tell her at last. "There's nothing for it but the tram."

So together you hunch forward through the sleet to board the Number 9, three corners away. The vehicle is a pickle jar of passengers. No choice but to stand with your daughter in a huddling embrace at the rear step, the frigid weather howling down upon you both. Ruth bears it gallantly.

Arriving at your rooms, you find her luggage already delivered. Together you'd judged it better to have the trunks portered than held all day at the station. The cost was only slightly more, and this way she can lighten her burden by keeping some things in your apartment when she goes on.

Ruth changes clothes as you prepare a kettle of tea. In moments she reappears in a heavy beige dress. Again she's another woman altogether. How many are her graces, this daughter with this destiny all her own? She says she's remembered something and steps to her frock coat hung up near the stove. From one inner pocket she brings out a bundle of cloth. Layer after layer she unswaddles it, then slips something from a woolen sock, and three perfect eggs lie clustered in the bed of her palms.

"From Mama."

You receive them one at a time. They bear the soft warmth of Ruth's body which cousined them close through her travels.

"And this," she says. A second inner pocket yields another mummied gift: a jar of honey. Clara, the dear!—she knows what spoils these are with commerce so strangled nowadays.

"There's a beekeeper near our house in Fischerhude," says Ruth. "The honey is five days fresh."

Clara recently had a house built for the two of them in the village neighbor to Worpswede. But now a commission has called the sculptress north to the Baltic shore, and Ruth is to be cared for by family friends in Dachau.

"Was it hard to leave home, my dear?"

"It would have been, but Mama will be gone anyway, so no. And in Dachau they keep bees too. They've already promised to teach me."

"I must thank your mother for this, Ruth. I've been without sweets for months. The neighborhood children here make such a noise I had to bribe them to silence. My chocolate was gone in a week."

Now Ruth seems to take note of your quarters. And just what does she see, you wonder, as she looks about the sparse room? What does she understand, now that she's old enough to understand?

"Do you care very much for this place, Väterchen?" she asks.

"For Munich?"

"*Ja,* and for these rooms?"

Her inquiry is pure, nothing but idle sweetness in it. You give some thought before answering, looking about the way Ruth has just done. You smile. "Not at all, my dear."

Ruth smiles too, and gives a wonderful laugh. It impresses you greatly that she does not ask, as you might have expected, the very sensible subsequent question: *Then why do you stay?*

Dinner with your daughter at the Odeon Restaurant. So poised she is, her slender wrists swiveling elegantly as she moves her fork and knife.

You wonder, were someone observing from a table across the dining room, would you and this young woman be taken for father and daughter? Or by deportment wouldn't Ruth appear to be a ladyfriend of whatever kind?—for there's a ceremony much like friendship between you now.

And how changed she is, though you saw her on her fifteenth birthday just last year. In Ruth's face, it seems to you, your own face is no longer evident—certainly nothing left of that doomed girlchild who once appeared to bleed across the border of a generation. Ruth is *of* you, yes, but for her own sake you needn't be *within* her. No, better for Clara to claim that place. And it appears that Clara does: now and then Ruth's decorous gestures betray most vividly the sculptress whose womb once carried her.

"Ruth," you say, "Ruth, your mother and you . . . you are both happy, yes?"

In lightest bewilderment, as if without thinking, she answers: "*Ja,* of course we are very happy, Väterchen."

And should you be surprised that this answer is no relief to you?

Do you care very much for this place? she asked you an hour ago. Might you have given a different answer than the one you gave? Might you have said: *I lived in Munich once before, my dear. In my youth. At the beginning of everything*—and then told her something of that beginning, and of what a beginning you feel yourself to be facing even now. Even now, as if you'd never left, as if the many years since then had never been.

Lumps of ashen slush coat the streets as you board a tram with Ruth again. Through the frozen twilit world of wartime Munich back to the Hauptbahnhoff.

Kisses traded once more and soon you stand by alone, watching as Ruth receives the conductor's hand and glides aloft into the carriage. And does that young man now helping her even suppose, in all the quiet interest of his glance, what decisive origins once cocooned your daughter's growth?—the story of all the many moments which have shaped this *now* that reveals her to him? Can he suppose that Ruth was not *always* this graceful member of womanhood now boarding his train, but that faraway days, inaccessible to her own young memory, were long ago at work in making her?

The whistle sounds. The engine draws its seething breath and the gears come astir in the arduous friction of metals, the resistance of gravity, the long labor of another departure. . . .

To Clara you write with assurances that Ruth has come and gone in safety. *"So I believe you can be entirely at ease in your work. . . . I wish you, dear Clara, health and peace and joyful labor. . . . All my love. Rainer Maria."*

.   .   .

Days later, on eighteenth November, arrives the blunt and woeful word of Auguste Rodin's death in Paris at the age of seventy-seven. With distressing quietness this passing occurs behind the welter of war. That great friend of your soul now doubly lost to you, buried in the garden of Meudon beyond a national boundary you're forbidden to cross. No stately ceremony mourns the Master, he is simply gone, as Paris has been gone for years.

In a letter to your publisher, you write: *"One hears and sees nothing but departure."*

epilogue

PARIS ~ MUNICH

RUE LINNÉ, PARIS: PRESENT DAY . . .

I have been in your letters. I mean amongst the sheaves of woven paper that you yourself withdrew from drawers, the paper you once laid flat across a desk to stain with words direct from your inner silence.

I'd made an appointment with the archivist. I arrived and had to answer only a few friendly questions. The archivist led me upstairs to a tiny garret space hidden high in the roof of the Hôtel Biron.

There were perhaps a hundred letters. I laid them out before me. Each one bore the dark eloquent script that had come of your first years with Lou. Bore the embossed tracery of your pen. And I felt I could see the silence of the rooms in which these lines had been written. Slow or fast, time had passed for you as it passes for me now. In your first weeks in Paris you wrote to the Master:

> *"It is not only to do a study that I have come to you,—it was in order to ask you: how must one live? And you have replied: by working. And this I understand well. I sense that to work is to live without dying."*

How you wanted it already in those days: this work you would pursue so tenaciously, through trials and triumphs alike, till the very end. And could you have seen, at that beginning, all that would fall away in this pursuit, all that would be gained?—the immense exchange a poet like you must face: divested of most everything for the sake of one thing beautiful, one thing to which you were destined above all else?

Amidst your letters were some receipts, some telegrams, your father's death announcement, a few of your calling cards. I took up each of the calling cards in turn—these small quotidian things you'd once carried in this or that pocket. One was black-bordered. They were all very plain. Several had been jotted over with notes or messages. The center of each read simply: *Rainer Maria Rilke.* And it was as though you'd turned your face toward this future of mine and had spoken very softly, very gravely.

"Da ist keine Stelle,/die dicht nicht sieht. Du Mußt dein Leben ändern."

There is no piece of this that does not see you. You must change your life.

I could never have known, fourteen years ago, when I first read your letters to Kappus on a silent afternoon in the midst of my youth, that I might one day find myself handling what had been yours.

But now I've come to Paris—your Paris and Malte's—and have been in your letters. My lodgings here bear a peculiar affinity to your own quarters of one hundred and some years ago in the rue Toullier, but four blocks away. The low rude-beamed ceiling and the modest square area of my room together create the compressed atmosphere of a ship's galley. And perhaps I *am* in a ship of kinds. Maybe I am sailing into the past, your past, and maybe this journey will endow me with new depths of feeling.

"That is our progress," you wrote. *"The materials are not so heavy anymore, not so important; we may use them and create whole dramas just to surround ourselves with a single conscious feeling, to become rich by a new feeling."*

I once saw you in Munich, during my first travels in Europe. Here it is again:

You come walking around the street corner toward the spot where I'm standing. To my left, on the wall of number 34 Ainmillerstrasse, a plaque has been hung. Your face in bronze relief. But you are approaching from a different time: 1918, in the days just before you will leave for Switzerland, never to return. You've written the Fifth and Sixth Elegies, and now the others await you out there. Restless with God, your hands stoved in your coat pockets, you come rounding the corner out of war, the heartache of thousands, your world long crazed. You've been loitering in this city, place of the damned, for years, one amongst the wounded many, and you're heading back to the shelter of this flat, this unchosen home and harbor.

I want to stop you before you go inside. I hope you won't mind. I'm not going to ask much of you. I just want to stop you with these hands from years beyond those that trouble you now, want to beg of you something small: the way to Saint Ursula perhaps (in my poor German, no less)—and then leave you, leave you struck by the sense, unmistakable, that I knew you already.

You're drawing close now. Words jostle up inside my head.

I am raising my hands.

Diablo Valley—Paris—Portland
2001–2006

CHRONOLOGY OF
RILKE'S WORKS
IN LOST SON

1897   publication of *Traumgekrönt (Dream-Crowned)*—poems
       Rilke writes *Christus-Visionen (Visions of Christ)*—poems, published posthumously

1900   publication of *Geschichten vom Lieben Gott (Stories of God)*—prose

1901   publication of *Die Letzten (The Last Ones)*—stories
       single performance of *Das Täglich Leben (Daily Life)*—a play, in Berlin

1902   publication of *Das Buch der Bilder (The Book of Images)*—poems

1903   publication of *Auguste Rodin*—a monograph

1904   Rilke begins writing *Die Aufzeichnungen des Malte Laurids Brigge (The Notebooks of Malte Laurids Brigge)*—a novel

1905   publication of *Das Stundenbuch (The Book of Hours)*—poems

1906   re-publication of *The Book of Images* (an expanded edition with thirty-seven new poems)
       publication of *Die Wiese vom Liebe und Tod des Cornets Christoph Rilke (The Lay of the Love and Death of the Cornet Cristoph Rilke)*—a prose poem

1907   publication of *Neue Gedichte (New Poems)*

1908   on All Souls' Day, Rilke writes *"Requiem für eine Freundin"* ("Requiem for a Friend")—poem

1910   publication of *The Notebooks of Malte Laurids Brigge*

1912   Rilke conceives the *Duineser Elegien (The Duino Elegies)* and writes the First and Second Elegies at Castle Duino, near Trieste on the Adriatic Sea

1913–1914 *Winter:* Rilke writes The Third Duino Elegy in Paris

1915   Rilke writes The Fourth Duino Elegy in Munich

1922   *February 11:* Rilke completes the full ten *Duino Elegies* at the Tower of Muzot in the Valais (Rhone Valley), Switzerland; between the second and the twenty-third of this month he also composes all of the fifty-five *Sonnette an Orpheus (Sonnets to Orpheus)*

1923   publication of *The Duino Elegies* and *Sonnets to Orpheus*

My driving ambition during the several years spent writing *Lost Son* has been to give readers an entirely human rendition of Rainer Maria Rilke the man and artist. While I've sought to render the poet's remarkable life as accurately as possible, I've been constantly in service to the narrative demands of a novel. *Lost Son,* therefore, should not be taken as biographical inquiry. Still, it is worthwhile to state that the lineaments of Rilke's life have been, with certain needful if substantial excisions as noted below, rendered accurately here.

A few characters in the novel are wholly imaginary: Karl of Saint Pölten, for example, as well as Rilke's young colleague in the Stiftskaserne, Wenzel; both, however, stand in for impressions or experiences Rilke spoke of, or is believed to have undergone, and represent several biographical figures or influences collapsed into a single character. At points I've been compelled to manipulate the order or substance of factual minutiae: Rilke's father, for instance, did not remain in residence at 19 Heinrichsgasse till his death but took quarters elsewhere in Prague, nor was Princess Marie von Thurn und Taxis single-handedly responsible for the poet's release from the Austro-Hungarian infantry—a petition drafted by Katherina Kippenberg and signed by numerous noteworthy literary figures of the day was of greatest effect in bringing about Rilke's transfer to the Vienna Imperial War Archives. Here and there I've shuffled the dates and details of correspondence or events, as well as the dates of certain poetical compositions. Immediately conspicuous to those familiar with Rilke's biography will be the omission in this novel of the poet's later love affairs, or near love affairs, with such women as Lou-Lou Albert Lasard, Magda von Hattingberg, Mimi Romanelli, and Baladine Klossowska. Despite their absence, I've endeavored to create a Rilke who is almost absurdly vulnerable and nevertheless relentlessly single-minded—which, I believe, is the ultimate impression derived from study of these romantic liaisons. If the overall thrust of *Lost Son* takes Rilke's autobiographical (and sometimes embellished) commentary as its basis, it is a portrait no less true to the poet's inner character for doing so: his impressions, fears, ambitions, failures, friendships, and triumphs. In the end, of course, as Rilke translator Willis Barnstone has put it: "The true Rilke is the poem." I might humbly amend Mr. Barnstone's comment: ". . . or the letter or the prose."

Finally, it is particularly important to note that *Lost Son* takes up a kind of direct discourse with Rilke's novel, *The Notebooks of Malte Laurids Brigge* (published in 1910 by the Insel-Verlag, Leipzig), being in many respects modeled upon *Malte,* which germinated from the poet's initial experience of Paris in 1902. The heart-piercing scenes here, for example, are inspired directly by those in *Malte,* as are the hospital vignettes and various other story elements. It's inevitable, then, that *Lost Son* should pay homage to the fine English translations of *Malte,* first by M. D. Herter Norton and later by Stephen Mitchell; readers are urged to explore Rilke's masterful novel in these rich renditions. All Rilke translations here, save two instances noted in the index below, are my own.

Lost Son was started in the summer of 2001 at the Hôtel de la Poste in Sierre, Switzerland; continued through the subsequent four years in northern California's Diablo Valley—and in the Quartier Latin of Paris in spring of 2005; and completed in Portland, Oregon, in autumn 2006.

—*M. Allen Cunningham*

ACKNOWLEDGMENTS

I owe thanks to numerous people, but most of all I am in debt to my wife, Katie, whose forbearance these last six years must be unparalleled in the history of happy marriages and whose readerly proclivities continue to bless my process as a novelist. I'm thankful to all my friends, family, and extended family for patience, understanding, and support throughout the long aloof period that engendered this book. The folks at Unbridled Books, all so steadfast in the act of championing their authors, continue to inspire feelings of great good fortune. Greg Michalson is a poetic and empathetic editor. He, Fred Ramey, Caitlin Hamilton Summie, and Alaine Borgias are among the best author advocates in contemporary publishing. Judy Heiblum, unwavering supporter and sensitive reader, has been a most encouraging steward of this novel. Many thanks to two very gracious ladies in Paris: Virginie Delaforge and Helene Pinet at the archives of the Museé Rodin. Humble thanks to Heather Lyon of Lyon Books in Chico, California, for forthright and discerning comments on the manuscript. Thanks to Jack Francis and Melanie Schauwecker, who offered invaluable advice regarding French usage.

My first brush with the world of Rainer Maria Rilke came through Stephen Mitchell's stellar translation of *Letters to a Young Poet* (W. W. Norton), complete with its remarkable foreword. I'll remain in Mr. Mitchell's debt for that formative introduction. I wish to note my appreciation of Eric Torgerson's book *Dear Friend: Rainer Maria Rilke & Paula Modersohn*

Becker (Northwestern University Press), which evokes the relationship of painter and poet with zest and insight and was of great assistance to me. I'm equally grateful for two translations by Edward Snow and Michael Winkler: *Diaries of a Young Poet* and *Rainer Maria Rilke & Lou Andreas-Salomé: The Correspondence* (both from W. W. Norton).

The body of scholarship on Rilke is staggering, and I consulted a number of titles too great to list here. In addition to those mentioned above, the following works proved extremely helpful: *A Ringing Glass: The Life of Rainer Maria Rilke* by Donald Prater; *Rilke: A Life* by Wolfang Leppmann, translated by Russell M. Stockman; *Rainer Maria Rilke: Life of a Poet* by Ralph Freedman; *Rilke: Man & Poet* by Nora Wydenbruck; *The Sacred Threshold: A Life of Rilke* by J. F. Hendry; *Portrait of Rilke, an Illustrated Biography* by Hans Egon Holthusen, translated by W. H. Hargreaves; *Rainer Maria Rilke: The Poetic Instinct* by Siegfried Mandel; *Rainer Maria Rilke: Creative Anguish of a Modern Poet* by W. W. Graff; *Rainer Maria Rilke: His Life & Work* by F. W. Van Heerikhuizen, translated by Fernand G. Renier and Anne Cliff; *Rainer Maria Rilke: Masks and the Man* by H. F. Peters; *Letters of Rainer Maria Rilke: 1892–1910* and *Letters of Rainer Maria Rilke: 1910–1926,* translated by Jane Bannard Greene and M. D. Herter Norton; *Wartime Letters of Rainer Maria Rilke,* translated by M. D. Herter Norton; *Rainer Maria Rilke: Selected Letters: 1902–1926,* translated by R. F. C. Hull; *Letters on Cézanne* by Rainer Maria Rilke, translated by Joel Agee; *Rainer Maria Rilke: Journal de Westerwede et de Paris, 1902,* edited by Hella Sieber-Rilke, French translation by Pierre Deshusses; *Ewald Tragy* by Rainer Maria Rilke, translated by Lola Gruenthal; *Visions of Christ* by Rainer Maria Rilke, translated by Aaron Kramer, introduction by Siegfried Mandel; *Auguste Rodin* by Rainer Maria Rilke, in translations by Jessie Lemont and Hans Trausil, and also by G. Craig Houston; *Reading Rilke* by William H. Gass; *Rainer Maria Rilke in Seiner Zeit* by Horst Nalewski; *Rilke's Leben und Werk im Bild* by Ingeborg Schnack; *Paula*

Modersohn-Becker: The Letters & Journals, edited and translated by Arthur S. Wensinger and Carol Clew Hoey; *The Letters and Journals of Paula Modersohn-Becker*, translated and annotated by J. Diane Radycki; *Paula Modersohn-Becker: Her Life and Work* by Gillian Perry; *Looking Back* by Lou Andreas-Salomé, translated by Breon Mitchell; *You Alone Are Real to Me* by Lou Andreas-Salomé, translated by Angela von der Lippe; *My Sister, My Spouse: A Biography of Lou Andreas-Salomé* by H. F. Peters; *Frau Lou: Nietzsche's Wayward Disciple* by Rudolph Binion; *Rodin: The Shape of Genius* by Ruth Butler; *Rodin on Art* by Paul Gsell, translated by Romilly Fedden; *Young Törless* by Robert Musil, translated by Eithne Wilkins and Ernst Kaiser; *Atget's Paris,* edited by Hans Christian Adam.

The following German editions containing Rilke's letters, diaries, and general prose were utilized for some translations. I am very grateful to Suhrkamp Verlag/Insel Verlag for permission to print translated quotations of copyright protected materials.

Rainer Maria Rilke/Auguste Rodin: Der Briefwechsel und andere Dokumente zu Rilkes Begegnung mit Rodin, ed. Ratüs Luck. Insel Verlag, 2001.

Rainer Maria Rilke: Tagbuch Westerwede und Paris 1902, ed. Hella Sieber-Rilke. Insel Verlag, 2000.

Rainer Maria Rilke: Shriften, ed. Horst Nalewski. Insel Verlag, 1996.

Rainer Maria Rilke, Ellen Key: Briefwechsel, ed. Theodore Fiedler. Insel Verlag, 1993.

Rainer Maria Rilke: Tagebucher aus der Frühzeit, eds. Ruth Sieber-Rilke, Carl Sieber. 2nd ed. Insel Verlag, 1973.

Rainer Maria Rilke: Sämtliche Werke, vols. 3 and 6. Insel Verlag, 1955–66.

Rainer Maria Rilke/Lou Andreas Salomé: Briefwechsel, ed. Ernst Pfeiffer. Insel Verlag, 1952.

Rainer Maria Rilke: Briefe, vols. 1 and 2. Insel Verlag, 1950.

Rainer Maria Rilke: Gesammelte Briefe, vols. 4 (pub. 1940) and 6 (pub. 1936), eds. Ruth Sieber-Rilke, Carl Sieber. Insel Verlag.

Rainer Maria Rilke: Briefe und Tagebücher aus der Fruhzeit 1899–1902, eds. Ruth Sieber-Rilke, Carl Sieber. Insel Verlag, 1933.

Rainer Maria Rilke: Briefe aus den Jahren 1906 bis 1907, eds. Ruth Sieber-Rilke, Carl Sieber. Insel Verlag, 1930.

Rainer Maria Rilke: Briefe aus den Jahren 1902 bis 1906, eds. Ruth Sieber-Rilke, Carl Sieber. Insel Verlag, 1929.

Rainer Maria Rilke: Gesammelte Werke, vol. 4. Insel Verlag, 1927.

INDEX OF RILKE QUOTATIONS

The following index lists Rilke quotations from *Lost Son* that are not readily cited in their context, together with the place in the Rilke corpus where they may be found. The Florence, Worpswede, and Schmargendorf Diaries are published collectively in *Rainer Maria Rilke: Tagebücher aus der Frühzeit* (Insel Verlag, 1973), and translated in *Diaries of a Young Poet* (W. W. Norton, 1997). Letters to Franz Xaver Kappus are collected in *Letters to a Young Poet* (*Briefe an einen jungen Dichter*). All original letters between Rilke and Lou Andreas-Salomé may be found in *Rainer Maria Rilke/Lou Andreas Salomé: Briefwechsel* (Insel Verlag, 1952) or in the excellent English translation, *Rainer Maria Rilke & Lou Andreas-Salomé: The Correspondence* (W. W. Norton, 2006). Other letters and journal entries cited below have been published in the innumerable editions of Rilke available in German or English. Most quotations may be found in one or more English translations (see annotated bibliography above), while a few have appeared in German or French only (see Insel Verlag bibliography above).